Patricia Bevin was born and raised in Northamptonshire, where she still lives. She is married to Keith and has three grown up sons and two grandsons. In 1977, she qualified as a state-registered nurse. Apart from breaks to have her children, she has spent her working life working in nursing homes where she has been a registered manager for over thirty years.

She has always been an avid reader of crime novels and has now achieved her ambition of writing one.

To Mum and Dad, who would have been so proud to see my name on my very own novel.

Patricia Bevin

A GOOD REST FOR SOME

AUSTIN MACAULEY PUBLISHERS™

LONDON * CAMBRIDGE * NEW YORK * SHARJAH

A CIP catalogue record for this title is available from the British Library.

ISBN 9781398434615 (Paperback)
ISBN 9781398434622 (ePub e-book)

www.austinmacauley.com

First Published 2021
Austin Macauley Publishers Ltd
Level 37, Office 37.15, 1 Canada Square
Canary Wharf
London
E14 5AA

I want to thank my husband, Keith, who put up with me pounding away on my laptop and coveting the kitchen table whilst writing the novel.

I also want to thank my sister, Lynsan, who I asked to read my novel to give me feedback before getting the nerve to send it away to a publisher.

"Are you sure this is the right place?" asked Ted as he pulled into the driveway, passing through black electric gates. "It looks more like a posh hotel and spa centre than a care home."

"Yes, it's definitely the right place, I only visited it last week, I'm not losing *my* memory!" answered Fiona with a smile.

The large house in front of them looked very imposing. It was nestled amongst lots of huge trees, which stood like giants protecting the house. "Aunt Ness will love it, remember she was brought up in that huge vicarage, she's used to large houses."

Ted stopped the car in front of the house. A large sign saying 'Goodrest Care Home' was above the front door. "Oh yes, you are right," he said with a grin. "Your memory is okay."

"Thanks very much for that!" said Fiona.

They got out of the car and looked around them. The grounds surrounding the house were lovely. The grass had been recently mowed, there were lots of colourful plants in the beds and magnificent baskets of petunias were hanging either side of the front door.

"They must have a very good gardener here," commented Ted. "Perhaps he would like to come and tend to our garden on his day off!"

"That's sexist," said Fiona. "It may be a lady gardener; anyway, we only have a small garden, which is very manageable for us."

"Hmmm, not sure about that," said Ted. "Right, let's ring the doorbell and see who comes to answer it."

He was just about to ring the bell when all of a sudden, the front door was flung open and an elderly gentleman came rushing through. He stopped suddenly when he saw Ted and Fiona in front of him. "Who the devil are you? Have you come to investigate?" he shouted.

"We are here to have another look around the home to see if it's suitable for my aunt to come and live here," said Fiona.

"Oh no, don't bring her here, they're all mad and they lock us in, funny things go on here, you can't trust anyone," he said.

"But you've just opened the door and come outside so it can't have been locked," said Ted.

"I've escaped when their backs were turned to keep myself safe," the man said. At that moment, a large, imposing, harassed-looking lady appeared at the door. She looked to be in her late fifties, dressed in a dark blue uniform, her dark hair swept up in a beehive hairdo and had a name badge on the front of her dress, which read 'Bridget O'Brien, Matron'.

"Wilfred, do come back inside, your tea is ready and it's going to be cold if you don't come back in and eat it," she said.

Ted and Fiona looked at the man who was now hesitating beside them. "Well, I might come in and eat my tea but I will leave afterwards. I cannot stay here any longer with such odd things happening."

"Just as you like," replied the Matron. She shooed him back inside before he could say anymore and then turned to the bemused couple on the doorstep. "Sorry about that," she said, but did not give any explanation as to why Wilfred had been escaping through the front door. "Hello again," she said, holding out her hand to Fiona, "and this must be your husband?" and shook his hand as well.

Ted replied, "Yes, my wife looked around last week and has asked me to come to give it the onceover to see if it's as good as it advertises on the website."

Fiona nudged Ted discreetly and gave a nervous laugh. "Don't mind Ted," she said. "He likes a joke."

"Yes, well, come in; come in," said the Matron in a firm voice. "We need to keep this door shut so we don't have any more people trying to escape. Someone must have not closed the door properly after they left."

She turned around to go through the door, expecting Ted and Fiona to follow her. They stepped through the front door, which the Matron then firmly closed after them.

"Follow me, come on," she said. Ted felt he was sixteen and back at boarding school. He remembered the sanatorium matron who had scared him half to death. He had tried never to be poorly as he felt he would feel worse in her care than the actual illness he was suffering from at the time. He gave a shudder thinking about those times. He had decided after leaving boarding school that his own children, if he had any, would go to a local school rather than a boarding school.

Ted and Fiona trailed after her, giving each other a furtive look. "She's a bit scary," mouthed Ted to Fiona.

"Shush," she whispered.

The Matron led them along a corridor and into her office. "Sit down," she said. They sat immediately in the two chairs that faced her large desk, feeling like schoolchildren in front of the headmistress,

"Now," said Matron, "I understand that you are here for a second viewing?"

"Yes," replied Fiona. "I thought my husband should make the decision with me as to whether aunt Ness would like it here."

"I'm sure she will love it here. We have some very nice ladies and gentlemen, many of whom have been here for a long time. We have one vacancy at the moment so I can show you the room if you would like to follow me; come on, I don't have too much time as I'm very busy."

Without waiting to see if they had any questions, she got up and walked from the office. Ted and Fiona stood up and followed her. They looked at each other but did not comment. Ted was trying, without success, to smother a laugh. Fiona nudged him to behave himself.

They trailed behind Matron. "You have lovely grounds here," said Fiona. "You must have a very good gardener."

"Yes," replied Matron. "She is good, she has been here for some time."

Fiona dare not look at Ted. She wanted to say I told you so, but kept quiet. She would save that comment for later when they were alone.

They walked along the corridor. They passed a dining room where some residents were eating tea. Fiona popped her head in and said a general 'hello' to the room. Faces turned and looked at her; some responded with a hello, others took no notice. She saw some staff in the room helping the residents who could not manage to feed themselves. *A good sign*, she thought. She had heard stories of care homes being very understaffed. She saw Wilfred at the far end of the dining room and gave him a little wave. He raised his hand in reply. The tea looked appetising from what she could see, nicely presented sandwiches, some residents had a hot meal, although Fiona couldn't identify what it was, and it looked like homemade cake. A large teapot and cups and saucers sat on a trolley.

"Come on," barked Matron so Fiona exited the dining room and followed her up the stairs. Ted was looking around and noticed some nice prints hanging on the walls. The carpets were good quality too, a bright red and green leaf pattern that looked good against the magnolia painted walls.

At the top of the stairs, they turned a corner and Matron stopped in front of a room. "This is Room 20," she said unnecessarily, as a plaque on the door stated this and it had a small slot beneath it, presumably where the resident's name would be. She opened the door and Ted and Fiona followed her.

It was a nice room. There was no smell other than a light whiff of paint. It was decorated to a good standard. There was a bed, nicely made up with a floral pink duvet cover and matching pillowcases, a wardrobe with a mirror on one of the doors, a bedside cabinet, chest of drawers and an armchair. All the furniture looked in good condition and was good quality.

The en suite bathroom boasted a shower basin and toilet, again all very nicely decorated to a high standard.

"Some of our residents bring their own bits and pieces to personalise their rooms, so if their furniture fits in, we will accept it," Matron said.

"Very nice," said Fiona. "What do you think, Ted?"

"I agree, it's really nice and well decorated," Ted replied. He went to the window and saw that the room overlooked the back garden. There were trees and flowerbeds, again very nicely maintained, and further away he could see a field of grazing sheep.

"Do you have many residents here with dementia or memory loss?" asked Ted. "Fiona's Aunt Ness suffers from short-term memory loss."

"Yes," replied Matron. "We have several residents with memory issues, she should fit in very well here."

"What about Wilfred trying to escape earlier? Does that happen often?" asked Fiona.

Matron replied, "He does not fully understand his illness, that is why he lives here. He gets very strange thoughts. We need to keep him safe."

Fiona said, "He said odd things happen here."

Matron shrugged and replied, "That's his concept of things due to his dementia. Now, if you have seen everything you need to, then shall we go downstairs?"

"But Wilfred appeared quite rational," said Ted.

"Take no notice of anything he says, it's mostly rubbish," said Matron.

"That's a bit harsh," said Ted. Matron glared at him but she did not comment further. Fiona was also surprised by the unprofessional comment from one in charge of such vulnerable people.

Once they had reached downstairs, Fiona saw that some residents were leaving the dining room. Some female staff in light blue uniforms were either pushing residents in a wheelchair or assisting them to walk with a zimmer frame. Some residents were making their own way out without the need for assistance. Fiona saw Wilfred coming out on his own and went up to him. "Are you feeling better now you have had your tea?" she asked.

"Not really," he replied.

"Why not?" asked Fiona.

"Strange happenings, it's not good here. The meals are alright though," he said in a whisper.

"What sort of things are strange?" asked Fiona.

"People disappear, one minute they are here and then they're gone," he said.

"Perhaps they have been poorly and died?" said Fiona.

"No, no," said Wilfred. "Odd things happen here."

"How long have you lived here?" asked Fiona.

"Too long," Wilfred replied. "I only came for a week but they kept me here."

He was about to expand on this when Matron came up to Fiona and Wilfred and said, "Come on, Wilfred, back to your room now." Wilfred glared at her and started to go up the stairs, presumably to his room. "Not that way, Wilfred, your room is number 10 on this floor," said Matron.

"But I want to see the room where Mary disappeared," replied Wilfred.

"Don't be silly, Wilfred, Mary did not just disappear, she was very poorly and died."

"No she didn't, she was alright the night before and then she didn't come down for breakfast, she just disappeared," said Wilfred.

Matron ushered Ted and Fiona along the corridor to her office. "Take no notice of Wilfred; it's his mind playing tricks," she said.

It made both Ted and Fiona feel uncomfortable. They felt Wilfred was really distressed and would like to have taken more time to talk with him.

Matron asked if they had made their mind up as to whether they would like to take the room for Fiona's aunt. Terms and conditions were discussed, which appeared very reasonable.

"I do like the available room and you appear to have quite a few staff for the amount of residents who live here," said Fiona.

"Yes," said Matron, "a lot of the staff have been here a long time and they look after the residents as if they are their own relatives."

Ted and Fiona felt reassured by this. Fiona said, "I think Aunt Ness would like it here, she wants to be in a country setting. Can we visit her any time we like?"

"We ask that relatives come at appropriate times and not during meal times or too late in the evening as the staff need to attend to them," replied Matron.

"We understand that, I think Aunt Ness would like the room?" said Fiona, looking at Ted who nodded at the unspoken question. "We should like take the room please. Can we bring her one day next week? She does have memory issues and she is relying on me and Ted to find a suitable place for her to live in and spend the rest of her days."

"Good," said Matron as she stood up to shake hands with both Ted and Fiona. "We look forward to seeing her next week. I will be in touch to get more details from you and we can decide on an admission day."

The phone rang and Matron answered it. She appeared flustered and said, "I cannot speak now Dr Johnson. I will ring you later when I have more time," and put the phone down with great haste.

Ted and Fiona left and made their way to their car. Matron stood on the doorstep looking as if she was making sure they actually left the premises.

"I feel sorry for Wilfred," said Ted as they made their way down the drive and through the electric gates.

"But he has dementia," said Fiona.

"I know," said Ted, "but he believes something odd is going on and it's distressing him."

"Oh well. When Aunt Ness is in residence there, perhaps we can talk with him when we visit her," said Fiona.

Once they arrived home, supper was discussed. It was gone six o'clock by now so they decided to have a meal that didn't take too long to prepare and cook. Ted decided to go for a quick run after asking Fiona how long it would be. "I'll do Chicken Korma so it will not take long to cook. You have about an hour before it's ready."

"Great," he replied as he went to change into his running gear. Fiona put a bottle of white wine in the fridge. She collected the ingredients needed for the supper and then went up for a shower.

Ted enjoyed his run and after showering, came downstairs to see if Fiona needed help with supper.

"It's ready now, go and watch your football on the television," she said.

Ted grinned, gave her a quick kiss and took a beer with him into the lounge, saying, "Manchester United against Liverpool."

Fiona grinned and heated the poppadoms and set the trays up. Ted preferred to have supper on a tray in front of the football so Fiona went along with this. She knew how much Ted enjoyed his football.

Fiona served the Korma up on hot plates and collected cutlery, which she put on the trays. She wanted to discuss the care home visit but Ted was too engrossed in the football match to talk. He thanked Fiona for the tray of food without taking his eyes off the match. Fiona went back into the kitchen and retrieved two wine glasses and then opened the Pinot Grigio. She handed a glass to Ted who again absently thanked her. Fiona took a sip of wine, enjoying the cool fruity taste. She enjoyed the Korma and finished it all as did Ted. They shared the wine between them.

After Fiona had finished eating, she told Ted she would ring Aunt Ness. Ted said to say 'hello' from him. Aunt Ness lived in a sheltered housing complex. She had been very happy living there but lately had been feeling scared on her own. She often believed someone had been trying to break in. After a series of tests, Aunt Ness, although only sixty-nine, had been diagnosed with dementia. Her short-term memory was quite bad but long-term memory was still excellent. Having paranoid thoughts was part of her dementia, the memory doctor had explained to Fiona. The manager of the complex had had many late-night calls from Aunt Ness but when investigating, there was no sign of anyone breaking in.

"Hello Aunt Ness, it's Fiona," said Fiona when the phone was picked up. "How are you?"

"Who are you?" asked Aunt Ness.

"Fiona, your niece," replied Fiona. She was used to her aunt asking who it was on the telephone. She was very suspicious of everyone. "I'm ringing to see how you are and to tell you about the care home visit Ted and I had this afternoon."

"What care home?" asked Aunt Ness.

Fiona replied, "The Goodrest Care Home that I visited last week. I did tell you about it. You are getting frightened living on your own so we had a talk and you agreed for us to find somewhere nice for you to live that had other people around you."

"I'm not sure," said Aunt Ness. "It's won't be my own home."

Fiona replied, "But you can take some of your own furniture and it's a lovely room. It looks over a garden. I even saw sheep in a field nearby. It's a big house, not unlike the vicarage that you grew up in. Why not try it and see how you get on. The Matron said you can have a month's trial there to see if you like it."

"Alright," said Aunt Ness. "But if I don't like it then I'm coming home."

"Good," said Fiona. "I will ring the Home and arrange for your admission on Friday next week, Ted and I will take a day's holiday from work to take you and some of your possessions over and help settle you in. You can write it on your calendar. Friday 12th August. Is that okay?"

"It will have to be, I suppose," sniffed Aunt Ness. Fiona didn't comment further on the move but went on to ask what she had been doing today. "Not much, I haven't seen anybody," said Aunt Ness. "No one ever comes and sees me."

Fiona knew this wasn't quite true as she had arranged for the sheltered housing manager to call in every morning. "Well, just think, you will have company all the time in the care home," said Fiona.

"I don't want to speak with people I don't know," said Aunt Ness.

"You will get to know the other residents once you settle in," said Fiona in what she hoped was a cheerful reassuring voice.

"We'll see," said Aunt Ness. "I must go now as *Casualty* is on."

"Okay, speak soon," replied Fiona and put the phone down.

She went back into the lounge where Ted was commenting on the football result and how Liverpool had deserved to win but had lost 3-1. "You should have seen the ref handing out yellow cards to Liverpool players when there was no need; sending off one player for a very minor tackle," moaned Ted. "Biased! He was biased!"

"Can we talk about Aunt Ness and the care home now?" asked Fiona.

"Did she agree?" asked Ted.

"Yes," said Fiona, "but only to a month's trial to see how she likes it."

"Fair enough, I suppose," answered Ted. "I wonder how she will get on with the frosty Matron. Both can be a bit sharp. Wonder if they will clash!"

"Shall we see if we can have a day's holiday next Friday so we can move her in and that will then give us the weekend to go and see her as well?" said Fiona.

"Should be alright," said Ted. "I will ask Geoff on Monday. It's fairly quiet in the office at the moment so it shouldn't be a problem."

Ted worked for a haulage company that organised drivers needed by firms who wanted his firm to supply agency drivers. He planned their routes as well. As it was August, many firms closed down for a summer break or had less staff so less workload around so fewer firms needed Ted's attention.

"It should be okay for me too," said Fiona. Fiona worked for the local council in the Environmental Health Department. She mainly organised recycling and rubbish collections and answered many queries and some complaints. "My bin hasn't been emptied!" was the main complaint. "I will check with Lynne on Monday but I can't see it being a problem taking Friday off," said Fiona.

"How is Lynne doing?" asked Ted.

"Alright. She's recovered well from the divorce. It's been two years now. It was a real shock to her when it happened. Came out of the blue, him saying he didn't love her anymore and moved out saying he had met someone else. Her two boys are doing okay too. They go to their dad's on alternate weekends, which helps them all. She actually had her first date since the divorce last night. She's joined a dating site called 'Find your perfect partner'. She showed me the website, you want to see some of the photos on there, talk about posing! Some blokes with no shirt on and holding a pint of beer! There are others with such brilliant profiles that you can tell they're fibbing or embellishing the truth! It's enough to turn anyone off!"

"Have you seen my photo on it yet?" joked Ted.

"Ha ha," said Fiona.

They had only been married for twelve months and were still in the first rosy glow of marriage. Fiona admired Ted's handsome looks. He was tall with dark hair that he liked to keep short. He had been out with plenty of girls before meeting blonde-haired Fiona in a pub. They had been out for the evening with separate friends in the same venue. Fiona had taken a bit of persuading to start dating him as she felt she may go the way of previous girlfriends. She had heard of Ted prior to meeting him in person, as he was well known locally for playing sports and frequenting the local pubs.

His relationships hadn't lasted longer than six months before Ted grew bored but once he met Fiona, Ted said no one could ever surpass her. He told her it was love at first sight over his pint and her gin and tonic!

Fiona had previously had a relationship that lasted three years but they had parted friends as they both wanted different things in life. Rob wanted to travel the world before settling down but Fiona was more of a home bird. Holidays were one thing but travelling for months on end, backpack in tow, did not appeal.

Ted and Fiona dated for two years before getting married. They had a wide circle of friends and liked to socialise.

They had discussed having children, and certainly wanted a family, but decided to wait a little longer. They liked to go out for impromptu outings for meals, weekends away and out for a drink but with a baby in tow, this would limit their activities. Both Ted and Fiona were in their early thirties and felt they had plenty of time for a family.

Both had lost their parents at an early age so that was why Aunt Ness was so important to Fiona. It was a family connection to her mother whom she had loved dearly. Losing her to lung cancer at only fifty-nine had devastated her. Her father had left the family home when Fiona was only two as he couldn't handle the responsibility of a family. He had died not long afterwards after getting in a fight when drunk. Fiona remembered a lovely childhood; her mother had more than made up for Fiona not having a father around.

Ted's parents had died five years ago whilst on holiday in Spain. They had been driving their campervan on the motorway when a lorry swerved to avoid another vehicle and ploughed into them, killing them instantly. Both Ted and Fiona were only children and had no close relatives apart from Fiona's Aunt.

Ted was very fond of Aunt Ness and willingly visited her. They had taken her out for pub lunches and shopping trips but recently, this had proved difficult due to Aunt Ness and her suspicious thoughts. "She's looking at me, she wants my purse," she would say about an innocent shopper. However often Ted and Fiona reassured her, the situation did not improve, which was why Fiona asked her aunt's doctor to investigate as to why her aunt was having these paranoid thoughts. Dementia was diagnosed. Medication had helped a bit but it was soon obvious that Aunt Ness needed professional care twenty-four hours a day. The doctor had advised Fiona to start researching care homes where her aunt could be looked after in a safe setting.

Goodrest Care Home had good reviews on its website and Fiona had arranged the preliminary visit before asking Ted to accompany her on a second visit.

Monday morning, after arranging a day off from work on Friday, Fiona rang Goodrest Care Home and asked to speak to the Matron. Whoever answered the phone had not identified himself so Fiona had no idea who she had spoken to and was just about to ask when the phone was put down with a loud clatter and she heard a loud voice calling, "Matron, it's for you!"

After a pause that seemed to extend past a minute, a voice spoke, "Matron here, how can I help you?" Fiona identified herself and Matron hesitated as if not remembering who Fiona was.

Fiona reminded her that she and her husband had visited on the previous Saturday about her aunt moving into the Home.

"Oh yes, I remember you both," Matron replied.

Fiona asked if they could move Aunt Ness in on this coming Friday. "Yes, that's fine," replied Matron. "Bring her in about eleven o'clock."

"We shall be bringing some small pieces of furniture, photos and a couple of pictures, if that's alright?" said Fiona.

"As long as they don't overfill the room and the handyman can put up the pictures, that will be fine," said Matron.

"Okay," said Fiona, "we will see you Friday then; by the way, how is Wilfred? We met him when we came to look around and he seemed very agitated."

"Oh, he passed away yesterday," said Matron.

"What? How did that happen? He seemed fine on Saturday," said Fiona with a rush of sadness.

"Naturally I cannot go into details with you. Suffice to say he is no longer with us," said Matron. "We will see you on Friday at eleven," said Matron and put the phone down.

Fiona was left feeling shocked, sitting with the phone in her hand. She was upset thinking about Wilfred. He had seemed so fit. Yes, he had had strange thoughts but surely, they wouldn't have killed him?

"Are you alright?" asked Lynne, who was sitting at the next desk.

"Not really," said Fiona as she replaced the phone on its cradle. "The care home where Aunt Ness is moving into just told me that a man we spoke to when we visited on Saturday died yesterday."

"Well, I should think that's a natural occurrence in a care home," said Lynne.

"But he seemed so fit when we saw him; he didn't look as if he would die a day later," replied Fiona.

She rang Ted to tell him. He too appeared surprised. "Perhaps he had a heart attack?" he said.

"I don't know," said Fiona. "I suppose it must have been, for him to die so suddenly."

The rest of the day, Fiona was quite busy, answering queries from the public. "Yes Mrs Smith, your bin collection day was changed last week from Monday to Tuesday. You were notified, as all your street was. Put the bin out tonight and it will be emptied tomorrow."

Mrs Smith said, "I don't like changes." Slammed the phone down.

Fiona offered to go to first lunch at twelve-thirty in a nearby café where she often went. She had an hour for lunch and then Lynne would go at one-thirty. She could sit outside in the sunshine. There were four tables and chairs outside the café. She was lucky to find an empty one. It was a nice day and other workers were also taking advantage of the fine weather. Last week it had rained on a couple of days, which was disappointing for August and its holiday makers.

A waitress came out of the café with her notepad and said, "Hello, what would you like?" She took Fiona's order of cheese salad in a brown roll, a bag of cheese and onion crisps and a flat white coffee.

Fiona was lost in thought, remembering the conversation she had had with Wilfred on Saturday at the care home. She felt very sad. He had not appeared unwell, only disorientated in his thoughts. She hoped he hadn't suffered. She also hoped her aunt would settle in and that she hadn't made an error of judgement in choosing Goodrest Care Home.

The waitress brought her lunch out and set it on the table in front of her, Fiona smiled her thanks. It was lovely to feel the sun on her face and she enjoyed her lunch hour before returning to the office so Lynne could go for hers.

Fiona arrived home at five-thirty. Ted usually got home just after six unless he had arranged to play squash with his friend Geoff. They worked together and had been good friends for the several years they had been working together. Tonight was a squash night so it would be seven-thirty before he arrived home. That gave Fiona time to have a shower, a quick call to Aunt Ness and prepare the evening meal. She looked in the freezer and found some lamb steaks, which she set out on the side to defrost. She went for her shower after a quick chat with her aunt and afterwards peeled some new potatoes and diced a cabbage. She tipped some frozen peas into a saucepan and got the gravy granules out of the cupboard. This reminded her to make the gravy as she had forgotten last week and the meal had not been as hot as it should have been as she had to hurriedly make gravy. "Memory loss at your age!" Ted had joked.

Fiona turned the six o'clock news on the television. It was halfway through a piece about hospitals. Not quite sure what the bulletin was about, Fiona was not listening carefully until she heard the name Dr Johnson. *Where have I heard that name recently?* she wondered. It was coming to the end of the bulletin but it showed a quick shot of him. He appeared to be in his early fifties, tall, grey-haired with dark-rimmed glasses. The newsreader then went on to speak about something or other that the government was planning to do about social care and the elderly in particular.

It was while she was simmering the potatoes, peas and cabbage and the lamb steaks were in the oven that she suddenly remembered where she had heard the name Dr Johnson. It was the name of the Dr who had been calling Matron at the care home, she remembered. Surely a coincidence she thought, Johnson is a common enough name.

Ted then arrived home, happy in the fact that he had beaten Geoff at squash for a change. Geoff was normally the better player but tonight, "he had an off day," reported Ted. "What's for dinner?" he asked.

"Lamb steaks and veg," replied Fiona.

"Are we having gravy with it?" smirked Ted.

"Go away!" said Fiona, shooing him up the stairs to get changed.

After eating their meal, Fiona told Ted about hearing the name Dr Johnson on the television. "It's a common enough name," said Ted.

"I know. It's probably just a coincidence. I didn't think to ask the Matron about GP services at the care home but they must have something in place for when residents are poorly."

"Bound to have someone they can call in," agreed Ted.

"I think I will ring up tomorrow and find out."

"Good idea," said Ted. "Now scoot over here for a cuddle, I haven't seen you all day."

"I'm really tired."

"Best have an early night then," said Ted with an exaggerated yawn. "I'm tired too so I think I need an early night as well!"

Fiona grinned at him. "Race you up the stairs," she challenged as she ran out the room. "Last one out the room washes and clears up!"

"Spoilsport," said Ted, following her.

"I'll be as quick as I can, don't fall asleep before I get there!"

Next morning after arriving at work, greeting Lynne and settling at her desk, Fiona asked her, "I forgot to ask how the date went on Saturday night."

Lynne smiled and said it went rather well. He seemed like a nice guy and they had got on really well. They had made plans to meet again this coming Saturday. "Good for you," said Fiona. "Hope it turns into something special."

"We'll see, we've only had the one date so far. I don't want to rush into anything too soon."

Fiona mentioned that she was going to contact the care home to ask about GP services. "I forgot when I was there and the Matron's a bit scary and makes you either forget to ask things or you don't like to interrupt her!"

"You should be able to ask anything you want to; after all, your aunt is going to be paying to be there so you have every right to know what she is being charged for," replied Lynne.

"I agree," said Fiona. "I'll call the home now."

She dialled the number. It took about half a minute to be answered. "Goodrest Care Home, Matron speaking," said the other end.

Taking a deep breath, Fiona asked, "Hello Matron, it's Fiona Chatsworth here. My aunt Ness is moving in on Friday. I realise that I forgot to ask about GP services there. Currently, my aunt has a very good one. Does she need to change once she's a resident in the care home?"

"Yes, she will change her doctor once she moves in. All our residents are under the care of Dr Johnson. He is a very experienced doctor who has looked after our residents here for many years."

"That's good to hear," Fiona replied. "But my aunt can be quite difficult with doctors. She is very suspicious of them but now has come to trust her current GP."

"She will soon become familiar with Dr Johnson. He visits the home most days and the residents all get to know him well and vice versa," said Matron.

"Alright then," said Fiona. "If that's the case, she will just have to get to know him."

"Any other questions?" asked Matron. "I am very busy as he is due to come and do a round in half an hour. I need to get on."

"No, not at the moment," replied Fiona. "Thank you, I will let you get on." The line went dead so Fiona put the phone down.

"Is everything alright?" asked Lynne.

"Not sure," said Fiona. "Matron's very abrupt at times. Aunt Ness will have to change to the Home's GP. She won't like it but it's something she will have to get used to."

Fiona had a busy day in the office and was more than ready to leave at five o'clock. She had planned to pop in to see Aunt Ness on her way home. Aunt Ness lived fifteen minutes away from Fiona's house. Fiona drove through rush hour traffic, cursing all the traffic lights, which changed to red as she approached them, *They see me coming and do it on purpose*, she muttered to herself.

It was nearly five thirty-five when Fiona eventually arrived at Aunt Ness's sheltered housing complex.

She pulled up in the carpark and zapped the car. She then spotted her seat belt was hanging out the bottom of the driver's door and had to unlock the car to push it back in.

She made her way to the entrance and punched in the code to allow entry. Her aunt's flat was on the first floor but Fiona climbed the stairs, forsaking the lift. *Good exercise*, she puffed to herself.

She knocked loudly on door number five and called out that it was Fiona. She heard her aunt come to the door asking who was there. "It's Fiona, your niece," replied Fiona.

A key was turned and a chain removed and the door opened. Her aunt stood there in her nightie and dressing gown.

"Oh," said Fiona, "are you going to bed?"

"No, of course not," said Aunt Ness. "I am making my tea." Fiona asked if she could come in. It appeared that her aunt hadn't got dressed that morning.

It's a good job she is going to have some proper care, thought Fiona.

She followed her aunt into the kitchen. She was preparing to make herself beans on toast. The beans were bubbling away in a saucepan. The bread had not yet been put in the toaster and there was no sign of any butter.

"Let me do this for you," said Fiona. "You go in the lounge and switch the television on. It's *Pointless*, you like that programme."

"I can do things for myself," sniffed her aunt.

"I know you can but while I'm here, let me help you," said Fiona.

Her aunt went into the lounge and Fiona heard her turn the television on. She could hear Alexander Armstrong speaking to the contestants.

At least it was the right channel, sometimes Aunt Ness watched a programme thinking it was the one she switched it on for but in fact, it was an entirely different one. One time, she watched *Eastenders* instead of a quiz programme, commenting that there weren't many questions in this programme, only a lot of shouting.

Fiona took her aunt's beans on toast through to her along with a cup of tea. Fiona poured one for herself and sipped it while watching her aunt eat. Her aunt laughed at *Pointless*, saying she could answer better than the contestants on tonight.

After the programme had finished and the beans on toast had been eaten, Fiona brought up the subject of the move to the Care home on Friday.

"No one told me it's happening on Friday," said Aunt Ness.

"We must have forgotten to tell you when it's happening. Sorry," said Fiona, knowing she had told her but her aunt had forgotten due to her short-term memory.

Fiona stayed for another hour, busy putting name labels into her aunt's clothes before leaving. She reassured her aunt, (and had written it on the kitchen calendar) that she and Ted would be over at nine-thirty on Friday morning to collect her and some of her belongings and take her to the care home. Other items could be collected when Aunt Ness had settled in.

Ted was at home when Fiona arrived back. He kissed her hello and asked after Aunt Ness. "Muddled and forgetful," answered Fiona. "It will be good to know she is safe and looked after at the care home. I said we will be over on Friday at nine-thirty to help get her things together before going to the home."

"Okay," said Ted. "Now, my culinary surprise for this evening is—"

"Fish fingers and chips!" interrupted Fiona.

"How did you guess?" asked Ted.

"Because your culinary surprise is always fish fingers and chips!" answered Fiona. "I'll have a quick shower first before this gourmet meal."

Ted swatted her with a tea towel, growling, "Be gone, wench!"

After dinner, Fiona told him about the phone call she had made to the Home that morning. "She will unfortunately have to change doctors when she's a resident there. Guess the name of her new doctor?"

"Dr Crippen!" joked Ted.

"Don't be silly! It's Dr Johnson," said Fiona. "It will be amazing if it turns out to be the Dr Johnson who was on the television the other evening. Matron was quite curt when I rang this morning; it's as if I was a nuisance calling with a question."

"You have every right to ask whatever you want to," said Ted. "She is paying to be there and we want to know that all is in order."

"Yes," said Fiona, "my sentiments exactly."

The phone rang. It was nearest to Fiona so she answered it. "Hi Geoff," she said. "I hear you got beaten by Ted last night! Never mind!" Fiona listened to Geoff talking. "Yes alright, it probably was a fluke!"

"Hey!" said Ted. "I heard that! The best man won!"

Fiona handed the phone to Ted. He was asking if he wanted a returns match tomorrow evening. "Okay, let me just check if the boss says it's alright!" Ted asked Fiona if they had any plans for tomorrow evening.

"No," she said. "Go off to your boys' games and get ready to lose the next match!" Ted laughed and asked Geoff if he was ready for another thrashing.

They chatted for a while so Fiona got up and went into the kitchen. She started to compile a list of all things they would need to take with them from Aunt Ness's house on Friday.

There was quite a lot: some photographs and pictures that held special memories for her aunt, a small table and a special bedside lamp her aunt was used to. Fiona wanted her to feel comfortable in her new surroundings. She knew her aunt would not be returning to her sheltered accommodation as her memory issues were increasing and it was not safe for her to live alone any longer. It was sad but Fiona hoped her aunt would make friends and settle into her new life.

This got her thinking about Wilfred and his sudden demise. *Very strange*, thought Fiona. What a shame that her aunt would not meet him.

"Any chance of a coffee?" asked Ted as he strolled into the kitchen.

"Of course, darling," said Fiona. "The coffee is there in the jar, the milk's in the fridge and I think I spy a mug on the mug rack!"

"Cheeky," responded Ted. "Do you want one?"

"No thanks, it would keep me awake," she replied.

"I think you should have one then," said Ted. "It would be good news for me as I will *definitely* stay awake if you are!"

"Go on with you," said Fiona. "Is that all you think about?"

Ted wiggled his eyebrows at her, which made Fiona laugh. "You're terrible!" she said. "I don't know why I love you so much."

"Because I'm so handsome," replied Ted with a leer. Fiona laughed.

They wandered into the lounge and spent the next hour sitting on the sofa together, holding hands and watching a documentary about riverboat cruises. It was something they thought they might like to try before starting a family. Having Aunt Ness in a safe environment also released them from calling in on her every other evening as they usually did whilst she was in her flat. They would visit her often in the care home but it would not be because they were afraid of finding her not dressed or not eating, as the care staff would oversee these needs. It would be nice to visit and take her for a walk in the grounds or take her out to a café for a cup of tea and a slice of cherry cake, which was her favourite cake.

After watching the news, Ted and Fiona retired upstairs where they spent the next little while in marital bliss.

Friday morning at nine-fifteen saw Ted and Fiona driving over to Aunt Ness. The previous evening, they had emptied their Volvo of all the paraphernalia that people collect in their boot and backseat. Having an empty car meant they could pack and transfer as many items as possible without making a second trip.

Aunt Ness had remembered it was the day of the move. Fiona had rung her the evening before, reminding her and saying it was also on her kitchen calendar.

They pulled up in front of the sheltered housing complex. They entered the building after punching in the code. They knocked loudly on Aunt Ness's door and the key and chain were heard as Aunt Ness removed both. "Hello Aunt Ness," said Fiona. "Today is moving day. Are you excited?" She was pleased to see her aunt was dressed in her day clothes.

"No," she replied, "I'm not."

Ted went ahead and started asking what he could do to assist with packing stuff up.

He retrieved a large suitcase from the loft. It was quite dusty, which made everyone cough as he wiped it. Fiona took Aunt Ness into her bedroom where they started packing some clothes into the suitcase. Ted wandered in and asked which photographs and pictures she wanted to take. Aunt Ness followed him into the lounge. She collected her wedding photo and the most recent photo of her late husband Jack who had died seven years ago.

She pointed out two pictures hanging on the wall. One was a scenic picture of a beach in Cornwall where she and Jack had spent many happy holidays. The other picture was of a vase of very colourful flowers. Fiona was not sure where that had originated from and Aunt Ness could not remember either. She just knew she wanted to take it with her as it was very familiar to her. The television set and remote control was taken into the hall to go with them.

Ted asked if she wanted to take any lamps from the lounge as well as her bedside lamp. Aunt said no. A small table was added to the collection piling up in the hall ready to be transferred to the car. Aunt Ness's radio went into a small holdall along with a couple of magazines and some small ornaments.

They all had a cup of tea before they left. There was a knock on the door. The manager had come to say goodbye and presented Aunt Ness with a card and a big bunch of flowers. "How lovely," said Fiona.

"We will miss you, Ness," said the manager, "but I won't miss your late-night phone calls!" But she was smiling as she said this.

Ted carried out Ness's belongings to the car. He used the lift for this. Fiona and Ness stayed in the flat until everything had been stowed in the car.

When they locked the front door, Fiona could see Aunt Ness was close to tears. "Think of it as a new beginning. You will make friends and there will always be someone around to help you," said Fiona, putting an arm around Aunt Ness.

As they got to the car, an elderly couple who lived next door came up to them and wished Ness luck in her new home.

Ness was assisted into the front seat in the Volvo and Fiona squeezed into the backseat. There wasn't a lot of room and the suitcase corner pressed into her knee. The television kept lurching to one side. Fiona hoped it was not going to be damaged. Fiona shifted around, which eased her knee a bit. Ted got into the driving seat, checked Ness and Fiona had their seatbelts on, put his own on and said "Well, here we go!"

The drive took twenty minutes and soon they were turning into the driveway of Goodrest Care Home through the electric gates.

"Look at that big house in front of you, Aunt Ness, That's your new home," said Ted.

"It's big, like the vicarage I used to live in as a child," murmured Aunt Ness. "I liked that house."

"I'm sure you will like this one too," said Fiona from the backseat. "Look at the gardens, Aunt Ness. They are very well maintained by a *lady gardener*," said Fiona with a smirk at Ted who noticed this in the driver's rear-view mirror. He returned the smirk with a wink.

Ted stopped the car just outside the front door. "I can move the car to the carpark when we have unloaded," he said.

Fiona scrambled out from the backseat, rubbing her knee where the suitcase had pressed into it. She helped Aunt Ness out of the front seat. Ted got out and rang the front door bell. It was opened almost immediately and to Ted and Fiona's relief, no elderly resident came rushing out. The door had been opened by a young lady in a light blue uniform. She had blonde hair tied back in a ponytail and looked like a nice person. "Hello," she said. "I'm Caroline and I've been expecting you." She went to Aunt Ness and said, "Welcome to your new home. I hope you will be happy here."

"I don't know you, who are you?" Aunt Ness said.

"I'm Caroline, one of the carers here. I will be looking after you," she replied.

"I don't need looking after," said Aunt Ness.

"Well, if you do need any help, then I will be here for you," said Caroline with a smile. "Please, all come in."

"You cannot leave your car here, we need it kept free for emergency vehicles," said a familiar voice. Standing at the front door looking cross was Matron. "We do have a carpark."

Ted said, "I will unload everything and then move the car, Okay?" Fiona could tell from his tone of voice that he was not happy at being spoken to like that.

"Well, hurry up and unload as I am expecting the doctor and he always parks here," she replied,

"Does he drive an emergency vehicle then?" asked Ted in a very calm polite voice. The voice that Fiona recognised as meaning 'Don't mess with me'.

Matron ignored his question and turned to Aunt Ness. "I am Miss Bridget O'Brien but you can call me Matron," she said.

Fiona smothered a laugh that she turned into a cough when Matron stared at her. Ted grinned because he could see through Fiona's cough.

"Come on in," said Caroline. "I will take you to your room now," she said, turning to Aunt Ness. Matron turned around and went back in through the door.

"Don't mind her," whispered Caroline. "She gets a bit funny when Dr Johnson is due, I think she's got a crush on him!"

Ted and Fiona looked at each other as if they could not believe that such a sour person could have romantic feelings.

"Right, let's get everything in before the good doctor arrives then," said Ted as he started unloading the car. "Aunt Ness, you go ahead with Caroline, and Fiona and I will bring your stuff."

Aunt Ness followed Caroline into the hall. Fiona and Ted unloaded the belongings from the car, which didn't take too long. They stacked them to the side of the front door so no one could trip over them. "Best take the car to the carpark now or I may be shot at dawn," joked Ted.

Fiona laughed and said, "Behave yourself!"

The front door remained open so after Ted returned after parking the car, he and Fiona started carrying things in. It took three trips before they had everything cleared from the doorway entrance. "There, nice and clear for Dr Johnson," said Ted.

Fiona remembered the way up the stairs to Room 20. She hadn't seen any staff or residents in the hall or dining room as she passed by it. She did detect nice cooking smells so obviously; lunch was being prepared. She couldn't remember where the communal lounge was and supposed most people were in there.

Aunt Ness was in her room looking out of the window. She turned to Fiona, saying, "Where are the sheep you said were here?"

Fiona was astonished that she had remembered about the sheep. "I don't know," she replied. "Perhaps they are grazing out of sight at the far end of the field today."

Aunt Ness looked around the room, asking where her belongings were. "Ted is bringing them in now," she answered. At that moment, Ted entered the room carrying the suitcase in one hand and holding a lamp in the other.

"Right," he said, "who is going to start unpacking?"

"Aunt Ness and I will unpack the suitcase," said Fiona. "You can bring the other things and we can decide where they can go."

Caroline asked if anyone would like a tea or coffee. "That would be nice, thank you," answered Fiona.

"Aunt Ness, what would you like?"

"Tea please," she said.

Fiona said, "Coffee for me and my husband please. None of us here take sugar." It still thrilled Fiona to say 'my husband' even after being married for a year.

Caroline returned with a tray of drinks. There was a plate of chocolate digestives on a small plate. "Look at this, Aunt Ness! Chocolate biscuits, no less!" said Fiona.

"Lunch is at one o'clock," announced Caroline. "Will you join us in the dining room, Ness?"

"I don't know anyone and I won't know where to sit," Aunt Ness said.

"I will show you and I will introduce you to the other residents too," said Caroline with a smile.

"We will leave at lunchtime and let you settle in, Aunt Ness," said Fiona. "We will come back tomorrow and take you for a walk in the garden."

"Don't leave me here alone," said Aunt Ness in a trembling small voice.

"You won't be alone. I bet by this evening, you will have made some new friends," replied Fiona.

Aunt Ness pulled a face, which without saying any words said "I bet I won't have."

They consulted with Aunt Ness as to where the photos and pictures would be going in the room. The wedding photo was placed on the windowsill where her aunt could see it clearly. The scenic picture was going to go on the wall above the television. Fiona wrote on a bit of paper where she wanted the pictures hung so Matt the handyman would know when he returned to work, presumably on Monday. She left the note on the chest of drawers where he should see it.

Being told that a handyman would hang the pictures irritated Ted because he was quite capable of banging a picture hook in the wall. He'd hung all the pictures in their own house and none had fallen down yet!

The small table was placed by the armchair and the lamp went on the bedside cabinet. Some red cushions, which they had brought with them, went on the two chairs. The colourful bedspread went over the duvet on the bed.

Two magazines went on the small table. Aunt Ness liked to read magazines rather than books as she could never remember what she had read in a book and had to keep returning to the previously read chapter! She joked that she would never finish a book because of this!

Ted placed the small Roberts radio onto the small table, making sure it was on Classic FM. This was Aunt Ness's favourite station. He set the television up and tuned it in. The picture was good. He set the remote control on the small table.

At five minutes to one, Caroline reappeared saying she would take Ness down to the dining room. Ted and Fiona said they would now leave but would return tomorrow afternoon. They all went down the stairs. At the bottom of the stairs, both Ted and Fiona hugged Ness and said they would see her tomorrow.

Caroline took Ness into the dining room and with a wave goodbye, Ted and Fiona went towards the front door. On the way, they had to pass Matron's office. The door was not quite closed but through the glass in the door they could see she was not alone. A man was with her. They appeared to be arguing. Matron looked flustered and the man looked cross. Fiona gave a gasp and said, "That's the Dr Johnson who was on television the other evening!"

"Are you sure?" asked Ted. "You said you only saw a shot of him at the end."

"I'm certain it's the same man," said Fiona. Just then Matron looked towards the door and immediately shut the door and pulled a blind down that covered the glass so the office interior was hidden.

"So that's Dr Johnson, Matron's flame," he said.

"Stop it!" said Fiona. "She obviously didn't like us looking in the office. Let's go."

They left through the front door. On the driveway, parked right outside, was a red Jaguar sports car. "Wow! Look at that," said Ted. "That would cost a fortune! If that's the doctor's car, then I wouldn't call it an emergency vehicle, would you?"

"No, I certainly wouldn't!" said Fiona. "Come on, let's go," as Ted was still admiring the car.

They made their way to the carpark and got in their car and drove down the drive and through the electric gates.

"I do hope Aunt Ness will be alright," said Fiona.

"It will take time for her to settle in but it's for the best. She couldn't carry on looking after herself for much longer," said Ted.

"I know you're right," said Fiona, "but it's a hard thing to do, putting someone in the care of strangers."

Ted suddenly said, "Let's go out for lunch. Save us cooking and it's a nice sunny day. Sitting in a pub garden with a plate of fish and chips that we haven't cooked ourselves will be a real treat."

"Sounds good to me," said Fiona.

Ted diverted from their normal route and drove to a small village not far from their home to a pub they had been to a few weeks ago. The beer had been decent and the menu looked appetising, although they hadn't eaten there on that occasion.

They arrived and parked up. There were quite a few cars in the carpark. "Let's hope we can find a table in the garden," said Fiona "It's too nice to be stuck inside."

They went in the pub through the entrance gate, glancing over in the garden. There were several tables in the nicely kept garden. Ted commented, "That family at the far table look like they're ready to leave. You stay out here and nab the table as soon as they get up. What do you want to drink?"

"Half a lager and lime please," replied Fiona.

She did as Ted suggested and stayed near the garden entrance, keeping a discreet eye on the family he had noticed. As soon as they started leaving, Fiona sauntered over to the table and asked if it was free. "Sure is," said the father. "Good meal and even better beer!"

The family left with their two sons arguing over what to do next. "The park with the big slide," said the younger boy.

"Skateboarding Park!" shouted the eldest. Fiona wondered who succeeded with their next destination. Probably the elder one!

Ted arrived with their drinks and sat down. "Good pint," he said with his top lip covered with foam. Fiona started to wipe it off but Ted stopped her finger by grabbing it and giving it a little bite.

"Hey," she cried, "that hurt." But she was smiling as he said it.

He released her finger and said, "You have permission to bite me back anywhere you like later."

"In your dreams," she retorted.

"You don't know what my dreams are like," he said with a smirk.

"I can guess!"

Ted said he had ordered fish and chips for both of them. "I wonder what Aunt Ness is having for lunch," Fiona said.

"Stop worrying about her, we will see her tomorrow and we can ask her then."

"She probably won't remember," sighed Fiona. "Mind you, the cooking smells were good, so hopefully it was nice. It was odd about the Matron pulling the office blind down and quickly shutting the door when she saw us, wasn't it?"

"Probably they were about to get passionate!" said Ted.

"I don't think so," said Fiona. "It didn't look very romantic to me when I saw them, they seemed to be arguing."

She tried to recall if she could remember what they had been arguing about before the door shut and the blind went down. She could remember raised voices and the odd words such as drugs, the word no and the word why.

"Oh well, as long as Aunt Ness settles in, I'll be happy," said Fiona. "And Caroline seemed kind."

"I'm sure the staff are okay, they have to be nice in that kind of work," said Ted.

"I didn't see too many residents or staff."

"They were probably busy."

The fish and chips Ted had ordered at the bar with their drinks were then delivered by a young waiter "Sauces?" he asked.

"Tomato ketchup and vinegar please," requested Ted.

"Okay, I'll bring them over," said the waiter, giving them cutlery wrapped in a napkin. Salt and pepper were already on the table.

The fish and chips were hot and looked excellent. Sauces were delivered and silence reigned as Ted and |Fiona started eating. "Another drink?" asked Ted, looking into his empty glass.

"Yes please," replied Fiona, draining the last of her lager.

Ted got up to go inside to the bar to order their second drinks. Fiona started her meal. Ted returned with their drinks. It was a lovely sunny day and families were making the most of it. There was lots of chat amongst the tables. Ted finished his meal, rubbing his stomach. "That was very good!" he commented. "We will have to come here again."

Fiona finished her own meal saying how nice it was.

"Do you want a pudding?"

"Just coffee please." replied Fiona.

Ted got up to return to the bar to order two coffees.

They dallied over the coffees, enjoying the fine weather.

"What time shall we visit Aunt Ness tomorrow?" asked Fiona.

"Well," said Ted, "I need to sort out the garage a bit tomorrow so let's visit in the afternoon."

"Okay, I need to do some housework tomorrow," said Fiona, "and I want to sort out what I need to send to the charity shop. They left a collection bag through the letter box yesterday."

"Don't throw anything of mine away unless I say so," said Ted.

"I wouldn't dream of it," said Fiona, "but you do need to look in your wardrobe for anything you haven't worn for a long time. They do say if you haven't used anything for a year then you probably won't wear it again."

"Who are 'They'?" asked Ted. "'They' don't know _my_ wardrobe!"

"When did you last wear that leather bomber jacket hanging in your wardrobe?" asked Fiona with a grin.

"A few years ago, but you never know," said Ted, "I might suddenly decide to wear it again."

"You were a teenager when you last wore it, so it probably doesn't even fit you now!"

"Well, just leave it here for now," said Ted.

Fiona grinned, knowing Ted wouldn't ever wear it again, but it reminded him of his youth.

Once they had finished their coffees and Ted had paid the bill, they left the pub and made their way to their car.

They drove home through lovely countryside. The trees were in full leaf, people's front gardens were in colour, a lovely time of the year.

Once they reached home, Ted pulled onto the drive and parked the car. They were lucky enough to live at the start of their road and had a driveway and garage. Some of the house owners relied on finding a parking space on the road.

Once inside, they opened the patio doors, which opened onto the garden. It wasn't a big plot, just large enough for two full-time working folk to manage. "I think I'll mow the lawn," said Ted. "I'll get changed first," as he went upstairs.

"Okay. I will sort out the charity bag as the collection is tomorrow," replied Fiona.

As she passed the phone in the hall, she saw it was flashing, which indicated someone had rung and left a message.

She picked it up and dialled 1571.

"Hello," said a voice. "This is Aunt Ness. They allowed me to use the phone to tell you I'm alright."

That's strange, thought Fiona. She wondered why it had been necessary for Aunt Ness to ring to say she was alright when she had only been there a few hours. Who had given her the use of the phone?

Fiona rang the Care Home. It went unanswered but she was able to leave a message. "Hello," she said. "This is Fiona Chatsworth. I've had a message from my aunt Ness to say she's alright. I hope that is the case. Please ring me if necessary and remind her we will visit her tomorrow."

She replaced the phone slowly. She really hoped it was all as innocent as it sounded.

Ted came downstairs and asked if she was okay as she appeared deep in thought. "Yes, I'm alright, but there was a message on the phone from Aunt Ness saying she's okay."

"That's good then."

"It just seems odd that she needed to tell us that after only being there for a few hours," said Fiona. "She will be seeing us tomorrow and can tell us then."

"She's probably forgotten she's seeing us tomorrow."

"Maybe," said Fiona. "Anyway, I returned the call but no one answered so I left a message reminding them to tell Aunt Ness we will visit tomorrow."

The rest of the afternoon was quite busy with the lawn being mowed and Fiona sorting out a bag of clothes for the charity collection.

At six o'clock, Ted asked Fiona what they should have for their tea.

"I'm not really hungry after the lunch we had. We can have a sandwich, if you like?"

"Okay by me," replied Ted.

The rest of the evening passed pleasantly, snuggled up together on the settee, eating a cheese sandwich and pickles and crisps and watching a film with Tom Cruise on Netflix.

The care home did not return Fiona's call so she presumed everything was alright.

Saturday morning dawned with bursts of sun appearing behind fluffy white clouds. The forecast was good with full sun appearing later according to the weatherman on Radio 2.

"That's good news. We will be able to take Aunt Ness for a walk in the grounds of the care home this afternoon," said Fiona.

"I think I'll go for a run this morning," said Ted.

"Okay, I need to sort the washing out. I ought to do some ironing too," said Fiona.

"A woman's work is never done!" joked Ted.

"Be off with you, or I will make you do the ironing; it's not my favourite job, as you know!"

Ted went to change into his running gear and Fiona went to get the washing basket from the bathroom. She shoved clothes into the washing machine, switched it on and then got the ironing board out.

She sang along to the tunes on the radio whilst she ironed. "You'll never get into a band with that voice," said Ted as he came downstairs.

"At least I can hold a tune," said Fiona. They had been to a few karaoke nights at their local since moving into the neighbourhood. Ted would only get up on stage after a few beers and the punters groaned and held their ears when he sang!

Ted went out the door, saying he would see her in an hour or so.

Fiona felt content. All seemed to be going well in her life. A happy marriage, a husband who she adored, a job she enjoyed and now Aunt Ness settling into a new home.

She finished the ironing and then hung the washing out on the clothesline.

Ted arrived back from his run, red-faced and sweaty. He went to give her a hug but Fiona pushed him away and said, "Shower first!"

"Spoilsport!" he said with a leer as he made his way upstairs.

After a sandwich lunch, Fiona went upstairs to change. She was looking forward to seeing Aunt Ness this afternoon.

Two o'clock saw them on the road to the care home. It was a lovely sunny day and they enjoyed the short journey through the countryside.

They arrived at the electric gates, waited for them to open and then made their way up the drive. "Is this an emergency vehicle or do we park in the commoner's carpark?" said Ted.

"Very funny, only the infamous Dr Johnson is allowed to park near the front door apparently," replied Fiona.

They parked up, noting there were several other cars in the carpark. Ted looked at the make of the cars, commenting on them. He parked their Volvo saying their car was just as good as most of them.

"Boys and their cars!" said Fiona. "As long as a car gets me from A to B, I'm happy."

"Not me," said Ted. "I like to make a statement."

"What, in a Volvo? You know what they say about Volvo drivers. Slow and elderly drivers!"

"Rubbish. They are very good, safe and economical cars and they go a fair pace, especially with me behind the wheel!"

"Yes, I remember the speeding ticket you got a while back! Three points and a fine."

"No comment," said Ted with a grin.

They got out of the car, locked it and made their way around to the front door.

"Do we have to ring, do you think, or do we just go in?" said Fiona.

"Not sure. Let's try the door and see if it opens."

They tried the door and found it wouldn't open. "In case someone escapes again!" commented Ted. They then noticed a small coded keypad on the side of the door. "Security," said Ted.

Fiona rang the bell. They waited for no longer than a few seconds and then it opened.

A young man, probably early twenties, stood there. He was dressed in a light-blue tunic and dark trousers similar to what Caroline had been wearing yesterday.

"How can I help you?" the young man asked.

"We have come to visit my aunt who was admitted yesterday," said Fiona. "Ness Allbridge."

"Oh yes, please come in. My name is Josh. Can you write your names in the visitor's book please, which is on the hall desk."

He turned and went inside. Fiona and Ted followed him and dutifully wrote their names in the visitor's book. Car registration details were needed as well. "Just in case we have people blocking other visitor's cars," the young man explained.

"I think your aunt is in her room. Follow me."

Ted and Fiona followed Josh through the hall. They saw a couple of female staff also dressed in a similar uniform. Fiona noticed a lady, obviously a resident, at the far end of the hall. She was walking slowly with a zimmer frame, singing softly to herself.

"That's Edna," explained Josh. "Always singing to herself. She's very happy."

Josh turned to the stairs with Fiona and Ted following.

Once at the top, they followed Josh to Room 20.

He knocked on the door and hesitated before opening it.

"Hello Ness, your family have come to see you," he said.

Aunt Ness was sitting in an armchair. She had the radio on but it was playing Radio One instead of Classic FM, which Aunt Ness listened to. Her face lit up when she saw them. "Thank goodness you are here to take me home," was her opening sentence.

"Hello Aunt Ness," said Fiona, "we have come to visit you."

"I'm all packed ready to go," said Aunt Ness. She had a small holdall by her chair.

"But we haven't come to take you home, only to visit and find out how you are settling in," said Fiona.

"I can't stay here; people are trying to break in all the time."

Fiona looked at Ted who shrugged and went over to Aunt Ness. He crouched down beside her and took her hand in his. "It's only the staff who are checking on you, I should think, no one is breaking in."

He re-tuned the radio to Classic FM. "That's odd. I left it on the right station yesterday."

"No, no, they are trying to break in. I'm not safe here."

Josh said, "She has been saying this a lot since she arrived."

Fiona said to him, "This is what she used to say at her sheltered housing flat. She got very scared."

"I am scared," said Aunt Ness. "I tell you I'm not safe here."

"Let's calm down," said Josh. "I will fetch a tray of tea for you all and you can have a nice chat together."

"Thank you," said Fiona. "That will be very nice."

Josh left the room, closing the door behind him.

Ted and Fiona sat down. Fiona took Aunt Ness's hand.

"You are safe here; the staff appear very kind. They are looking after you."

"No, they are not. They don't like me."

"I'm sure that's not true, Aunt Ness. How did you sleep last night?"

"Not good because of all the lights."

"What lights?" asked Ted.

"The ones outside my room in the garden."

"Perhaps they are security lights?" said Fiona.

"I think someone wanted to break in," said Aunt Ness.

"Well, I hope you sleep better tonight," said Fiona.

Josh returned with a tray of drinks. Fiona mentioned to him that her aunt had not slept well last night due to some lights outside.

"Not sure what they would have been," he said, looking puzzled. "There's only the garden outside this window. There's a security sensor light outside the front of the house but there aren't any lights in the garden."

"Oh well," said Fiona. "Let's hope Aunt Ness has a better night tonight. Let's have our drink and then we can take a walk outside."

Once they had finished their cups of tea, Fiona asked Aunt Ness which jacket she wanted to wear for their outside walk.

"I don't know," she said, "you choose."

Fiona went to the wardrobe and extracted a green jacket that she had seen her aunt wear many times.

"This one?" she asked as she held it up.

"Yes, that's mine," said Aunt Ness.

Fiona helped her aunt put her jacket on. They exited the room and closed the door behind them. They made their way down the staircase. In the hallway, they encountered another resident along the passage.

"Hello," said Fiona. The elderly gentleman murmured something Fiona could not understand.

"Come on, Bert," said a voice. "Don't dally in the hall; you need to come and sit in the lounge with the others." A female carer appeared. She took Bert's arm and steered him through a doorway that Fiona presumed was the communal lounge.

Fiona had not seen the lounge on either of her aunt's pre-admission visits so she followed them in. She saw about twelve elderly people sitting in chairs. Some were reading, others were just gazing around the room. Josh was in there attending to a lady, giving her a drink. There appeared to be more ladies than men.

The television was on, some sort of quiz show, but only one or two residents were watching it. Bert was taken to a chair at the far end of the lounge, which overlooked the garden.

The room was nicely decorated with pale green wallpaper and a floral carpet. The residents were quiet; no one was really talking to each other. Fiona felt sad as she surveyed the room. *Is this what we all come to?* she wondered. All these people had lived long lives, had experienced many events but ended up sitting in a lounge chair looking into space. She shuddered at the thought of ending up like this.

"Hello," said a voice from the doorway. A man leaning on a walking stick was entering the lounge. "Who are you?"

Fiona turned. He was probably in his late seventies with a cheerful face. "I'm Fiona," she replied. "My aunt moved in here yesterday."

"Good for her," he said. "I'm John. Pleased to meet you."

Fiona was pleased to see a resident who was able to converse without any obvious signs of dementia. "What number room is she in?" he asked.

"20," replied Fiona.

"Oh dear," John said. "That was Mary's room. She was a lively one. She was very outspoken. She disappeared one day about two weeks ago. We were expecting her down for breakfast, we were waiting for her but she never arrived and then we were told she had died, God rest her soul."

"She must have been poorly," said Fiona.

"No, no," said John, "in quite good health she was. Fit as a fiddle apart from her diabetes and just a bit slow walking. Matron informed us after breakfast when we asked where she was. We couldn't think where she had got to. We always sat at the same table and had a good chat over our eggs and bacon. We are allowed a tomato and sausage as extras on a Sunday!"

Ted put his head inside the door, obviously wondering what was keeping Fiona. "Are you coming?" he asked.

Fiona said, "Nice to meet you, John," as she went out of the lounge back into the hallway where Aunt Ness was waiting near the front door.

"That was odd," she said to Ted in a low voice, not wanting Aunt Ness to overhear. "His name's John and seemed perfectly alright. He was telling me about an unexpected death here."

"What, Wilfred, you mean?"

"No, someone called Mary who had the room Aunt Ness is in now."

"Two odd deaths then," said Ted. "Doesn't sound too good, does it?"

"Must be a coincidence," said Fiona. "Come on, let's go out for our walk."

Ted opened the front door. There was a code on the right-hand side that identified how to open it, and Fiona helped Aunt Ness down the two steps. She was a bit unsteady and held her walking stick tightly in her right hand. Fiona followed and closed the door behind them.

"No sign of Matron today," she commented. "Her office door is closed."

"She must have a day off," said Ted. "I bet she's out on a date with Dr Johnson!"

The day was warm and sunny with a light breeze. They made their way towards the front garden. The beds were full of flowers and there was a wooden bench beside a water feature. The grass was cut short and the pathway they followed was block paved so as to make it nice and even to walk on.

"Lovely grounds," said Fiona. "They must spend a fortune on keeping it as nice as this."

Aunt Ness was enjoying being outside. She used to be an avid gardener and appreciated the lovely garden. She could name some of the flowers, which pleased Fiona. Her long-term memory was good; it was just her short-term memory that was the problem.

They made their way over to a bench overlooking the driveway and front garden. It was large enough for them all to sit on. Aunt Ness raised her face to the sun and gave a contented sigh.

"Lovely," she said. "The vicarage had a big garden like this. My sister and I had a swing that we played on whenever it was fine. We had competitions to see who could swing the highest. She usually won!"

It was nice to hear Aunt Ness reminiscing about days gone by.

There was the sound of a car coming up the drive. "Look at that," said Ted. "It's none other than Dr Johnson!"

They all watched as the red Jaguar came to a halt outside the front door of the house.

"Emergency vehicle, my foot!" murmured Ted.

They watched as the doctor got out of his car, bent down and retrieved a briefcase from the backseat and zapped the lock on the car. He was dressed more casually today. He had worn a suit last time they had seen him but today, he had cream chinos and a light blue open-necked polo shirt on. He appeared younger in casual clothes than he had when wearing a suit.

He went up to the front door and punched a code into the keypad, which opened it.

The door closed behind him. "Matron will be upset she's missed him!" said Ted. "I wonder where she lives."

They spent another thirty minutes sitting on the bench. They chatted and they could tell that Aunt Ness was less agitated and enjoying their company and being in the sunshine.

They rose from the bench and were just about to go and explore the back garden when the front door opened and Dr Johnson appeared. He looked up and gave a brief nod of his head as an acknowledgment when he saw the three of them in the garden.

He zapped the car open with his key and got into it, throwing his briefcase on the backseat. He reversed the car and drove down to the gates, which opened towards him when he approached them.

Ted, Fiona and Aunt Ness slowly made their way around the house towards the back garden. Like the front garden, it was beautifully maintained with borders of flowers and a couple of benches. There were trees that stood majestically high and framed the sides and back of the garden.

After a walk and a short rest on a bench admiring the flowers and lawn, they returned to the front of the house. "Shall we go back in now?" Fiona asked Aunt Ness.

"I suppose so," she said.

They rang the doorbell, which was opened very quickly by Josh.

"Have you had a nice walk?" he asked.

"Lovely. We enjoyed looking at the gardens," replied Fiona.

They all went in and followed Josh down the hallway. "We know the way to my aunt's room," Fiona told him.

The three of them went up the stairs back to Room 20.

"Shall we come back to visit you tomorrow?" asked Fiona to Aunt Ness.

"Yes please."

They settled Aunt Ness into her armchair, read to her what programmes she might like to watch on the television that evening and then said goodbye and left.

Ted and Fiona were told the code on the inside keypad by Josh so they could let themselves out the front door, and went down the steps. Just then, a large black estate car arrived and parked outside the house. A couple of darkly suited men got out.

"Uh huh," said Ted as they stood to one side. "I think they are undertakers."

"Not another death!" said a shocked Fiona. "How many is that?"

"I suppose they must have quite a few considering it's a care home for the elderly," replied Ted.

"But that's three recent deaths that we know of and Aunt Ness only arrived yesterday!"

The suited men were admitted inside after ringing the doorbell.

"Come on, let's go quickly," said Fiona "I don't want to watch them bringing a body out."

They hurried round to the carpark, got in the car and went down the drive. Once through the gates, Fiona shuddered and said, "I hope Aunt Ness will be alright."

"She's in good health, except for her dementia."

"Even so, it's a bit disturbing, so many deaths in a short time."

They fell silent and drove home.

Once inside the house, Fiona asked what should they have for their tea.

"Don't mind," said Ted. "Something simple?"

"Spaghetti Bolognaise?"

"Perfect."

Ted went upstairs to change into older clothes as he was planning to do some weeding in the garden, after asking if there was anything he could do to help.

"No thanks, I can manage," said Fiona.

Fiona collected the ingredients required to make the bolognaise later. They needn't eat straight away. She was worried, musing on the events at the care home. She hoped Aunt Ness didn't get wind of what had been occurring at the home in the last few weeks, or it may make her more agitated about living there. Fiona supposed that those residents able to understand might wonder about their own mortality each time a death occurred.

She turned the radio on so she could be distracted from her thoughts.

Ted came downstairs, switched the kettle on and made a cup of tea for both of them before going outside.

Fiona could hear him talking to their next-door neighbour Fred over the garden fence. He was a widower whose wife had passed way a few years ago. He was always ready for a chat. He got a bit lonely but a couple of afternoons a week, he went to the local community hall where elderly people gathered for chat, tea and cake.

The rest of the afternoon passed pleasantly enough. It was nice to have a bit more free time now that they did not have to keep going to check on Aunt Ness in her sheltered housing flat.

Ted came in from the garden at six o'clock and went to shower before supper.

The spaghetti bolognaise was good, especially with the bottle of Shiraz that Ted opened.

Fiona went up to shower and got into bed around ten o'clock leaving Ted to watch a sports programme, which was not Fiona's favourite television programme. She liked to read in bed and was currently reading a good thriller.

The next day, they woke up to drizzly rain. The forecast had predicted light showers and very little sun today and for once, the forecast appeared to be correct. They relaxed in bed, not needing to rush getting up, reading the Sunday newspaper, which had been delivered earlier. Ted immediately bagged the outside of the paper as the back contained the sports pages. Fiona perused the inner pages. They only had a newspaper delivered on Saturdays and Sundays. They relied on their mobiles and the evening news on weekdays.

"What time shall we visit Aunt Ness?" asked Fiona.

"Shall we go this morning so we can have the afternoon to ourselves?" said Ted.

"Okay, fine by me."

They got up, washed and dressed then ate a light breakfast of cereal and toast. "Shall I get some pork steaks out for supper?" said Fiona.

"Good choice."

"I haven't shopped much this week so will need to call in at Tesco's after visiting Aunt Ness. I need vegetables, milk and bread."

"Okay."

Fiona collected some washing and turned the machine on.

"I'll sort this out when we get back. No good waiting for it to finish as I can't put it outside today because of the weather."

They were ready to leave just before eleven. They locked up and went out to the car. They heard the church bells calling folk to church. They saw some people hurrying along with umbrellas up the hill towards the church. Fred was just leaving his house so Ted offered to run him to the church. "Thanks," said Fred, "I'm running a bit late this morning."

They all got in the car and drove to the church. Fred got out just as the bells stopped ringing.

"I would have been late! Thanks again," he said.

Ted reversed out of the church carpark and drove back down the hill and turned at the roundabout, taking a right turn towards the main road.

"Our good deed of the day," he remarked.

Fiona laughed. "He's a nice man and a very good neighbour," she said.

"I wonder if Matron will be working today?"

"Perhaps she doesn't work weekends," replied Ted. "Management often don't."

They arrived at the care home and drove through the gates.

"I hope we don't see another black car arriving again today," said Fiona.

"Me too."

Ted parked in the carpark, they got out and locked the car and made their way to the front door. It was still drizzling.

"My hair is getting wet," cried Fiona. "Let's hurry."

"A bit of rain won't hurt it."

"You're a man, you don't understand female hair!"

Ted rang the bell. It was answered quickly. This time a carer whom they hadn't seen before opened the door to them.

"Yes?" she said.

"We are here to see my aunt Ness, Mrs Allbridge," answered Fiona.

"Oh yes, our new lady. Come in." Her name badge read Alice.

She turned and Ted and Fiona followed her into the hallway.

"You have to sign in the visitor's book."

They did as they were told. "We know the way to her room," said Fiona.

"She's not in her room, she's in the lounge," Alice said.

Alice took them through into the lounge. She looked around the room.

"There she is, over in the corner at the far end."

They made their way over to Aunt Ness. The lounge looked over the back garden. It had patio doors that enabled the residents to look out onto the lovely garden. It was full of colour with the summer flowers.

"Ness, you have some people to see you," stated Alice. She had raised her voice as she spoke as if Aunt Ness had a hearing problem.

"She's not deaf," remarked Fiona.

"Most of them are so it's automatic to raise our voice," said Alice.

"Well, Aunt Ness has excellent hearing."

"Yes, I have. I can hear perfectly well so there is no need to shout," said Aunt Ness.

"Alright, calm down, dear."

"I will not be told to calm down when I've done nothing wrong."

Fiona intervened as she could see Aunt Ness starting to become agitated.

"Perhaps you can relay to the rest of the staff that Aunt Ness does have good hearing."

"If you say so. I normally work at night but they were short today so I got called in. I don't like day shifts as there's too much to do." Alice shrugged and walked off.

"I don't like her," said Aunt Ness. "She thinks we are all fools here."

"I'm sure that's not true, but I must admit I didn't much take to her. She's not as nice as Caroline and Josh," replied Fiona in a low voice so as not to be overheard. "Shall we go to your room?"

"I'm not allowed to be in there."

"Why not?" asked Ted.

"Don't know. I was told to come in here."

"I will ask if we can go to your room as we want to visit you without everyone around. You wait here, Ted."

Fiona went out of the lounge to look for a member of staff. No one was around so she went back towards the lounge when she suddenly saw Matron appear from a door of another room.

"Matron," called Fiona, "we have come to visit my aunt and should like to take her to her room while we are here."

"Why?" asked Matron.

"Because we want to. Surely there is not a problem, is there?"

"No, no, but we don't encourage room visits. We like to be around in case we hear our residents telling tales."

"What? That's outrageous! My aunt is paying good money to be here and she has every right to use her room whenever she wants to."

"Well, don't believe all she tells you, that's what I'm trying to say."

Fiona was lost for words. She stood there unable to move for a few seconds. She then turned and went back into the lounge before she said something she may regret later, and went over to Aunt Ness and Ted.

"Come on, we are going to your room now."

She helped Aunt Ness up out of her chair, handing her the walking stick. They passed several residents in chairs. Some were looking quite vacant; others were looking interested in what was going on. The television was on loud, at such a volume presuming everyone in the room was deaf.

They went out of the lounge and started climbing the staircase.

"Where are you going?" asked a voice.

Fiona turned and saw it was the carer Alice.

"We are going to my aunt's room."

"Matron won't like that," said Alice.

"Tough, because that's where we are going and no one can stop us."

Ted looked at Fiona. He didn't know about the run-in Fiona had had with Matron and was surprised to hear Fiona speaking like that. She didn't raise her voice very often.

"I'll tell you in a minute," she said to Ted when she saw his questioning look. "Let's carry on to Aunt's room."

They reached Room 20 and opened the door.

Aunt Ness walked in and went straight to her chair, breathing a sigh of relief.

"I didn't like sitting there with people I don't know," she said.

"There's no reason why you can't stay in your room if you want to. This is your home now and you have the choice of where to spend your day," said Fiona.

Ted murmured his agreement.

Fiona relayed her conversation with Matron. "That's so out of order!" he agreed.

Fiona looked around the room. "Some things have been moved around," she commented. "We left Aunt's wedding photo on the windowsill and now it's on top of the chest of drawers. Did you move it, Aunt Ness?"

"I don't remember moving it but that doesn't mean to say I didn't!"

Fiona moved the photograph back onto the windowsill.

She saw that the note she had left stating where the pictures should be hung had disappeared. She wrote another note and placed it on the chest of drawers again but this time placed a small ornament on it so it wouldn't get lost. She wondered whether it had fluttered onto the floor and a housekeeper had picked it up thinking it was rubbish.

Fiona then realised one of the cushions was missing.

"Do you know where the red cushion has gone?" she asked Aunt Ness.

"Did we bring it from home?"

"Yes, we definitely did. We brought two. One's here but the second one has disappeared."

"Well, I don't know then."

Fiona thought she must remember to ask one of the staff about the cushion and also to remind them to ask the handyman to hang the pictures.

She opened her aunt's wardrobe to check that all her clothes were still there. "Where's your blue lambswool cardigan?" she asked.

"Did I bring it?"

"Yes, I remember hanging it in the wardrobe on Friday."

"I don't think I've worn it."

"You weren't wearing it yesterday and obviously you are not wearing it today."

Ted was fiddling with the television as when he turned it on, there was no picture or sound.

"It's saying no signal," he said "I'll retune it again. It was perfectly alright when I set it up on Friday."

"I will ask the staff about the cardigan as well as the cushion," said Fiona. "It's very odd that two items are missing. All the clothes have her name in so they shouldn't get lost."

They stayed chatting until there was a knock on the door, which then opened and Josh walked in.

"Time for lunch!" he said.

"I'm not hungry," said Aunt Ness.

"It's roast beef and Yorkshire pudding today and I do believe its apple pie and custard for afters."

"Sounds good!" said Ted. "I think we'll stop as well," he joked.

"Not allowed unfortunately," said Josh. "Other visitors have asked before and Matron refuses. She says the food bill will soar if we feed anyone other than residents."

"Shame! We'll just have to have dry bread crusts and cheese at home then, Fiona!"

Fiona laughed, saying he was a tease and that is what she would serve him if he didn't behave, which made Aunt Ness and Josh laugh.

Fiona and Ted got up and Josh went to help Aunt Ness out of her chair, making sure she had her walking stick.

"Oh, before I forget," said Fiona, "we have noticed a cushion and a cardigan are missing and also some items in the room have been moved around."

"Also," said Ted, "her television had lost its signal so I've retuned it and the radio station had been changed to Radio One from Classic FM."

"I don't know anything about any of that but I'll make enquiries to see if any of the staff can shed a light on it."

"Her cardigan has her name in it," said Fiona.

"Should turn up then, it's probably in the laundry."

"But she hasn't yet worn it here yet!"

Josh shrugged and repeated that he would ask around.

They exited the room and went downstairs. There was a nice smell of cooking permeating in the hallway as Josh led the way into the dining room and led Aunt Ness over to a table where two other ladies were sitting. Fiona followed them.

"This is Alma and Freda, they are sisters who live here," introduced Josh.

"Hello," they cried in unison.

"Hello back," grinned Fiona. "Nice to meet you both."

"And you, back!" they replied together. They all laughed.

A couple of carers including Alice were in the process of serving out the lunches. It looked really appetising. Fiona hoped her aunt enjoyed it.

Fiona said goodbye to Aunt Ness and her dining companions, saying to her aunt that she would ring the home to tell her as to when she and Ted would visit again, and made her way out of the dining room.

On the way out, sitting at a table near the door, she saw a lady wearing what appeared to be an identical cardigan to her aunts missing one.

She didn't stop but, in the hallway, told Ted what she'd seen.

"Must be a similar one. Why would someone else be wearing Aunt Ness's cardigan? She hasn't even worn it herself here, so it hasn't gone to the laundry and been put back in another resident's wardrobe by mistake."

"Don't know. It must be a coincidence."

They made their way to the front door. As they passed Matron's office, she was just coming out.

"Goodbye," she said and went to turn into the hallway.

"Just a moment," called Fiona. "There are two things missing from my aunt's room. A red cushion and a blue cardigan, which is exactly the same as another lady is wearing in the dining room."

"What are you insinuating? That this lady went to your aunt's room and took it? Are you accusing her of stealing it?"

"Of course I'm not accusing her of stealing it!" stammered Fiona. "I was just saying that it looked just like my aunt's."

"She must have a cardigan exactly the same then. Goodbye," snapped Matron who then made her way along the hallway and disappeared through a door into a room at the far end.

Fiona stood there open-mouthed.

"How incredibly rude!" she said to Ted. "There was no need for that!"

"No, there wasn't," said Ted. "Come on, let's go."

They pressed the keypad, which allowed the front door to open.

They made their way around to the carpark and got into the car. It had stopped raining but there were dirty grey clouds in the sky that suggested that another shower was not far off.

Ted manoeuvred the car out of the carpark, down the drive and through the gates.

"I don't know what to say!" said Fiona. She felt outraged and was seething. Ted knew that his wife was not one to get mad normally but he knew she was upset as well as angry.

"Tesco's?" he asked, wanting to distract her so she calmed down.

"No, the nearest pub! I could do with a stiff drink after that!"

"Really?"

"No, not really. Let's go to Tesco's. We can pick up a bottle of wine and have a drink at home."

They grabbed a trolley outside the supermarket and made their way around the aisles. They came across Lynne with a half-full trolley in the cereal aisle.

"Hi you two," she greeted them. "Enjoying shopping on a Sunday?"

Ted laughed. "I don't enjoy shopping any day of the week but we were running out of things."

"Me neither, but with two teenage boys in the house who are always hungry, I'm usually running out of something!"

"I hear you've joined the dating scene," said Ted.

Lynne blushed. "Well, I miss some real adult conversation after I finish work. The conversations at home generally are about football, cricket, the latest trainers and who fancies which girl at school! The last one when they think I'm not listening!"

They all moved on down the aisles filling their trolleys as they went. They said goodbye to Lynne with Fiona saying she would see her at work in the morning.

"I hope she meets someone really nice on the website," commented Ted.

"I do too," replied Fiona.

Once home, they put the kettle on and Fiona made a sandwich for both of them.

"No dry crusts and cheese?" teased Ted.

"No, not this time," said Fiona with a smile.

She put the shopping away. *Funny how you always bought more than you go into a supermarket for*, she thought.

They spent the rest of the afternoon watching a film on the television. It was nice to relax and cuddle up on the sofa together. They kissed and Fiona wriggled out of his embrace saying stop as they were missing the film.

"What film?" replied Ted. "Who wants to watch a film anyway?"

"I do. I know I've seen it before but I like it."

"There's something you may like even better."

Fiona swatted his hands away. "Stop it, I'm concentrating."

"Well, I may as well get prepared for tomorrow. We have a new contract I need to do some work on."

He reluctantly got up and went upstairs to the spare bedroom he used as an office, leaving Fiona who was now stretched out on the settee.

It was still overcast with a fine drizzle outside so Fiona felt no guilt about lying on the settee on a lazy Sunday afternoon. *Gardening can wait for fine days*, she thought.

After the film finished, she went into the kitchen to make preparations for their supper. She then remembered the washing in the machine so she took it out and hung it on a free-standing clothes airer in their dining room.

The pork steaks were nicely defrosted. She peeled potatoes, shredded cabbage and cut cauliflower into mouth-size florets.

She got the gravy granules out of the cupboard in case she forgot again. She made some stuffing balls and found a jar of apple sauce in the cupboard.

The meal was ready for seven o'clock. She called upstairs to Ted. He came down and they sat with the meal on their trays in front of *Countryfile*.

"Delicious, thank you," he commented patting his stomach. His plate was as clean as a whistle. Fiona liked the fact that Ted appreciated and ate her meals with obvious enjoyment. Until they were married, she had not cooked much but now she enjoyed preparing and serving meals to an appreciative recipient.

By ten o'clock, Fiona was ready for bed. Ted watched the news and then came up to shower and join Fiona. She was half asleep so he settled to holding her close and breathing in her familiar fresh smell. He knew how lucky he was in finding his soul mate. He had his perfect world.

Monday morning arrived. The weather outside was sunny and clear. It was a good start to the day but showers were forecast again for the afternoon.

The alarm trilled at seven-thirty, waking them both.

Fiona turned to Ted and murmured, "Morning."

"Morning to you too," as he leaned over to kiss her. They enjoyed a five-minute cuddle.

"Early night tonight?" smiled Ted.

"We'll see," Fiona grinned as she got up to go into the bathroom.

Ted stayed in bed whilst Fiona used the bathroom and when she returned, he got out to use the bathroom. Fiona returned to the bedroom, made the bed and then went downstairs.

They had breakfast of muesli and toast and marmalade. Zoe Ball was on Radio Two with incessant chatter that went over their heads. Some of the songs were good. Take That singing *Patience* was a good one as was Queen's *Bohemian Rhapsody*.

"See you tonight," Fiona said as she kissed Ted goodbye. She went out of the front door and got into her small Corsa car. She had owned the car for a few years and was reluctant to change it for a newer model. While it still went well, she would hang on to it.

Ted went out to his car to drive to work five minutes later. This morning routine was familiar to both of them.

Fiona arrived at work just before nine. Lynne was already at her desk. Fiona shrugged off her jacket and put it on the back of her chair. "Good morning," she greeted Lynne.

Lynne replied, "Morning."

The two had shared an office for over four years. They had gotten to know each other well. Occasionally, they had been for a drink after work but since Lynne's marriage had broken up and Fiona had married, Lynne was needed at home as soon as the work day was over to look out for her two sons.

"Apart from shopping in Tesco's, how was your weekend?" asked Fiona.

"Not bad at all," said Lynne with a smile. "I had a second date on Saturday night."

"Details please!"

"I don't want to jinx anything by saying too much but it went well."

"What's his name?" asked Fiona.

"Kevin."

"What does he do?"

"He's a doctor."

"Wow, sounds like a good catch!"

"He's very nice. A bit older than me but that doesn't seem to be a problem." She started sorting her desk out ready for the day ahead.

Lynne obviously didn't want to say any more about her date and Fiona respected that so didn't ask any further questions.

The office phone rang at that point. Lynne answered it. The first of many calls that day.

At lunchtime, they went out on separate breaks as usual. Ted rang Fiona for a quick chat while Fiona was eating a sandwich on a park bench in the garden at the back of the council offices. It was starting to look as if a shower was imminent.

"I may be late home tonight as we have this new contract to sort out, which is being a bit tricky," said Ted.

"Okay, I will get supper for eight instead of seven then."

They chatted for a few more minutes.

"See you tonight. I love you," said Ted.

"Love you too."

It was time for Fiona to return to the office. The rain shower arrived just as Fiona got back at the office.

"That was lucky!" she told Lynne, shaking a few rain droplets from her hair. They had a busy afternoon answering telephone enquiries and sorting different schedules out.

Fiona got home just after five-thirty. She parked up on the driveway. Fred was in his front garden pulling weeds. The sun had come out now and the evening weather looked promising.

"Hi Fred," called Fiona. "I hope you didn't get too wet returning from church yesterday."

"I got a lift back so I was alright. Better weather today. By the way, you had a visitor today. Kept knocking on your door. I told him you worked in the day but he said he needed to see you."

"I wonder who that was," said Fiona. "What did he look like?"

"Young fellow, looked like a nurse. Had a blue uniform on."

"How odd. Still, knowing I work in the day, perhaps he will either ring me or come around in an evening."

"Maybe."

Fiona let herself in, feeling puzzled as to who her visitor may have been. The only nurse-type people she had encountered were the care home staff but why on earth would they be coming around to her house?

She had a shower and changed into casual clothes. What to do for supper was her next thought.

She was starting to prepare a salad and getting out the new potatoes to start scraping them when there was a knock on her front door.

She opened it and was very surprised to see Josh, the carer from Aunt Ness's care home.

"I called around earlier today but the man next door said you worked in the day so I've come back this evening," he said.

"What on earth do you want with me?" Fiona asked.

"Can I come in and talk to you?" he said with a furtive glance behind his shoulder. It was if he didn't want to be seen.

Fiona opened the door wider and stepped back to let him in. She led him into the lounge and gestured for him to sit down. Fiona sat down in the chair facing him.

"Is Aunt Ness alright?"

"Yes, she's fine."

"Then what can possibly be the matter?"

Josh hesitated as if he didn't know where to start.

"I have only been at Goodrest Care Home for three months but there's some very strange things going on there," he said. "I thought you should know as your aunt is the newest resident and I like her. I don't want anything to happen to her."

"What sort of strange things?" asked Fiona, starting to feel very alarmed.

"I don't trust the Matron. She's always sucking up to Dr Johnson," Josh said.

"Why don't you trust her?"

"They're always in her office talking in low voices. The residents are a bit scared of her, the way she talks to them. He's actually quite nice. Lots of her rules, which shouldn't be allowed."

"What sort of rules?" asked Fiona.

"Some of them are not allowed to be in their rooms in the daytime, for one."

"I know when we arrived for a visit yesterday, my aunt had been told to sit in the lounge and not stay in her room."

"There you are then."

"But it could be for their own safety. If they have some sort of dementia, it may be better for them to be where staff can keep an eye on them."

"It's not just that," said Josh. "They are not allowed on their own outside unless someone is with them."

"Again, it's probably for their own safety," repeated Fiona.

"I don't think so. There some odd things going on they don't want the residents to know about."

"Have you any evidence?" asked Fiona.

"Not really, only things that the residents have told me. That is, the ones who can tell me anything and there aren't many of them that can do that. Some have lost some of their belongings since being admitted. Some have seen a light outside at night. A light where there shouldn't be any."

"Well, there's probably a logical explanation, perhaps someone got out and they were being looked for, or perhaps the night staff heard a noise outside and went to investigate," replied Fiona.

"I think not. I just thought I ought to warn you that things are not as simple as they appear!" He got up and said he needed to go.

Fiona saw him to the door. "I'm planning to visit Aunt Ness tomorrow evening."

"I'm on shift tomorrow evening. I will see you then."

Fiona opened the front door and saw him out. He walked down the drive turning left at the end. There was no car parked nearby so she presumed he had walked or parked around the corner in the next street.

She closed the door after he had gone. She went into the kitchen and sat down. *What a strange visit*, she thought.

She picked up the phone and dialled the number for the care home. It was answered quickly but the person did not identify themselves so Fiona asked to whom she was speaking to.

"Marie," said the person. "How can I help you?"

Fiona was still no wiser as to whom she was speaking to but she didn't pursue it.

"My name's Fiona. Can you tell my aunt, Ness Allbridge, that I am coming to visit her tomorrow evening at about six o'clock please."

"Alright," said Marie and put the phone down with a firm hand.

Fiona put her own phone down carefully.

She got up and went back to preparing the evening meal.

Ted arrived home at seven o'clock. He was tired from his long day but not too tired to give Fiona a big hug and kiss. "I've missed you," he said, nuzzling her neck.

"Go and shower," she said.

She would tell Ted about Josh's visit while they ate.

They sat down to eat at seven-thirty. The salmon salad and new potatoes were served. Crusty bread and butter accompanied the meal. No wine this evening. They tended to open a bottle just with their weekend meals.

"I had a visitor earlier this evening," started Fiona.

"Oh yes? Not your secret lover, I hope!"

Fiona smiled and said "And if it was?"

"I would have to kill him," replied Ted with a grin.

"No, not my secret lover, his wife won't let him out on a Monday night!"

"Nor any night, I hope!"

"Seriously; Josh, the carer from the home, called round. Apparently, he came in the day but Fred told him I was at work, which is why he came back this evening."

"What on earth did he want?" exclaimed Ted.

"To warn me that some strange things are going on at the care home. Lots of rules for the residents, residents' missing items and strange lights outside at night."

"How very odd."

"Yes, that's what I thought. Very strange, he said he likes Aunt Ness and he doesn't want anything to happen to her."

"I should hope not! What did you say?"

"I said I will be visiting her tomorrow evening. In fact, I rang the home to tell Aunt Ness that I will be there tomorrow about six."

"I'm playing squash with Geoff tomorrow after work so I can't come with you."

"That's okay. I don't mind going on my own."

Fiona got up to clear the plates away. She put them in the dishwasher and then wiped the table.

"Shall we go for a quick walk to the park?" asked Ted.

"Okay. Let me get my jacket."

She went to the cupboard to retrieve her jacket. She glanced in the hall mirror, smoothing down her blonde hair. *She needed a trim*, she thought. She would ring the hairdresser tomorrow to arrange an appointment.

They made their way down the road towards the local park. There were one or two families there with children playing on the swings and slide. One little boy of about seven was on the roundabout, urging his father to push faster.

The park looked lovely after the recent rain showers. The colourful flowers in the numerous beds were glistening with water droplets and the trees were in full leaf.

"We are lucky to have this park," said Fiona as she and Ted strolled along holding hands. "We will be able to bring our children here."

"Anything you need to tell me?"

"No, we did say we wanted to wait a while before producing any."

They wandered past the play area that led to a wooded area. The tall full leafed trees made it darker here. They could hear a dog barking. A couple appeared around the corner with a chocolate-coloured Labrador on a lead.

They wandered on the designated pathway that was well worn by the many feet that had walked the same route over the years. As they neared the centre of the wooded area, they spotted two people sitting on a bench.

"Look," said Ted, "that's Matron!"

"So it is. I wonder who that is with her."

"Wonder if she lives near here?"

Ted pulled Fiona to one side so they were shielded behind a massive tree trunk.

"Don't let her see us," whispered Ted. "Let's watch."

They peered around the tree to see what was happening.

Matron and a lad of about twenty appeared to be in a deep discussion. The lad was wearing blue overalls and a cap pulled low so his face couldn't be seen. Then Matron put her hand in a bag she had with her and handed him something. He put it in his rucksack.

"What is it?" whispered Fiona. "I can't see."

"I can't see either. Looks funny business to me," said Ted in a low voice.

Just at that moment, a black and white dog suddenly appeared and bounded up to them, greeting them with short sharp barks.

Matron looked up at the noise, staring in their direction.

A man and a lady in their late fifties appeared, shouting, "Harvey! Harvey!"

The lady spotted her dog and came over to Ted and Fiona. "Naughty boy, Harvey! Sit!"

"I'm so sorry," she apologised. "I hope he didn't jump up at you."

"No, it's fine, he didn't jump up, just surprised us!" replied Fiona, looking at the couple. The dog appeared to be of a mixed breed, probably mostly a collie.

The lady attached a lead to the sitting dog's collar, admonishing him for running off, apologised again and left to walk in the opposite direction.

Fiona looked up and saw the empty bench. Matron and the lad had gone.

"Blow!" she said to Ted. "I wonder where they went."

"Didn't see with all the commotion," replied Ted.

"Shall we carry on into the wood?" asked Ted.

"No, let's turn back and go home."

They turned around facing the way they had walked. Some rain clouds were dotting the sky.

"Let's get back before it rains," Ted said as he slung his arm around Fiona's shoulder and pulled her close against him.

They made their way back through the main park. The play area was more or less deserted now. A lone teenager was on the swing flying as high as he dared.

Once home, they settled down on the settee, cuddling up together. It was gone nine by now and they were both tired.

"I'm visiting Aunt Ness tomorrow after work and you're playing squash. Do you want to pick up fish and chips when you've finished?"

"Good idea," agreed Ted. "We should both be back about eight."

"Save cooking," said Fiona. She yawned. "I'm going up, I'm very tired."

"I'll watch the news and then I'll be up."

He turned to kiss her. "Sleep well. If you're not awake when I come up, I'll see you in the morning."

Fiona went upstairs and got ready for bed. She set her alarm for seven o'clock. She usually read for about half an hour but after the second page, her eyes started closing. She was comfortable, warm and cosy. Rain battered against the windows. She put the book away and fell quickly asleep. She didn't hear Ted come up. He snuggled up to her but she was oblivious.

Ted fell asleep almost at once.

Tuesday morning dawned bright with a promise of sunshine later. The alarm went off, waking the pair of them.

"I missed our cuddle last night. You were well away when I came up," said Ted.

"Well, there's no time now either," smiled a sleepy Fiona.

"There's always time for a cuddle."

"Bags the bathroom first!" cried Fiona as she rose from the bed after the quickest of cuddles.

She washed and dressed and went downstairs, leaving Ted to his ablutions.

She opened the lounge curtains then put the bread in the toaster ready for when he appeared downstairs. She made a pot of tea and got the cereal out of the cupboard. She took bowls, cutlery, mugs and plates out and laid the kitchen table.

Ted appeared five minutes later.

They ate their breakfast, cleared up and kissed each other goodbye, with Fiona reminding him not to forget to bring fish and chips home that evening.

Fiona arrived at work. Lynne was not yet in, which was unusual. She arrived in a rush a few minutes later. She sat down at her desk, stuffing her handbag in the bottom drawer of her desk.

"Thought I was going to be late."

"It's not like you to be in after me," said Fiona.

"I had another date last night and got home a bit later than planned. Then I couldn't sleep, tossed and turned and finally dropped off in the early hours," Lynne replied.

"A date with the doctor?" asked Fiona.

"Yes."

"Going well then?"

"Yes. I really like him. He's off to a conference in Bournemouth today so last night was the only free night we could see each other this week."

"I'm glad for you," said Fiona. "You'll have to come around for a meal with us one evening so I can meet him."

"It's still early days," smiled Lynne. "Perhaps in a few weeks when we know each other a bit more."

"I'll hold you to that; what do the boys think of him?"

"They haven't met him yet but they seem okay with me seeing someone. Now their father has a new girlfriend, they probably feel sorry for me."

The phone rang and Lynne picked it up, the first of many calls that day. The working day went well, no crises for once.

Fiona went to second lunch at one-thirty. She bought a tuna and salad sandwich and a bottle of fruit juice from the delicatessen she often went to. She sat on a park bench soaking up the sun. It was a much better day today, sunny and warm. Many of the park benches were occupied with what looked like other office workers. Some were eating alone but there were some benches with two or three people on, talking and eating their lunches.

She thought about Aunt Ness and the forthcoming visit planned for this evening.

After a busy afternoon, Fiona left the office and retrieved her car from the carpark. She realised she had forgotten to ring for a hair appointment. *Must remember tomorrow*, she thought.

She drove through the rush hour, noting this time the traffic lights were being kind to her for once.

She pulled up at the care home's electric gates just before six o'clock, waited for them to open and then drove around to the carpark. She got out and locked the door.

She went to the front door of the home and rang the bell. She hadn't yet been given the code to enter the home without ringing the bell. Perhaps visitors weren't allowed the privilege of knowing it!

The door was answered by a carer who she hadn't seen before. Her name badge read Rosalyn.

"Yes?" Rosalyn asked.

"I'm Fiona and have come to visit my aunt Ness. Mrs Allbridge."

"Come in. Please sign the visitor's book."

Fiona duly signed as Rosalyn kept watch while she did so.

"Where will Aunt Ness be?" she asked.

"She's in her room. She has been a bit unsettled today and wouldn't have her tea in the dining room with the other residents. I'll take you up."

"There's no need. I know the way to her room."

Rosalyn shrugged and went further down the hall.

Fiona went down the hall and climbed the stairs. She went to her aunt's room knocking on the door before entering.

"Go away!" said her aunt's voice as Fiona entered the room.

"It's me, Fiona," said Fiona as she made her way over to her aunt.

Aunt Ness was sitting in her chair. She was sitting in silence; no radio or television was on. There was a tray on the table in front of her but the meal was untouched as far as Fiona could make out.

"What's the matter?" she asked.

"They're poisoning me. I can't eat anything here,"

"Nonsense. That looks a really nice salad on the tray."

Aunt Ness said, "That's what they want me to think but I know it's poisoned."

"Why do you think that?"

"Because of what I know," said Aunt Ness with a quiver on her voice. She looked on the verge of tears.

"What do you mean?"

"I don't know."

"Calm down and tell me everything." said Fiona. She grasped her aunt's hand, pulled a chair up and sat down in front of her.

"It's because of the lights."

"What lights?"

"Outside at night. They know that I have seen them so they will break in and get me."

"No one is out to get you and no one will break in. This is a care home where you are safe and being looked after," reassured Fiona.

She was worried looking at her aunt. She was very worked up and trembling.

"Shall I go and ask the nurse about this?"

"No! No! It will be worse for me if you do that."

"Have you taken your tablets today, the ones that your previous doctor prescribed for you when you had these thoughts when you lived in your flat?"

"I don't know. They give me something but I don't know what they are."

Fiona said, "I will go and ask if you are taking your tablets, they really helped you before."

"Alright, but come back, won't you?"

Fiona asked if she should turn the television on. She hoped some distraction might calm her aunt down. She agreed so it was switched on. The BBC news was on. The newsreader was speaking about something that had happened in London. There had been some sort of incident outside the Houses of Parliament late in the afternoon.

Fiona left her aunt watching it. She appeared to be settling down now.

Fiona picked up the tray with the untouched meal on it and made her way out of the room and went downstairs.

She looked around her and wondered where she would find a member of staff.

Rosalyn appeared just then, coming out of the communal lounge. She looked at Fiona with a raised eyebrow.

"Can you help me?" asked Fiona. "My aunt has not touched her tea as she believes it is poisoned. She's very worked up. I wonder whether she has had the tablet today that calms her down when she's like this."

"I would think she has, if she is written up for it, but I can go and check."

"Also, can she have a sandwich and a cup of tea please and I will stay with her while she eats it."

"Alright, the kitchen is closed now, but I can make one for her."

"Thank you and please don't forget about checking if she has had her tablet today."

Rosalyn turned away and went through a door at the end of the hallway.

Fiona went back upstairs to her aunt.

Aunt Ness did appear more settled now she was being distracted by the television.

"I have spoken with a carer called Rosalyn who is checking about your medication and she also making you a sandwich," said Fiona.

Aunt Ness smiled and said how nice it was to see her as she hadn't seen her recently. Fiona didn't correct her.

"Ted sends his love."

"Ted?"

"My husband, remember?"

"Oh yes. The tall man who brought me here. It's all his fault."

"We both brought you here last Friday," Fiona reminded her.

Fiona looked around the room and saw that her aunt's pictures were on the wall.

"That's good; the handyman put your pictures up for you."

"He had a secret bit of paper when he did it. I think it was telling him things about me."

"No," laughed Fiona. "I left instructions on a bit of paper telling him where we wanted the pictures hanging."

"No, I don't think so. It was some sort of secret message."

Fiona left the subject of the pictures alone. She saw the wedding photograph was still on the windowsill.

The red cushion was still missing though.

She looked in the wardrobe to check if the blue lambswool cardigan had been returned but she couldn't find it.

There was a knock on the door and Rosalyn entered carrying a tray with a sandwich, a piece of fruit cake and two mugs of tea on it. Fiona thanked her and took the tray and putting it on the table in front of Aunt Ness.

"I checked the drug chart with the nurse and your aunt did have all her tablets today," she said.

"Perhaps she needs to have her medication reviewed," said Fiona.

"I will check with Matron tomorrow to find out when Dr Johnson can do that but I think he's away this week. A locum doctor is covering," said Rosalyn, leaving the room.

Fiona unwrapped the cling film covering the sandwich and offered the plate to her aunt. She started to eat it, much to Fiona's relief. They both drank their mugs of tea. Aunt Ness then ate the fruit cake.

"I'm glad you brought some food in with you, I can't eat the poisoned stuff they give me here."

Fiona didn't correct her as she was afraid her aunt may become agitated again. Fiona saw that her aunt's radio was on her bedside table. She went over and switched it on to check the channel and was very annoyed to see it was showing Radio One again instead of Classic FM.

"Have you played your radio today?" she asked.

"I don't remember."

Fiona tuned it in again to the correct programme. Next time she visited, she would bring a small label and would write on it, "Classic FM only, do not change channels."

She went back to sit with Aunt Ness and they watched the rest of the news. The local news then came on, which they watched together.

"I have to go soon," said Fiona. "Will you be alright?"

"I suppose so."

"Shall I help you into your nightie?"

"No, thank you," said Aunt Ness in a firm voice. "I want to remain dressed in case I need to leave here tonight."

Fiona could tell that her aunt was not going to be persuaded so she got up and moved her chair back.

"I'll ask someone to come up a bit later and help you into bed."

She kissed her aunt goodnight and said she would visit again in a few days. Fiona hoped that she would see an improvement next time she called in.

She made her way downstairs and seeing Rosalyn in the hallway, asked if someone could assist her aunt to get ready for bed later. She also reminded her about the medication review when a doctor next visited the home. "Is Josh on shift this evening?"

"No, he rang in sick, making us short-staffed."

Fiona made her own way out of the front door after punching in the code on the keypad.

She drove home at a steady pace thinking about her aunt. It was very early days and hoped she would begin to settle in.

She arrived home before Ted. It was nice not having to prepare a meal. She hoped Ted remembered to pick up the fish and chips after his squash match.

She had a shower and dressed in her nightie and dressing gown ready for a cosy evening in. She prepared a couple of trays ready for their meal and put two plates on a low oven heat to warm. She went into the lounge and turned the television on. *Eastenders* was on. Not a programme she normally watched but Lynne did and had said there were some good storylines going on at the moment. Fiona didn't really know the characters; *it was all a bit confusing*, she thought. There was lots of shouting and people falling out with each other.

Ted arrived home just before eight. She could smell the delicious aroma of fish and chips as he came through the front door.

"Hello darling," called Ted. "I've remembered our supper!"

"Hello to you too! I'm glad you did or it would have been the bread and cheese!"

He took them through into the kitchen then returned to the lounge where he dived at Fiona on the settee, giving her a big kiss.

"Who won the match?" she said, returning his kiss.

"Don't ask!"

"Never mind, you can't win them all!"

Ted went into the kitchen and returned with the trays of food. He brought in ketchup, vinegar and salt.

They sat together on the settee and thoroughly enjoyed the fish and chips.

"How was Aunt Ness?" he asked.

"A bit confused. Thinks she is being poisoned and that people are out to get her. The radio had been tuned again to Radio One, which is very annoying, and her cardigan and cushion is still missing."

"That's not on; I should report it to Matron if it keeps happening."

"I didn't see her this evening."

"Perhaps she's having another clandestine meeting in the park!"

"I asked if Dr Johnson can review her pills but was told he's away this week," said Fiona.

"There must be another doctor on call," replied Ted.

He got up and removed their trays. "Very good!" he said. "I enjoyed that."

"Me too."

"What shall we watch this evening?" he asked.

"There's a new series on at nine, which looks quite good, on Channel Four. A family who have gone to live in France after buying a dilapidated house and are doing it up."

"Okay, sounds worth watching."

They spent the next hour engrossed in the programme. The family renovating the house in France were very entertaining and it made good viewing.

At half past ten, after the news, they locked up and made their way upstairs. They lay in bed, cuddled up together, chatting about their day until they fell asleep.

When Fiona reached the office the next morning and settled at her desk, she rang the care home. She wanted to know what sort of night Aunt Ness had had.

"Very good," she was told by whomever answered the phone. "She was agitated before bedtime so a sleeping tablet was prescribed for her and she slept all night."

"But she's never had a sleeping tablet before," said Fiona.

"Well, it soon settled her."

"Did the doctor look at her other tablets?" asked Fiona.

"No, as it wasn't the usual doctor. Dr Johnson is the doctor who will do that but he isn't here this week."

"Alright, but when he returns, I should like him to look at them."

"I will tell Matron that you have asked."

Fiona put the phone down.

"Everything okay?" asked Lynne.

"I suppose so. They gave Aunt Ness a sleeping tablet last night. She was very agitated when I visited her and apparently, she was still agitated later."

"I'm sure she will settle down when she's used to being there," said Lynne.

"I hope so."

Fiona rang her hairdresser and managed to secure an appointment for a haircut on Saturday morning.

The day passed quickly and Fiona left work on time at five o'clock. She and Ted were meeting some friends this evening. She wanted to get home to shower and wash her hair.

Ted arrived home just after Fiona and waited for her to come out of the bathroom so he could have his shower.

Fiona dressed in a summer dress and light jacket and waited in the lounge for Ted. He came downstairs with slicked back wet hair. They went out of the house and walked to the local pub. They were meeting friends who they had known for some time.

"Are we eating?" asked Fiona.

"Let's see if the others are," replied Ted.

They entered the Red Lion. Hugh and Moira were already at the bar and hailed them as they saw Fiona and Ted. Hugh was tall with blond hair and chin stubble and Moira was an attractive redhead. They had been good friends ever since Fiona had started dating Ted. Hugh had been to university with Ted and after meeting and marrying Moira, they often met up as two couples. Hugh and Moira hadn't yet started a family, just like Ted and Fiona.

"What are you drinking?" Hugh asked.

Ted turned to Fiona. "Lager and lime?" he asked.

"Please."

"A pint of Abbot and a half of lager and lime please," he asked the barman.

They took their drinks and found a table at the far end of the pub. It was a bit quieter there, away from the bar so they could hear themselves talk.

They hadn't seen each other for a couple of weeks so they chatted about what they had been doing since they had last met. Hugh was something in the finance world and Moira was a nurse in the local hospital. She had recently decided to leave the NHS as she was tired of working double shifts due to under staffing. She had another week of working her notice before finally leaving.

Fiona told Moira about her aunt Ness moving into the care home.

"My grandmother went into one several years ago and really liked it," said Moira.

"Aunt Ness is quite unsettled at the moment," said Fiona. "I hope she settles. She's really not enjoying being there at the moment. She says strange things are happening at the home, which she cannot understand."

"I'm sure things will improve soon," said Moira.

They spent a very pleasant evening and ordered food from the bar. Scampi and chips with a side salad for Ted and Fiona; Moira, being a vegetarian, chose mushroom pasta and Hugh ordered a medium rare steak with all the trimmings. It was what he ate each time he went out for a meal, which caused great hilarity and teasing as he always studied the menu at length, far longer than anyone else, but always ended up ordering the steak. Ted got in another round of drinks. The pub was pretty full and the noise levels increased as the night wore on.

At ten o'clock, they called it a night as all had to get up for work in the morning.

They said goodbye outside and made their way home. It was quite dark. The nights were pulling in now but it was a pleasant walk home. Hand in hand, Ted and Fiona strolled down the main street before turning into their road.

"Nice evening, good company," commented Fiona as they reached their front door.

"Yes, it was."

They didn't switch on the television but went straight to bed after locking up as they were both tired.

The next day, Fiona arrived at work at nine o'clock as usual. Lynne was already there. They had a chat about what they had been doing the previous evening.

"Have you heard from your doctor friend?" asked Fiona.

"Yes, he rang me for a chat," replied Lynne. "He's at his Bournemouth conference and due home on Friday."

"He must be important to go on conferences. What sort of doctor is he?"

"He's a geriatric consultant. I know he gives lectures to junior doctors."

"You stick in there; it all sounds good!"

"The boys are going to meet him this weekend."

"Has he been married?" asked Fiona.

"He's been divorced for many years. He has a teenage son called Tom."

"Well, I hope it goes well. If it carries on, perhaps we can all meet up one evening."

"We'll see how it progresses before I start introducing him to friends!"

That evening after supper, Fiona told Ted about Lynne and her new doctor friend.

"She's really upbeat, which is great. I hope it goes well for her."

They watched a programme about monkeys in the wild. It was amusing and made them laugh.

An early night rounded off a very pleasant evening.

Next day over breakfast, Fiona suggested to Ted that they visit Aunt Ness that evening.

"Okay, we'll go more or less as soon as I get home so we won't be too late back."

They both went off to work.

Fiona was home a bit before Ted. She got some lamb chops out of the freezer and quickly peeled some potatoes. She remembered to find a label so she could attach it to her aunt's radio.

Ted arrived back and after a quick wash and change, they set off to the care home.

"I wonder how we will find her this evening," murmured Fiona. "I hope she's more settled."

They drove through the gates and parked in the carpark.

They rang the doorbell and a male carer who they hadn't seen before admitted them. There was no name badge on his tunic to identify him.

"She's just finishing tea," he said.

"I hope she's in the dining room starting to make friends," said Fiona.

"Yes, she is."

He took them through into the dining room, after they had signed in, and asked them to wait at the door and went up to Aunt Ness. There was an empty plate in front of her. She was at a table with two other ladies who were still eating. There were several other residents in the room, some were finishing their meal, some were being helped to eat by staff and others had finished eating.

The carer said something to her aunt and she turned her head towards the doorway.

She didn't appear to respond when seeing them. The carer helped her up from her chair, retrieved her walking stick from the back of the chair and guided her towards the door.

She looked at them without recognition.

"Hello, Aunt Ness," said Fiona.

Aunt Ness looked at her and asked who she was.

"It's Fiona and Ted."

"But who are you?" she repeated.

"I'm Fiona, your niece, and this is Ted, my husband."

Aunt Ness looked at them and said, "I don't think I know you."

Fiona asked the carer if they could go upstairs to her aunt's room with her. He said yes of course they could.

They exited the dining room and the carer guided Aunt Ness and her walking stick towards the staircase. He went first and her aunt climbed the steps slowly with Fiona and Ted following. When they reached her room, the carer left to go back downstairs.

Aunt Ness went straight to her chair.

Fiona pulled a chair up close to her and took her hand. Ted sat in the other chair.

No one said anything for a few seconds and then Fiona asked her aunt what was troubling her.

"I don't know," she answered. "I don't know anything anymore."

Fiona was concerned as Aunt Ness did not seem to be able to concentrate. Her eyes kept closing and she looked very tired.

"I think she's been given some sort of pill to keep her sedated, she's really quite out of it. I wonder if it's the aftereffects of the sleeping tablet she was given last night," she said to Ted.

"Maybe."

Aunt Ness appeared to be falling asleep.

"I think I'll help her into bed so she can sleep it off."

She collected her aunt's nightie from under the pillow on the bed and gently woke her and led her into the bathroom. She helped her aunt wash her face and hands. She left her to use the facilities and when the bathroom door opened, she assisted her into bed. Aunt Ness was quickly asleep.

Fiona closed the curtains leaving the bedside lamp on. She remembered to attach a label on the radio asking that it be kept on Classic FM. She noticed that it was on the correct channel this time.

They left the room and made their way downstairs.

Fiona saw the carer and voiced her concerns.

"She's just very tired," he said. "She is an elderly lady."

"I think it's more than that, she's really out of it, as if she's sedated."

"I'm sure she will be alright tomorrow," he said. "We will keep checking on her."

Ted and Fiona let themselves out of the front door and went to the carpark.

"I will ring the Matron tomorrow and ask how Aunt Ness is. She really needs her medication checked by a doctor," said Fiona.

They drove home and after showering, prepared and ate their supper. They watched television and retired to bed after the news.

Next day just before leaving work, Fiona received a phone call from Moira.

"Is it Goodrest Care Home that your aunt has moved into?" she asked.

"Yes."

"I have seen an advert advertising for nurses to work there so I'm thinking of applying."

"That would be good. Less stressful than hospital work and you could also keep an eye on Aunt Ness!"

"I will let you know if I get an interview," replied Moira.

Fiona mentioned this to Ted over supper. She also told him that she had rung up the home that morning asking how Aunt Ness was. She had been assured that her aunt had slept all night without any sleeping tablet and appeared much brighter this morning.

"It would be very convenient, having someone you know working there. She could be a spy!" he said.

"I agree. It would be nice, having Moira keeping an eye on things," said Fiona.

Moira rang a couple of evenings later, saying she had been to the care home for an interview and was hopeful of securing a post. They would be letting her know in the next day or so.

She said she had been interviewed by the Matron who had appeared quite formal. The post sounded interesting with fewer hours that she had been working at the hospital. The pay was good too.

"I hope she gets the job," said Fiona to Ted after she had finished talking to Moira.

Fiona rang the care home to check how Aunt Ness was and was reassured that she was alright.

The evening passed pleasantly enough and they went to bed after the news.

Goodrest Care Home was a busy place. There were forty residents who lived there and the home employed plenty of staff to cater for their different needs. There was a mixture of nurses, carers, housekeepers and kitchen staff.

There was a handyman called Matt who attended to jobs requiring maintenance attention. He repaired items, painted and decorated and generally made himself useful around the home. He was in his late fifties, grey haired, and was fit and strong. He had worked there for two years and really enjoyed his job. He used to have an office job but he had hated being cooped up inside, doing the same things day after day, so had chucked it in and started using his maintenance skills doing odd jobs for friends and neighbours. He had applied for this post when he saw it advertised and was really pleased to secure the position. He lived locally and was happily married to Nancy, a carer who visited vulnerable people in their own homes.

He was a little bit afraid of the Matron who barked her orders, expecting him to jump when she spoke to him. Matron had been in post for just over a year. He had much preferred the previous one but she was now retired and had handed over the reins to the current Matron, who had been her deputy. Matt liked to chat to the staff and loved to hear about any gossip that was circulating. He had been a bit perturbed recently as he felt there was an atmosphere that hadn't been there before this Matron took over.

He did not know too much about Dr Johnson who attended to the residents' medical needs. He seemed pleasant and always said hello when he met Matt in the home. He and Matron were often closeted in her office as if their many conversations were not meant for any listening ears that may pass by the door. He had heard the Matron speaking quite harshly to some of the residents, which Matt thought was uncalled for. They were in the home because they needed care and attention and it was not their fault if their diagnosis of dementia made them act a bit odd at times.

He had heard from some of the care staff who also thought things were not quite right in the home since Matron had taken over.

Nick, one of the trained nurses, worked many shifts and said he had voiced some concerns to Matron but had been told to get on with his job for which he was employed.

Matt was quite friendly with Nick and together they had discussed these concerns. Nick said he had considered leaving but it was a well-paid position and he may not be able to get another position so locally to where he lived. He was nearing retirement age and needed to earn and save enough money before finishing work completely, as his state pension wouldn't support him and his wife. He contributed to the works pension as a top up. Nick was a small man, easily overlooked if there were other people in the room. He was quietly spoken and didn't say a lot.

The care home was owned by a large consortium. Occasionally, a big boss called Mr Smith called in. Matron was different again when he visited. She was less abrupt and appeared much friendlier with the staff than when the boss was not there.

Dr Johnson was not often present on these visits but if he happened to be there, he was amenable and pleasant. He seemed like a decent man and a good doctor and the staff liked him.

The staff were a bit apprehensive when the big boss visited and didn't converse much with Mr Smith if they could help it. He didn't pay a lot of attention to them as most of his visit was taken up with Matron.

Matt kept out of his way as well, finding jobs—when he visited—that he could do without bringing attention to himself.

He heard that there was to be a new nurse joining the team soon. He had seen Matron taking a lady around the home a few days ago and heard them talking about her nursing experience. She had looked nice and Matt hoped she would be taken on.

There was another nurse called Jane who worked part time, who Matt didn't care for. She was in her sixties and could be very sharp and not very kind-hearted. She strutted about ordering the staff to do things that she could easily do herself. The carers didn't like to object to her orders as they felt she was a nurse and therefore more experienced than them.

Matt had had a few run-ins with her and always came off worse.

A maintenance man was 'under her' and should do as he was told was her attitude.

As she was part time, only working three shifts a week, he put up with it as he was not the argumentative sort but he had to bite his tongue on many occasions.

He moaned at home to Nancy about her, who told him he should stand up for himself a bit more.

"I try to, but she gives me a stare without saying anything," he said.

Nancy laughed at this and said, "Wimp."

Matt worked Monday to Friday, nine till five. He was a good handyman and really liked the residents.

"There's a new resident called Ness who arrived last week," he told Nancy on Thursday evening. "She seems really nice even if she is a bit muddled. I put some pictures up in her room. There was a bit of paper, presumably from a relative, saying where the pictures should go in her room but I did ask her if she was happy with them where I hung them. She seemed pleased, which was nice."

"There's a wedding photo in her room. It's really interesting seeing pictures of long ago. We just see the person as they are now; almost forgetting they were young once."

"Like we were?" Nancy asked.

"Just like we were," Matt smiled.

"Matron wasn't at work today, which was good. It's a much nicer atmosphere when she's absent. Dr Johnson didn't come in either."

"Oh well, let's forget about work, we're at home now," said Nancy. "Let's ring George up and speak to Maisie if we can. Our very talented six-year-old granddaughter is in a musical play the holiday club put on. Such a shame they live so far away that we can't attend but perhaps George has recorded it."

They rang their son George on FaceTime and were delighted to hear that it had been recorded, and then spent the next hour watching Maisie singing and dancing in the play. Maisie then appeared on their computer screen and told her grandparents all about her performance.

Nancy asked after her eighteen-month baby sister, Sophie.

"She cries most of the time," replied Maisie. "I will be glad when she's old enough to play with me."

They had a good chat with George and his wife Marie and then closed the computer down. They lived about fifty miles away so visits were not as often as they would all like but talking and seeing them on FaceTime cheered them all up.

They enjoyed the rest of their evening watching television.

Saturday morning arrived and after breakfast, Fiona got ready to go the hairdressers for her appointment. Ted was planning to go for a run whilst Fiona was out. "We'll plan our weekend when you get back," said Ted.

"I'll go to Tesco's after the hairdressers and pick up some bits we need. Anything special you want me to get?" Fiona asked as she was writing her shopping list.

"Beer and wine and can you pick up some shaving foam please?"

"Well, those items won't feed us!"

She checked the fridge and cupboards, jotting items down on the list. She collected shopping bags and kissed Ted goodbye.

"See you later!"

She drove to the hairdressers and spent an enjoyable couple of hours having her blonde hair washed, trimmed and her roots touched up. She chatted to the stylist Isobel who had looked after Fiona's hair for some time now. She told her about her aunt moving into Goodrest Care home.

"My godfather Robert moved in there about six months ago," said Isobel. "He died quite suddenly two months later. He was a real character. He called a spade a spade and wouldn't stand any nonsense. He stood up for himself and also for the other residents if he thought they needed it. We were not expecting him to go so soon even though he wasn't in the best of health."

"What did he die of then?"

"The death certificate said heart failure and diabetes."

"What did you think of the Matron there?"

"Not a lot. She didn't have much time for relatives. She could be a bit abrupt so I didn't have much to do with her. She was always more interested in the doctor who looked after the residents' health needs."

"Dr Johnson?"

"Yes," said Isobel, blow-drying Fiona's hair. "He was the one who signed the death certificate. He said it was natural causes, but I had my doubts."

"How come?"

"Well, we had only visited him the day before and he'd been quite bright. A bit confused, kept talking about a strange light outside in the garden at night. Also, some of his belongings kept disappearing and we never did find them when we collected his belongings. Matron said he probably hadn't even brought them in with him but I know he did have them when he moved in."

"That's very odd. Aunt Ness has also mentioned lights and some of her things have gone missing too."

"Most of the nurses and carers seemed nice. A couple were not so nice though."

"A friend of mine is a nurse and is going to work there soon," said Fiona as Isobel asked her to close her eyes as she trimmed her fringe.

"That's handy; she can keep an eye on things for you."

"That's what Ted and I thought."

"All finished!" said Isobel as she whipped the robe off Fiona's shoulders, brushing a few stray hairs off as she did so.

"Thank you, that feels great and looks much better!"

She got up from the chair and walked with Isobel over to the reception desk. She paid the bill, adding five pounds as a tip. It was good to have a reliable and competent stylist. She'd had a few hair disasters before finding Isobel! She bid farewell saying she'd see her again in a few weeks.

Fiona then drove to Tesco's in the high street. She made her way into the carpark. It was busy and she had to circle around a couple of times before finding a vacant space. Having a smaller size car did make parking a lot easier. Looking around, she could see a fair few larger vehicles that took up more parking space within the allotted white lines than her car did. One shopping trip a few weeks ago, she had actually been unable to get back in her car as she returned with her shopping, as her car had been tightly wedged in between two large ones so her door wouldn't open wide enough for her to get in after depositing her shopping in the boot! It had taken ages till the driver returned and moved his car.

She grabbed a trolley from the front of the store. She checked her list and made her way around the aisles.

She found everything she wanted and then queued at a checkout. It was very busy even with most of the tills open and took about ten minutes before her turn arrived.

She stacked her shopping in the boot, noticing with relief that she would have enough room to get in the driver's seat!

She hadn't bumped into anyone she knew, which was quite unusual for a Saturday.

She drove home thinking about what they could do this weekend. They would visit Aunt Ness either this afternoon or sometime tomorrow. Perhaps they could take her out for a drive. The weather forecast was good.

She arrived home and Ted must have seen her pull up on the drive because he came out and helped take the shopping inside.

"Good run?" she asked.

"Very good. Your hair looks nice." He grabbed her and gave her a kiss. "A new woman!" he commented.

"Go on with you! Stick the kettle on and then we can decide what to do this afternoon."

Fiona put the shopping away while Ted made a cup of coffee for them both.

"Shall we see Aunt Ness today or tomorrow?" she asked.

"Let's go this afternoon. We could take her out somewhere. That will leave us a free day tomorrow to do something."

"That's what I thought. Great minds think alike," she grinned.

"And fools never differ!" replied Ted.

Fiona punched his arm. "Cheeky!"

She made a ham salad sandwich for them both, with a couple of bags of crisps, taking it to eat outside in the sunshine. Ted set up two folding chairs on the patio that overlooked their small neat garden.

They ate contentedly and agreed to visit the care home at three and take Aunt Ness out for a drive.

Three o'clock saw them parking in the care home carpark. The red Jaguar was parked by the front door. "Well, look at that!" said Ted. "Dr Johnson's emergency vehicle parked up at the weekend, no less!"

"I hope nothing's wrong," said Fiona. "He would probably only be here at a weekend if he was called in to see a resident."

They rang the doorbell. They stood there waiting for a minute or so and then Ted rang it again as no one was answering it.

It opened after their second ring by Josh.

"Hello, come in quickly. It's all kicking off here!"

"What's going on then?" asked Fiona.

He closed the door behind them.

Ted and Fiona could hear some raised voices coming from the communal lounge.

"Is Aunt Ness alright?" she asked quickly.

"Yes, she's fine," reassured Josh. "It's the sisters, Alma and Freda. Freda is accusing staff of pinching some of Alma's things from her room. She's very agitated and won't calm down. Alma's in tears saying it doesn't matter but Freda is screaming for someone to call the police. Dr Johnson has been called in by the nurse in charge as no one can calm her down. He is in there now wanting to give her something to calm her but Freda's having none of it."

"The other residents are unsettled hearing all this. Those that can understand what's going on are also saying that they have had things gone missing and they want the police to come to investigate their thefts."

Fiona could hear Dr Johnson trying to reason with Freda but it wasn't having any effect. "Get the police now!" Freda was yelling. "I need to report a crime."

Fiona peered into the lounge with Ted looking over her shoulder.

Freda saw them and shouted, "Here are the police now. About time! Help me."

Residents and Dr Johnson turned towards the door and saw Ted and Fiona.

"Yes, it's the police," said Dr Johnson. "Come outside with me, Freda, and you can tell them all about it."

He cast a pleading look at Fiona.

Ted nudged her and said quietly, "Play along. Pretend you are the police." Fiona looked around the room but couldn't see Aunt Ness.

"Come with us, Freda. We need peace and quiet to listen to you. Let's find a room where we can talk and get the details," said Fiona, hoping she sounded reassuring. Freda turned to Alma and told her to wait there and that she would go with the police and report the thefts. She walked to the door and Dr Johnson followed her. He had a briefcase with him.

Josh turned to the room of residents who were quietening down now and said he would make them all 'a nice cup of tea'. The nurse in charge, who Fiona didn't recognise but was wearing a dark blue tunic on so she assumed he was the nurse, was also in the room but looked to be lost for words. Josh appeared to be more in control.

Dr Johnson led Freda, Ted and Fiona into a room at the end of the hallway. Inside was an office desk and chair and half a dozen arm chairs lined up against two walls. A laptop and monitor were on the desk. There was a window looking out onto the back garden.

"Sit down here, Freda," said Dr Johnson after closing the door and steered her towards an armchair. She was red in the face, a bit breathless and looking very flustered. She did as he asked. There was a gush of air from the plastic cushion on the chair as she sat down heavily. He pointed to a couple of chairs and gestured Ted and Fiona to sit down.

They did so, carefully settling onto the chair cushions. He went over to the desk and sat behind it. He put his briefcase down on the floor, opened the laptop in front of him and turned it on. He was in casual clothing. He was wearing dark blue jeans with a light blue open-necked shirt with the sleeves rolled up to the elbows.

Freda looked at Fiona and asked if she had a notebook with her so she could take notes.

At this point, the door suddenly burst open and Matron rushed in. "I've just been informed of what's going on and came straight over. Why did you not ring me earlier?" she accused Dr Johnson. "And why are these people here?" pointing to Ted and Fiona.

"These are the police," said Freda. "They are here to take my statement about a theft. Alma has been a victim of a robbery. It's not your business. It's police business now."

"What a load of old rubbish!" Matron said in a loud voice and was about to say more when Dr Johnson stood up and suggested that she leave the room.

Matron looked at him in astonishment "How dare you! This is my nursing home and I demand to stay and hear what is being said."

Ted stood up and said he agreed with Dr Johnson that it would be best if she did leave the room and that they would speak with her afterwards. Freda also said she wanted her to leave as she wanted to speak privately to the police.

There was a very uncomfortable silence and then Matron stuttered, "This is preposterous!" then turned and went out, slamming the door behind her.

"Now," said Dr Johnson, looking at Freda, "you need to calm down. You are quite breathless and getting so worked up will not help your condition. What exactly is the problem?"

Freda turned to Ted and Fiona. Fiona had taken a diary from her handbag, so with pen in hand, she looked as if she was preparing to take notes.

"I will only speak with the police," said Freda to the doctor. "I don't trust you."

She turned back to Fiona. "Alma has had a clock taken from her room. She has also had some biscuits stolen. Are you writing this down?" she asked Fiona.

Fiona scribbled in the diary. She had never ever before been taken for a policewoman and part of her was finding this amusing but she also felt sorry for Freda. She glanced at Ted, who was also looking amused but trying to hide it.

"What sort of clock?" she asked Freda.

"It's one of those clocks that has birds' noises that sound on the hour. It's been taken off the wall in Alma's room. There's just a picture hook on the wall now. The thief didn't take that! They've probably got their own hook to hang the clock on!"

"And what sort of biscuits have been taken?"

"Custard creams. It was a brand-new packet. It's not good enough. We were going to have one each with our hot chocolate drink tonight."

"I'm sure there should be some biscuits here that can replace the ones gone," said Fiona. "As to the whereabouts of the clock, we will ask about and see if we can find it. When did you last see these items?"

"This very morning when I called in to see Alma. I'm sure the clock was on the wall; at least I didn't notice it wasn't there, and the custard creams were on her little table by her chair. I went up to her room after lunch to fetch her a cardigan as she was feeling a bit chilly and the clock certainly was not there then, as there was no bird whistle at two o'clock when I was in the room. That's what made me look at the wall, the silence of the blackbird. He's the two o'clock bird. That's also when I noticed the custard creams had been stolen.

"Can I have a report number? I have seen on the television that when a crime is committed, the police give some sort of number to make it official."

"Your crime reference number will be 1287. We will investigate," replied Fiona.

Freda appeared to be satisfied with Fiona's reply.

Dr Johnson stood up and said if that was all then maybe Freda should return to Alma. The thefts had now been reported and Freda would be kept abreast of the investigation. She should now leave it to the police to do their job.

"You had better find them. I shall go higher if you do not do your job properly," she threatened Fiona.

Ted got up and opened the door to let Freda leave. "You didn't say much, I suppose it's because she is your boss," said Freda to Ted.

"Yes, she is my boss," replied Ted.

Fiona hid a grin as Freda turned to thank her before leaving the room to return to Alma in the lounge.

Dr Johnson thanked Ted and Fiona for going along with pretending to be the police. He turned the laptop off and picked up his briefcase. "I'd better go and see Matron before I leave and smooth things over. I can't stay much longer. I have an appointment later that I don't want to miss."

He left the room leaving Ted and Fiona looking at each other. "How on earth did that all happen?" asked Fiona. "I've never been mistaken for the police before!"

"Nor me, boss!"

"Just remember your place, I'm in charge! We'd better go and find Aunt Ness now."

They left the room and went upstairs, planning to go to Room 20. They saw Josh on the landing and related to him the events that had gone on in the room downstairs. He told them that the other residents had eventually calmed down but some were saying they wanted to report their own thefts to the police now they were in the building.

"We don't really want to get involved anymore," said Fiona. "It wasn't very nice pretending to be someone that we obviously aren't."

"Matron was furious. She stormed into the lounge telling everyone to shut up! She then told me she had been chucked out of the room by Dr Johnson. He's in her office now trying to make it up to her," said Josh.

"It is strange though that other people were saying that they had had things taken too. Fiona's Aunt Ness has some things missing too," said Ted.

"Perhaps you ought to investigate!" said Josh. "I've been here three months now and have heard residents talking about missing items. Mostly trivial things but even so, it's still disturbing. I have no idea what's going on. There are a lot of staff employed in the home but it's not nice thinking there might be a thief working here."

"I suppose it could be a resident taking things but we generally know the ones that may wander into other people's rooms. We keep an extra eye on them and I can't really see a resident taking a clock off a wall. We would find them in their rooms surely if it was a resident taking things. I think there is something not quite right about this home, which is why I called around to your house."

"Well, we'll see," said Fiona, "but we are here today to see Aunt Ness, not to take notes and investigate thefts!"

They carried on to Room 20. Fiona knocked on the door before entering.

"Hello, Aunt Ness," she called as they entered.

Aunt Ness was sitting in her chair listening to the radio. Fiona was relieved to hear it was playing Classic FM. Hopefully her sticky label on the radio had done the trick!

"How are you?" she asked, going up to her and taking her hand. Ted came to stand in front of her so Aunt Ness could see him too.

"I'm alright. It's Fiona and Ted, isn't it?" said her aunt in a small voice.

At least she recognises us today, thought Fiona.

"Would you like to come out for a drive in the country?" she asked.

Her aunt's face lit up. "Yes please, you could then drop me off at home afterwards."

"We can't do that. You live here now," Fiona reminded her.

Her aunt's face fell. "I don't like it here. People are strange and I don't know them."

"I'm sure you will get to know them before long."

Ted got her jacket out of the wardrobe. Aunt Ness shrugged it on and looked around for her handbag.

Ted found it in her bedside cabinet. He retrieved her walking stick beside the chair that she had been sitting in.

They left the room and went downstairs. Fiona looked around for a member of staff to tell them that they were taking her aunt out for a couple of hours.

She popped her head in the lounge and saw Josh helping a resident with a drink.

He put his thumb up when Fiona told him they were taking her aunt out for a bit. "We'll have her back by six. Can you keep her tea back please?"

They passed by the Matron's office on their way out but it appeared empty and the door was closed.

They went through the front door and walked around to the carpark. Dr Johnson's car had gone from outside the front.

The next couple of hours were spent driving around the countryside. Aunt Ness sat in the front with Ted driving. He pointed out various points of interest during the journey.

They passed a stately home, which boasted a caravan site in an adjoining field. Ted pulled up so they could have a look. He wound the window down. There were a lot of people about. The smell of barbeques and cooking floated in through the car window. Some of the caravans looked really large and modern, many with awnings attached. Families appeared to be socialising with each other and the atmosphere appeared really nice and friendly.

"Have you ever considered a camping holiday?" Ted asked Fiona, meeting her eyes through the wing mirror.

"No, not really. I think I prefer my home comforts," she replied.

"I should think it would be a bit difficult to get away with your police work!"

"Police work?" asked Aunt Ness.

"It's a long story but no, I'm not in the police!" laughed Fiona.

Ted wound the window back up and restarted the engine. They carried on with their drive. Aunt Ness appeared to enjoy all the scenery. They travelled through a couple of small villages. One of them looked as if they had had a fete on in the afternoon. People looked very busy dismantling stalls and clearing away unsold items, although a bouncy castle was still being used by obviously excited children while their parents watched. Ted stopped the car and was able to purchase a jar of homemade raspberry jam from a produce stall, which he handed to Aunt Ness to take back to the care home with her.

They arrived back at the care home just before six o'clock.

They parked up by the front door, hoping Matron was not around to tell them off.

Ted waited in the car while Fiona rang the bell to be admitted. Josh answered it. "Nice afternoon out?" he asked Aunt Ness.

"Lovely," she replied.

"Has it quietened down here now?" Fiona asked Josh.

"Only because Freda thinks the police are investigating the thefts."

Fiona kissed her goodbye and said she would see her soon. She asked Josh if he could label the pot of jam as being her aunt's and keep it in the kitchen.

The door closed behind them and Fiona got in the car.

"Well, that was a busy afternoon in more ways than one!" she commented to Ted.

"It certainly was, Officer!"

Fiona grinned at him. "Any more of that and I'll have to arrest you."

"Will you get the handcuffs out later?" he said with a leer.

"Stop it! It's a bit worrying though, thinking there may be a thief in the home."

Ted asked if she fancied going to a pub for a drink and something to eat.

Fiona said she did, so they drove to a pub called The Roosters Arms just a couple of miles away. They had noticed a board outside it when they had passed it earlier, advertising a new menu that sounded very good.

They entered the pub and found a free table by a window. It looked out onto the beer garden. Some families were there sitting at the bench tables. There was a play area and from inside, they could hear children's laughter.

"I think I'll have a white wine please," when Ted asked what she would like to drink.

"I'll bring the menu over," he said.

He came back with her wine and a foaming pint of beer.

They looked over the menu. Fiona decided on lasagne and chips and Ted opted for a medium rare steak with all the trimmings. "Just like Hugh orders!" she grinned.

They chatted about their day out and then the waiter brought over cutlery, serviettes and a basket with packets of different sauces in. The pub was *olde worlde* and had a nice atmosphere. Table lamps were switched on in corners of the room, and although there was still enough daylight not to really need them, it was a nice cosy touch.

It wasn't long before their meals arrived. They were excellent, hot, homemade and tasty, which they both enjoyed. Another drink later and they made their way out to the car.

"We'll have to go there with Hugh and Moira one evening. He'll enjoy the steak," said Ted, driving home and making his way across the roundabout that led into their street.

"That reminds me, I wonder if Moira got the job at the home. I'll ring her tomorrow and find out."

When they got in, Fiona saw the light flashing on the house phone, which indicated a message was on it.

It was from Moira saying she had been accepted for the nurse post at the care home and would be starting a week on Monday.

"That's good, both for her and us," said Ted. "Perhaps she can do some sleuthing and find the thief. You can then cut out your second job as a police officer and leave it to her!"

"Very funny."

They wandered out onto the patio with a glass of wine, discussing what to do the next day.

"A long walk somewhere?" said Fiona.

"Good idea, we can take a pack up and have a picnic. Why not try that National Trust place over near Southfield. It's about thirty miles away but it's a nice ride out that way as well."

"Sounds good to me."

They spent the rest of the evening watching the James Bond film, *Live and Let Die*. They had both seen it before but still enjoyed it as they did all the Bond films.

They went to bed at eleven.

Monday morning woke up to light drizzly rain. Grey clouds were low in the sky promising showers later. Yesterday had been a lovely sunny day, just right for a ramble in the countryside. The picnic had gone down well and they had arrived back home early evening, tired but fulfilled.

Fiona arrived at work just after Lynne. She stored her wet umbrella in the stand near the door with a few drips landing on the floor. She got some tissue and wiped them up.

She smiled good morning at Lynne.

"Good weekend?" she asked.

"Very good. Kevin met the boys on Saturday afternoon. It was going very well until he had an urgent phone call and had to disappear for a couple of hours but he came back later. He didn't say why he'd been called away and I didn't like to ask. The boys liked him and he scored even more points when he offered to get a takeaway of their choice!"

"McDonald's or KFC?" guessed Fiona.

"What else would they chose! Kevin and I had a Chinese. What was your weekend like?"

"It was quite exciting in parts! I had to pretend to be a policewoman at the care home on Saturday. We arrived to a lot of commotion. One of the residents was missing some items and refused to calm down until the police came. The doctor was there and she wouldn't listen to him. When she saw me and Ted, she thought we were the police and would only discuss it with us. We went into a room where I had to take details of the thefts. She believed I was Ted's boss so would only talk to me, which was amusing!"

"What was taken?"

"A wall clock and a packet of custard creams."

"Crime of the century then!" said Lynne.

"It really upset the lady because they were taken from her sister's room and she was standing up for her."

"How was it left?"

"I'm supposed to be investigating! It is odd though, because other residents say they have had things gone missing from their rooms as well. Aunt Ness had a cushion and cardigan go missing the day after she was admitted."

Fiona mentioned that her friend Moira was going to start working as a nurse at the home next Monday. She hoped Moira may be able to throw light on some of the alleged thefts once she started work there.

The day passed quickly. They both stayed in for their lunch breaks as the rain showers had arrived. There was a small café within the council offices where they worked. The sandwiches were quite good for a change. A new company had recently taken over the catering and was a big improvement over the last lot.

Both Lynne and Fiona usually preferred to take their breaks away from the office to have a walk and some fresh air.

Their working day finished at five and they left the office together. The rain had stopped now. They said goodbye and retrieved their cars from the carpark. Other council workers were collecting their cars and making their way out.

Fiona drove home stopping only for a couple of red lights, which was not bad for the time of day. Ted was playing squash this evening with Geoff so Fiona had a couple of hours to herself before he got home.

She showered and washed her hair and then sorted out some washing to go into the machine, switched it on and prepared their meal. She planned steak pie, cabbage and new potatoes this evening.

She rang the care home to ask after Aunt Ness. Matron answered the phone, she hadn't identified herself but Fiona recognised her voice.

"She's perfectly alright. There's no need for you to keep phoning to see how she is."

"Well, I do worry about her. She is my aunt after all and I think I've a right to make sure she's settling in okay, particularly after Saturday's events. How is Freda today?"

"I can't disclose any information about other residents."

"Fair enough. I can ask her myself when I next come in to visit."

"I'd prefer you didn't speak with her, there's absolutely no need to upset her."

"I would not want to upset her but because I was involved with her predicament. I should like to make sure she's feeling better," said Fiona.

Matron put the phone down very sharply without further comment, the force of it ringing in Fiona's ear.

Fiona replaced her own phone more gently on the cradle.

She returned to the kitchen and poured herself a glass of wine. She didn't normally drink in the week but felt she needed one.

"What an awful woman. She should never be in the caring profession. Not a sympathetic bone in her body," she said to Ted when he came home.

Ted had been beaten yet again by Geoff so he wasn't in the best of moods.

"I thought I would beat him tonight but he was on fire!"

"Never mind, I'm sure you'll beat him next time. Go and change, dinner will be ready in twenty minutes. I'll have a beer ready for when you come down."

"Now you're talking!" He leant in for a kiss before going upstairs.

Fiona got the clothes out of the washing machine and hung them on the dining room airer.

They ate their meal while watching the *One Show*. Fiona admired the dress that Alex Jones was wearing, black and white check with a large white collar.

It was interesting tonight; there was a section on care homes and how to choose the right one. There were some interviews with relatives who all seemed happy with the choices they had made for their relatives.

"Bet none of them are in Goodrest," commented Fiona.

"It's early days," said Ted. "If things don't improve, we can always move her."

"That would probably disorientate her even more," replied Fiona. "I'll be glad when Moira starts working there so she can give us her opinion on the home."

They stayed in for the evening. Monday nights always found them a bit tired after a busy weekend so they watched the news and then retired for the night.

Tuesday morning, Matt signed in for work at Goodrest Care Home at his normal time of nine o'clock. He was anticipating a busy day as he had been asked to redecorate an empty room before a new resident moved in. He went to the paint shed and collected the paint, brushes, masking table and floor rags and made his way to the empty room.

Room 18 was two doors away from Ness's room. He thought he'd pop in to say hello to her. She seemed like a real nice lady and he had heard she had a caring niece who visited. He had chatted to Ness when he had hung her pictures up. Some of the residents here had very few visitors, which he thought was a shame.

Wilfred had been the resident in Room 18. It hadn't been redecorated before he moved in as he had been admitted only the day after the death of the previous resident who had been in the home for a couple of years.

He pondered on this. There had seemed to be quite a few deaths recently. He shrugged, thinking it was probably the nature of the business but Wilfred had appeared to be fit and well. Obviously, Matt wasn't privy to all their medical details but even so, it had been quite sudden.

He recalled Mary had died suddenly recently; again like Wilfred, she had appeared quite fit but obviously, he didn't know what medical conditions they had.

He took his paint and paraphernalia into Room 18. It was a nice room overlooking the back garden as Mary's had in Room 20. He looked out of the window. The lawn was nicely mowed and the flowerbeds were in full bloom. There were trees that bordered onto a field where a flock of sheep were grazing, nibbling at the grass. There was a shed at the end of the garden. He had never been in it in all the years he had been employed at the home. He had been told it was out of bounds to him and had never questioned this. He now wondered what was in the shed.

He started painting the room. Light green colour on the walls and the skirting boards would be glossed white.

He turned his radio on and began applying the paint. He liked painting, it was soothing and he was generally left alone to get on with the job.

The door suddenly opened without any knocking and a lady appeared. She looked surprised to see him in the room.

"Hello Annie," he said. He recognised her as one of the many housekeepers who worked at the home. He had not had much to do with her as she always appeared sullen and reluctant to talk. Most of the other housekeepers were friendly and always up for a chat.

"What are you doing?" she asked.

"Well, you can see I'm painting," he replied. *Surely it was obvious*, he thought.

"Is someone moving into this room?" she asked.

"Not sure," answered Matt. "I've just been asked to freshen the room up."

She gave him a strange look and went out of the door.

How odd, he thought but then returned to his painting and started singing along to the radio. He had finished painting two walls by lunchtime and then went for his break. He went into the staff room where a couple of carers were having theirs. Most of them were nice and enjoyed a chat.

He got out his lunch of cheese and pickle sandwiches and bag of cheese and onion crisps that Nancy had packed up for him that morning, and switched the kettle on to make a cup of tea. He had a nice slice of cherry cake for afters.

"Did you hear about the commotion here on Saturday afternoon?" asked the elder housekeeper called Belinda. She had reached the age of sixty-five and was considering retirement. She was a bit slow when working and only did as little as she could get away with.

"No?" said Matt.

"I heard the police were called," said Thelma. She was a lady in her fifties who had worked at the home for several months now. She was well liked amongst the staff, always happy and willing to do extra jobs.

"No. I haven't heard about it," said Matt "What happened?"

Thelma told him what she knew about the incident. She hadn't been on shift but had been told all about it from Josh that morning.

"Crikey," said Matt. "I wish I'd been here. I bet Matron was fuming at being chucked out of the room."

"Serves her right," said Belinda. "She would have wanted to stay if Dr Johnson was there. She idolises that man."

"Fancy the police coming!" said Matt.

"I don't think it was the proper police from what I heard, it was someone coming to visit and Freda thought they were here to investigate the thefts," said Thelma.

They discussed the incident whilst eating their lunches.

Matt returned to Room 18 to carry on with his painting. He was called away mid-afternoon to repair a wheelchair where the brake had seized up. He really enjoyed his work helping out where needed.

At half past four, he had finished painting all the walls and started tidying up, ready for the doors and skirting boards glossing next day.

As he came out the door, he saw that Room 20's door was open. He heard some raised voices coming from within the room.

"You will come down for tea," he heard Matron's voice. "I insist you come out of your room."

"I don't want to come down. I want to stay here," he heard Ness say.

"Come along, stop being difficult."

Matron was coming out of the room and saw Matt.

"Just collecting Ness to come into the dining room for tea," she told him but in a much more pleasant tone of voice than what he had heard a minute ago.

"I want to stay here in my room where I feel safer. I'm scared downstairs," said Ness.

"Nonsense, you are safe enough downstairs. We can keep a better eye on you in the dining room."

Ness was coming out of the room, walking slowly with her walking stick but looked very unhappy. She saw Matt and asked him if she could stay in her room.

"He is just the handyman. There is no need to ask him," said Matron.

Matt felt his temper rising. There was no need for Matron to have said that. He didn't lose his temper very often but felt sorry for Ness.

"Why can't she have tea where she wants to?" he asked Matron.

"Oh, very well, stay in your room if you must, but your tea may be late because the staff have enough to do without bringing trays upstairs to all and sundry." She went downstairs and Matt led Ness back into her room.

She sat down in her chair, looking upset. Matt took her hand and told her that she had the right to choose where to eat her meals. He asked her if he should turn her television on while she waited for tea.

"I like *Pointless*," she replied. He turned it on to BBC One ready for when it came on. His wife Nancy liked *Pointless* too, he told her.

He left her watching her programme and went downstairs. He saw Rosalyn and asked her about taking Ness her tea in her room. "No problem," she said. He mentioned that Matron had been very short with Ness about it.

"That sounds about right. She had a run-in with Dr Johnson earlier and has been in a foul mood ever since," said Rosalyn in a low voice.

Matt collected his coat and bag from the staff room and went out to his car. *Poor Ness*, he thought as he drove home, *fancy being spoken to like that. It's not fair and it's not right.*

He told Nancy about it over their tea.

"How awful, feeling scared at her age," she said. "Matron shouldn't be allowed to get away with it and who does she think she is calling you 'just the handyman'! As if you're no one."

"I can look after myself but I'll keep an eye out for Ness," replied Ted. "She's a nice old lady."

They cleared up after their meal and settled down to watch television. *Eastenders* was a favourite of theirs and they soon became engrossed in the many storylines.

Next day Matt arrived at work and returned to Room 18 where he started glossing the skirting boards. He wondered if a new resident would be moving in any time soon. The room was looking good. The home's furniture was of good quality. A lot of residents brought in their own small items of furniture to make the room more familiar to them. *It must be sad leaving their homes and settling into one room*, he thought.

He wondered how Ness was today. Later, he would knock on her door and pop his head in to say hello.

He left off painting at lunchtime and knocked on Room 20's door. There was no answer so he slowly opened the door after knocking again. She was not in her room so supposed she had gone downstairs for lunch.

He would try and catch her later.

He took his packed lunch into the staffroom. He switched the kettle on to make a cup of tea. Annie was in there but she didn't acknowledge him when he walked in. He said hello but she didn't reply, only giving him a stare. He felt the uncomfortable silence and hoped someone else would join them in the staff room.

He made his tea and unwrapped his ham sandwiches and opened his salt and vinegar crisps. He tried to eat them quietly but could hear the loud crunch as he ate them. Annie was not eating; presumably she had finished her lunch. She was not doing anything, just staring at him.

To his relief, the door opened and a carer came in. He recognised her as a new employee who had started the previous week. He didn't know her name but she looked nice.

"I'm Matt," he introduced himself. "I'm the maintenance man for the home." He wanted to start a conversation to relieve the silence.

"I'm Sue. I started here last week. How long have you been here?" She opened her sandwiches and took a bite of what looked like cheese and onion going by the smell.

"Been here a couple of years here now," replied Matt.

"What do you think of Matron?" she asked. She appeared very forthright and Matt didn't quite know how to reply with Annie listening.

"She's alright," he said.

"Bit strange, to my way of thinking. She's not very caring towards the residents."

"Well, the nurses are okay, she's management so probably doesn't have as much to do with them," said Matt. The staffroom door opened and Josh stuck his head inside the door.

"Matt, Matron wants to see you now," he said.

Matt finished his lunch. He was entitled to half an hour and was determined to have it. He didn't get paid for his breaks so didn't see why he should jump the minute Matron called. Sue and Annie left the room in the next ten minutes and he was left on his own.

He got up after his half hour and disposed of his lunch wrappings in the bin. He washed and dried his mug out and replaced it in the cupboard.

He made his way to Matron's office wondering what she wanted; he couldn't think of anything he had done wrong.

He knocked on her door and was invited to enter.

"I asked to see you fifteen minutes ago. Where were you?"

"I was on my lunch break," Matt explained.

"I need Room 18 finished as there is a new resident coming in tomorrow. I will allow you to do some overtime so you can get it finished today."

"I will have to ring Nancy to tell her I will be late home as she will have tea ready at our usual time."

"I will allow you to use my phone to call her."

Matt rang Nancy and said not to expect him till about eight o'clock. She said she would hold back tea till he arrived home.

He went back to Room 18 and continued to paint. He took pride in his work and liked to do a good job.

He took a break about half past five. He was gasping for a cup of tea so went over to the staff room. There was no one in there. He switched the kettle on and got a tea bag out of the tea caddy.

He made his brew and sat down. The staff room was quite sparse with a table and six chairs. There were no pictures hanging to break up the plainness of the walls, except for a cork noticeboard on the wall near the door. It had posters and notices pinned to it. There was no television or radio to relieve the silence. Management obviously didn't intend the staff to stay any longer than necessary in the room. The window looked out onto the carpark. Matt could see a few cars parked so presumably there were some visitors in the home.

He took a ten-minute break before making his way back to Room 18.

He was almost at the room when he heard someone coming up the stairs. He turned around and saw a blonde-haired woman heading towards Room 20. "Hello," he said to her.

"Hello," she replied. "I'm Fiona, I'm visiting my aunt Ness."

"Oh yes, I know her. I'm Matt, the maintenance man; I put your aunt's pictures up when she moved in."

"Thank you for doing that."

She knocked on her aunt's door and went in. Matt went into Room 18.

He carried on painting applying white gloss on the skirting boards. He hoped he should be finished by eight o'clock. He would be more than ready for his supper by then. Nancy would be pleased to see him back so they could spend a couple of hours together until bedtime.

He heard Room 20's door open, footsteps and then there was a knock on his door.

He put his paintbrush down carefully across the top of the paint tin and opened the door. "I'm sorry to disturb you," said the blonde lady, "but I wonder if you know where one of my aunt's pictures has gone. It's the scenic one of Cornwall. It was on the wall but has now been removed."

"I haven't taken it down. I remember hanging it on the wall," said Matt.

"I wonder where it is then."

"I have no idea," replied Matt.

"There have been other things missing from her room as well and from what I hear, other residents have had items go missing too."

"You'd best ask Matron if she knows anything."

"Have you heard of things going missing in the home?"

"I know there was a theft reported over the weekend and the police were called in."

"Well, that's a bit of a long story, but I'm not happy about this. These rooms are the residents' own and their belongings should be safe."

"I agree."

"Is Matron here, do you know?" asked Fiona.

"She's gone home now but I can ask her in the morning."

"Please do and I will also ring her first thing."

Fiona thanked him and went back into her aunt's room.

"I will ring up in the morning and speak to Matron," she told Aunt Ness.

She spent another hour with her aunt watching television. She was very annoyed about the missing picture.

She had heard good reports about the home before moving her aunt in but was now wondering if she had made an error of judgement but her aunt did appear to be more settled than of late and it would disorientate her if she had to move out.

She said goodbye to her aunt at seven o'clock. Ted would be home by now so she wanted to go so that they could spend the evening together. She didn't see any staff as she made her way to the front door.

She went out of the home but as she was leaving the carpark, she saw a black estate car park up near the front door.

Surely not another death, she thought.

She drove down the driveway and made her way out through the gates.

She arrived home and greeted Ted who was in the process of making a macaroni cheese for their supper. His culinary skills were minimal but he could prepare some dishes as long as she left instructions.

"Serving up in ten minutes," he said, twirling around to show off his apron that said 'Master Chef'. He kissed her and asked how her day had been.

"Work was fine but not so good with the visit to the home. I'll tell you about it while we eat. I'll have a quick shower first."

Fiona showered and came downstairs in her nightie and dressing gown.

Ted served up the macaroni cheese on warm plates. He had buttered some crusty bread. They sat at the kitchen table.

"Very good!" said Fiona as she tucked in. "I'm impressed."

They had a yoghurt for afters and then Ted made coffee for them both.

"Tell me about the home visit," he said.

Fiona related the tale about her aunt's missing picture. "I met the handyman who knew nothing about it."

"How odd," said Ted. "It seems there's a thief about in the home."

"Also, a black estate car pulled up by the front door as I was leaving."

"Blimey, not another death!"

He could tell Fiona was worried. He took her hand and agreed she should ring up in the morning to speak with Matron.

Ted told her to go into the lounge, switch the television on and he would clear up in the kitchen. They spent the next hour watching *Blue Planet* with David Attenborough. It took Fiona's mind off her aunt for a while.

They snuggled up together on the settee and went to bed after the news.

Matt was also telling Nancy about Fiona's concern about the missing picture from her aunt's room. "It is strange. I keep hearing about things going missing from residents' rooms. I also think there was a death this evening. I didn't see anyone to ask but as I went to my car after work, I saw a black estate car going through the gates."

"There's been a few deaths recently, haven't there?" commented Nancy.

"I know. I wonder who died this time, I expect I will find out tomorrow."

Nancy then told him that one of the elderly folk that she looked after was going into the home tomorrow. "He can't manage on his own now even with us carers going in several times a day."

"I bet he's going into Room 18 that I've painted."

"He's a really nice man. He lost his wife last year and is finding life difficult without her."

"How sad. I hope he settles in. There will be company for him there that should help him."

They chatted about their granddaughter Maisie who Nancy had spoken to on the phone earlier that evening.

"She's really growing up now, talks very well, but still not too keen on baby Sophie!"

"That'll change once Sophie gets a bit older and they can play together."

They watched the news and went to bed.

Next day dawned fine and clear and the forecast for the next few days was favourable.

Matt arrived at work and checked whether Room 18 was ready for the new occupant. He heard that it was a man coming in. He was probably the one that Nancy had mentioned last night. He organised the furniture and was pleased to see how nice the room looked with the fresh paint. He looked out of the window and was surprised to see the small shed at the very end of the garden had the window slightly open. He had never seen it open before. He tried to look into it but it was a fair way away from where he was looking and the bit of inside that he could see appeared dark so he couldn't make anything out.

He saw Kirsty the lady gardener was weeding a flowerbed. She was aged around forty-five. He didn't know much about her. She did not open up much about anything of a personal nature but was eager to discuss anything to do with gardening. Perhaps the small shed was also her domain but he knew there was a large shed that was on the edge of the car park that held all her gardening equipment. He had seen her going in and out of it. There was a large lawn mower, a strimmer and lots of flower pots.

The greenhouse alongside the large shed was often full of plants that she grew from plugs, which, when ready, she transferred into the baskets, tubs and flowerbeds. She took pride in her work and received many compliments from residents and visitors. She kept the lawns well mowed and the edges trimmed. She tended to keep to herself and didn't use the staff room. He had heard she was single and lived a couple of miles away. She drove a Mini Cooper van that she always parked on the far edge of the carpark. He had seen her sitting in her car drinking from a flask so he presumed she had her breaks in it rather than use the staffroom.

Matt had some maintenance jobs to do. He needed to fix an extractor fan in Room 12. It was making a racket whenever the bathroom light was switched on that annoyed the resident. After fixing it by giving it a good clean, he then went and sorted out a vacuum cleaner that kept cutting out when being used.

He was then called to service a couple of wheelchairs that had loose brakes. He enjoyed the diversity of his job as no two days were ever the same. He liked to have a chat to the residents and staff.

He saw Josh in the staffroom at break and asked him who had passed away yesterday.

"It was Freda, one of the sisters. Quite unexpected it was. It actually happened in the morning. A locum doctor eventually came out much later because Dr Johnson isn't around this week but they took her away to the hospital, not the funeral home, which is what usually happens, as there's talk of a coroner's inquiry. Alma is beside herself with grief. Someone's had to sit with her all day, she's so distressed."

Matt pondered on this news. He remembered hearing from Thelma about Freda and the theft incident at the weekend. He wondered whether Freda may have had a stroke brought on by being so worked up. He had heard this could happen. He supposed they would find out in due course.

After break, he was asked to go into the lounge to replace a ceiling bulb. He took his ladder and climbed up to reach the light fitting.

He could hear a couple of residents talking to each other about Freda.

"I can't believe she's gone," said an elderly man called Tom. He was a nice old boy who had been a resident at the home for the past three years.

"Nor can I," replied the other man in the adjoining chair. He was called Arthur who had been a resident at Goodrest for about a year. The men were usually found sitting together and did the Daily Telegraph crossword. It was nice, listened Matt as he unscrewed the light fitting and replaced the bulb, when residents made friends.

Arthur said, "It was very sudden, I hope she didn't suffer. I wonder if it was a heart attack."

"Her heart was alright, I think. She had a few breathing problems and diabetes but surely that wouldn't kill her. I hope Alma will be alright without her," said Tom.

"She hasn't been down for any of her meals today. She's probably lost her appetite with the sad news," replied Arthur.

Matt climbed down his ladder and said to the men that indeed it was sad news about Freda.

Arthur said, "That's about four people gone in just a few weeks. Hope you and I won't be next, Tom."

"So do I. It's my birthday in a couple of weeks and my daughter is planning a get together. Be a shame to miss it!"

Arthur agreed and then asked Matt if he knew four down in the crossword as he and Tom were stuck.

Matt had a look at the crossword and said, "I think the answer's murder."

"Well done!" said Arthur. "I hope that's not an omen with all the deaths going on here!"

Matt grinned and was leaving the room just as Matron was coming through the door. "What were you talking to Arthur and Tom about?" she asked.

"The crossword," he replied.

"Just get on with the job that you are being paid for. I think you were talking about more than just the crossword."

"They are upset about Freda," said Matt. He felt his temper rising. "It is obviously a subject that they want to talk about. Several deaths in just a few weeks is making them nervous."

"It's none of yours, or their, business," she snapped.

"Actually, I think it is our business. If anything odd is going on here then we all want to know about it."

"Odd?" she said. "Who said anything about things being odd?"

"Well, the people who have recently died were not particularly poorly, from what I can tell."

"I'm sorry; I didn't know you were a trained nurse! Now get on with your own job, which is purely maintenance and stop gossiping."

She turned around and went out of the room.

Matt looked flabbergasted as did Arthur and Tom who had listened to the exchange of words.

"There's something not right about that woman," said Tom. "I don't take to her at all."

Matt nodded agreement without further conversation and went down the hallway to put his ladder away in the closet where he kept his tools. He was fuming at being spoken to like that.

He closed the closet door and saw the blonde lady who had visited Ness yesterday.

"Hello again," he called. Fiona looked up from signing the visitor's book.

"Hello," she said. "I've taken the afternoon off work to spend time with my aunt. She's quite unsettled since coming to live here and I'm worried about her. I was going to ring but decided to visit instead."

"I think she's in the lounge sitting by the window," said Matt.

"I hope she's making friends. Company is what she needs. I also want to ask someone about Freda and whether her bird clock has turned up. I don't know whether you heard about her mistaking me for the police at the weekend?" Fiona said.

"You obviously haven't heard the news. Freda died yesterday morning."

"What?" said a shocked Fiona. "How?"

"Not sure. I heard it's gone to the coroner though," whispered Matt.

Fiona was stumped for words. She didn't know what to say. She turned and went into the lounge where she spotted Aunt Ness sitting looking out of the window into the garden. The television was on with its usual loud volume. Some residents were watching it but some appeared to be dozing in their chairs. A female carer was sitting with one resident assisting her with a cup of tea.

Fiona pulled up a chair by her aunt. Aunt Ness did recognise her, which relieved Fiona, and she seemed pleased to see her.

"Thank goodness you have come to take me away."

"I've come to see you for a chat but not to take you away," said Fiona. "Shall we take a walk in the garden?"

"Yes, but we can only go a little way in the garden or I will get into trouble."

"What on earth do you mean?" asked Fiona.

"Because I might see the lights."

"What lights?"

"The lights I see at night. I was told there aren't any lights but I've seen them from upstairs. They come from the end of the garden."

Tom had wandered over to collect a box of tissues from a table near to where Aunt Ness was sitting. He was using a walking stick to aid his mobility.

"I can't help overhearing," he said in a low voice, looking around to make sure no one overheard *their* conversation. "I've seen the lights too but was told I was imagining it as well."

"Who told you that there are no lights?" asked Fiona.

"Moody Matron, of course!" he replied with a grin. "I have seen the lights a few times. I may be old but I've not lost all my marbles. I know what I saw. Others have seen them too so we can't all be wrong, can we?"

"Where do you think the lights are coming from?" asked Fiona.

"The only place they could possibly come from is the shed at the end of the garden. I'm sure I've seen someone with a torch going down there when it's dark."

"We are going out for a walk in the garden so I may go down to the shed and see if I can find out what's in there," said Fiona.

"Don't let 'she who is in charge' see you or you'll be for the high jump!" grinned Tom. "Let me know if you spot anything."

"I have heard about Freda," said Fiona. "I'm so sorry."

"Awful," said Tom, looking sad. "Bit sudden, like it was with Mary and Wilfred. One minute they're alright and the next minute gone."

Tom wandered back to Arthur where he picked up the paper and resumed puzzling over the crossword.

Fiona helped Aunt Ness to her feet, retrieved her walking stick and went out of the lounge. She told her aunt to wait on a hall chair while she ran up to get her a light jacket from her wardrobe.

She came downstairs to find Matron standing by Aunt Ness asking what she was doing sitting in the hall.

"We're about to take a walk in the garden," Fiona informed her. She asked her about the scenic Cornwall picture that was missing from her aunt's room.

"I have no idea where it's gone," replied Matron. "I can't be held responsible for everything in the residents' rooms."

"But you are responsible; you are in charge of the home. We brought my aunt's things in here believing everything would be safe."

"Perhaps another resident took it," said Matron.

"I think it's highly unlikely that a resident would wander into another person's room, reach up and remove a picture off a wall. I want it found. It means a great deal to my aunt. I shan't let this rest until it's found. I'm also upset and shocked to hear about Freda dying."

Matron shrugged and disappeared into her office. Fiona helped her aunt into her jacket and made their way to the front door. Fiona could see into Matron's office. She saw she was talking on the phone.

Fiona opened the front door and helped her aunt down the steps. They made their way around the side of the house into the back garden. They walked slowly but the path was level so as to avoid the risk of any trips and slips. It was a nice sunny afternoon with a light breeze.

They wandered along the path that wound through the garden. They admired the colourful flowerbeds and Aunt Ness could name some of them. "That's a dahlia," she told Fiona, "and that's a dianthus."

They came to a bench and sat down. Fiona saw a lady who she presumed was the gardener. She was pulling up weeds from a flowerbed near the end of the garden. She was kneeling on a firm cushion that she kept shifting along to get to the next bit of bed as she weeded.

Fiona got up from the bench and went over to her. "Hello," she greeted her. "May I say how nice you keep the gardens. It must keep you very busy." The lady turned and looked up at her.

"Yes, it does. I'm Kirsty. I'm glad you like them. It's not easy keeping on top of it but I try my best."

"Do you have any help? It's an awful lot for one person."

"I have a bit of help sometimes from the residents' doctor's son. He's quite good at weeding. He's at university but does holiday work here."

"Dr Johnson's son?" asked Fiona.

"Yes. He's on holiday at the moment, somewhere abroad. Spain, I think he said, but should be back here next week to give me a hand."

Fiona asked if the small shed at the end of the garden held her gardening equipment.

"No, it's not big enough to hold everything. I have a larger shed over near the greenhouse on the edge of the carpark."

"What's kept in that small shed?" asked Fiona, pointing to it.

"I'm not sure. I've never needed to go into it. It's probably a storage area. It's padlocked."

"My aunt thinks she's seen lights in it some nights."

"Really? I didn't think there was electricity in the shed."

"Torches, she thought."

"I really don't know. It's none of my business," said Kirsty abruptly. She got back down on her kneeling pad, signalling that the conversation was over.

Fiona went over to the shed, saw the padlocked door and pressed her face up against the window. She couldn't see anything as it was dark inside.

She went back to her aunt who was still sitting on the bench and had turned her face up to the sun, enjoying the warmth on her face. It was a cloudless blue sky. Fiona thought perhaps she and Ted could go for an evening walk after tea.

She told her aunt that she hadn't been able to see anything in the shed.

They sat on the bench for another half hour before returning inside the home. Sue answered the doorbell and let them in without saying anything.

Fiona guided her aunt up the stairs towards her room. She settled her in the chair, turned the television on and then went out to see Matt who was on the landing a bit further down the corridor, on his ladder, cleaning out a ceiling light fitting. "Hello," he called. "I saw you out in the garden."

"It's lovely out there," said Fiona. "I had a chat with the lady gardener as well."

"She does a great job," replied Matt as he climbed down his ladder.

"I tried to look in the small shed at the end of the garden but it was padlocked. Aunt Ness and other residents say they have seen a light in there at night."

"Weird," said Matt. "There can't be any electricity in there. It's too far away from the home."

He folded up his ladder, glancing up at the light. "Another job ticked off!"

"We haven't found the missing picture yet. I spoke with Matron who implied that another resident went in and took it off the wall," said Fiona.

"I can't really see that happening."

"That's what I told her. I hold her responsible. She does run the home after all. I also mentioned Freda, and that I was really shocked at the news."

"We all were. It was very sudden and unexpected. Apparently, the coroner's involved, which means it may not be natural causes."

Fiona was about to speak when she heard footsteps coming up the stairs. She looked over her shoulder and saw Matron and Dr Johnson coming up the stairs. They were talking in low voices but stopped when they saw Fiona and Matt.

"Have you quite finished?" Matron asked Matt. "I'm sure you must have plenty to do without gossiping."

"I'm just passing the time of day," replied Matt. He clutched his ladder, saying goodbye to Fiona and went downstairs.

Fiona went into her aunt's room. Someone must be poorly she thought if Dr Johnson was here. She wondered who it was.

She spent another half an hour chatting with her aunt. Her eyes kept going to the bare wall where the picture had once been. She didn't mention it to Aunt Ness in case it upset her. She checked the radio on the bedside table and saw it was on the correct station. She then went to the wardrobe to see if the missing cardigan had been returned.

It wasn't in there but she couldn't see anything else had gone walkabout. She also saw the red cushion was still missing from the chair.

She turned the television over to Channel Three at four o'clock to *Tipping Point* for her aunt, who appeared to be quite settled. "See you in a few days," she said, kissing her goodbye. Aunt Ness looked at her and smiled.

Fiona left the room and went downstairs. Matron and Dr Johnson were in the office with the door open. Fiona could hear them talking. "She should be comfortable now she has had the injection," Dr Johnson was saying. "It may not be too long now."

Matron was saying she would ring the daughter.

Must be someone nearing the end of life, thought Fiona.

She let herself out of the front door but just as she was about to close it after her, it was pulled open and Matron was there.

"Please don't gossip with the staff," she said. "They exaggerate and get the wrong end of the stick."

"What do you mean?" asked Fiona.

"Matt, the maintenance man. He likes to gossip. The staff need to keep their thoughts to themselves. I also saw you talking to the gardener in the garden."

"I was only having a chat with both of them, not gossiping."

"Well, it's best if you don't chat with him or her in future," Matron said as she turned away, closing the front door.

Fiona carried on down the steps wondering what all that was about.

Dr Johnson's red car was parked outside the front door. She went around to the carpark, got in her car and drove down the driveway and through the gates. *There's something very odd about that home*, she thought.

She arrived home about five. Ted wasn't yet back from work. She showered and washed her hair and then went into the kitchen to start preparing their evening meal.

Ted came through the front door just before six. He kissed her hello and asked about her visit to Aunt Ness.

"Strange," she replied. "There is definitely something not right about that home."

"Let me shower and change and then you can tell me all about it."

Fiona grilled sausages and added them to a casserole mix that she then put in the oven. She scraped some new potatoes and took out some frozen mixed vegetables. She located a cheesecake in the freezer that she left on the side to defrost.

As they ate their supper, she told Ted about the visit to the home and that Freda had died. "There's something really not right." Ted was shocked to hear about Freda.

"Matron is obviously afraid someone is going to say something, which she would rather not have said, if that makes sense!" she said.

She related the conversation she had had with Tom in the lounge. "He has seen lights at night in the garden too. He appeared to be with it, he even said he had got all his marbles!"

"Aunt Ness was okay this afternoon, which was good. We went into the garden and I spoke to the lady gardener who seemed nice. I went to look in the shed where the lights have been seen but I couldn't see anything as it was too dark inside. Matt, the maintenance man, says there's no electricity in there so it must be torches that are the lights that people have seen at night. Oh, and Dr Johnson was there with Matron, saying something about an injection and it wouldn't be long now."

"Wow," said Ted, "that's a lot of conversations you had!" He finished his meal and patted his stomach. "Very nice, thank you!"

Fiona got up and cleared the plates away. She brought the cheesecake to the table. It was still a bit frozen inside but they ate it anyway. Ted got up to make them both a coffee.

After stacking the dishes in the dishwasher and cleaning the worktops, Ted asked if she wanted to go for a walk.

"Just a short one, I'm a bit tired," replied Fiona.

"Early night then tonight!" he grinned, raising his eyebrows.

Fiona laughed and batted his hands away as he grabbed her as she got up. They went to the park for an hour, enjoying the evening sunshine and then returned home to watch some television before going to bed.

Matt was also telling Nancy about the afternoon. "That Matron is getting worse," he grumbled. "I think she's got it in for me. Whenever she sees me talking to someone, she accuses me of gossiping. I think she must have something to hide as she's so suspicious of what we're talking about." Nancy agreed with him but told him to forget about it for the evening.

Fiona drove to work next morning in glorious sunshine. She told Lynne about her visit to the care home yesterday afternoon. "Something's going on there but I'm really not sure what," she said. "Aunt Ness seems a bit more settled though, which is good."

"It will be better when your friend starts working there next week. She can be a spy for you!" remarked Lynne.

Fiona agreed with her. "I think I will ring her this evening for a chat and share my concerns with her."

She had a busy day at work and when she arrived home at half past five, she rang Moira before Ted came home to distract her and she forgot to ring. Moira answered after a couple of rings. It had been her last day working at the hospital and she was looking forward to a few days off before starting at the care home.

Fiona relayed her concerns about the home and also the fact that there had been several unexpected deaths in recent weeks. She told her that her aunt was worried about lights in the garden at night.

Moira listened and reassured her that she would be on the alert once she started working there. Fiona felt some relief that someone would be there on the inside looking out for any suspicious activity. They had a good chat and arranged for the four of them to meet up on Saturday night for a drink. Ted arrived home and she told him what she had arranged. "That's fine by me," he said.

Supper was prepared and eaten and then they watched television for the rest of the evening.

The next day was overcast. Showers were forecast for later in the day. "Not the best August we've had, one day good and the next day rubbish," said Ted. They both drove off to their respective works. He was very busy at work but liked his job, and was looking forward to the weekend. He and Fiona enjoyed spending time together; they liked doing the same things such as going for walks and socialising with friends.

He was very happy with his life. Until he had met Fiona, he hadn't been able to imagine being married and being with just one person, but now he realised what he had been missing. She didn't complain when he met up with his friends for sporting activities and she was also a good cook! She was a lovely person; he loved her loads and he thanked God that he had met and married her.

The remainder of the working week passed pleasantly enough and by Friday evening, both Ted and Fiona were looking forward to two days of rest.

The weekend forecast was good and Saturday dawned fine and bright. The temperature was rising and no rain was due for a good few days.

They discussed what they should do over the next two days. "Don't forget, we are meeting Hugh and Moira tonight," Fiona reminded Ted. They decided to do a Tesco shop first and then afterwards take a ride out into the countryside and find a walk before returning home to get ready for their evening out.

Tesco's was busy. They did their shop, queuing for a good ten minutes at a checkout and then returned home to put it away.

They had a quick sandwich, changed into appropriate walking attire and set off in the car. Ted drove about ten miles to a small town called Morton. He parked up and they changed into walking boots and set off for a country walk. The weather was lovely, sunny with a very light breeze, and there were a lot of families about, obviously having the same plan as them.

They followed a footpath leading into a wood. The trees were in full leaf, making it quite dark in some areas. The bracken brushed against their legs as they made their way into the wood. They met several people coming towards them, some with young children and some with dogs on leads. The majority of people were polite, nodding or smiling to acknowledge them, the dogs even more friendly. Some tried to jump up at them but their owners intervened, much to Fiona's relief. She had been attacked by a dog in her teens and had been quite nervous of them ever since.

They ventured further into the wood. There were not so many people around now; there were varying routes through the wood according to the signs.

They walked for a while and then came across a clearing. It looked onto a field of grazing cows There was signage to say walkers could go through it. "I'm not going through that field of cows," said Fiona. "I've read of people being attacked."

"It's usually when there are calves with them; there aren't any in there," said Ted.

"Even so, I'm not going through. Let's go back now."

They turned around and started to make their way along the path they had come from.

They were halfway back going through the wooded area when they heard a yell. They saw a young man lying on the floor, holding his left arm. "Help," he called to them. "I've tripped on a tree root and hurt my arm; I think I've broken it." They went over to him. They looked around but no one else was about.

"Can you move your arm?" asked Fiona. She knelt down by him. He looked to be about eighteen. "Can you wriggle your fingers?" She remembered doing a first aid course when she was in the girl guides.

"No. It hurts too much," he said. Ted helped him to his feet. He was obviously in a good deal of pain. The young man held his arm with his other one, guarding it against his chest.

"You need to have it X-rayed at the hospital," he said.

"I can get my dad to take me. He's a doctor so will know what to do."

"Have you got a car here?" asked Ted.

"Yes, it's in the carpark but I won't be able to drive it."

"Where do you live?"

"Just outside Morton, not far away," he replied with a groan of pain.

"We can take you home," said Fiona.

They walked through the rest of the wood and into the carpark. "That's my car," he said, pointing with his good arm at a dark blue Kia. Ted went over to check it was locked up.

He came back and assisted him into the front passenger seat of their car and helped him put on the safety belt as gently as possible, avoiding touching the injured arm. "What's your name?" Fiona asked.

"Tom," he said with a grimace.

"I'm Fiona and this is my husband, Ted."

Fiona got into the backseat. Ted drove out of the carpark, asking Tom for directions to his house.

"Carry on along this road for a couple of miles and then turn left at the crossroads. It's the red brick house halfway along on the left. My dad's red Jaguar should be on the drive."

Fiona sat up with a start. "A red Jaguar?" she repeated. "Is your surname Johnson?"

"Yes, how did you know?"

"I've seen him and his car at Goodrest Care Home where my aunt is a resident. His car has been parked there a couple of times when we've visited."

"Small world," said Tom. "He looks after the people at the home."

They turned at the crossroads and drove along until they saw the red car outside a very large detached house. It had bow windows both upstairs and down. The window frames were painted dazzling white. The front door was bright red, which matched the car on the drive. The front garden looked immaculately maintained. There were a couple of beds blooming with flowers that bordered a nicely mowed lawn.

Ted pulled up onto the driveway beside the red Jaguar. It was large enough to hold at least four cars. He turned off the engine and got out, going to the passenger side to help Tom out of his seat. Fiona got out of the backseat. Tom thanked them and said he could make it into the house on his own.

He started making his way to the front door when it suddenly opened. Dr Johnson stood there. He was in casual clothes and as he did before when they had seen him wearing similar clothing, he looked younger than when wearing a suit.

He saw Tom favouring his injured arm and came out onto the driveway, asking what on earth had happened.

"Tripped over a tree root in the woods and I think I've broken my arm. These people helped me and drove me home."

Dr Johnson looked at Ted and Fiona, recognising them at once.

"Thank you very much for helping Tom. I know you; I've seen you at the care home."

"Yes," said Fiona, "my aunt is a resident there. We saw you last weekend when Freda was so upset. I'm so sorry to hear she's since died."

"Yes, it's very sad."

He told Tom to go inside the house and that he would come and look at his arm.

"Thank you for helping and bringing him home. I presume Tom's car is still in the carpark?"

Tom disappeared through the front door.

"Yes," said Ted. "It's all locked up so should be safe enough until it's collected."

Fiona got into the passenger seat of their car and Ted went to the driver's side.

"Thanks again," said Dr Johnson and turned to go back into the house.

Ted reversed out of the driveway and turned onto the road.

"Well, well," said Ted. "Fancy that!"

"He could have invited us in for a cup of tea, I would have liked to see what the house is like inside," said Fiona.

"He doesn't want to mix with the likes of us! We are way out of his league, judging by the size of that house," replied Ted with a grin.

"You're probably right but we did help his son. I wonder if he has broken his arm."

They drove home. Fiona had first shower and afterwards looked in her wardrobe, wondering what to wear for their evening out. She was looking forward to seeing Hugh and Moira again. They were good company.

She came downstairs and made a cup of tea while Ted had his shower.

She decided on wearing a blue floral calf-length dress and cream kitten-heeled mules. Ted sported a cream polo shirt and tan-coloured chinos.

"Don't we look good!" remarked Ted, standing admiring himself in the hall mirror.

"Good enough to mix with the Johnsons?" she laughed.

"Of course, we look good enough to mix with the elite!" grinned Ted.

They left the house at seven and drove to the pub in the next village where they had arranged to meet their friends.

Ted and Fiona entered the Red Lion. It was a quaint country pub owned and run by a couple called Mike and Nick. They were in their late forties and were a couple in their personal lives as well as their business life.

"Nice to see you both," hailed Mike. He generally served behind the bar and Nick tended to look after the catering side.

Ted asked Fiona what she wanted to drink. She opted for a glass of chardonnay and Ted chose a pint of Doombar.

Ted paid and they wandered over to an empty table. Fiona looked around the room. Most of the other tables were occupied either with people eating or just enjoying a drink.

Five minutes later, the door opened and in walked Hugh and Moira. They saw Ted and Fiona and waved a hand in greeting. Hugh asked Moira what she wanted. She told him and then went over to the table and sat down. She looked fresh and summery in a cotton green dress and wore her red hair up in a high ponytail.

"Been here long?" she asked.

"Just got here," replied Fiona, sipping her wine.

Hugh came over with a white wine for Moira and beer for himself.

"Good pint!" he said to Ted. He took a long swallow, emerging with foam on his upper lip. Moira laughed, saying she didn't like his moustache!

They decided to stay inside to eat. There was a family garden outside and they could hear the sound of children shouting and playing. They couldn't see the garden from the window by their table as was at the back of the pub. Their window looked out to the front.

Ted went to the bar to grab some menus and to get a round of drinks in. Fiona opted for a soft drink so Ted could have another pint later. She would drive home.

They looked at the menu choices.

"Scampi and chips for me please," said Fiona.

"Me too," said Ted.

Moira chose vegetable lasagne with chips. Hugh took ages to make up his mind what he wanted to eat and the others teased him about the length of time it was taking him. "I think I will have a medium rare steak and all the trimmings," he finally said.

"That's what you choose every time we eat out!" laughed Moira. "I don't know why it took you so long to choose what we all knew you would order in the end!"

Mike came over with his notepad, asking if they had chosen their meals. He took down their orders, saying it would be about fifteen minutes, and went into the back of the bar to the kitchen. He brought over a basket of sauces and condiments and put it on their table.

Fiona saw a girl in her early twenties serving at the bar. "I'm sure I've seen her working at the care home," she murmured to Ted.

He looked up. "I can't say I've seen her before," he replied.

"Perhaps it was when I visited the other afternoon on my own. I'm sure she was in the lounge giving someone a drink."

She turned to Moira asking if she was looking forward to starting work at the home on Monday.

"Yes," said Moira. "It will be different to what I'm used to but it will be nice seeing the same people and getting to know them. In hospital, just as you start getting to know someone, they are discharged. Patients don't stop in for long nowadays. As soon as a bed becomes empty, within a couple of hours someone else is in it!"

Ted and Hugh were making arrangements to play a round of golf the next day. ("If it's okay with you, love!" he said aside to Fiona.) Ted had recently taken golf up. He wasn't very good yet but was hoping to improve with practice. Hugh played quite often and was willing to coach Ted.

Their meals arrived, carried over by the girl from behind the bar. She distributed cutlery and asked if they required any more sauces.

"Haven't I seen you working at Goodrest Care Home?" asked Fiona.

"I finished there last week," the girl replied. "I had had enough of the Matron and the funny things going on there and people having their things go missing."

"What sort of funny things?" asked Moira. "I'm a nurse and due to start work there on Monday."

"Well, good luck to you, that's all I'll say. I stuck it out for three months. Too many deaths, things going missing and accusations being hurled about and residents not being listened to."

"Goodness!" said Moira. "I hope I'm not making a mistake in going to work there!"

"My aunt is a resident there," Fiona said to the girl. "Is she safe?"

"As long as she doesn't complain, she should be alright. It's the ones that kick up a fuss that are in danger."

She looked at Moira. "Good luck."

She turned and went back to the bar, collecting empty glasses as she passed tables.

The meals were good and silence reigned as the four of them ate. Fiona was feeling unsettled after hearing the girl's comments about the home.

"I'm glad you are going to work there. Please let me know if you hear or see anything that's not right or if things continue to go missing. I will move Aunt Ness if it comes to it," she said to Moira.

"I will let you know anything I find out. I'm on a month's trial and if I don't like it, I will look for something else."

Fiona felt reassured that her aunt would have someone in the home that would look out for her. They all enjoyed the rest of the evening. Another round of drinks was ordered and brought over by Mike.

"Compliments to Nick for the delicious meals," Ted told him.

"I'll pass them on," replied Mike. "Glad you enjoyed them."

The evening broke up about ten-thirty. They left the pub with Ted and Hugh arranging to meet at ten o'clock tomorrow at the local golf club. Fiona told Moira she would be visiting Aunt Ness tomorrow and she hoped all went well on Monday.

"I will be in touch," replied Moira.

They got in their cars and drove home.

Matt was called by the care home on Sunday morning. He had been enjoying a lie in with Nancy when the phone had rung at nine-thirty. It was Sally, the nurse in charge, asking him to come and look at a leaking radiator in one of the resident's rooms. "I can't stop it dripping even after isolating it," she explained. "Sorry to drag you in on a Sunday."

"No worries. I'll be there in the next hour."

He told Nancy he shouldn't be too long. They were going out later to visit a cousin of hers who had not been too well lately. "We'll take her a nice bunch of flowers. I'll pick some up from the garden centre on my way back from the home," he said.

He washed and dressed, had a quick coffee and a slice of toast and marmalade and then left to drive to the home.

He let himself in and went to find Sally. She was in the Matron's office, looking a bit puzzled. "I've just had a phone call from Dr Johnson saying he is on his way in to see one of the residents who is not very well. I didn't call him though. I'm not sure who asked him to come. There's something wrong with Arthur, he's not his usual cheery self, but not ill enough to warrant a visit from him on a Sunday. Matron won't be pleased he's coming in. She likes to be here and she's not in today."

She told Matt that the leaking radiator was in Room 16. "It's Toms room. He's in there now holding a bowl to catch the drips. I've said it's not necessary for him to hold the bowl but he insisted."

Ted collected his toolkit from the closet and made his way up the stairs to Room 16. He knocked on the door and heard Tom say to come in.

He was crouched in front of the radiator with a half bowl of water in his hands.

"Let's have a look then," said Matt. Tom stood up with a bit of help from Matt. His walking stick was near the bed so Matt handed it to him for support.

"Won't stop dripping," Tom told him.

Matt went to the end of the radiator and gave the knob a good turn. It had been turned off but not fully, which explained why it was still dripping water. Matt looked under the bottom of the radiator and could see a small rusty area that must have a small hole in it. He asked Tom for a tissue so he could wipe excess water up from the bottom of the radiator. Tom handed him one. "I'll have to drain the radiator and fill this hole," explained Matt. "Lucky you don't need the radiator on, it's not cold outside."

"You haven't got old bones like mine!" replied Tom with a grin. "My bones never warm up these days!"

"I'm sorry to hear your mate, Arthur, is not very well today," said Matt. He knew the two of them were friends. He often saw them in the lounge chatting and doing a crossword.

"He was alright yesterday until he had the row with Matron in the lounge."

"What was the row about?" Matt asked curiously.

"Arthur was sticking up for old Gwen who was moaning about something missing from her handbag."

"What was missing?"

"A magnifying glass. She needs it to read with. It makes the print much bigger. Her eyes are not so good so she uses it a lot. Matron told her that she must have lost it herself. Gwen told her that it was always in her bag so she knows where it is when she wants to use it. Arthur told Matron she should look for it as Gwen hadn't lost it herself so it must have been stolen. Matron went mad and told him to keep out of it and mind his own business. Arthur stood up and waved his walking stick at her. Everyone was watching!

"Matron told Gwen that she would try and find her another one but not to hold her breath as she couldn't think where a spare one would be found. Gwen started to cry. Arthur told Matron she was cruel and horrible and didn't care about the residents. He said she shouldn't be in charge and the previous Matron had been so much nicer. Some of the residents started to agree with what Arthur was saying. A couple of others also started waving their sticks at her."

"Wow, sounds like a big row!" said Matt. "What happened next?"

"Matron left the room, dashing out as if the hounds of hell were after her! It all then started to quieten down, just Gwen sobbing still. Arthur went up to her and put his arm around her. He said he would ring on his mobile and ask his son to buy her a new one. He would be visiting on Monday and could bring it in then."

"That's good then," said Matt. "Do you think Arthur is poorly today as a result of the argument? He's an old man and shouldn't get worked up like that."

"I know. He has something wrong with his heart, I think," replied Tom.

"Dr Johnson is calling in to see him, I heard Sally the nurse say."

"I hope he's alright, it's not like him to miss his breakfast. He likes his eggs and bacon of a morning and today being a Sunday, we are also given a sausage and tomato for a treat."

Matt collected his tool bag, tipped the bowl of water down the sink in the en suite bathroom and said cheerio to Tom, saying he would see him tomorrow and repair the radiator.

He went out of the room in time to see Sally and Dr Johnson coming up the staircase. He presumed they were going to see Arthur in his room. He knew Arthur had the room next to Tom's.

He stood to one side at the top of the stairs and let them pass. Dr Johnson nodded at Matt.

"Thanks for coming in on a Sunday," said Sally.

"The radiator has stopped dripping now and I'll repair it tomorrow," replied Matt.

He went downstairs and put his toolkit away in the closet in the hall. He saw Josh coming out of the lounge.

"Tom's been telling me about the big row between Arthur and Matron in the lounge yesterday."

"Yes, I heard about it today when I came on shift," said Josh.

"I hope Arthur's alright. I've just seen Sally and the doctor going up to see him."

"I saw Arthur earlier this morning and he didn't seem too bad," said Josh. "He looked a bit more tired than usual but that's all."

Matt mentioned that there was tension and a strange atmosphere in the home lately and most of it revolved around the Matron. Josh agreed, saying she wasn't much liked by anyone. Staff tended to keep out of her way and that went for some of the residents too.

They heard someone coming down the stairs and looked up to see Sally and Dr Johnson coming down. They were talking in a low tone but Matt heard the doctor say he thought Arthur should be better soon. "It's as if he had been given a sedative but he isn't written up for anything so I can't be sure without a blood test. I'm glad he rung me though to check him over."

Matt thought, *So it was Arthur himself who had rung the doctor!*

Sally showed the doctor out of the front door. She saw Matt coming along the corridor.

"How is Arthur?" he enquired.

"Very sleepy, which isn't like him. He's normally the life and soul of everything but he's been checked over and all seems normal, apart from being very tired."

"Good. See you tomorrow!" said Matt and carried on towards the front door.

Just as he was opening it, the blonde lady who he recognised as Fiona, who had her aunt Ness here, was about to put her finger on the doorbell.

"That's good service! I never even rang the bell!" she exclaimed with a smile.

"At your service," he bowed and grinned as he let her pass through the door. He then left to collect his car. He remembered to pick up a really nice bunch of flowers from the garden centre for Nancy's cousin.

Fiona signed the visitor's book and popped her head in the lounge to see if her aunt was in there. She couldn't see her so went upstairs, presuming she was in her room. She knocked on the door and went inside. Her aunt was pottering about in her room. The radio was playing and was still on the correct channel.

She was pleased to see Fiona and they had a hug to say hello. "I've just put some clothes away in my wardrobe," she told Fiona. "A nice lady has washed them for me."

Fiona asked if she wanted to go for a drive in the car. Aunt Ness's face lit up and said that sounded nice. "Ted's playing golf this morning," she told her aunt. "He's not very good but is hoping to improve with practice."

She got her aunt's light jacket out of the wardrobe and helped her put it on.

"You look happy this morning?" she commented.

"I had a good night's sleep last night. There were no lights outside to keep me awake."

Fiona didn't comment on this, just said that was good.

She gave her aunt her walking stick and they went downstairs.

Fiona saw Josh and told him she was taking her aunt out for a drive. "You should have been here to witness a big row in the lounge yesterday," he said. "Matron again, and someone having something go missing."

"More things going missing?" queried Fiona. "It's getting beyond a joke. Surely something needs to be done about it. Did I see Dr Johnson's car leaving just as I arrived?"

"Yes, he came to see Arthur who was all worked up as he was in the middle of the big row."

"I hope he's alright?" asked Fiona, looking worried.

"He's just very tired, which is unusual for him. He's normally quite sprightly for his age. In fact, he was the one who rang on his mobile for the doctor to come out to see him."

"That seems very odd, surely it's more usual for the nurse to ring for a doctor's visit," said Fiona.

"It looks as though he was given some sort of sedative," whispered Josh. "He's not prescribed one so it's a bit odd."

Fiona looked alarmed. "And this is after the row yesterday!"

"Exactly," said Josh. "Makes you wonder, doesn't it? He knows Matron doesn't work on Sundays so must have thought it safe to ring for the doctor. She would never have rung him just because he's more tired than normal." Josh said to enjoy the drive and would see them later.

"I'll have Aunt Ness back for lunch," replied Fiona.

They walked slowly round to the carpark. She helped Aunt Ness into the passenger seat of her car and helped her put the seatbelt on.

They drove through the gates and turned right at the end of the road. It was a lovely day. She wondered aloud to Aunt Ness how Ted was getting on with his golf match.

Fiona was a competent driver and drove at a steady pace. She pointed out things of interest to her aunt. They saw some lovely front gardens, obviously very well-tended by their owners, as she drove through the villages. She realised then that she was approaching Morton where Dr Johnson lived. She told her aunt about finding the young lad with an arm injury yesterday afternoon during a walk in the woods.

"I wonder how he is and whether he has broken his arm?" she pondered to her aunt. She came to the crossroads and then turned left to drive down the road where the Johnsons lived. There was no red Jaguar on the driveway but she saw Tom's blue Kia parked up. Fiona slowed down, thinking if she should pull up to enquire after Tom and his arm.

She stopped the car opposite the house. She switched off the engine and told Aunt Ness to stay put as she was going to knock on the door to see if Tom was at home. Fiona crossed the road and went to ring the doorbell.

After half a minute, the doorbell was answered by Tom. His left arm was bandaged but not in a plaster cast.

"I was just passing by and thought I'd ask after your arm," explained Fiona.

"How kind," said Tom. "Dad took me to the hospital where the X-ray showed no break but it's just heavily bruised. It's strapped up as you can see but should recover in a couple of weeks."

"That's good then," said Fiona.

"Thanks again for helping me yesterday," he said.

"No problem, glad we were able to help." Fiona turned and went back to the car.

Tom went back inside the house.

She told Aunt Ness that Tom had not broken his arm after all but it was heavily bruised. Fiona restarted the engine and carried on with their drive.

She returned Aunt Ness to the care home just before one o'clock. Josh answered the door and helped Aunt Ness inside. "Roast Lamb and mint sauce for you today," he told her.

She returned home where Ted regaled her with shot by shot of his golf lesson with Hugh. He had really enjoyed it and couldn't wait to go again. Birdies, eagles, wedges, putters were talked about. Fiona had no idea what all these things were but didn't want to appear ignorant so just nodded and smiled.

When he paused for breath, she told him about taking Aunt Ness out for a drive and calling in to see Tom and his arm. "Dr Johnson wasn't there but he'd been to the home earlier this morning to see a resident who may have been sedated after a row with Matron yesterday. According to Josh, he wasn't prescribed anything like that so it's a bit of a mystery."

"What was the row about?" asked Ted.

"Another resident's item has gone missing, and it turned out that the poorly resident, Arthur, had called the doctor in himself!"

"That must be unusual; surely a nurse would call the doctor in?"

"That's what I said to Josh, who agreed with me. Anyway, Aunt Ness was in good spirits today and really enjoyed the drive out."

"Good."

They had a sandwich lunch and then Ted said he was going out to mow the lawn. Fiona got a chair out of the shed and sat on the patio, half watching him and half reading her book. It was sunny and warm and her eyes kept closing and before long, she was dozing off.

She woke up an hour later, her book having slipped off her lap ending up by her feet, to find Ted in a chair alongside her, also dozing off!

They sat on the patio for a couple of hours before Fiona went inside to start preparations for their evening meal. Roast chicken, fresh vegetables, roast potatoes, an evening in front of the television and an early night would round off their weekend nicely.

Monday morning arrived with the sun shining and the promise of fine weather all week.

Moira was preparing for her first shift at the care home. The alarm had gone off at six-twenty. The shift started at half past seven. It was only two miles away so she had plenty of time. Hugh stirred and muttered something as she quietly got out of bed. His alarm was set for seven. He didn't need to be at work until nine.

She was looking forward to a new challenge. Surely it would be easier than working in a hospital?

She showered and dressed in the navy dress that the nurses wore at the home. She pinned on her fob watch and made sure she had a pen in her pocket. She had a cup of tea and a bowl of cereal. At seven, she heard Hugh's alarm go off and took him a cup of tea.

He was stirring awake. She kissed him and handed him his tea.

"See you later," she said. "I'm going now as I don't want to be late on my first day."

"Good luck!" he said, which reminded her of the girl in the pub on Saturday night who had said the same thing.

She went out to her car and drove the two miles to the care home. She went through the electric gates and parked in the car park. There were a few cars already parked there, *some would belong to the night staff,* she thought.

She had not been told the keypad code on the front door so she rang the bell. It was answered by a carer whose name badge identified her as Alice.

"I'm Moira, the new nurse."

"Come in, we were told someone new was starting today. I'm Alice. I work here three nights a week."

Moira was shown the staffroom where she could store her bag. It was very sparse and not the most inspiring staffroom she had ever been in.

"I'll take you through to the nurse on day shift. You will be shadowing her," said Alice.

She took Moira into the dining room where the day nurse called Sally was. They introduced themselves. Sally showed Moira where to sit. "The day shift will be here soon. We have a handover from the night nurse."

By half past seven, there were several staff in the dining room ready to hear the night report. Moira was introduced by Sally as a new day nurse.

The nurse, a man called Graham, handed over. He had worked the night shift with three carers who were just finishing up before going home. He named all the residents and related what sort of night they had had. The only concern was Arthur who the doctor had been called in to see yesterday morning. "He's still a bit out of sorts, not his usual self," said Graham. "He had had a restless night, muttering but not making a lot of sense. He got out of bed a couple of times, rang the call bell but when we answered it, he wasn't sure why he had rung it."

He finished his report and then left as his shift had finished.

Sally organised which staff was allocated to getting up which resident, and then the carers left the room to start work. Sally then took Moira with her to start dispensing the medications. She explained about the usual routine and that some residents needed some of their medication half an hour before eating so they were dispensed first. The medication sheets for each resident appeared quite straightforward to Moira. She had used similar in the wards at the hospital. There didn't look as if there were any medications that she hadn't come across before.

Sally and Moira were very busy for a couple of hours. Sally explained that there would be some dressings to be done later on but medications were dispensed first. Moira's impression was that it was well organised and something she would feel comfortable doing on her own in time.

One of the carers asked if Arthur would be coming downstairs or would he be staying in his room like he had done yesterday. Sally said she would be going to see him shortly and would let her know.

They went into Room 14, which was Arthur's room. Sally knocked on the door before entering. Arthur was still in bed but awake.

"Good morning, Arthur," said Sally. "This is Moira who is a new nurse starting here today. How are you feeling this morning?"

"Better than yesterday," he replied. "What was in that tablet that I was given on Saturday night? It made me woozy and I didn't feel very well."

"I was here on shift Saturday evening and I didn't give you any tablets that you don't normally take."

"Matron said if the extra tablet was not taken then I possibly could have a heart attack," said Arthur.

"That's strange," said Sally. "She didn't say anything to me about you needing an extra tablet. I will check your medication sheet to find out what it was."

She asked Arthur if he felt well enough to come downstairs today.

"I think so," he replied. Sally said she would send a carer to help him get washed and dressed. He didn't usually need help but she couldn't be too careful. He still appeared not quite himself and she didn't want him falling if he felt woozy. He accepted his tablets, which she handed to him with a glass of water. He looked into the small pot that held them. "They look about right," he said and took them with a glass of water.

They left the room with a promise that someone would be with him shortly. "How odd," said Sally to Moira. "Matron doesn't normally dish out the medication. It's always the nurses that do that."

"Let's look at his medication chart," said Moira. "If any medication is given then presumably it has to be documented on the chart."

They went back to the medicine trolley and got out the charts. Sally found Arthur's and with a finger scrolled down the list of his medications.

"There's nothing documented about any extra tablets he may have been given. He had his normal ones at six o'clock that I gave him and signed for."

"How odd," said Moira "Do you think he dreamt it? What's his cognition like?"

"Very good normally. He's quite on the ball. He recognises the tablets that are prescribed for him and takes them quite happily. I will have a word with Matron when she comes in."

They completed the medication round with no further problems.

Moira met Fiona's Aunt Ness who was sitting in the lounge and told her she was a friend of Fiona's. She was also introduced to Matt the maintenance man. He smiled warmly and greeted her with a firm handshake. *He seemed a cheerful person to have around,* Moira thought. A care home needed a good competent handyman and it seemed Goodrest had one, if first impressions were anything to go by.

Moira asked Sally if she could sit and study the medication charts so she could get an idea of what ailments the residents had.

Sally agreed that was a good idea. "Let's grab a cup of coffee and sit together so I can answer any questions you may have."

They spent the next hour looking through them. Moira asked questions about each of the residents and now had a fair idea of what was wrong with each of them.

At eleven o'clock, Matron arrived at work. She went straight into her office without greeting any of the staff.

Sally knocked on her door and entered with Moira following.

"Ah, the new nurse," said Matron. "I hope Sally is looking after you?"

"Yes, she is, very well," replied Moira.

Sally asked her about the tablet that Arthur said had been given to him on Saturday evening. Matron denied giving him any tablet. "Why would he say that?" asked Matron.

"Well, he wasn't very well yesterday, which he has put down to some extra tablet that he says you said he needed to avoid a heart attack."

"How dare you question me! If I say I didn't give him anything then that's because I didn't."

"He rang Dr Johnson from his mobile yesterday and he came in to see him," said Sally.

"He did what? How dare he! I will be having very strong words with Arthur Colshaw about this. How did he get his number?"

"I have no idea," said Sally. Sally privately thought Arthur must have asked a carer for his number that was displayed on the board in Matron's office but she wasn't going to say this and get someone into trouble.

Moira was listening to this exchange. She was seeing the Matron in a different light to the one when she had been interviewed.

"There must be an explanation," said Moira. "Arthur seems to know what he's on about. He's convinced you said he needed an extra tablet on Saturday evening."

"I suggest you both leave my office and return to your work. I do not want to hear any more about this matter. I know nothing about this tablet he says he was given," Matron said, raising her voice. She turned away from them, sat down at her desk and opened a file indicating the conversation was over.

Sally and Moira left the office. They looked at each other but did not comment and walked down the hall.

They went into the room where the locked drug trolley was kept and only after closing the door did they speak.

"How strange," said Moira. "Is she normally so abrupt and rude?"

"Quite often," replied Sally. "Except when Dr Johnson is around, then she's all sweetness and light!"

"Well, I won't stand for it if she speaks like that to me again. I can give as good as I get!" said Moira.

They worked well together for the rest of the morning. Sally was a good mentor and Moira enjoyed her friendly company. Sally was a large girl with dark hair with a streak of pink in the long fringe that she swept to one side. She was in her late twenties, not married but had been dating Jack for three years. They had travelled prior to her working at the home and they were both working hard to save up for more travelling, this time to Australia. Jack worked as a car mechanic. "What he doesn't know about cars isn't worth knowing!" said Sally with a grin. She lived with Jack in a rented cottage in the next village and she had worked at the care home for six months.

Moira thought the residents seemed to be very nice and although she couldn't remember all the staff's, names most of them appeared very friendly. She didn't particularly take to one of the housekeepers. Moira thought her name was Annie. She appeared sullen and not very communicative. When Sally had introduced Moira to Annie, she just nodded without any comment. The other staff had said they were pleased to meet her, welcome to the team and the usual things that people say when a new member of staff arrives, but Annie was silent.

Moira took herself off to look around the home and try to familiarise herself with the layout. She saw Annie pushing her housekeeper trolley into Room 20 where Fiona's Aunt Ness lived. She noticed she hadn't knocked on the door before entering. Moira didn't know whether Ness was in there or not. Moira went to the door and gave it a knock before opening it quickly.

Annie was sitting on the bed, looking at her mobile phone.

"I didn't think we were allowed to have our mobile phones with us while we are working?" she said to Annie.

Annie shot up from off the bed. She appeared flushed, probably from being caught flouting the rules. She shoved the phone in her tunic pocket.

"I am new here so I'm familiarising myself with everyone and everywhere. I've also read the employee handbook and it definitely says 'No mobile phones on shift except on breaks'." Moira didn't want to come over all authoritative but she felt she should make a point.

Annie glared at her and muttered that she would go and put her phone in the staffroom. She left the room, leaving her trolley in the middle of the room. Moira moved the trolley to one side as she didn't want Ness coming up and tripping over it. She also noticed the bedside cabinet drawer wasn't quite shut. Had Annie been looking in it?

Moira noticed a magazine in the side of the trolley. It was this week's edition of *Hello*. Kate and William were smiling from the front cover. The royal couple had visited a children's nursery a couple of weeks ago, announced the cover's headlines, and there were plenty of pictures of the visit inside on pages fifteen to eighteen.

She put the magazine back where she found it and looked inside the trolley. She saw a selection of cleaning products and cloths. An aroma of polish wafted up.

Moira looked around the room, noticing the solitary picture hook on the wall from where a picture was obviously missing. She would certainly keep her eyes and ears open. Residents' belongings should be safe in their rooms. It was awful to believe someone, presumably a member of staff, was taking them from the vulnerable people living here.

All staff had police checks prior to be taken on so a person with a history of stealing would certainly not be suitable for working in this environment.

Moira left the room, closing the door behind her. Annie had not yet returned from putting her phone in the staffroom.

She would mention this to Sally when she went downstairs. She continued her tour of the home, opening cupboards to see what was in them, checking where the fire exits were and generally trying to familiarise herself. She knew there were currently two empty rooms in the home.

Presumably, advertising the empty rooms would be dealt with by Matron. She must be pleasant when showing potential residents and their families around or her attitude would put people off moving in.

She went into Room 10, which was one of the empty rooms. It looked very impersonal with only the bare minimum of furniture in there. It was lovely to see how the rooms became more personal when residents moved in with their own possessions. They moved into care homes after leaving their own homes because they needed someone to look after them, it must be very daunting but having their own possessions around them must help them to settle in.

She found Sally in the dining room having a cup of tea while she was looking at the staff rota.

"Molly, a night carer, has rung in sick so I'm trying to get cover for tonight," she told Moira.

"Is that our job, to organise cover? I would have thought that would be down to Matron."

"It is usually but she says she's too busy and told me to sort it out," replied Sally with a grimace. "It's not always easy. Some staff are willing to work extra shifts but others don't want to."

She took the hand phone out of her pocket, punched in a number and waited for it to be answered.

"Hi Rosalyn, it's Sally," she said. "Are you free to cover a night shift tonight? Molly has rung in sick." She listened to whatever Rosalyn was saying. "Yes, I know that's twice in a week she has rung in. You can? That's great, thank you very much!" She switched the phone off and wrote in the rota. "Sorted," she grinned with relief. "Sometimes it takes several tries to get someone to agree to come in at short notice."

"Surely we have enough to do with our own duties without the responsibility of sorting rotas out? Matron should know that. What does she do in the day?" commented Moira.

"Not really sure. She's closeted in her office a lot."

Moira told Sally about Annie and her phone. "She's a strange one," said Sally. "Always looks miserable and doesn't say much to anyone. I'm glad you pulled rank. Shows her who's in charge."

"I also saw a *Hello* magazine in her housekeeping trolley. It was this week's edition."

"Gwen was saying she was missing her *Hello* this morning. I wonder if it's the one Annie had. I will ask her."

She got up and motioned for Moira to follow her. They went upstairs and saw Annie coming out of Room 8. She was slowly pushing her trolley. Sally asked if she had a *Hello* magazine in the trolley.

"No," said Annie. "Why would I have one in here? Take a look for yourself," and pushed the trolley, which was on wheels, rolling it towards them.

"I definitely saw it earlier when you left the trolley in Room 20," said Moira, stopping the rolling trolley.

"Why were you looking in the trolley anyway? It's nothing to do with you what I keep in it. You're a nurse. I don't look in your drug trolley!" said Annie.

"Don't be so silly, Annie!" said Sally. "Where has the magazine gone? Gwen is missing her *Hello*."

"I don't know and I don't care, now let me get on with my cleaning or I will get behind and Matron will be on my back." She grabbed her trolley and went into the next room.

"What number room is Gwen in?" asked Moira.

"Room 12," replied Sally. "Let's go and see if the magazine is in there."

They knocked on the door of Room 12. There was no reply so they went in. The *Hello* magazine was peeping out from under '*TV Choice*' on a table by a chair.

"Annie must have come and put it back," said Moira. "She probably realised I had seen it and when she came back after putting her phone in the staffroom, nipped back and hid it here, making us believe it had been here all the time."

Sally took the magazine to return it to Gwen who was in the lounge. Gwen was very pleased to see it and thanked them for finding it. "It was definitely missing," she said. "Where was it?"

"It was in your room. I don't know what happened but you have it now. You enjoy it!" said Sally kindly and touched her arm in a comforting way. Gwen immediately started reading it with obvious pleasure.

She turned to Arthur who was sitting in his usual chair by Tom.

"How are you feeling now?" she asked him. They were doing the crossword in the Daily Telegraph.

"Better today. I don't know what that pill was but I don't want another one. Made me really woozy and even worse, I fair lost my appetite! Missed my Sunday breakfast of eggs, bacon, sausage and tomato!" he said with a grin.

"Glad things are back to normal," said Sally with a smile.

"That reminds me, I was going to have a visit from my son today but he's rung and told me something's cropped up and now can't come till the weekend. I forgot to ask him to buy a new magnifying glass for Gwen to replace hers that was stolen."

"I can buy one for her," said Sally. "I'm planning to go into town after work. I will bring it in tomorrow."

Moira was looking at the interaction between Sally and the residents. She was a natural carer and very kind. She could see the residents liked her. She hoped the other nurses and carers were as kind.

The shift ended at two-thirty. Nick was the trained nurse on the afternoon shift. He was a quiet man and didn't say a lot. He said he was pleased another nurse had started as sometimes they were a bit short-staffed.

The afternoon staff listened to the handover that Sally delivered. There were six carers on with Nick. Moira was introduced to them but realised it would probably take a few shifts before she remembered all their names.

She hadn't seen Matron since the office encounter earlier. *Good thing*, she thought, wondering what she had been doing since arriving at eleven.

Sally and Moira collected their bags from the staffroom. They would be working an afternoon shift together tomorrow.

She said goodbye to Sally, thanking her for looking after her, saying she would see her tomorrow and went to collect her car from the carpark.

Glad my first shift is over, she said to herself as she drove down the driveway and through the electric gates.

She arrived home and put the kettle on to make herself a cup of tea. She cut herself a slice of fruit cake and took the tea and cake into the lounge and sat down. She had a lot to think about. She had really liked Sally and thought her first shift had gone reasonably well, considering some of the events of the morning. She recalled the magazine episode with Annie and the conversation about Arthur's tablet with both him and the Matron.

That was very odd, she thought. Cognitively, Arthur had appeared fine and he was absolutely adamant about being asked to take the extra tablet on Saturday evening.

She had an hour's sit down in peace and quiet and then went upstairs to get changed. The day was warm and sunny and she went out into the garden to pull up a few weeds. Hugh usually got home around half six so she had plenty of time to think about what to prepare for dinner. She liked to cook and he was an appreciative recipient of her meals. Hugh was used to her working shifts and on the evenings she was working, he was competent in getting his own meal.

Matt had also had a busy day at the care home. He repaired Tom's radiator in the morning. He had a captive audience with Tom watching him and offering advice. Tom had worked in the building trade all his working life, he told Matt, saying he had a lot of experience in maintenance. He suggested that if Matt should ever need an extra pair of hands with anything then he was only to ask. "I'll remember that," grinned Matt.

With the radiator repaired, he got on with his other jobs. He needs to re-tune two residents' radios that somehow had changed channels. He had two wheelchair brakes to mend, a couple of ceiling lights to change, a noisy extractor fan to clean and a slow flushing toilet to attend to.

He took an early lunch break in the staffroom. He was on his own, made himself a mug of tea and took a newspaper out of his bag to read while eating his cheese and pickle sandwich. He was just reading about a Labrador dog that had given birth to twelve puppies when the staffroom door opened and Annie walked in. Matt looked up and said hello. She muttered something that he couldn't hear and went over to a locker. She pulled out a large black holdall and looked at her phone.

Matt looked back at his newspaper. She was always looking miserable, as if she would rather be anywhere than at work and so unfriendly, he thought. He liked nearly all the staff but there was something about Annie that he didn't like. He didn't trust her but had no evidence as to why. It was just intuition and he was usually right.

She often looked unkempt in appearance and he was surprised Matron let her get away it. Staff should look neat and tidy. Her hair was grey and straggly and always looked in need of a good hairdresser. Her housekeeper's overall was stained that a hot machine wash should sort out, he thought.

She didn't acknowledge him and went out of the room. He was glad she hadn't been on a lunch break as she made him feel uncomfortable, even more so if it was just the two of them. The other staff were friendly and up for a chat when they had their breaks.

The door opened again. Matt looked up and saw Josh come in for his break. He switched the kettle on asking if Matt wanted a coffee or tea. "No thanks, not long had one," he replied, holding up his mug.

Matt liked Josh. He was generally cheerful but recently he thought he had seemed a bit distracted.

"Everything alright?" Matt asked him. Josh tossed a tea bag into a mug, poured in boiling water and then added milk from the fridge. He added a spoonful of sugar, gave it a good stir and then came over to sit at the table.

"I'm not really sure," he replied. "I think something is going on here at Goodrest. I can't put my finger on it but things are not like they used to be when I first came."

"What sort of things?" asked Matt.

"Well, residents having things taken for a start. I think there's a thief on the staff. Also, there have been a few deaths recently and they were people who were in fairly good health as far as I can tell. Take Wilfred and Freda, for instance. Both reasonably well but they suddenly died."

Matt said, "But surely a doctor has to sign a death certificate with a cause of death?"

"Yes, I know. Freda's death went to the coroner from what I heard. That means there was no obvious reason why she died so suddenly."

"But didn't Dr Johnson see her the day or so before? There had been that row about the missing bird clock and biscuits."

"But he didn't come out when she died. I think I mentioned to you at the time that it was a locum doctor who came to see her but obviously he couldn't see a reason why it was so sudden so he couldn't sign it off."

"Well, it must have been discussed with Dr Johnson at some stage as he was her usual doctor," said Matt.

"I suppose so. I hear the coroner has now released her body so a death certificate must have been signed now. Wilfred was another unexpected death too," said Josh with a frown. "He seemed fine one day and the next minute he'd gone too. It seems that all these deaths are after some sort of confrontation with Matron."

"Good grief, Josh!" spluttered Matt. "You're not thinking she's bumping off the residents, are you?"

"I'm not saying that, but it seems a big coincidence."

The door then opened and a couple of carers came through for their lunch break. "Shush," said Josh, looking at Matt.

Matt looked at his watch and saw he'd had his half hour he was entitled to. He got up and put his mug in the dishwasher. He folded up his newspaper and packed it away in his bag. He glanced at Josh, saying he would see him later.

Matt left the staffroom, feeling worried. Was there anything going on here? He would certainly be keeping his ears and eyes open from now on. He returned to his maintenance jobs. He needed to go outside and look at some loose guttering. He got his tall ladder out of the large shed where Kirsty kept all her gardening equipment. There was no sign of her. He took a hard hat from the shelf.

The loose guttering was above the side of the house that looked onto the back garden. He positioned the ladder, giving it a shake to make sure it was firm enough for him to climb up on.

He went up the steps very carefully. He had once fallen off a ladder so was always a bit nervous of it happening again. He had twisted his ankle and it had never recovered fully.

He reached the guttering. He could see a bit into the bedroom window that was above it. He realised it was Arthur's room. He could see Annie in there. She appeared to be rummaging in the top drawer of Arthur's bedside cabinet. Matt couldn't see if Arthur was in the room. Annie cast a look around at the door and then turned back to whatever she was doing in the drawer.

Matt ducked down a bit. He didn't want to be seen. His heart started beating faster. There was a net curtain covering the window but he hoped she hadn't spotted him. A bright yellow hard hat was not easy to miss. He stayed where he was for a few moments and then risked another peep into the room.

It was empty as far as he could tell. The bedside drawer was now closed. There was no sign of Annie or anyone else in the room.

Matt leaned forwards as much as he could, peering as close to the window as he felt safe to do so. Definitely no one was in there now.

He looked at the guttering and could see it had become dislodged. He manoeuvred it back into position.

He descended the ladder, relieved that he hadn't fallen off. The sight of Annie rummaging in a resident's drawer had surprised him. It had looked sneaky to him. She obviously hadn't wanted to be seen, judging by her glance towards the door of the room. He wondered what she had been looking for. There might be a clear explanation for her being in the room doing what she had been doing but he couldn't think of one right now.

He returned the ladder to the shed. Kirsty was in there, sorting out some tools she used for her gardening. "Hello," she called, "keeping busy, I see," pointing to the ladder. Matt returned the hard at on the shelf.

"Keeps me out of mischief," he grinned at her.

They had a chat about the gardens and Matt complimented her on how well she kept them.

"Thank you. It's not an easy task on your own," she replied. "I have a bit of help sometimes but Tom's hurt his arm and can't work for a couple of weeks."

"Yes. I've seen a lad out here sometimes," Matt replied. "He looks quite fit."

"He apparently tripped on a tree root when walking in some woods!" she said. "I think I'll get him some glasses!" She laughed.

"Good idea. Nice to see you. I'd better be off now in case Matron thinks I'm skiving," said Matt with a laugh.

He walked back up the garden and went through the back door into the home. He passed the lounge and popped his head in and saw Arthur and Tom ribbing each other about who had answered most of the crossword today. Matt thought again about seeing Annie in Arthur's room. He saw Nick the nurse in charge this afternoon at the far end speaking to Ness.

He was asked by one of the carers called Caroline to look at a television in Room 6. "Frances says that *Countdown* was spoiled by the picture going on and off. The sound was there but she wanted to see the letters to guess the word and without the picture, she couldn't!"

Matt went up to Room 6. Frances was one of the few residents who always stayed in her room. She was eighty-eight and looked very well for her age. She wore her long grey hair up in a topknot. She didn't like to mix with the other residents in the lounge, she only liked certain television programmes and liked to watch them without people talking or interrupting. She had her meals in her room as she said she couldn't bear to look at people being fed by staff. She didn't have a lot of compassion and called a spade a spade. Some of the younger staff were a bit in awe of her, as she could be very abrupt with them.

Matt knocked on her door and waited for her to tell him to go in. He had once made the mistake of going in after knocking but not waiting for the command to enter. He had never made that mistake again after the telling off she gave him!

Matt heard the order to enter the room. Frances was sitting in front of a television with sound but no picture.

"Sort this out!" she ordered him. "How can I be expected to watch, or in this case not watch, my programmes with only sound?"

Matt turned the television off. He re-tuned it but the same thing happened. Sound but no picture!

"I will swap this one for a different one. We have some spare ones in the home," he told her.

"I hope it is of the same quality as mine. I can't watch an inferior one, not with my eyesight."

"I will find one that is just as good," he promised, keeping his fingers crossed.

He took the aerial out of the back and unplugged the television. He carried it out of the room, reminding her that he may not knock on returning to the room as he would be carrying a television.

"Very well, but give a loud cough when you open the door so I know it's you," she barked at him.

Matt took the television out of the room. He knew there was one in an empty room so he collected it, leaving the broken one in there to sort out tomorrow.

He returned to Room 6, opened the door giving a loud cough as he entered. He set the new television up and tuned it in. Thankfully, a picture appeared along with the sound!

"Thank you," she said. "You've done very well. Just in time for *Tipping Point*."

Matt left the room, feeling relieved he had escaped without any telling off!

He finished his working day doing small odd jobs. He didn't see Josh again but wanted to come back as soon as possible to the conversation they had had in the staffroom at lunchtime.

Fiona woke up on Tuesday morning, feeling a bit under the weather. She had not had a good night's sleep, which was unusual for her. Ted had slept with no problems judging by the light snoring she had heard hour after hour. She had finally dropped off about four in the morning so she felt tired and sluggish when the alarm woke her.

She climbed out of bed wondering if she was coming down with something. Summer colds were not very nice. It was warm anyway without sweating a cold out.

She took two paracetamols with her breakfast cup of tea. She normally had cereal and toast but she didn't fell hungry and had to push her cereal down as she felt slightly nauseous.

Ted was full of beans. Mornings were usually good for Ted. He sometimes went for a run before going to work.

Fiona had never wanted to go for runs. She enjoyed walking. She wasn't particularly sporty but she was fine with Ted wanting to do his sports. He liked to keep fit as often as possible and she was all for it for him, but it was not for her. Walking was her way of keeping fit, not sweaty runs or playing squash!

Ted noticed she looked tired. "Are you okay to go into work?" he asked.

"I hardly slept last night. I don't know why. If I feel rough later, I'll come home. It's probably just a summer cold," Fiona replied.

She drove to work and parked up in the council carpark. She saw Lynne arrive and waited for her. They walked to their office together.

"You look a bit tired," she commented to Fiona.

"I feel it. I didn't sleep much last night. I'm not sure if I'm coming down with a cold. I'll see how the day goes and if I don't feel better later, I'll leave work early."

They went into their office and prepared for the day.

"How's the romance going?" Fiona asked Lynne. "I haven't asked lately."

"Good," replied Lynne. "I really like him. He's kind and the boys like him too."

Fiona really hoped it worked out for Lynne. She deserved being happy after her divorce and if the boys liked him then that was a bonus.

She struggled on throughout the morning but by lunchtime felt quite unwell. Lynne told her to go and not return until she was better.

Fiona returned home. She rang Ted at work to tell him she was home and going to bed to try and have a sleep.

"Don't worry about a meal this evening. I'll get something for us when I get home," he told her. Fiona rang off and went upstairs to bed.

She immediately fell asleep and was only just waking up when Ted returned home. He came upstairs and bent over her. He kissed her but Fiona shooed him away in case he caught whatever she had.

Ted was a bit worried. Fiona was never normally ill and he hated seeing her unwell now. He asked if she wanted anything but she said just a glass of water. She wasn't hungry; she just wanted to rest.

Ted went to fetch her water but when he returned, Fiona was fast asleep. He put the glass of water on her bedside table, kissed her forehead and went downstairs.

The phone rang later in the evening. It was Moira asking for Fiona. Ted explained that she wasn't feeling too well and was asleep in bed. Moira commiserated and said she would ring back in a day or two.

Ted asked her how her first day at the care home went. "Not too bad," she answered. "The Matron is not the best one I've come across but we'll see how things go."

She said to tell Fiona when she woke that her aunt appeared fine and she would ring her in a day or two.

Ted got himself a ready meal and spent the evening going up and down the stairs checking on Fiona. She was fast asleep every time he checked.

He got into bed beside her at half past ten, hoping she would feel better tomorrow.

Next morning, Nick was the nurse in charge at the care home. He was a competent nurse but the carers found him quiet and he never interacted with them in the way that Sally or the other nurses did. He listened to the handover from the night staff and made sure the carers knew their tasks for the day. Nick started dispensing the medications when Sue came and asked him to look at Arthur as he didn't appear to be his usual self.

Nick followed Sue up to his room. Arthur was in bed looking rather flushed. Nick asked Sue to fetch a thermometer and the blood pressure machine so he could take Arthur's observations. Whilst she had gone, Mick took Arthur's pulse. It was quite rapid, way above the normal range. He asked Arthur how he was feeling. "Rough," replied Arthur.

Sue arrived back and Nick took Arthur's temperature and blood pressure. He had a temperature but his blood pressure was normal. "I will get you some paracetamol for your temperature," Nick told him. "Stay in bed and rest."

He went out of the room to get the paracetamol. Sue put her hand on Arthur's forehead. "Let's take the duvet off you and just have a sheet over you instead. I can get a fan for you as well. That will cool you down."

Nick returned with the paracetamol and helped Arthur sit up to take them with some water.

Sue fetched a fan and set it going in the room.

"Keep checking him," said Nick. "Come and get me if anything changes."

He left the room to return to dispensing medications. Sue made sure Arthur was comfortable and then left to attend to other residents.

When Nick saw Matron a little later, he reported that Arthur was unwell and in bed. "I will go up and see him," she said. Arthur was asleep when she went into his room. He was not as flushed as Nick said he was earlier as the fan was cooling him down.

She pulled open his bedside cabinet drawer but at that moment, Sue came into the room. Matron slammed the drawer shut and said it had been open and she was shutting it. "Arthur must have opened it then because it was closed earlier," said Sue, looking down at the sleeping Arthur. She felt his forehead. "I think his temperature is coming down," she told Matron.

Matron left the room. Sue went out after her and reported back to Nick that Arthur was cooler now.

Nick and Sue kept popping back to see him throughout the morning. He woke up a couple of times and had a drink. Nick documented the visits and took his observations again later in the morning. They were all quite normal now. He appeared to be over the worst. He was more awake and drinking quite well. He didn't want anything to eat though.

Tom had asked after Arthur and been told he was having a day in bed as he was feeling a bit rough. He was advised not to visit him as they didn't want Tom to catch anything in case it was contagious. Tom pondered over the crossword on his own but it didn't hold much appeal without his friend.

Nick handed over to Sally and Moira when they came in for the afternoon shift. He relayed the observations that he had taken and suggested she take them again during their shift.

Sally bristled a bit at being told this. "Of course, I will take them during the shift," she told Nick.

The morning shift departed and the afternoon shift began. It was quite busy as Dr Johnson was doing a round. Matron had been asked to go out and assess a potential new resident in the local hospital so she wasn't about for Dr Johnson's visit, which she was not happy about.

He sat with Sally and Moira and discussed all the residents. He checked their medication charts. He made a few changes to a couple of them.

When it came to Arthur's chart, Sally informed him of Arthur repeatedly saying that he had had an extra tablet on Saturday evening and that's why he was ill on Sunday. "I didn't prescribe anything extra for him," he told her.

Moira told him that Arthur had insisted that Matron had said he needed it to avoid having a heart attack.

Dr Johnson looked at her in disbelief. "Are you sure? Arthur didn't say anything to me on Sunday but I must admit he was more asleep than awake when I saw him."

"That's what Arthur said and he was very adamant about it."

"I will check it out with her," he said.

They finished looking at the charts and then Dr Johnson saw the residents. He went into the lounge and greeted a lot of them by name. He then saw the few residents who were in their rooms, including Arthur. He spoke to him, checked his blood pressure and reassured him he should be up and about in no time.

Moira thought he was nice. Remembering the residents' names made it more personal, which was appreciated. He listened to what they were saying to him even though some had dementia where the conversation didn't make a lot of sense.

Matron arrived back just as the round was finishing. "Might I have a word with you in the office?" he asked her.

She beamed at him, apologising for not being around for his visit. "I was looked after very well," he replied, smiling at Sally and Moira. Matron gave them a look that could have been interpreted as something other than praise for them.

Dr Johnson followed Matron into her office and closed the door behind them. Unfortunately, Sally and Moira could not hear the conversation.

When he came out of the office ten minutes later, he left the home.

Matron came bustling along the hallway and found Sally and Moira in the lounge. "A word with both of you in my office, now!" she snapped.

They followed her in and Matron shut the door. She asked them what they had been telling Dr Johnson about this extra tablet of Arthur's that she was meant to have given him on Saturday evening.

"I only told him what Arthur has been saying," said Sally.

"I did not give him a tablet," said Matron, getting very red in the face.

"Alright, calm down," intervened Moira. "Dr Johnson was asking after Arthur and it was only right to tell him what Arthur had said about having the tablet to avoid having a heart attack."

"I repeat for the very last time that I did not give him any tablets on Saturday evening. Go now and I don't want to hear another word about it." She sat down heavily in her chair. "And close the door behind you."

Sally and Moira left the office, closing the door after them and went to sit in the dining room.

"What on earth is going on?" asked Moira. "I almost believe her, don't you?"

"I really don't know what to believe any more," said Sally. "If Matron didn't give him the tablet then who did give it?"

They looked at each other in horror.

"Did Arthur actually say it was Matron who gave it?" asked Moira.

"Let me think," said Sally. "No, from what I can remember, Arthur didn't actually say Matron gave it, only that he was told Matron said he needed it. We have presumed that she gave it but someone else could have given it saying Matron said he must have it."

"We now need to ask Arthur who gave it to him then and then the mystery is solved, except it doesn't tell us what the tablet was."

They went upstairs to Arthur's room. Sally knocked on the door and they went in. Arthur was fast asleep.

"Bother!" said Moira.

They went out of the room and made their way downstairs.

It was now time for the teatime medications to be given out so the next hour was pretty busy.

They had a cup of tea and a sandwich at around half past six. They sat in the dining room. Sally made sure that the carers took their breaks. They worked hard and deserved a rest between their tasks. Some of the residents were quite demanding, which took up a lot of their time, but the carers were kind and patient and didn't mind.

Arthur had slept through tea so at seven o'clock, Sally and Moira took up a tray with a sandwich, yoghurt and cup of tea on it. He was sleepy but rousable. Sally asked if she could take his blood pressure and temperature. He agreed. They were satisfactory and she made a note for his file downstairs. She helped him to sit up in bed and laid the tray across his lap.

"While we are here, can we ask you about the extra tablet that you were given on Saturday night?"

"I might have been mistaken about that," he said. "Perhaps I was dreaming I had one. I know I had more visits from a carer in the night than usual though."

"But you were so certain that one was given to you to prevent having a heart attack."

"No. I think I was mistaken." He didn't meet her eyes but stared ahead as he was telling her this.

Sally didn't believe him but she couldn't just come out and say this. She looked at Moira for help.

"Has someone told you to say you didn't have the tablet when in fact you did?" Moira asked him.

"Course not. I tell you I must have been mistaken. Now leave me alone to eat my tea." He looked down at the tray, picked up the sandwich and took a bite and then lifted his head to look straight ahead.

"Okay, we'll leave you now. Just ring the call bell if you need anything," said Sally. They went out of the room.

"I'm certain someone's told him to say that," Moira said. "He wouldn't look at us when he was saying it."

They went downstairs.

The rest of the evening passed quickly. After a doctor's round, there were notes to write up. They shared this between them. "It's nice having another nurse on shift with me," commented Sally.

Their shift finished at nine o'clock. Sally left Moira to do the handover to the night staff. They then collected their bags from the staffroom and went home.

Moira told Hugh about her day and how concerned they were about the extra tablet that Arthur now said he hadn't had.

"You'd best ask Police Constable Fiona to investigate," suggested Hugh.

"It's not funny, it's very puzzling," replied Moira.

They watched some television and then went to bed.

Fiona felt a little better the next day. She hadn't come out with a cold after all. She rang Lynne and said she was taking the day off to recover more fully.

Lynne told her to take as long as she needed. Fiona said she hoped to be in the next day.

She saw Ted off to work. She managed to eat a bit of breakfast and drank a couple of cups of tea.

Ted had told her that Moira had rung up the previous evening saying her aunt was fine, which reassured Fiona.

She spent a lazy morning, still in her night clothes, lying on the settee watching some daytime television. She showered later in the morning and got dressed afterwards. She sat in the garden enjoying the sunshine for a while. It was quite nice to be off on a weekday. There were no noisy lawnmowers disturbing the peace, which was what usually happened on a Sunday afternoon!

Matt was at the care home, carrying on with his many jobs. There was a bedside cabinet cupboard drawer to fix as the hinge had become loose, light bulbs to replace and a couple of sinks that had dripping taps.

He enjoyed the variety of maintenance jobs that he did. There were routine monthly tasks such as checking showers, lights and wheelchairs that he fitted in around the other jobs that arose on a daily basis.

He saw the new nurse Moira talking to Ness in the lounge, as he was going in with his ladder to change a ceiling light bulb. She seemed very pleasant from what he had seen of her. Ness was talking back with her.

He saw Tom sitting on his own with the newspaper in his hands. "No Arthur today?" he enquired.

"He was poorly again yesterday and I haven't seen him yet today. I hope he'll come down later. He's missed his breakfast again and I need his help with the crossword," replied Tom.

Matt changed the ceiling light bulb and went out of the room with his ladder.

He had his lunch break and spent the rest of his day doing routine jobs. Matron checked on his progress, which he wasn't impressed with. He knew what he had to do and always completed his jobs on time.

Moira was also having a good morning. There were no unwell residents, apart from Arthur feeling more tired than usual. She was the only nurse on shift today. She had completed the medication round in good time, considering it was the first time doing it on her own. Sally was on the late shift and Fiona looked forward to seeing her later.

The carers performed their variety of tasks well, with Rosalyn asking Moira to check whether Arthur was well enough to go downstairs today. She went to his room and took his temperature and blood pressure, which were fine. She didn't want to upset him by mentioning the Saturday evening tablet again. He said he would stay in his room for the morning but would go down for lunch. He didn't seem as distracted as he had been the previous day.

Moira handed over to Sally and the afternoon carers at two o'clock. Sally asked if she had had a good morning as she had been the only nurse on duty.

"I was fine. I remembered most of what you have shown me. I hope I did everything right!" replied Moira. "The carers are very supportive and Matron kept out of the way, which was a good thing!"

"She should have been supportive as well," said Sally. "You being new here and being the first shift on your own."

"I didn't mind," said Moira.

Moira left and drove home. She was enjoying the new job and the staff was very nice. It was just odd about Arthur and the tablet and also no one had gotten to the bottom of the residents' things going missing.

She would ring Fiona later this evening and report in. She hoped she was feeling better today.

Fiona was in the kitchen preparing the evening meal when Ted arrived home. He kissed her and gave her a hug. He had rung at lunchtime and was relieved to hear she was feeling better. He hated it knowing she was feeling unwell, it was so unlike her. She was normally very well and in all the time he had known her, she had only been ill once when she had had the flu.

"I'm feeling much better," she told him. "I'm not sure what was wrong with me but I think I will go back to work tomorrow."

"Only if you're sure," replied Ted.

"I'm sure," she said as she kissed him.

Ted felt much relieved and went upstairs to shower and change.

They ate their meal on trays in front of the *One Show*. Fiona's appetite was back and Ted cleared his plate as usual.

The phone rang and Fiona answered it. It was Moira.

"Just checking in to see how you are," said Moira.

"I'm feeling much better today, thanks," Fiona replied. "How is the new job going?"

"It's going alright actually. The staff is really nice and helpful. The Matron is not particularly accommodating but I'm keeping out of her way as much as I can. There a few odd things going on but nothing about your aunt worries me."

"That's good then," said Fiona. "What sort of odd things?"

"Well, things still going missing and a resident having a tablet that he's not prescribed for."

"Sounds worrying," said Fiona.

"Leave it to me," replied Moira. "I will get to the bottom of all this!"

They chatted for a further ten minutes and then ended the call.

Fiona relayed the conversation to Ted. "I'm glad Aunt Ness seems to be alright. I will see her later in the week when I'm feeling back to normal."

She rang Lynne to tell her that she was feeling better and would be back at work tomorrow. She had an early night and was fast asleep when Ted got into bed.

Sally was on the early shift the next day. She had the handover from Graham. It had been a peaceful night, he said, and most of the residents had slept well. There had been some call bells rung by some residents throughout the night but nothing untoward. Arthur was feeling better.

She spoke with the carers on shift with her and they went off to get their allocated residents up for the day. She had just started dispensing the breakfast medications when Matron suddenly appeared. "What do you think of the new nurse?" she greeted Sally.

"She's very nice and a very good nurse. She will be an asset to our team," replied Sally.

"I'm not sure," said Matron. "She seems a bit forward."

"In what way?"

"Well, this business with Arthur. I don't think she believed me when I said I didn't give him that tablet."

"Actually, she did believe you but it made us both wonder if someone else gave him it, saying it was on your orders."

"Who would do that and for what reason?"

"We don't know. All we do know is that Arthur was adamant about it being given to him at the time, but yesterday, he denied actually having it."

"That's very strange, but it's good to hear that you believe I was not responsible for giving it to him," said Matron. She went off without further comment.

Sally thought that was almost the most reasonable conversation she had ever had with Matron. She normally was barking her orders out and not staying around to chat to the nurses.

She must be a bit worried, thought Sally. She continued with the drug round.

When she saw Arthur in his room, he said he wanted to get up and come downstairs today. He seemed quite bright and said he was looking forward to his eggs and bacon and also doing the crossword with Tom. Sally smiled and said she would see him downstairs.

Sally went in to see Ness in her room. Sally thought she was looking a bit tired. The carers hadn't yet been in to assist her getting up for the day.

"How are you today?" Sally asked her.

"Well, I didn't sleep much last night. The light in the garden kept me awake."

"What light?" asked Sally.

"The one I saw in the garden. I can see it shining through the window from my bed. The curtains aren't very thick. The light showed up in my room. I get frightened thinking someone is going to break in."

"It's very secure here," said Sally. "The night staff are about and no one could come inside without them knowing."

She gave Ness her morning tablets and said someone would be in soon to help her get washed and dressed.

She felt sorry for Ness. She had read her pre-admission records and knew that Ness had been afraid in her own flat, thinking someone was going to break in. She hoped she had reassured her.

Sally continued with her medication round.

She went into the lounge to see who was in there, and went over to the far end window as she heard a noise. She saw that a window catch was broken. It was a bit breezy outside today and the window wasn't closing properly, causing it to rattle due to the broken catch.

She went to find Matt who she knew was in the dining room fixing a light.

He followed her into the lounge to see the window catch. "It looks like the window has been forced open. There's a bit on it to stop it opening too wide but someone has forced it to open very wide," he said. "The screws are out." He looked on the floor and found them on the carpet.

He picked them up and went to get his screwdriver from his toolbox. He put the screws back in and tested that the catch secured the window.

"It's a bit odd," he said to Sally. "Why has someone really pushed on the window causing the screws to come out?"

"Oh well, it's secure now," Sally said.

Sally looked through the window onto the back garden. She could see Kirsty mowing the lawn. She hadn't had much to do with her but she did admire the work she did in the gardens. The flowerbeds were lovely. Tall trees bordered part of the garden throwing shade onto the far end. There was a small shed at the end in the corner. Sally wondered what it held. Gardening tools, she imagined. Sally turned away from the window and saw Arthur and Tom come through the door. They sat in their usual chairs and Tom opened the newspaper he was holding. They placed their walking sticks by the side of their chairs.

"How were the eggs and bacon?" she asked Arthur.

"Excellent," he replied with a grin. "You can't beat a good breakfast!"

It was nice to see him downstairs again with his friend Tom. Arthur started telling Tom that his radio channel had been altered when he had turned it on that morning. "Can't think how it changed, it's normally reliable."

Sally went out and sat in the dining room, filling in reports. She was looking forward to seeing Moira later who was due on the afternoon shift. She might suggest meeting up for a drink one evening with their other halves. She felt they might become good friends.

Moira arrived for her shift. She had had a busy morning. She had done the weekly shop and afterwards met a friend for a coffee. She had ended up having a cheese and tomato toastie with her coffee as well, to save getting something to eat at home before work.

Sally handed the shift over. Moira was pleased to hear that Arthur had recovered and was in the lounge again.

Sally left saying she had the next two days off. She was decorating her lounge, a job she wasn't keen on but Jack was even less keen on decorating then she was, but she had volunteered to do it.

Moira went to see the residents in the lounge. She saw Gwen was happily using her new magnifying glass that Sally had bought for her. She went up to Ness who was sitting at the far end, peering closely out of the window. Her nose was almost touching the glass. "What are you looking at?" asked Moira.

"The garden…to see if I can see where the lights are coming from."

"But it's daytime. There aren't any lights," replied Moira.

"No, not now. The lights at night."

"At night?" repeated Moira.

"Yes. Not every night but some nights."

"But there's nothing out there that would have a light on it."

"I know what I see. There are lights and I sometimes hear voices as well."

Moira knew that Ness's room upstairs overlooked the garden.

"Well, if you see them again, why not ring the call bell so the night staff can see them too?"

"I might just do that," Ness said.

She turned to Moira and asked for a cup of tea.

Moira went into the kitchen and made her one and took it through to Ness. She was looking towards the television now, as if losing interest in the garden.

She recalled Fiona mentioning that her aunt had seen lights in the garden.

Moira spoke with the other residents in the lounge. She was tempted to ask those with rooms looking onto the back garden if they had seen any lights at night but decided not to.

She had a good and uneventful shift. The carers were extremely helpful and when she asked questions, they readily answered. Matron stayed in her office and didn't appear until she left at five o'clock. She did come and find Moira to say she was leaving.

The night staff arrived just before nine o'clock. It was not Graham tonight but a lady called Nina. She was in her early thirties. She told Moira she had worked three nights a week at the home for the last two years. She had three preschool-aged children and nights suited her better for child care than day work. She admitted she got tired as she had to be awake in the daytime to look after her children. She said her husband worked long hours and often didn't arrive home early enough for her to have a rest. She always hoped for a quiet shift. *She looked tired*, Moira thought, and this was before she had worked the shift.

Nina asked Moira how she liked it so far.

"It's good," replied Moira. "Everyone is being very helpful. It's always difficult starting somewhere different and you have to get to know so many new people."

She was about to ask Nina if she had seen any lights in the back garden at night but the other night staff came into the room. Alice was on shift as was three other care staff. There was a young male carer called Carl and two women, Nadia and Amy, who looked to be in their forties.

She began her handover of her shift. She left soon afterwards and drove home. She was tired and would have a quick shower and sandwich and go to bed as she was on the early shift again in the morning.

Moira arrived at work the next morning but was told by Nina that one of the carers, Anita, had rung in sick. This caused a collective grumble from the other carers. "We are always covering for her. She rings in sick a lot. She does have a disabled husband to care for as well as working here but she should reduce her shifts if she can't cope," Josh told Moira.

Moira was used to working with staff that regularly called in sick. That was one of the reasons why she had left the hospital. The managers expected the staff that did always turn up to cover the shortages. Sometimes, agency staff were used but by the time they were shown what to do, it was quicker to do the work yourself.

The handover was completed and the carers, still grumbling, left the room to get the residents up for the day.

Moira decided to ask Nina if she had seen any lights in the garden at night.

"It's strange that you ask me that because I have seen something on the odd night. I close the lounge curtains soon after we get here if they've not been closed earlier and occasionally thought I've seen something towards the end of the garden. I have presumed that it's someone walking their dog in the field at the end of the garden. It's like a torch beam as it flickers, as if someone is holding a light. I haven't been out to look as I don't want to be nosy."

"Is it near the small shed that's in the garden?" asked Moira. "It's just that some residents mention seeing lights there and also hearing voices."

"It is usually around that area, now you come to mention it," replied Nina. "Oh well, as long as whoever it is doesn't come up the garden to the home, we should be alright." She didn't appear to be particularly concerned.

She collected her bag from the staff room and went home.

Matt arrived for work at nine o'clock. He greeted Moira with a cheerful good morning. He and Nancy had been to the pictures last night and then after the film finished had had a bite to eat in Frankie and Benny's nearby.

He was always pleasant and amenable and well-liked by residents and staff alike. It was well known amongst the staff that he didn't much care for Matron but then many of the staff felt the same as well. They tended to keep out of her way as much as they could. She never usually greeted them by name and certainly never made small talk with them.

Moira asked him if he knew what was kept in the small shed at the end of the garden.

"I don't actually know," he answered. "My things are kept here in the closet or the bigger things like my large ladder is kept in the large gardening shed of Kirsty's at the end of the carpark."

"Could you have a look in the shed?" asked Moira. "It's just that some people have seen a light at night near it and I'm intrigued as to what may be stored in there."

"I will go and look later on when I've done some of my jobs," he told her.

Moira finished the medication round. All the residents appeared well and in good spirits. There was a singer who came in at eleven to entertain them that always went down well. She sang songs accompanied by music that they could sing to from a good few years ago and it was always a very popular performance. The lounge was packed with residents coming to watch her. They enjoyed a cup of tea afterwards. It was lovely to see them happy and animated, thought Moira.

The morning shift finished and the next shift arrived for work. Nick was the afternoon nurse in charge. Moira hadn't had much to do with him yet. He was quiet but listened attentively to her reports.

He asked a few questions about some of the residents, as well as asking about Arthur and whether he had recovered now from the weekend. Moira said it had been very strange about the tablet episode. Nick just said, "Quite."

She collected her bag, wishing him a good shift.

As she was leaving the home, she remembered about asking Matt to look in the shed. He hadn't returned to tell her if he had seen anything so she presumed he hadn't yet looked. She would ask him tomorrow, which was her last shift of the week.

Moira drove home thinking she had done the right thing in taking this job. She really liked working with Sally and most of the other staff were very nice. She couldn't get a grasp on Nick yet but as she got to know him better, she was sure she would find him just as competent as the other nurses.

Fiona returned to work on Thursday as she was feeling much better now. It must have been a twenty-four-hour bug, she thought. She hoped Ted wouldn't catch it.

She caught up with things that had mounted up over the couple of days whilst she had been off. Lynne had been busy in her absence, covering some of Fiona's work, and was very pleased to see her back at her desk. They worked well together and missed each other when one of them was off.

"Have you had any doctor dates this week?" she asked Lynne with a grin.

"He came over on Tuesday for tea with me and the boys," she smiled. "It was good to cook a roast chicken dinner for a change. The boys enjoyed it as well. Normally, their choice of chicken comes in pieces covered with batter around it, in a tub with a jolly looking chef on the side!"

Fiona laughed. "I'm so glad things are going well! Have you met his son yet?" asked Fiona.

"Not yet. Apparently, he had an accident on Saturday and hurt his arm. He tripped over a tree root when walking in some woods."

Fiona shot up in her seat. "No! I don't believe it."

"Why on earth not? Kevin wouldn't make something like that up."

"Is Kevin's surname Johnson?"

"Yes."

"It's the same Dr Johnson from the care home. Ted and I helped his son Tom when we were walking in the woods. We found him on the ground with an injured arm and took him home. They live in Morton."

"Well, I never, what a coincidence!" exclaimed Lynne. "What do you think of Kevin?"

"He seemed really nice. He was very patient and considerate with a resident called Freda when she was so upset about her missing things. He also ordered Matron out of the room, which took some guts!" said Fiona. "I haven't really had much to do with him, but I know he looks after all the residents at the home. The most dealings I've had with him was when I was pretending to be a policewoman when Freda said her clock and biscuits had been stolen. The poor woman died not long after that."

"To be honest, he doesn't really talk about his work much when I see him. He's quite high up in his profession and gives conference talks. Like most people, you want to relax and forget about it as much as you can when you're off," said Lynne.

"Well, I really can't believe this!" said Fiona. "He has a lovely big house in Morton and his son Tom seems a nice lad. I also saw him being interviewed on television one night."

Wait till I tell Ted tonight, she thought.

They returned to answering the phone calls and dealing with general enquiries for the rest of the day.

Fiona told Ted all about it over their evening meal. They ate it on the patio. It had been a very warm day so they had quiche and salad.

"She's done well for herself there," commented Ted. "I bet he's on a good whack."

"Trust you to think of money and how much he may earn," teased Fiona. "I'm really happy for Lynne. I hope it goes somewhere. Her boys like him too, which is a bonus."

"We'll have to meet up with them for a drink. We can discuss the residents' missing items, lights in the garden at night and sudden deaths!"

"Stop it!" said Fiona with a laugh. "Mind you, I would like to get to the bottom of all those things. I need to know Aunt Ness is safe in the home."

They went inside with their plates and stacked them in the dishwasher. It was half past seven.

"Quick walk?" asked Ted.

"Alright but not too far."

It was a lovely evening, light blue sky with only a plane's vapour trail marring it. They headed out on the path, choosing the opposite way from the park where they normally had a walk in the evening. They strolled along, holding hands.

There was not a lot of traffic about. The rush hour had been and gone. They met other people walking out enjoying the fine evening. It was a long path on the edge of the main road that ran alongside some fields. Some sheep were grazing and a couple of horses were trotting around a field.

They walked a couple of miles and then turned back. The evenings were starting to pull in now. Autumn was just around the corner.

They discussed having a few days away in September. They mildly argued about where to go.

"Wait for children to go back to school before we go anywhere," said Ted. "It will be a bit cheaper."

They arrived home at a quarter to nine. Ted put the chairs away from the patio in case it rained. It wasn't forecast but you can never trust the weather forecast, he said.

They spent the next hour before going to bed cuddled up on the settee watching a documentary about the Queen. It showed footage of her childhood, teenage years and marriage leading up to her coronation in 1952.

Matt went to work at nine o'clock on Friday and as he was driving through the gates and parking his car in the carpark, he suddenly recalled the conversation yesterday with Moira. *Damn, I forgot to look in the shed*, he thought.

He had been very busy yesterday and it had completely gone out of his head.

He went into the home, putting his bag containing his packed lunch in the staffroom. *Nancy looked after him very well*, he thought with a smile He was more than capable of preparing his lunch but she insisted on doing it every evening.

She knew exactly what sandwiches he liked, added a slice of cake and a packet of crisps. Sometimes there was a chocolate bar! It was his lucky day when she had agreed to marry him all those years ago!

He wasn't sure if Moira was on morning or afternoon shift but he would soon find out.

He wandered into the dining room but only a few residents were in there eating breakfast. They looked up as he entered and he called good morning to them. He looked in the lounge but again, only a couple of residents were in there. The television was off for once and silence reigned.

He said hello to them and wondered where to find Moira if she was on duty.

Nick came down the stairs. "Is Moira around?" he asked.

"Afternoon shift," Nick replied as he carried on walking. *A man of few words*, thought Matt. He didn't know Nick like he knew the other nurses. He seemed competent as a nurse from what he had seen of him but not a great conversationalist.

Matt looked in his maintenance book to see what jobs there were for him to do. He read about a couple of light bulbs, a sticking door and a window in Room 2 that wouldn't shut properly.

He decided to go down to the garden shed before he forgot and before Moira came on shift later. He didn't want Moira to think he couldn't be trusted to remember what she'd asked him to do.

He went out of the back door and made his way down the garden. There was no sign of Kirsty but he wasn't entirely sure what hours she worked. She may start later than him he thought.

He reached the shed. There was a coded padlock on the door. He had no idea of the code. He tried to open it using the main home's door code but it didn't open.

He pressed his face to the window. It was dark inside and he could see some shapes but could not identify what they were as couldn't see much at all.

"What are you doing?" said a sharp voice.

Matt quickly turned around. He saw Kirsty. He hadn't heard her coming.

"I'm just wondering what is in this shed," he replied.

"I have no idea either. I don't know the padlock code. I have been told it's not anything to do with me so I tend to ignore it."

"But it must contain something or why would it be padlocked?" he asked her. "There some things in there but it's too dark to see what they are."

Kirsty put her face to the window. "I can't make anything out either. It's too dark inside," she said.

"Apparently, some residents have seen lights on or near in this shed at night," said Matt.

"But there's no electricity in there as far as I can tell," she said.

"I know, it must be a torch light that they have seen. Some torch beams can shine really brightly."

They both continued pressing their faces to the window but eventually gave up as neither of them could identify anything inside.

Matt went back up the garden and went into the home. Kirsty went off to her own shed to sort out which gardening implements she needed for the day.

Matt wandered down the hallway and saw Nick in the lounge. He seemed to be talking quite earnestly to Arthur. Tom wasn't there. Matt couldn't hear what they were saying as they were talking in a low voice. Arthur looked a bit worried, which in turn worried Matt.

Nick looked up and saw Matt standing in the doorway. Matt retreated out of the room. He might speak with Arthur later to make sure he was alright.

He got on with his maintenance jobs. There was always something that needed repairing.

He saw Moira arrive for her shift in the afternoon. He knew she had a handover from Nick at two o'clock so he would speak with her later when she was free. Matron was in the home so he kept out of her way as much as possible. Every few days, he had to see her to report on maintenance issues. Instead of issuing a summons to see her in her office that she normally did, she came to find him this Friday afternoon.

"I saw you in the garden this morning. What were you doing?" she asked.

He was in Room 4 looking at the shower that was reported to be spurting water out at an alarming force.

He wasn't sure what to say but had a quick think and ended up telling her the truth.

"I went to the bottom shed as some residents thought there were lights shining in it during the night."

"What nonsense," she replied. "There is no electricity in that shed. It's just a storage area."

"It could have been a strong torch," said Matt.

147

"They must be imagining it. Some of our residents don't always know what they are saying. That's why they are here at Goodrest. Their minds are playing tricks on them. You cannot believe all you are told. I suggest you ignore them and get on with the job that you are employed for, which are maintenance problems."

"It's not me that they are saying it to. It's to the nurses, carers and family as well," said Matt.

"Well, I will speak to the staff and tell them to ignore it as well. They should know better than to listen to idle gossip."

She turned and went out of the room.

Matt examined the shower head. It just needed cleaning. He then tested it and it now worked perfectly. He went out of the room but spotted Moira about to go into Room 2.

He caught up with her before she went in. He told her he had been to the shed in the garden but couldn't get in as it was padlocked and he didn't know the code to open it. He said Kirsty had come along as well and didn't know anything about the shed either. She didn't keep any of her equipment in there. They hadn't been able to see anything when they looked in the window as it was so dark inside.

Moira thanked him for looking but as to what the lights were remained a mystery, she said.

Matt finished his shift at five. He was looking forward to the weekend. They were visiting their son, his wife and granddaughters tomorrow, which was always a treat. It was quite a drive but worth it.

He told Nancy about his day and about looking into the shed to see if he could see anything and then about Matron accosting him in Room 2. "Funny business," she said. "Forget work now, it's the weekend."

Ted was having another round of golf with Hugh on Saturday morning so Fiona invited Moira over for coffee.

It would be good to have a catch up without the men there.

She tidied the house and put some washing on. It was another warm and sunny day. They could sit outside on the patio so she got two chairs out of the shed. Ted had mown the lawn the evening before and there was still plenty of colour in the garden.

Moira arrived at eleven. She looked cool and summery in pink shorts and a matching vest. "Nice to wear something other than a uniform," she chuckled when Fiona told her how nice she looked.

Fiona made coffee, opened some chocolate biscuits and they went to sit outside.

"So how's the new job going?" asked Fiona.

"Not bad really. The staff are nice, Matron's an ogre and the residents are lovely," Moira replied.

"How's Aunt Ness?"

"She's good, appears to be quite settled from what I can tell so far. She sits in the lounge with the other residents, eats well and doesn't appear to be stressed in any way."

"That's a relief then," said Fiona. "Has she mentioned anyone trying to break in? That was the problem when she was in her flat."

"Well, she has mentioned seeing lights in the garden, which worries her, but I've tried to reassure her that she's safe."

Moira then told her about asking Matt the maintenance man to have a look in the shed where the lights were meant to be coming from. "He couldn't get in for a proper look as there's a padlock on the door and it's too dark inside to see anything. No one seems to know what's inside the shed."

"It's a bit worrying about the residents' belongings going missing though," said Fiona. "It must be someone in the home who is taking them."

"It's not a nice thought," replied Moira. "I'm getting to know the staff now and don't like to think of one of them thieving."

They continued chatting until Ted and Hugh arrived back from golf just after one o'clock. Ted was full of it and thanked Hugh for the lesson.

"We'll make a golfer of you yet," he laughed. "I enjoyed this morning too."

Fiona went into the kitchen to make a sandwich for their lunch. Two more chairs were brought out of the garden shed. They ate their lunch and had a cold drink afterwards.

Hugh and Moira left at half past two as they needed to do a Tesco shop.

Ted and Fiona spent the rest of the day in the garden. Fred kept popping his head over the fence and offering advice to Ted as he was weeding.

Fiona invited him around for a cup of tea, which he eagerly accepted. He was a nice person but lonely so they tried to be as sociable as possible.

Next day, after a very satisfying lie in, they decided to visit Aunt Ness. They had breakfast and then drove to the home arriving about eleven. Dr Johnson's red Jaguar was parked outside the front door.

"I wonder why he is here on a Sunday?" wondered Fiona to Ted.

She rang the front door bell and waited to be admitted.

Rosalyn answered and let them in. They signed the visitor's book. Fiona asked her where she would find Aunt Ness.

"She's in her room. She didn't have a very good night. She has been quite agitated and so Dr Johnson has been called in to see her."

This alarmed Fiona and she raced up the stairs with Ted following her.

Fiona knocked on her aunt's door and without waiting for an answer went straight in.

"Dr Johnson was in the room with a male nurse who Fiona hadn't seen before."

They both turned around to see who had entered the room. Her aunt was sitting in her chair. A cuff was on her aunt's arm that was attached to a small machine. "Is my aunt alright?"

"I'm just taking your aunt's blood pressure," Dr Johnson told her. "She has been very agitated and I've been called in to see her."

Fiona went over to her aunt and took her hand. "What's wrong?" she asked Aunt Ness.

"I don't know," she replied, looking at Fiona. "My heart started racing and it wouldn't stop. I was frightened."

"Her blood pressure is slightly raised," said Dr Johnson. He popped a thermometer into her ear.

"That's normal," he said.

He removed the cuff on her arm.

"It must have been the tablet that I had last night," her aunt said. "I was alright until I took it."

"What tablet?" asked Fiona.

"The one that would stop me having a heart attack."

"A heart attack?" said Fiona. "But there's nothing wrong with your heart."

"I was told if I didn't take it then I would have a heart attack."

"Who gave you this tablet?" asked Dr Johnson.

"I don't know the person who gave it to me, I was half asleep. I think I was woken up and told that Matron had ordered me to take it. I was looked after very well though."

Both Fiona and the doctor looked puzzled.

Aunt Ness appeared to be calming down. She looked sleepy; her eyes kept closing.

Fiona told Dr Johnson that she would sit with her aunt. Ted sat down in a chair.

"I will speak to Matron tomorrow and see if I can find out about this tablet," the doctor said as he left the room.

Ted and Fiona stayed for an hour but Aunt Ness didn't speak much as she appeared really sleepy. They left her to sleep and went downstairs.

Fiona went to find the nurse in charge. He was in the lounge talking to Gwen.

Fiona asked if she could have a word with him. He left Gwen, who was using her magnifying glass to read a magazine. A resident called Vera called out to him asking if he had seen her multicoloured rug as it was missing. He told her he would look for it.

They stepped out into the hall.

His name badge read Robert. Fiona said her aunt was now sleeping and had he any idea about the tablet that her aunt said she had been given.

"No idea," he replied. "She's not prescribed any night time tablets. I am only part time here but I know what tablets the residents are prescribed. All medication is written on their records."

"I will ring Matron in the morning," she told him, "but please can I be informed if she continues to be unwell?"

"I will pass it on to Nick this afternoon as well," Robert said.

She and Ted left the home.

"I don't know what's going on but I feel something is not right," she said to Ted as he drove home. "I think I will ring Moira tonight and tell her about this."

She worried all afternoon. She rang the home early evening and enquired after Aunt Ness. She was told by the nurse that she was still sleepy but had managed to eat a small amount of tea. Fiona asked if she could relay to Aunt Ness that she had called and sent her love.

Fiona rang Moira and told her about Aunt Ness and the tablet that apparently Matron had said she needed to prevent a heart attack. Moira said she would try and find out tomorrow what it was all about. She was on the early shift and would ring Fiona in the evening.

"I'm so glad Moira is there," Fiona said to Ted.

Moira was concerned after the phone call. It was very like the situation with Arthur and his extra tablet. He had also been told that the tablet was to prevent a heart attack. It was too much of a coincidence.

She told Hugh of her concerns. "I should speak to the Matron in the morning and tell her how concerned you are," he said.

"I will," she said, "but whether it will get me anywhere remains to be seen; she's certainly not the easiest person to talk to."

She kept thinking about it all evening and also woke in the night, which was unlike her as she normally slept well.

Kirsty arrived for work on Monday morning. She planned to spend some time in the greenhouse today sorting it out. There were lots of empty plant pots and spillages of old compost that needed sweeping up. There was also a broken pane of glass that needed replacing. She may need to ask Matt about helping her with that.

She lived on her own in a small rented cottage in the next village. Her mother had lived with her but had died after a short illness last year. She had a cat for company, a ginger and black tabby that had suddenly appeared, moving in with her one winter three years ago. She had no idea where he had come from and despite putting up posters, no one had ever claimed him so he stayed.

She didn't have friends, just the odd acquaintance. She didn't encourage friendships and never had done She had been an only child and was used to her own company, and was fine living on her own with just Joey the cat. She knew some people at Goodrest found her a bit standoffish with not a lot of conversational skills but it was probably because she lived alone and worked alone. She liked nice things and her furniture and non-working clothes were of good quality. She enjoyed good food and cooked a wholesome nutritional meal for herself every night. She liked reading biographies rather than fiction and watched very few programmes even though she had a large smart television in her perfectly decorated lounge.

She had worked in an office environment for several years before changing job direction. She hadn't liked mixing with the staff. They gossiped, which she disapproved of. She had always enjoyed gardening and finding this position at Goodrest was her dream job. She was left alone to get on with her job and enjoyed the many compliments she received.

She made her way over to the greenhouse with a bristle broom, brush and dustpan intending to sweep up the spilled compost. She saw something red on the ground and bent down to pick it up. It was a torch. She picked it up and switched it on. It appeared quite powerful as it had a strong beam of light even in daylight.

It hadn't been there when she had left at four o'clock yesterday as she was certain she would have noticed it because of its bright red colour.

She looked up to see if anyone was around in the garden that might have dropped it but couldn't see anybody at all. She could see up the garden to the home and could spot some residents and staff through the windows.

Kirsty took the torch into the greenhouse and laid it on a shelf. She got on with her sweeping up. She then recalled that Matt had been told that a light had been seen in or near the small shed by some of the residents. She wondered now if the light seen was actually a torch light. The beam certainly would be powerful enough to be seen from the home. When she went to find Matt to help her with the broken windowpane, she would tell him about finding the torch.

She continued working in the greenhouse and by lunchtime it was clean, neat and tidy and ready for the many corms she would keep from the dahlias when the flowers were over. Usually, the first frost got them but at least she had the greenhouse ready for autumn and winter. She wintered other plants and bulbs such as begonias and also grew hyacinths in pots later in the year that she took into the home before Christmas for the residents to enjoy the recognisable perfume. Once the flowers withered, she planted them in the garden. Springtime found her greenhouse abundant with growing plants. She bought them as plugs and nurtured them until they were strong enough to plant out in the garden.

Kirsty went to the staffroom knowing Matt generally took a break about one o'clock. She hoped he was alone as she didn't want to make idle talk with anyone.

She found him in there eating a sandwich and reading his newspaper. She guessed cheese and onion by the smell!

There were two carers and a housekeeper also in the room. She recognised the housekeeper as Thelma. She was a cheerful person and always ready for a chat if they met. She was pleased that the housekeeper Annie wasn't in there as she felt uncomfortable around her. She had attempted to make conversation with her on a couple of occasions but had only received grunts in reply. She had seen her that morning putting some stuff in the large dustbin outside so she knew she was at work.

She asked Matt if he could come and look at the broken windowpane in the greenhouse after his lunch break.

"Of course I will," he answered. "Give me ten minutes."

Kirsty returned to the garden. It was a fine day again. She took the long hoe from her shed and started hoeing between the rose bushes.

Matt came out to find her. She took him into the greenhouse and showed him the broken windowpane. He said he would remove it and measure for a replacement. He should be able to collect some glass later and fit it tomorrow.

Kirsty then showed him the red torch that she had found earlier that morning. Matt switched it on, commenting on the powerful beam.

"How odd," he said. "It has to belong to someone who uses this garden; I can't see how a dog walker using that field behind the garden would have dropped it."

"Well, it certainly wasn't here yesterday when I left at four o'clock."

"Can I take it with me?" he asked. "I'll see what I can find out."

"Course you can take it. If you find out whom it belongs to, please let me know as I'm intrigued!" said Kirsty.

Matt went back into the home. He could see into the lounge as he walked from the garden and saw some of the residents and he saw flashes of blue uniforms moving around as well. He also saw a person looking out from an upstairs window but could not recognise them from this far away. He looked down again at the torch, recognising it to be quite an expensive model.

He put it in on a shelf in his closet where he kept his tools. He would ask around if anyone had lost it.

The afternoon passed slowly. Nick was the nurse in charge for the afternoon but Matt found him quite hard to talk to. General maintenance repairs required his attention but nothing he couldn't handle.

On his way home, he called at the wholesalers where he usually bought his supplies from. He picked up a pane of glass, applied bubble wrap around it for protection and carefully laid it in the boot of his car.

He arrived home and gave Nancy a big hug. "Good day?" he asked.

"Very good. I managed to finish my round early for once so got home at three o'clock."

Matt was pleased to hear this. Nancy worked hard and she always went the extra mile for her clients. She was popular and they always enjoyed seeing her arriving at their homes to assist them.

He told her about his day and also about Kirsty finding the red torch in the garden.

They spent the evening in, watching television after tea and enjoyed a phone call from Maisie who was still grumbling about how often baby Sophie cried!

Nancy commiserated with her and said she was sure she would things would be better when she was a little older and could play with her. Maisie said she wasn't sure she could wait that long.

Next day, Matt arrived at work and carefully removed the pane of glass from the boot of his car. He took it to the greenhouse and laid it on the shelf. Kirsty wasn't around yet. He went into the home and opened the closet where he kept his tools to fetch a cloth, a pot of putty and a knife. He was closing the door when he realised that the red torch was not on the shelf where he had left it yesterday.

He looked to see of it had dropped on the floor but there was no sign of it at all. *How weird, I know I put it on the shelf yesterday*, he thought to himself.

He closed the door after collecting the putty and knife.

He went down the garden to remove the broken glass pane in the greenhouse. Kirsty was in there.

He told her that the torch had gone missing from his closet where he had left it the previous day.

"Who goes in there apart from you?" she asked.

"I suppose many of the staff would know the code on the door. It's not a secret. Someone may need something out of it like a screwdriver or something if I'm not there. There's a code on the door so residents can't get in."

"Do you think someone saw us with it in the garden yesterday?" asked Kirsty.

"I suppose if someone had seen us with it and it was theirs and wanted it back, they would have assumed I would put it in the closet."

"I wonder who it could have been?" said Kirsty. "Seems a bit suspicious, I think. They could have waited for you to come in today and asked you for it back instead of just taking it."

"I agree."

Matt removed the broken glass pane and prepared the window for the new one. He then fitted the new glass. It didn't take long but reminded Kirsty that the putty would take a while to harden off.

He went back to the home.

He supposed that whoever took the torch from the closet would have been on the afternoon or night shift.

He looked around as he was doing his jobs, trying to recall which staff had been on shift yesterday afternoon. He saw and asked Josh but he denied knowing anything about it.

Matt then thought that it could actually have been someone who had been working in the morning as he had put the torch in his closet after lunch. There would have been about half an hour before the morning shift would have finished and the afternoon staff started. Or it could have been taken early this morning by a member of the night staff before he started work at nine.

He supposed from this that it could have been any number of people who had taken the torch from the closet.

Nick was the nurse in charge so Matt asked him if he knew anything about the missing torch.

"Are you accusing me of taking it?" he asked.

"Not at all, but you were here yesterday afternoon and I wondered if you saw any staff going into my closet."

"No, I didn't see anyone."

Nick went on with whatever he was doing and Matt went to Room 1 that had a loose toilet seat that needed fixing.

Harry was the occupant of Room 1. He had lived at Goodrest for about four years. He was a very sprightly gentleman for someone of ninety-two and didn't need any aids to mobilise but had some sort of dementia that made his short-term memory very spasmodic. His memories were more in the past that he unknowingly confused with today's events.

"I'm going out this morning," he told Matt.

"That's nice, where are you going?" replied Matt.

"I've got an appointment at the bank. They have asked to see me. They want to talk about my money. I'm looking for my car keys but can't seem to find them."

Matt knew that Harry didn't drive anymore and hadn't driven since living in the home but he helped him search for the elusive keys.

"Perhaps the car is in a garage being repaired and they have the keys," he told Harry.

"I think you may be right. I remember now, the brakes were sticking. I shall have to cancel my appointment till I get my car back. I can't find my phone either so can you ring the bank to cancel the appointment for me?"

"Will do."

"Good man, I can always rely on you," said Harry. He sat down and opened his newspaper. "I can now relax and have time to read this without going out now."

Matt agreed with him and after repairing the toilet seat said cheerio to Harry.

How sad, thought Matt, *but at least he's happy enough and not depressed or agitated as he knew some people with dementia could be.*

Matt went to the staffroom for lunch. Brenda was in there eating out of a Tupperware container. It looked like some sort of rice dish. "That looks and smells nice," commented Matt as he put the kettle on.

"Leftover Chinese takeaway from last night," she grinned.

Brenda was always telling staff that she was going to be retiring soon but as yet she hadn't handed her notice in. She had been talking about retirement for about a year now. She had been at Goodrest for several years and over the last couple of years had been increasingly slower in moving about due to arthritis. She looked after an elderly mother who lived with her. The staff suspected she wanted to continue working to have a break from being at her mother's beck and call.

Matt made his cup of tea and unwrapped his sandwich. Chicken and stuffing. They had eaten a roast chicken dinner last night that had been much appreciated. He enjoyed Nancy's cooking, she looked after him very well.

The door opened and Annie came in. She looked at them both as they said hello but didn't say anything back.

Brenda raised her eyebrows at Matt.

Annie went to her locker, opened it and looked in her large bag. It occurred to Matt that the bag was not of a handbag size so why bring such a large one to work?

He had an idea.

"Did you hear about the torch that was found in the garden yesterday?" he innocently asked Brenda.

"No?"

"A red torch was found in the garden by Kirsty. She showed it to me and neither of us could think where it could have come from." He was watching Annie as he spoke. She seemed to go very still and appeared to be listening to the conversation.

"I put it in my closet where I keep my tools but it's since disappeared."

"How can it just disappear?" asked Brenda.

"I don't know but I'm trying to find out who took it."

Annie shoved her bag back in the locker and went out of the staffroom.

"I have a very strange feeling that Annie knows about the torch. I'd like to look in her bag but I don't want to get caught or I'll be in trouble," said Matt.

"I'll cover for you if you want to look now," said Brenda.

Matt was very tempted. He finished his sandwich and ate his slice of cherry cake. If anyone came in the staffroom, he would have to explain what he was doing looking in a bag that obviously wasn't his. He could be in big trouble. He was just starting to get up to go to the locker when the staffroom door opened and Thelma came in. "Hello," she said, "can I join you?"

Matt quickly sat down while Brenda smothered a grin.

"I'm gasping for a cuppa," she said as she switched the kettle on. "Anyone want one?"

Matt said he didn't but Brenda accepted her offer.

Thelma sat down with them at the table. She was a chatty soul and started talking about her morning. "Matron caught me in Ness's room and accused me of skiving to get out of doing my share of the work. How dare she! I had just finished cleaning it and was about to go out and start in the next room when she came in. No knocking on the door before she entered. She who sits in the office all day twiddling her thumbs acting as if she's busy when she's not."

Brenda laughed and Matt grinned.

"It's not me who skives, it's that Annie. She's a lazy so and so. I've seen her just flicking a duster around a bit, not actually using it to polish anything. She doesn't move things either but does Matron go after her? No, she doesn't! I caught her in your closet this morning, Matt."

Matt sat up straight.

"When was this?" he asked.

"First thing, not long after we arrived at eight o'clock this morning. I asked her what she was doing in there and she said she was looking for a screwdriver to tighten a screw on her housekeeping trolley. Bit odd, I thought, she would normally wait for you to mend something like that."

"I have had a torch go missing from the closet," said Matt. "Did you see her take anything, or was she holding anything when you saw her?"

"She did put something in the trolley but I assumed it was a screwdriver but I didn't actually see what it was, she was too quick. Do you think it was your torch?"

"Well, it's a big coincidence that she was in there and the torch is now missing," he replied.

His half-hour break was up so he needed to leave. "Keep an eye on her, will you?" he said to them. They nodded and said they certainly would.

He didn't see Annie again before she left work but he would speak with her tomorrow.

Ted was playing squash with Geoff on Wednesday evening so Fiona decided to go and visit Aunt Ness after work. She had spoken to Matron earlier in the week about the tablet episode and had got nowhere. Matron insisted that she knew nothing about it. She said she knew Dr Johnson had been called in to see her but that was because she was unusually agitated but no reason was found.

Moira had told her the same thing. She had also spoken to Matron who denied knowing anything about a tablet.

Fiona arrived at the care home just before six o'clock. She rang the bell and it was answered by Rosalyn.

"Hello, come in," she greeted Fiona. She signed the visitor's book. She recognised a name written in the book as a lady who had been a neighbour of her aunt's at the sheltered housing complex.

Her aunt was in the lounge in her usual chair by the window.

"Hello," she said, giving her aunt a kiss. She gave her some chocolate and also a bunch of flowers that she had picked up on her way over.

"I see Dorothy came to see you this afternoon."

"Yes, it was lovely to see her," replied Aunt Ness. "We had a cup of tea together."

"Good, that will have been nice. How are you feeling?"

"I think I have been very tired for a couple of days but I feel better now."

Fiona looked around the room and waved at Tom and Arthur. They waved back and then turned back to *Eggheads* on the television.

"You were tired because you had a tablet that you don't normally have and it made you very sleepy."

"No, I didn't have a tablet. I got mixed up. I think I'm just feeling my age," said Aunt Ness.

"The doctor was called in to see you because he was concerned."

"I don't remember."

"Well, never mind. It's good you are feeling better now."

"Hello," said a familiar voice. Fiona turned around and saw Moira.

"Hi Moira," she replied. "Aunt Ness is telling me she's feeling much better now."

"Yes, she's got more energy now, which is good to see."

"She's also saying she didn't have a tablet; she was getting mixed up."

Moira asked if she could have a word with Fiona outside the lounge. She left Aunt Ness starting to unwrap the chocolate bar.

"Did she say she was mixed up and didn't have the tablet, which made her unwell?" asked Moira.

"Yes."

"That's very strange. Another resident had the same experience as your aunt, saying he was given an extra tablet to prevent a heart attack but a couple of days later, he also said he had been mistaken."

"What are you implying?" asked Fiona, looking worried.

"There's something going on and I intend to get to the bottom of it. Fortunately, he and your aunt are okay but it's really odd that both were very sleepy after taking this tablet and then both saying they must have been mistaken. There were also some unexpected deaths recently here that worried some of the staff. Death certificates were issued so the doctors must have been satisfied with the cause of their deaths."

Fiona was looking very alarmed. "Should I move Aunt Ness out of here?" she asked Moira.

"It would unsettle her and probably disorientate her so let me see what I can find out," said Moira.

Thank goodness Moira was here, Fiona thought with some relief.

She went back into the lounge. Aunt Ness was talking to the lady resident who was sitting in the adjoining chair. They both looked happy. Aunt Ness was obviously starting to make a friend, which was good. She had been lonely prior to coming here and Moira was right in believing she would be unsettled if she moved her now.

Fiona asked her aunt if it was alright for her to go up to her room and put the flowers in a vase. She said she would come back downstairs after arranging them. Aunt Ness said that was fine and she didn't need to come up with her as she was chatting to Betty. Fiona took the flowers upstairs and went into Room 20.

She had seen Rosalyn in the dining room and asked for a vase for the flowers.

Fiona arranged the flowers and put them on the chest of drawers where Aunt Ness could see them when sitting in her chair. She looked in her aunt's wardrobe.

The blue cardigan was still missing and Fiona believed she would never see that item of clothing again. She then thought that there were fewer clothes in the wardrobe than there should have been.

She moved the hangers and tried to remember which clothes she had packed when coming into the home.

A pale mauve jumper with buttons on the front and a blue wool tartan skirt appeared to be missing. The skirt was dry clean only so even if her aunt had worn it and it had gotten stained, then it wouldn't have been washed in the laundry here at the home. It would surely have been left in a bag for Fiona to collect to take it to the dry cleaners.

Fiona closed the wardrobe. She went to her aunt's bedside table. The radio channel was still Classic FM so that was alright. She pulled open the bedside cabinet drawer. There were some tissues, a few hairgrips and a book in there. She knew her aunt had brought a handbag in with her and looking in the bottom of the cabinet, she saw it.

Fiona opened it and saw that the purse was missing. It was quite a large green-coloured purse that her aunt had used for several years. There was a clear bit in the side bit of the purse where you could slide a small photo. It was a picture of Jack that occupied the space. Fiona looked in the chest of drawers to see if it was in any of the four drawers. It wasn't in any of them. There had been two twenty-pound notes and some loose change in the purse when she had been admitted here.

There was nowhere else to look. She went into the bathroom and saw her aunt's pot of Boots No 7 moisturiser was not on the shelf above the sink. It couldn't have all been used up because it had been new when her aunt came in and it usually lasted for at least a couple of months.

Things were clearly being taken from her aunt's room. There were too many items missing for them just to be mislaid.

She went out of the room. She went downstairs to look for Moira. She found her in the dining room writing on what looked like medication sheets. Fiona told her about the missing items.

Moira made a note of everything that was missing and said she was on shift the next morning so would report it to Matron and also ask the staff if they knew anything. She would look in the laundry as well to see if the missing clothes were in there.

"Thanks," said Fiona. "I won't mention any of this to Aunt Ness. It would only worry her and I don't want that."

Fiona went back to see her aunt in the lounge. She sat and chatted with her for another half an hour, said goodbye and then went to find Moira to say she was going home now.

Fiona drove home worrying but relieved that Moira was working at the home.

Thursday morning dawned bright and sunny. Moira showered, dressed in her uniform and then took Hugh a cup of tea. He was just stirring. She kissed him and said she would see him later.

She drove to work and parked in the carpark.

She was determined to see Matron and discuss the missing items taken out of Ness's room. Matron didn't seem unduly concerned when Moira saw her about ten o'clock. "She must have mislaid them," she said.

"I'm sorry but there are too many things missing for her to have mislaid them. I believe someone on the staff is thieving."

"Who would that be?"

"I've no idea but I'm going to ask around," replied Moira.

Matron didn't look too impressed with Moira's reply.

"Well, don't you go upsetting the staff, I don't want them leaving, it's hard to recruit."

"But if someone is stealing from the residents then we need to find out who it is. They should not be working here."

"Alright, but keep me informed," Matron said and turned away from Moira to indicate that the conversation had finished.

Moira finished her medication round and started to write up some notes. She did this in the dining room. The residents had finished their breakfast and most had retired to the lounge. There was a musician coming later on in the morning to entertain the residents and they wanted to get good seats ready for it.

Matt popped his head in the dining room to say hello.

"Matt," said Moira, "can I have a word with you?"

He came in and sat down opposite her.

Moira told him about the missing items from Ness's room.

"Have you heard about any missing things from some of the residents' rooms?" she asked him.

"I have actually. I also had a torch stolen from my closet."

"Any idea as to who it might have been?"

Matt hesitated before replying. Moira noticed this and asked again if he had any suspicions.

"Well, between you and me, Annie the housekeeper comes to mind," he said. "But I've no proof it's her, just a feeling."

He explained that she had heard him talking in the staffroom to Brenda about the torch he had found and the fact it had disappeared, and although he insisted to Moira that he had no evidence, he said Annie, from her body language, had seemed interested without asking any questions. "She was looking in her locker and I know she was listening to our conversation. I should think most staff would have asked me about it."

"Could you see what was in her locker?" asked Moira.

"No, I couldn't. I know she had a large bag in there but I don't know what was in it or why she would bring such a large bag to work."

"Perhaps to put stolen things in it?" said Moira.

"Maybe," said Matt.

Moira told him that she was going to try and find out who was responsible for the thieving.

"Count me in," said Matt. "I will keep my ears and eyes open too."

He left Moira to finish her reports. He pondered over the conversation with Moira as he carried on working.

Moira handed over to Nick who was nurse in charge for the afternoon. She found it quite difficult to connect with him on anything but a professional level. The other staff were more open and liked a chat.

She spoke about the residents and how they were on her shift. There were no poorly residents and they had enjoyed the musical entertainment that morning.

When the carers had left the room, she mentioned to Nick about the residents' missing items.

He shrugged and said due to dementia a lot of them may hide things and then say they were stolen.

"But the missing items aren't in their room. If they were hidden then surely, they would be found?" said Moira. "Also Matt had a torch taken from his closet yesterday."

"I don't know anything about it," said Nick and got up without saying any more.

Moira didn't say anything more to him other than, "Hope you have a good shift." Collected her bag and left.

Sally was on shift the next day and she would discuss it with her. She may have some ideas.

Next day, Lynne was telling Fiona that Kevin had introduced her to his son Tom yesterday. He had driven by Lynne's house as he was giving Tom a lift to his friend who lived nearby on the outskirts of Morton. They called in at Lynne's on the way so Tom could meet her and they had stayed for a coffee.

Tom's arm was improving and he hoped to be free of the support bandage next week. He told her that he worked a few hours helping Kirsty in the garden at the care home in his university holidays and that it had been a nuisance hurting his arm as he needed the money but couldn't work until it improved.

Lynne said that he seemed very friendly. Her boys had not been at home at the time, they were out visiting their dad.

She'd mentioned to Tom that Fiona was a friend of hers and had been glad to help him when he hurt his arm in the woods.

"Small world," Tom had grinned. They hadn't stayed long but Kevin was going over on Saturday to take her and the boys for a day out. "You won't all fit in his Jaguar and I haven't seen him driving anything else," said Fiona.

"He's coming over in Tom's car," said Lynne.

Fiona was really glad that all was going well for Lynne. It would be nice to all go out together one evening so Fiona could get to know Dr Johnson and pump him for information about the care home! He probably wouldn't say much but even a bit of inside information would be welcome.

Moira was on late shift and Sally handed over her morning report to her. Moira asked if she could have a word with her after handover before she went home.

The afternoon carers left the dining room and Sally asked what she wanted to ask her.

"It's about things going missing in the home. Ness's niece, Fiona, who is also a friend of mine, visited yesterday evening and found more things gone from her room. Her purse, moisturiser and some clothes were missing."

"This is serious," said Sally. "We need to report this to Matron."

"I have, this morning, but I didn't get anywhere. I also spoke to Nick yesterday and he didn't have much to say about it. He intimated someone with dementia could have hidden the things but one item missing from her room is a picture so that isn't an easy thing to hide if a resident took it, or Vera's multicoloured rug as it's quite large," replied Moira.

"I agree. It has to be a member of staff who is taking them and getting them out of the home," replied Sally.

Moira said she had also spoken with Matt about it. "He's had a torch taken from his closet where he keeps his tools. It was taken sometime between lunchtime yesterday and this morning at nine when he came to work. Also, it's not just the missing things that are worrying; it's the sudden deaths that have been in the home in the last few weeks."

Sally said, "I too have wondered why some of the residents died so suddenly. They were all reasonably well even with their underlying health conditions, but death certificates were issued so it must have been clear as to why they died."

"All those that died, as far as I know, had some sort of run in with Matron not long before."

They looked at each other.

"We have to investigate this ourselves. Matron obviously isn't taking it seriously," said Moira. "We have Matt onboard as well."

"Let me go and find him while we are all here," said Moira.

She found him up his ladder on the upstairs landing, replacing a ceiling light. "Can you come into the dining room for a chat?" she asked him.

He looked puzzled but came down his ladder and carrying it with him followed her downstairs. He returned it to his closet.

Sally motioned for him to sit down with her and Moira.

"We have been discussing the residents' items that have been disappearing from the home and also the sudden deaths here in the home in the last few months," she told him. "Matron isn't interested but we are very concerned. We hope that between the three of us, we can find out what's going on."

"Of course, I will assist you in any way I can."

"We need to make a list of all the missing items that we know about. We also need a list of all the residents who have died suddenly," said Moira.

Sally grabbed some paper and a pen.

Together, they tried to remember all the items missing. Ness was missing several items of clothes, a picture, a red cushion, a pot of moisturiser and her purse. Vera was missing her multicoloured rug. Gwen was missing her magnifying glass.

Sally recalled other residents who had reported missing items before Moira started working at the home.

Sid had a picture go missing, a fleece blanket and some loose change that had disappeared from his bedside cabinet drawer. Mary had said her nice hand mirror went missing along with her makeup bag full of cosmetics. Sheila had reported missing a red cushion, a cardigan, a skirt and some magazines. Sarah had mentioned she had lost her eyedrops that she kept in her room as she administered them herself, two jumpers and a pair of trousers, some magazines and some hairspray.

Wilfred had reported he was missing some handkerchiefs, a small alarm clock and a ten-pound note. Jane had reported she was missing two blouses and an underskirt and a hairbrush. Freda had her bird clock and biscuits go missing. Matt said not to forget about the torch that had been taken from his closet.

It was quite a large list when written down. There may have been more but she couldn't be sure enough to add to it. They pored over the list trying to make sense of it. It would be very hard to find out any dates when things went missing though.

Sally then made a list of all the residents who had died suddenly in the last few months. There had been a couple of expected deaths so she didn't count those.

There was Mary, Wilfred and Freda recently. Matt said that Josh had also voiced concern over the deaths.

Sally said a resident called Robert had died about four months ago quite suddenly as well. "It was a shock and I remember he had also reported some things missing. He made quite a fuss about it, accusing everyone and anyone. He even accused Matron. Dr Johnson was called in to help calm him down. I can't recall what was taken though, I'll try and remember."

"If we had the exact dates of when they died, we could match it to whoever was on shift at the time," suggested Matt.

"The rotas are kept in Matron's office. Each completed week of rota gets filed every Monday morning," said Sally. "We would have to wait until she's not here before going in there to look."

"Where would we find the dates of deaths?" asked Moira.

"Again, they're stored in the office. The files of past residents are kept in a filing cabinet for a time before they're archived."

"We could send Matron on a false outside assessment so the office would be empty for at least an hour," suggested Moira.

"Good plan," said Sally. "I can ask Jack to ring up pretending to have a grandfather who wants to come in as a resident and ask her to go and assess him in his own home."

"Has he got a grandfather?" asked Matt.

"Yes, but not living around here," she grinned. "He lives in Scotland. We could send her there and it would give us a couple of days of her office being empty!"

"I don't think she would fall for that!" said Matt with a laugh.

"We would give a false address for Grandfather, fifteen miles or so from here, and that would give us about an hour and a half with an empty office," said Sally.

They all agreed to this plan. Sally would ask Jack to ring up on Monday morning suggesting Matron go off to carry out an assessment about two-thirty. Moira, Sally and Matt would all be in the home then. Moira was on the morning shift and Sally on the afternoon. Matt would be in the home as usual as his hours were nine until five.

Moira left to go home and Sally continued with her afternoon shift.

Moira rang Fiona in the evening to tell her about the plan. She said Sally and Matt were in on it too.

She discussed what the plan was and hopefully they would be a bit closer getting some answers about the sudden deaths. Fiona listened carefully, feeling relieved that something was being done. She agreed that it would be almost impossible to identify any dates regarding the missing items.

They finished the call and then Fiona relayed the conversation to Ted.

Monday morning arrived. Moira took the night handover from Nina. There was nothing untoward, the residents had slept well.

Nina and her night carers left to go home and Moira started the medication round. She was a bit apprehensive about the proposed plan and wondered what time Matron would arrive for work.

Matt arrived for work at nine o'clock. Matron hadn't yet appeared.

"What if she's off today?" she asked him.

"Hopefully not," Matt replied. He went off to see what jobs were ready for him to do that day.

At ten o'clock, Matron arrived. Moira rang Sally as arranged so she could tell Jack to make the phone call asking for his grandfather's assessment to be carried out at two-thirty.

Moira was passing the office to answer the front doorbell at half past ten and could see Matron speaking on the phone and writing something down. The office door was closed so she couldn't hear what was being said.

Moira let the visitor in and then went into the lounge. She was speaking with Ness when Matron walked in.

"I have to go out early this afternoon," she said to Moira "Someone just rang up asking me to go and assess a potential resident in their own home."

"Okay," replied Moira.

Matron went out. She hadn't spoken to any of the residents in the lounge, which Moira considered very rude.

Moira went to find Matt to tell him that Matron was going out later to carry out the 'assessment'.

"Good," said Matt. "The first part of the plan is going well!"

They continued with their various jobs for the rest of the morning.

At one forty-five, Matron told Moira she was leaving. Sally had just arrived for her afternoon shift.

After Matron had been gone for five minutes, Moira, Matt and Sally entered Matron's office.

Sally went to the first filing cabinet where she hoped to find the filed rotas. She directed Moira and Matt to the second cabinet where past residents' files were stored.

Moira found Robert's file on the top shelf and then saw Mary's, Wilfred's and Freda's files.

Matt took Robert's file and Moira looked at Mary's. The last documentation in the files was the day of their death. They quickly told Sally the dates who then looked at the rotas for those days.

Moira and Matt then looked in Wilfred's and Freda's files to find their dates of death.

They wrote the dates down as well as telling Sally.

Sally was frantically going through the past rotas. She pulled out each rota for days that the residents had died and photocopied them.

Matt kept watch at the door. Moira replaced the residents' files where she had found them.

The photocopier did its job and the four rotas were quickly copied. Sally returned the rotas in the file and grabbed the photocopies, stuffing them in her pocket, and they all went out of the office.

They were very relieved to get out without being spotted.

The afternoon carers were in the dining room waiting for Moira and Sally. They were wondering where they were as they needed to get on with their shift. Moira apologised to them saying she had needed to speak with Sally before handover.

After handover, the carers departed. Moira and Sally looked at each other and grinned. "We did it!" said Sally with a high five. "Now we need to match which staff were on shift when the four residents died."

Matt popped his head into the dining room and seeing they were alone; he went over to sit with them.

Sally got the photocopies out of her pocket. She smoothed them out as they had gotten a bit crumpled and looked at them.

"Do we look now or shall we meet up in an evening where no one will see or hear us?" said Moira.

"That's a good idea," said Sally. "Let's meet at my house at half past five on Wednesday as neither of us is on the afternoon shift. Is that okay with you, Matt?"

"Yes, that's fine by me." He got up and left the dining room after being given directions to Sally's house. Moira went home with the same directions and Sally began her shift.

Matron arrived back at the home at three o'clock in a foul mood. "It was a false address. There was no such number house on the road. Someone is playing tricks on me. What a complete waste of my time," she fumed and stormed off to her office, slamming the door behind her.

Sally crossed her fingers hoping they had left everything in the office as they had found it.

She didn't see Matron again on shift so assumed everything was alright.

Moira had a day off on Wednesday and did a morning shop at Tesco's. She disliked food shopping but they were running short of items in her fridge and cupboards so she had to go. It was quite busy for midweek and she had to queue as only a few checkouts were open. She returned home and prepared a lasagne that she and Hugh could heat up when she returned from Sally's. She had told him about what they had done in Matron's office and he had said he hoped they would be successful in finding something out.

Sally spoke with Jack and told him that all had gone according to plan. He was intrigued and had been glad to play a part in it. Matt told Nancy and she wished them luck. She would delay their evening meal until he returned.

Sally worked the morning shift. Matron was not there, which was nice. The atmosphere was definitely better when she was missing. Matt whistled as he went about his various jobs, looking forward to the detective work later on at Sally's house. Annie was working and he tried to keep an eye on her but he kept being called away to repair things so he wasn't able to see her much.

Half past five saw them all in Sally's kitchen. She had a table and four chairs that they sat around. She made them all a coffee and opened up a packet of chocolate digestives.

She laid the rotas on the table. She had the list of the dates when the four residents had died.

"Right, let's take Robert first. He died on May 2nd in the morning." She checked the rota. "There is a lot of staff on shift from morning till night. We'll make a list and then compare it with the others."

"Nina was the night nurse; Nick was the nurse on in the morning and Robert in the afternoon. Housekeepers were Thelma, Brenda and Annie; carers were Rosalyn, Caroline, Sue, Mavis, Dawn, Amy, Charles and Josh in the morning.

"In the afternoon, the carers were Wendy, Sarah, Lorna, Johnny and Ken. I think we can disregard the kitchen staff at the moment," she said.

"Next we will look at Mary as she was the next to die," said Moira. "She died on August 1st in the morning, according to her records."

Sally looked at the rota for that day.

"Graham was the night nurse; Nick was the nurse in the morning and Jane in the afternoon.

"Housekeepers were Annie, Brenda and Fred. Morning carers were Rosalyn, Caroline, Josh, Lynda, Jackie, Margaret and George. Afternoon carers were Wendy, Lorna, Ken, Heather and Jenny."

Matt said, "Now we will look at Wilfred. He died on August 11th in the morning."

Sally looked at the rota for that day. "Right, Nina was the night nurse, the morning nurse was Frank and the afternoon nurse was Nick. Housekeepers for the day were Annie, Brenda and Muriel. Morning carers were Caroline, Amy,

Josh, Paul, Lynda, Dawn, Marie and Jackie. Afternoon carers were Jackie, Teresa, Rosalyn, Sue and Ken."

"Now for Freda," said Moira.

Sally looked at the rotas for the morning of August 20th, the day that Freda had died.

"Here we go again. Nina was night nurse; Jane was the morning nurse and Nick was the afternoon nurse.

"Housekeepers were Annie, Thelma and Brenda. Morning carers were Alice, Rosalyn, Heather, Lynda, Charles, Sue and Natalie. Afternoon carers were Josh, Jenny, Margaret, Jackie and Ken. We now need to compare who was on shift on all the days of the four deaths."

This took a bit of working out but eventually, after another coffee, a list was drawn up.

Nick had been on shift on all the days. Annie and Brenda had been on shift on all of them too. Rosalyn, Josh, Ken and Jackie were carers who had also worked on all the days of all the deaths.

"We now have our list." said Sally. "Now we need to work out what the next stage of our plan is."

"We need to speak to all this staff to find out what happened on their shift. Some may already have had concerns but not said anything," said Moira. "I know Josh has been worried. He spoke with Ness's niece, Fiona. He actually called around at her house."

"Then let's start with him. I can do that."

"We must be very careful too as one of them could be hiding something," said Matt.

"We also need to talk about the residents' missing things," said Sally. "And was Matron there on the day of the deaths? I don't think she was because she doesn't tend to work weekends and two of the deaths were on a weekend."

"I can't see how we can find out who was always on shift when things went missing. They are random items that have been occurring for quite some time now," said Matt. "I think it's just a case of being vigilant and if anything else goes missing then we make a note as to what is missing and who is working when it happens."

They called it a day at seven o'clock. Moira and Matt needed to go home and eat. Jack arrived home from work and Sally said she would tell him over supper what they had discovered.

Moira got home and talked it over with Hugh as they ate their lasagne. He told her to be careful how they approached the staff. She wouldn't want Matron to get wind of this.

"I agree. With being new and on a month's trial, it wouldn't look good for my career prospects!"

"You could always change careers and go into the police force like Fiona."

"Very funny!"

They cleared up their plates and took a coffee into the lounge where they spent the rest of the evening watching a film.

Matt also told Nancy that they had now established who had been on shift on the days of all four deaths. She urged him to be careful when asking any of the staff about the deaths. "I don't want you bumped off." Matt promised her that he would watch his back.

Thursday morning, Sally arrived for her morning shift. Jack had warned her to be very careful about how she was going to ask the staff about the deaths in the home. After all, he said, it could all be just a coincidence all four dying suddenly like that as they were elderly and probably not in the best of health. She reassured him she would be careful.

She was going to let Matt speak to Josh but she would speak with Nick as he would be coming on the afternoon shift and after the handover might be the best time.

Matron was in work this morning but spent most of it in the office, still grumbling about Monday and the false assessment. Dr Johnson was coming in later to do his weekly round. Sally knew Matron would cheer up then and appear pleasant and attentive whilst he was there.

He arrived at eleven o'clock. He asked Sally to accompany him while he saw the residents. Matron hovered around until he suggested she return to her office as Sally was with him and could answer any questions he may have about the residents and that he would see her in her office after his round. She gave him a smile and retreated but only Sally saw her face change to anger as she made her way to the office.

The round lasted an hour and then they sat in the dining room with the residents' records and medication charts. He made a few medication adjustments and thanked Sally for her time. He made his way to the office where Matron was waiting for him.

Sally completed all her tasks and just before two o'clock, Nick arrived for his shift. She handed over the morning report to Nick and his five afternoon carers.

The carers left to attend to the residents, Sally asked Nick if she could have a quiet word with him. He looked a bit startled. Sally didn't usually find him easy to talk to. He always appeared reserved and not particularly friendly.

"I have been thinking about the sudden deaths we have had here in the last few months, There have been four of them and I'm bit concerned that there was not more of an investigation at the time. I know you were on shift when they died."

"What are you suggesting?" Nick asked. His face gave nothing away.

"Well, weren't you a bit concerned? All of them were in reasonable health for their age and then they were suddenly gone."

"Natural causes. Old age. Nothing more than that," said Nick and he got up and left the room.

Sally sat there, feeling stunned. She had expected Nick to be more interested. She went and collected her bag and left to go home.

Sally rang Moira in the evening and told her about her futile conversation with Nick. She said she hadn't seen Matt to hear if he had spoken with Josh.

"Do you think Nick has something to hide?" Moira asked.

"Well, I would have thought he would be interested in what I was saying but he dismissed it saying it was natural causes in all the cases and nothing else."

"It sounds a bit suspicious to me. You would think he would want to discuss it in more detail. Let's keep a close eye on him."

"Surely a trained nurse wouldn't be involved?" said Sally.

"Stranger things have happened, you only have to read the newspapers," replied Moira.

"Let's see what the other staff on shift at the times of deaths think."

They had a chat and then Sally rung off saying she would see her tomorrow at work.

Moira told Hugh what Sally had said. He said forget about it for now until any real evidence showed up.

They had their evening meal and planned to watch a film. Moira rang Fiona before settling down to give her an update.

Matt was also speaking to Nancy over their evening meal. He said he had not seen Josh on his own today so hadn't been able to ask him anything about the deaths. He hoped to see him tomorrow.

Fiona had spoken with Moira the previous evening and on Friday morning was telling Lynne about their suspicions and how they were going to ask the staff about the sudden deaths. She said that a list had been drawn up with the staff on shift at the time of the deaths. Lynne said this was serious and they should proceed with caution.

"If there is something going on and one of them is involved then there could be trouble."

"But if there is something going on and one of them is involved then it should be made known," said Fiona. "I'm looking out for my aunt and the other residents."

"Do you think I should ask Kevin about it?" said Lynne.

"Not yet, let's see what the others find out first."

Moira had told Fiona that she would keep her updated.

Fiona was going to visit Aunt Ness this Friday evening as she and Ted were planning to go away for the weekend. They were going to the Lake District and had arranged to stay in a bed and breakfast overnight. They would take walks in the daytime. The weather forecast was good and both were looking forward to it.

She left work at four instead of five to allow time for the visit and then get home in good time to pack for the weekend away. They were planning to leave at seven in the morning to try and avoid the traffic.

Fiona arrived at the care home just after half past four. Josh answered the door when she rang the bell. Fiona wondered whether Matt had spoken with him but didn't ask him as she wasn't sure if he knew he was aware of the plan to ask some of the staff about the sudden deaths.

She passed Matron's office and saw she was in there sitting at her desk. She was on the phone.

Fiona found her aunt in the lounge. There were several residents in there. The television was on but no one appeared to be watching it. Aunt Ness was in her usual chair by the window. A lady was sitting in the chair beside her with a magazine on her knee. Fiona hadn't seen her before.

"Hello, Aunt Ness," said Fiona. Her aunt smiled at her. Fiona turned to the lady in the next chair and introduced herself.

"I'm Margaret," the lady replied. "I moved in a few days ago."

"Pleased to meet you. I hope you are settling in alright," said Fiona.

"Yes I am. It's a bit strange but everyone seems nice."

"My aunt has been here a few weeks now."

"You couldn't do me a favour, could you?" asked Margaret.

"Of course, I could. What can I do for you?"

"Can you ask if anyone has seen my bracelet? It's proper gold and I can't find it. I only wear it on special occasions. I thought it was in the jewellery box in my room but was told it must have fallen off my wrist when I was wearing it but I'm sure I haven't worn it since being here. I'm told that it's my memory playing up but I'm certain I haven't worn it since I arrived as there's not been a special occasion," said Margaret.

Not another mislaid item, thought Fiona.

Fiona looked around and saw Rosalyn coming into the lounge. Fiona went up to her and repeated what Margaret had said. "She's got memory problems," said Rosalyn.

"She says it was in her room and cannot recall wearing it since being here," said Fiona.

"She must have mislaid it then," said Rosalyn. She went off to attend to a resident who was calling for attention.

Margaret shook her head. "No, I only wear it on special days. I know it was in my room," she told Fiona.

"Do you have anyone come to visit you?" asked Fiona.

"I have my daughter Diane coming tomorrow. It's her first visit. I will ask her to search my room."

"I hope she finds it for you."

Fiona turned to Aunt Ness. "How have you been since I last saw you?" she asked.

"Alright, I think." Fiona thought she didn't sound too sure.

"Has anything happened?"

"I got told off for asking where my picture and cushion is," she said.

"Who told you off?" asked Fiona.

"I can't remember."

"Have you seen any more lights outside your window at night?"

"I don't think so."

"I saw a light last night," interrupted Margaret. "I was getting into bed when I saw something shining in the garden. I looked outside as I drew my curtains."

"Could you see where the light was coming from?" said Fiona.

"The shed at the end of the garden," said Margaret. "I think it was a torch light. It wasn't an electric kind of light. It was more like a beam."

"My aunt has seen the same kind of light."

"What's in the shed?" asked Margaret.

"I went to have a look one day but couldn't see as it was too dark inside to make anything out," replied Fiona.

Fiona thought that for someone who was supposed to have memory problems, Margaret was coming across as very lucid.

She would relate all this to Moira when she next spoke to her.

Nick, the nurse on afternoon shift, came into the lounge and announced that tea was ready and everyone should make their way to the dining room.

Margaret got up and asked Aunt Ness if she was coming so they could sit together for tea. Fiona helped Aunt Ness out of her chair and handed her walking stick.

They made their way out of the lounge into the dining room. Fiona asked Aunt Ness if she could go up to her room and make sure everything was alright. Aunt Ness said yes of course she could.

She saw her aunt and Margaret settled in the dining room, discussing what they think they had ordered.

Fiona went upstairs to her aunt's room. She went inside and had a look around. Everything seemed as it should be. The radio was set on Classic FM. She opened her wardrobe and nothing else seemed to be missing, which was a relief. She closed the wardrobe door. There was still no sign of the picture or red cushion in the room.

Fiona went downstairs into the dining room. Aunt Ness and Margaret appeared to be eating well.

Fiona said goodbye, kissed her aunt and she would see her next week. She left, noticing that Matron's office was empty now. Fiona drove home. Ted was there and they started packing for their weekend away.

Moira rang about seven o'clock to update her on the plan. There wasn't much to report, she told Fiona.

Fiona told her about Margaret and her missing gold bracelet. Moira said she would have a look in Margaret's room tomorrow if she had her permission and also speak to her daughter, Diane.

She rang off, saying she would speak next week.

Ted and Fiona finished packing ready for their early getaway in the morning.

Moira reported for her morning shift on Saturday. She had the handover from Graham who said the night had been quiet and the residents had slept well. When the carers had left the dining room, Moira asked Graham if he had ever noticed any lights in the garden at night. She told him that some residents who had rooms overlooking over the garden had seen lights, apparently coming from the shed. She said they thought it was a torch light.

Graham said he hadn't noticed any lights. He said he didn't normally look out onto the garden during his shift but would keep an eye open in future.

He left to go home.

Moira spent the next couple of hours dispensing the medications. She spoke with each resident and all seemed okay.

Being a weekend, Matron wasn't in, which the staff were quite happy about. Around eleven o'clock, the front door bell rang. Moira answered it and admitted Margaret's daughter, Diane. Moira gave her an update on how Margaret was settling in and then mentioned the bracelet that Margaret said was missing.

"She did bring it in with her," said Diane. "I will have a look in her room. It's gold so I hope it turns up. She usually only wears it on special occasions because it was expensive."

"Margaret did give me permission to look in her room but I haven't had time yet so I will leave it to you. Please let me know if you find it," said Moira.

Diane went into the lounge where Margaret was sitting with Ness. Moira saw a few residents looking at Diane as she was not known to them. Tom and Arthur spoke between themselves while looking at her. They were so used to the regular visitors that anyone different would interest them.

Diane went out of the lounge and went upstairs to her mother's room. She was there a while before coming down to find Moira.

"The bracelet is neither in her jewellery box nor anywhere in her room. I've looked everywhere for it," she told Moira.

"I will ask the staff if they have seen it," said Moira. She wasn't going to inform Diane that items had been going missing as it would alarm her. Moira was going to make a note of the missing bracelet along with all the other missing things as planned with Matt and Sally.

Moira finished her shift with a handover to Nick and the afternoon carers. She did mention Margaret's missing bracelet and asked them all to keep their eyes open for it.

Moira left and drove home. She realised that when they were finding out which staff were on shift at the time of deaths, they hadn't identified the night staff on shift apart from the nurse. The missing items could have gone missing during the night, which when thinking about it could be more likely. Someone could have gone into the residents' rooms while they were asleep. She would discuss this with Matt and Sally. They would need to look at the rotas again to see who had been on shift with the nurse.

Sally had a copy of the rotas so Moira decided to ring her up.

Sally answered the phone when Moira rang her at four o'clock. She told her about the missing bracelet and asked her to check the rota. As Margaret had only been a resident for a week, the bracelet could have been taken by someone at night in her first week of residence.

Sally and Jack were about to go out to visit Jack's parents but Sally said she would look at the rotas tomorrow and ring Moira in the evening. Moira said she was on the afternoon shift so Sally said she would ring her at work.

Moira then rang Matt but there was no reply from his home phone or mobile. She left a message on his mobile saying she would ring him in the morning.

Moira had a lie in on Sunday morning as she wasn't on shift until two o'clock. She got up at nine and cooked a breakfast for herself and Hugh. Hugh was planning to go for a round of golf later when Moira went to work. He said he had paperwork to do after the golf and would have a light meal waiting for her when she got home. Moira did some vacuuming and dusting. Not her favourite activity but still needed to be done. She had a sandwich lunch with Hugh before leaving for work.

Moira arrived at the care home just before two and took the handover from Jane. Jane was a part-time nurse and had worked at the home for several years. She was planning to retire soon. She was quite abrupt and gave a short handover with the minimum of information. Moira asked a few questions about the residents and received answers but without any elaboration. Moira didn't particularly take to her and she had heard carers say the same. Moira would have liked to ask her about residents missing items but felt uncomfortable in her presence so didn't say anything.

Jane left and Moira went to see the residents in the lounge. Tom and Arthur were there with their crossword. Gwen was reading a magazine with her new magnifying glass. Ness and Margaret were by the window in their usual chairs. John was wandering around, picking objects up and then putting them down. Moira asked him if she could help him with what he was looking for. "My wallet," he replied. "I've lost it."

Moira asked him when he last saw it. "Last night," he replied. "I've been looking for it all morning. It has twenty pounds in it." He looked worried and unhappy.

"I'm sure it will turn up," she reassured him. He didn't look convinced. He said he would go and look again in his room. He left the lounge, going up the stairs with a dejected air. Moira thought she would give him time to look and then she would go up to him.

She went to speak to the other residents. The lounge was quite full, some of them watching the television, others just staring into the air and some were asleep. The carers on shift brought the tea trolley in and gave out tea and biscuits. Some residents required help with their drinks and Moira was pleased to see that those needing help received it.

At seven o'clock, Dr Johnson walked in. He told Moira he was passing and thought he would call in to see if everything was alright. Moira told him that all residents were well. She mentioned that John was unhappy that he had lost his wallet. She took this opportunity to tell him that several residents had items been going missing for quite a while. He seemed concerned and said it was the first he had heard of it other than when Freda had reported her clock and biscuits missing. Moira said it had been reported to Matron but nothing had been done about it. He asked what the items were.

"Money, makeup, clothes, pictures, a bracelet, cushions, a torch, a magnifying glass, magazines to name just a few," she replied.

"How disturbing," he said. "This needs investigating. I will call in tomorrow to have a word with Matron."

He thanked Moira for telling him and then left.

She wondered whether she should have mentioned the sudden deaths. She would ask Sally about it.

Sally rang at eight o'clock saying she had looked at the rotas. She discovered that two night carers were on shift on the night before the day of the sudden deaths, Alice and Carl. Moira told her about Dr Johnson calling in this evening and she had spoken with him about the residents missing items but hadn't mentioned the deaths.

"Best not to at the moment until we gain more information," said Sally.

Nina was on the night shift. Her carers were Alice, Carl, Sue and Amy. Moira handed the shift over to them. It was the same combination of staff as the previous night. Moira said goodbye and would see them in the morning.

She drove home where Hugh was just finishing preparing a salad for their supper. He had enjoyed his game of golf and had had a good evening sorting out paperwork.

Moira was tired so went to bed after supper.

She arrived at the home next morning and received the handover from Nina. It had been a quiet night and the residents had slept well. She stayed sitting in the dining room when the carers left to start their work helping residents get up for the day. "I wanted a quiet word with you," she said to Moira.

"I saw a light in the garden late last night. It was down near the shed. I asked the staff if they could look and they also witnessed it but all were too scared to go down the garden. I couldn't find Carl to ask him so I presumed he was attending to someone. By the time I found him and looked out in the garden, it was all in darkness. Carl looked a bit alarmed when I asked him about it. Do you think it was just a coincidence that he was missing at the time the rest of us saw the light or do you think he may have been out there?"

"Did you ask him what he was doing when you couldn't find him?"

"He said he was helping a couple of residents to the bathroom and it took a little while. He said not to worry about the light as it probably was someone with a torch walking their dog in the field behind the garden."

"A bit late to walk a dog!" remarked Moira.

"That's what I thought," said Nina. "He's not here tonight but I will keep my eyes on the garden and him on his next shift."

Nina collected her bag and went off home.

Moira had a busy Monday morning. She completed her medication round and was just locking up her drugs trolley when Matron appeared. "Everything alright?" she asked Moira. Moira replied that it was. She told her that Dr Johnson had called in to the home last evening.

"What on earth for?" said Matron. "I hope you didn't call him in."

"No, I didn't, he said he was passing the home and just popped in to make sure everything was alright."

"What did you tell him?"

"That the residents were well but we also discussed the missing items," said Moira.

"Why did you do that? It's nothing to do with him."

"It is if the residents are upset about things going missing as it can have an impact on their health," replied Moira.

Matron looked at Moira and turned away with a huff and went out of the room. *Surely*, thought Moira, *she should be more concerned about someone, most likely a member of staff, who may be stealing from the residents. If I was in charge of the home, I would be launching an investigation and if someone was found to be stealing, they should be dealt with.*

Moira went around talking to the residents. John was still looking for his wallet and Margaret's bracelet had not turned up. She saw that Sarah appeared a bit quieter than usual.

"Is anything the matter?" Moira asked her.

"I am missing my *Woman and Home* magazine. It only came yesterday. It was in my room but it's gone. I haven't read it all yet."

"Did you bring it into the lounge?"

"No, I always like it to be in my room so I can read it in the evening before going to bed. If I bring it in the lounge, other people want to read it."

"Did you read it last night before bed?" asked Moira.

"Yes, and I left it on my table by my chair but it had gone when I woke up."

Another missing item, Moira noted, something else to be added to the list. It had to have been taken by a member of the night staff. Moira promised Sarah she would pick up another one on her way home and would bring it in tomorrow.

Sarah cheered up and thanked her.

Matt wasn't around this morning but was due in after lunch. Nancy had an outpatient appointment that Matt had wanted to go to with her.

Sally was on the afternoon shift. After handover and the carers had left the room, she told Sally about Sarah's missing magazine and the fact that it had to be taken by one of the night staff. She told her as well about Nina and three of the staff seeing a light in the garden but Carl had not been around to see it.

"Right, we may be getting somewhere. What do we know about Carl?"

Moira, being new, didn't know much about him and suggested, "You can ask Nina tonight when she comes in. She must know him quite well as they work nights together."

"Good plan," said Sally.

"Also, I told Matron that I spoke with Dr Johnson last evening about the missing things and she wasn't best pleased. She said it wasn't his business, but I said it was, as it causes residents to worry, which can impact their health."

Sally hooted at this. "You didn't!"

"I certainly did," grinned Moira.

Moira left saying she had a day off tomorrow so would catch up with Sally the following day after she had spoken with Nina. "We must update Matt as well. He wasn't in this morning."

"I 'll see him this afternoon," said Sally.

She found Matt collecting some tools from his closet. A wheelchair brake was loose and needed his attention.

Sally updated him on recent events. He repeated what Sally had thought, they may be getting nearer to solving the mystery of the missing items.

Sally had a quiet shift. Matron was in her office all afternoon and didn't appear at all.

Nina and her night carers arrived for their shift. Sally handed over and after the carers left the room, she told Nina about Sarah's missing magazine and that it had to have been taken during last night's shift. She repeated what Sarah had said about reading it before bed and it had been taken from the table in her room during the night as it wasn't there in the morning.

Nina at first thought Sally was accusing her of taking it.

"No! Of course I'm not accusing you at all!" said Sally. "I just wondered if you had seen one of the carers with it?"

"No. I didn't."

"What do you know about Carl? Moira told me about you seeing lights in the garden last night and he was missing when you asked the staff to see them as well."

"Yes, I couldn't find him at the time we saw the lights. Carl's about forty, I think, never been married and he lives with his mother and she's a bit of an invalid and has been for a few months. I don't think she ever goes out of the house from what he says. They live a couple of miles away in Seaton, the next village to here. He's worked here for about six months. He used to work in another care home near Morton but he has never said why he left there to come here."

"How many nights does he work?"

"He works four nights a week but will always work more if he's needed. He says he needs the money. Do you think he's taking these things? And what have the lights got to do with him?"

"I have no idea, there's no proof unless he's found with something that a resident has missed."

Nina said she would watch him carefully and tell Sally if she found out anything.

Sally thanked her and left to go home.

She drove home a different way. She passed through the next village called Seaton. It was more a hamlet than a village as there were only a few houses on the main road and no church. It was getting dark but there were some streetlights opposite the houses. Sally wondered which house Carl and his mother lived in. She was just driving slowly past the last couple of houses when she spotted Carl through her driving mirror. He was pulling a black wheelie bin out from the side path of the last but one house and onto the front. It must be dustbin day tomorrow. She didn't stop as it may have looked a bit odd but she now knew where he lived but why that mattered, she didn't know yet.

She arrived home about ten minutes later than normal due to her altered route.

Jack came out of the front door when he saw her car arrive home. He had been getting worried, he told her.

"Sorry," she said. "I'll tell you why I'm late when we get in."

He hugged her and listened to her account of the latest missing item from Sarah's room. She told him about her talk with Nina, about the garden light and that Carl had not been around to witness it. She said she had wanted to try and find out a bit more about Carl and she now knew where he lived.

"You be careful," he warned her. "If he is the one stealing things then he's not going to want to be found out and if he hears you are suspecting him being the thief then there could be trouble."

"I'll be careful," she promised him.

She was going to discuss with Moira and Matt what the next course of action should be.

Moira had the next day off. She met a friend for coffee and then they did a bit of retail therapy. Moira bought a dress and cardigan and then saw some shoes that were in a sale. She couldn't resist them, she said to Hugh.

"But do you really need them?" he asked.

"A girl can never have enough shoes," she replied with a grin.

She rang Fiona in the evening and asked how the weekend away had been.

"Lovely break," said Fiona. "The weather was kind; we walked a lot and the bed and breakfast was great."

Moira updated her on the latest missing items and they now had a possible suspect in Carl. There was no proof yet but hopefully it was only a matter of time. She said they needed to somehow visit Carl's home to see if any of the items were there.

"How on earth are we going to do that?" said Fiona.

"We need someone, who Carl doesn't know, to visit on some pretence. He works nights so will be there. Whoever goes must remember some of the items that have been taken and look to see if any are in the house."

"The obvious people are Ted, Hugh or Jack because he doesn't know them. Discuss it with the others and let me know who pulls the short straw!" replied Fiona.

"It might be better if it was a woman because he has a housebound mother."

"I wonder whether my friend Lynne would do it," said Fiona "Shall I ask her at work tomorrow? Have I told you she is dating Dr Johnson?"

"No! Really?"

"Yes, a real surprise for me too when I found out!"

"Why not ask her? She can be pretend to be doing a survey or something."

"I will ask her tomorrow, I'm sure she will be up for it."

They chatted for a bit longer and then rang off.

The next day, Fiona told Lynne about the plan and asked if she would visit Carl's house.

"I certainly would!" she replied instantly. "I have always fancied myself as a Miss Marple!"

"I will give you a list of all the missing items and you need to see if you can spot any of them."

"Give me the list and I will memorise as many as I can!" said Lynne.

"Don't mention this to your doctor though," warned Fiona.

"Of course not," Lynne promised. "Let me know when you want me to go. It will have to be in the day time so I'll have to go out from work."

"I'll cover for you," said Fiona. "If Big Boss comes in, I'll say you had an appointment. I'll ring Sally tonight and tell her you'll do it."

Fiona rang Sally that evening and said Lynne had agreed to visit Carl's house. She needed a day or so to memorise the items she needed to look out for. Sally said she would email the missing items over to Fiona so she could give them to Lynne. They also needed to plan what Lynne was going to say as to why she was visiting the house.

"Lynne will think of something without arousing suspicion," Fiona assured Sally.

Fiona gave the emailed list of residents' missing items to Lynne the next day. "Homework!" said Lynne.

"I will call around on Thursday morning saying I am doing a survey on small villages and what the pluses or minuses are for living in a village opposed from living in a town. Hopefully, I will gain access. I'll go in the morning when her son is in bed after working a night shift."

"Good idea," said Fiona. "I will just check with Sally that he will have worked Wednesday night."

Fiona checked with Sally who said she would check the rota to see if Carl was on shift Wednesday night. She was working tomorrow morning and would ring Fiona at work.

Next day Sally checked the rota and saw that Carl was working tonight. She rang Fiona at work to say for Lynne to go ahead with the visit on Thursday morning when Carl would presumably be asleep in bed. He should be as he was working Thursday night as well.

Lynne had the list of missing items that he needed to look out for at his house. Fiona tested her on them, which caused great hilarity. It reminded of them of a childhood game where items were placed on a tray and then covered and the person who remembered the most won a prize! As long as Lynne remembered a few of them, it should be alright, Fiona said.

It was arranged that Lynne would call at the house at eleven o'clock next day with a clipboard and survey.

Next day, Lynne left the office at half past ten. She had tried to remember most of the items that she needed to look out for.

She found the house but parked up a little way down the road. She wondered whether she ought to call at another house after visiting Carl's in case Carl or his mother checked up on her. If she only went to one house, it may cause suspicion.

She walked up to Carl's front door and knocked. She didn't ring the bell in case it woke Carl up.

After waiting for about a minute, she could hear someone coming to answer her knock. Lynne waited for the door to open. A lady stood there, leaning on a walking stick. She was around eighty, grey-haired with what looked like with a very lined face and a nice smile. She wore a reddish coloured dress with a blue lambswool cardigan and had fluffy pink slippers on her feet. *Was the cardigan the missing one from Fiona's aunt's wardrobe?* Lynne wondered.

"Hello," said Lynne, returning the smile. "I'm in this area carrying out a survey on what it's like to live in a small village as opposed to living in a town. Have you got ten minutes?"

"Come in, sorry it took a while for me to answer the door." said the lady. "I don't leave the house much as I have difficulty walking since I had an accident about six months ago. We must be quiet though as my son works nights and is asleep upstairs. Follow me, it will be nice to have someone to talk to."

She turned to walk slowly down the hall so Lynne closed the front door and followed her into the lounge where the lady turned into.

"Sit down," she said. "My name's Lydia, what's yours?"

"Lynne." She saw no reason not give her real name as Carl would not associate her with the care home.

"What do you want to ask me?"

"How long have you lived here?" asked Lynne.

"Nigh on forty years. My son was born in this house. We never thought we could have children and then at the age of forty, Carl arrived. His father died when he was ten so we've been on our own a long time."

Lynne looked around and said what a lovely lounge she had. The walls were painted pale green and had several framed pictures and photographs hanging and the carpet was a slightly darker green colour that complemented the walls. There was a beige-coloured three-piece suite, a large television and a glass cabinet filled with lots of knickknacks, paperweights and photographs. She saw two red cushions on the sofa and a multi-coloured blanket draped over the back of the sofa. There was a coffee table with a plant on and a small table by each chair. *Two items spotted,* she thought, as well as the blue cardigan.

Lydia stretched her right arm up and pointed to a photograph hanging on the wall. "That's me and Ray on our wedding day. He was a good man. Shame he died and didn't see our Carl grow up."

Lynne saw Lydia's sleeve of her cardigan ride up as she pointed. A shiny bracelet decorated her wrist.

"What a pretty bracelet," she remarked.

"It was a present from Carl. He's a good boy, loves to give his mum presents." She looked at the bracelet and smiled. "I tell him not to spend his money on me but he says he enjoys it. I said it was too expensive but he said it's fake gold so didn't cost much. Can you see the lovely coloured blanket on the back of the sofa? He knows I love bright colours. He bought it in a sale, he said."

Lynne said he was indeed very generous.

She thought she ought to conduct the survey and asked questions about the village.

"Never lived in a town and I don't want to," said Lydia. "Noisy, lots of traffic, too many people, no, it's not for me. I like peace and quiet."

Lynne wrote the answers down.

Lydia was obviously enjoying the company and conversation and Lynne felt very guilty knowing she was there under false pretences. She noticed *Hello* and *Woman and Home* magazines on the small table next to the chair where Lydia was sitting. "You enjoy reading magazines?" she asked.

"Carl picks them up for me. They pass the time away but my eyes aren't what they used to be," replied Lydia. She reached down into a bag by her chair and extracted a magnifying glass. "Carl got me this and it helps with reading the small print. I like the television but tend to watch it more in the afternoon and evening. Can't do with those loose women and the news is always depressing. I like a bit of Philip and Holly on *This Morning* but they're off on a summer break at the moment. I like *Tipping Point* but find some of the questions a bit hard and I really enjoy *The Chase* at five o'clock but again, I don't know a lot of the answers but I do like Bradley!"

A magnifying glass was another missing item on the list, thought Lynne. Lynne asked her a few more questions relating to living in the country and wrote Lydia's answers down.

She then asked if Lydia knew if her neighbours would be in so she could ask them questions for her survey.

"No, they all go out to work. You would have to come back in an evening."

Lynne chatted for a while longer and then got up and thanked Lydia for her time.

"What am I thinking of! I never offered you a cup of tea. You must think me very rude," said Lydia.

"It's fine and I've really enjoyed chatting with you," said Lynne. "But may I make you a drink before I leave?"

"No thank you, Carl will be up soon, he gets up about one o'clock and we have one with our lunch. He does all the cooking as I find it hard to stand for more than a few minutes. He is such a good boy."

Lynne told her she would see herself out and thanked her again for her time. As she was walking through the hall, she was startled to hear a sound like a cuckoo coming from the kitchen!

She heard Lydia chuckle and called out it must be twelve o'clock.

"Yes, it is," called Lynne from the hall. "It made me jump. Goodbye, Lydia."

She closed the front door behind her and took a deep breath. Some of the missing items were definitely in the house, which made Carl the thief. *What a shame*, thought Lynne, *I hope Lydia never finds out that he has stolen the presents that he says he buys for her. She would be devastated.*

Lynne made her way to her car and drove back to work.

She related her findings to Fiona who made a note of all the missing items she had seen and heard in Carl's house.

"There may have been others but I only went into the hall and lounge. His mum is really nice and she enjoyed me being there. I felt really sorry for her when she was telling me about the generous gifts Carl buys for her."

"What a shame!" said Fiona. "I will ring Sally this evening and tell her all this. Thanks for going."

"No problem, I really liked chatting with her. She is a very nice person. She hardly ever goes out since apparently having had an accident she told me but I could tell she enjoyed the company. Let me know what happens next, won't you?"

"Of course I will."

Carl got up fifteen minutes before one o'clock. He showered and dressed and went downstairs. His mother was in the lounge using the magnifying glass and reading the *Woman and Home* magazine.

"Hello son," she greeted him. "Sleep well?"

"Like a log," he replied. "What shall we have for lunch?"

"Beans on toast?" suggested Lydia.

Carl went into the kitchen. A thrush started singing. He glanced up at the clock and grinned. One o'clock!

He heated the beans, put bread in the toaster and called his mum in when it was ready. He made a pot of tea and placed it on a cork mat in the middle of the kitchen table with a milk jug and two mugs. He sorted out cutlery and plates and spooned the beans onto the toast.

Lydia sat down, picked up her knife and fork and started to eat.

"I've had a visitor this morning," she told him.

"Have you, that's unusual. Who was it?" he said as he poured the tea into the mugs. He added milk, stirred and passed a mug over to his mother.

"A very nice lady called Lynne. She was carrying out a survey on the benefits of living in a village rather than a town. She came in for about an hour and we had a lovely chat."

"That's nice."

"She asked lots of questions. She also admired my bracelet."

"Did she?"

"I told her you said it was only fake gold but she thought it was pretty. She also liked the coloured rug that you bought me. I told her that you often buy me things. I showed her the magnifying glass that you bought me to see my magazines small print."

"What questions did she ask you?"

"About living in the village and how I liked it."

"No, not the survey but the other questions about the presents that I bought you."

"She agreed you were very generous to your old mum. The cuckoo clock sounded at twelve o'clock and I know it startled her as she was leaving. You don't expect to hear a cuckoo in a house, do you?" she chuckled.

"You shouldn't have let her in. You didn't know her and she could have been anybody. Did you ask for her identification?"

"No, I did not. That would have been rude!" said Lydia.

"Next time someone calls, it's best not to let them in."

"I enjoyed the chat. I get lonely. With you working nights, I don't see anyone else."

No more was said about the visitor but Lydia thought Carl seemed a bit distracted. She asked him if he was feeling alright and he said he was fine.

Carl went out for a walk in the afternoon. He was thinking about his mother's visitor this morning. She seemed mighty interested in the presents he gave to his mum. He wondered who she really was. He hoped this wasn't going to be a problem. He needed to be careful and watch his back for a while. He would not use the shed to store the items in, just in case someone had suspicions.

The shed was very useful and he could easily transfer items to it at night without being spotted and then he collected them early morning and transferred them to his car while the other staff were busy in the home. Sometimes he had to leave them in the shed for a day or so if he got his timing wrong. The carpark floodlight was on a sensor timer and he would be spotted if he put the things in his car as soon as he took them as it lit up very brightly that could be seen easily. He always parked as near to the garden as possible. It had been a nuisance when he lost his torch but thankfully had found it in the maintenance man's closet. It was an expensive torch and he couldn't afford to buy another one like it.

He loved his mother and wanted her to have nice things but he couldn't afford much so taking them from residents who wouldn't really miss them was the next best thing. He was careful of who he took them from. It was easier if they had dementia as mislaying things and forgetting when they last had them was part of their illness. The gold bracelet was easy, a new resident in the home, she probably thought she hadn't even taken it in with her.

Magazines were also easy to take. Clothes that would fit his mother were also quite easy. They would be presumed to be in the laundry and then lost. He couldn't resist the red cushions or multicoloured rug. His mother liked bright colours. He just wanted to make her happy. He would do anything for her. She had been in a car accident six months ago and had been more or less housebound ever since. He had been caught taking small things for his mother in his previous job at the other care home. They said if he resigned immediately then they would take no further action. That was a relief.

He quite liked working at Goodrest Care Home. The staff was okay, the shift patterns were fine and it was convenient for travelling. It was a big enough building to be able to disappear on shift without causing suspicion and stash the goods in the shed late evening and retrieve them early morning when the mornings were getting lighter and the floodlight in the carpark didn't come on.

He arrived back at home and prepared the evening meal of pork steaks and fresh vegetables. His mum enjoyed her food and he liked to look after her as well as he could. He was grateful for all her care of him since his father died when

Carl was only ten. She had gone without things so he could have a good childhood and he wanted to repay her back especially now she was dependant on him to provide for her.

After their tea, he spent the evening watching *Eastenders* and then *Midsomer Murders* with his mum. He was not on shift tonight or tomorrow.

Fiona told Ted about what Lynne had seen in Carl's house. "What's going to happen now?" he asked.

"I'm not sure. I expect Sally will inform Matron and she will deal with it. He's surely going to be fired now that the missing items have been seen, it's evidence of his stealing."

"But it was discovered by underhand means," Ted pointed out. "It needs to be discovered by someone from the home who knows which items went missing."

"I will wait to hear from Sally to see what happens next," she said.

Sally rung Matt up that evening and told him what Lynne had seen in Carl's house. He said the same as Ted. "Without one of us seeing these things, how can we accuse him?" he asked.

"One of us will need to have an excuse to visit him. We have to think how."

Matt said he would go around if there was a plausible reason for calling at the house. Sally said Carl was not on shift again until Saturday night.

"How about if Nancy and I have a walk on Saturday afternoon and just happen to pass his house. I or Nancy could stumble outside, spraining an ankle and knock on his door and ask for some help, pretending we need a lift back home or could he call a taxi for us."

"I suppose that could work," said Sally, "but does he know you?"

"No, because our paths don't cross, with him on nights and me working in the day, but during a conversation, I can express surprise that we work at the same home. I could then appear shocked to spot some items that have been taken and see how he reacts."

"Would Nancy go along with this?"

"Yes, I've told her all about it and she's on the side of the residents. It's stealing from vulnerable people."

"Okay, I will run it past Moira and let you know at work tomorrow."

Sally spoke with Moira the next afternoon after handover. She agreed that it could work. They found Matt repairing a television in a resident's room. The resident was in the lounge so they could talk without being overheard.

"Okay, let's do it," said Sally. "Once you see the items and tell him that you believe they have been stolen, you will have to leave the house quickly. He will know that the sprained ankle was faked. Have your car nearby."

"But being a Saturday, Matron will not be at the home for us to tell," said Moira.

"I'm on shift Saturday afternoon," said Sally. "I will call her in on some pretext. You can come to the home, Matt, and tell her what you have seen at Carl's. Call me on your way in so I know what time to ask her to come in."

"After this is sorted then we must concentrate on trying to find out about the sudden deaths. We've overlooked them a bit with all this going on," said Moira.

The plan was agreed by all three of them.

Saturday was a fine day. "Just the right weather for a walk!" Matt said to Nancy. Nancy was in complete agreement with the plan.

Matt drove to Seaton just after two-thirty and parked the car in a road just off the main road where Carl lived.

He and Nancy ambled down the road towards Carl's house. No one was about. "I hope someone's in," said Matt. It was agreed that Nancy would fake a stumble and clutch her ankle just outside the house.

They reached the house and then Nancy performed a realistic looking stumble. Matt bent down to look at her ankle, in case anyone was looking, and then looked around for help. He helped Nancy limp to Carl's house and he rang the doorbell. The door was opened by Carl. Matt explained that his wife had hurt her ankle while they were out for a walk and was it possible to come in while he called a taxi to collect them. Carl's mother appeared over Carl's shoulder and exclaimed, "Come in, you need to sit down. Carl, move out of the way and let them pass." Carl stood to one side and let them enter into the hall. Nancy limped after Carl's mother, who slowly walked holding her walking stick into the lounge.

Nancy sat down on the sofa.

"You poor thing," exclaimed Carl's mother who introduced herself as Lydia. "Put your foot up on this footstool."

Matt said he didn't have his mobile phone on him and could he call for a taxi using their phone? "Fetch it, Carl," said Lydia. "Then make a cup of tea for us all."

Carl went out of the room without saying anything. Lydia started asking their names and where did they live.

Matt started talking about where they lived and dropped in the conversation that he worked in a care home nearby.

"What a coincidence, Carl is a night carer at Goodrest Care Home."

Matt pretended to be surprised. "No, that's where I work! I'm the maintenance man."

Carl came in the lounge with a tray of tea and the phone. He handed a mug to his mother and then to Nancy and Matt. He hadn't brought one in for himself.

"What a lovely multicoloured blanket," Matt remarked, seeing it on the back of the sofa.

"Yes, Carl bought it for me," said Lydia. "Carl, guess what! Matt works at Goodrest care home too!"

"I'm admiring your mother's blanket," Matt said, looking at Carl. "A lady resident had one like it at the home but it went missing."

"Tell Matt where you bought it, it was in a sale, then perhaps the lady can replace it," said Lydia.

"I can't remember," said Carl.

"I like your red cushions," remarked Nancy.

"Carl bought me those as well, he's so thoughtful. He bought me this lovely bracelet as well."

She stretched out her arm for Nancy and Matt to admire it.

"A lady at the home lost one just like that the other day," remarked Matt, looking at Carl.

"It's only fake gold but it is very pretty," Lydia told Nancy.

Carl gave Matt the phone and suggested he call a taxi.

At that moment, a sound like a blackbird trilled from the kitchen.

"Three o'clock!" chuckled Lydia. "It's not a real bird but a clock that has bird sounds every hour."

"What a coincidence," said Matt, looking at Carl. "A lady in the home had a bird clock but it went missing just like the blanket and cushions."

Carl stood up and said they needed to leave now.

Lydia told him not to be so rude. They hadn't even called a taxi yet.

Nancy got up from the sofa and said her ankle felt so much better now she had rested it a while and she thought she could now walk on it. She thanked Lydia for the tea and she and Matt made their way out of the lounge into the hall. Matt placed a hand on Carl's shoulder in the doorway and quietly said, "What a shame your mum has a thief for a son. You should be ashamed."

Matt opened the front door and he and Nancy left.

They went to their car and Matt rang Sally saying they would be with her in about ten minutes. Sally said she would ring Matron to come to the home.

As soon as they left, Carl went into the kitchen. He looked at the bird clock. He returned to the lounge where his mother was saying how pleased she was that Nancy's ankle was better now she had rested. She didn't mention anything Matt had said about the blanket, bracelet, cushions or clock.

Carl said he was going for a walk and would be back to make their tea. Lydia replied she was content to watch the television as *Family Chase* was on soon.

Matt and Nancy arrived at the home. Sally said she had contacted Matron on the pretext of a resident feeling very unwell and she couldn't cope without backup. Matron had sighed and said she would be in shortly but couldn't understand why Sally couldn't cope with it.

Matron arrived at three-thirty. She was not best pleased she told Sally. It was her day off and she shouldn't be called in by a nurse who was paid good money to cope with all events that occurred on her shift.

When Sally could get a word in, she asked Matron if they could go into her office as she had something to tell her. Matt and Nancy followed them into the office.

"What on earth are you doing here?" she asked them. She sat down at her desk.

"Listen up," said Sally. She related where Matt and Nancy had been this afternoon and what they had discovered at Carl's house. "Some of the stolen items were there in the house. It's evidence of who is responsible for taking the items from the residents."

"It may be pure coincidence that they have similar things," said Matron.

"No way. They are the items from our residents," said Matt. "What are you going to do about it?"

Matron was stumped for words.

Sally said she should call Carl in and ask him to explain how the items ended up in his house. Surely, he should be suspended while an investigation was carried out?

Matron could see that the three of them were not going to drop this.

"I will speak with him when he's next in." She looked at the rota and said he was next in on Sunday night.

"But surely he should not be allowed to be on shift before being spoken to?" said Matt.

"Leave it to me. I am in charge of the home and I will deal with this as I feel fit," said Matron.

Sally said she was speaking on behalf of the residents as many could not speak for themselves. She would inform the police if Matron did not take it seriously.

Matron said she would deal with it and stood up, indicating the meeting was ended. Sally said, "I expect to be informed of what happens next."

Matt and Nancy left the office and went home. Sally also left to return to her shift duties.

Matron remained in her office and made a phone call.

Sally rang Moira and told what had happened and what Matron had said.

Moira said she was on the afternoon shift the next afternoon and would see whether Carl arrived. Sally had the day off so would wait to hear if Carl arrived for the night shift.

Matron left the home without seeking Sally out. Sally handed over to Nina but did not mention anything about the afternoon's events.

The next afternoon, Moira arrived just before two for her shift. Nick was the morning nurse and handed over to her. He only commented on the residents' morning shift and did not make any other talk. There was no message to say that Carl was not coming in for the night shift. Moira hoped his shift had been covered if he was not coming in or they would be one carer down for the night. She worried all afternoon.

At nine o'clock, Graham arrived for the night shift. The carers clocked in but there was no sign of Carl. There were four carers on. Alice had not been on the rota to work so she assumed Matron had rung and asked her to cover the night shift.

Sally handed over to them. No one asked why Carl was not on shift. Perhaps they assumed he had rung in sick.

Moira left the home and drove home. Ted asked her whether Carl had turned up and Sally said no. She hadn't heard from Matron either.

Carl was at home after receiving a phone call from Matron that afternoon. She had asked him not to come in for his shift as there was a concern about residents' missing items that may be in his house. He denied it but she said unless it was proved otherwise, he was suspended from work. He told his mother that he had forgotten he had applied for annual leave and that was why he was not at work. He was worried he would lose his job. He spent the evening watching television with his mother.

He went to bed with thoughts spinning around in his head.

Carl started to collect up the items that he had taken from the home. His mother was still in bed. He would have to think of an explanation that his mother accepted. He took the bird clock from the kitchen, the red cushions and the multicoloured blanket. He somehow needed his mother to hand over the bracelet. He retrieved the magnifying glass from her bag. He placed them all in a black bin liner and stored them under some sacks in his garden shed.

His mother woke, dressed and came downstairs. She went into the kitchen where Carl had prepared breakfast.

She tucked into cornflakes and marmalade on brown buttered toast. She asked Carl what he would be doing today as he was on annual leave.

"I need to go into Morton," he replied. "I have been thinking about your bracelet. I want to get it valued to find out if it's valuable."

Lydia looked at her bracelet and took it off. She handed it over to Carl. "It would be good if it's worth something," she said.

Carl took the bracelet and put it in his pocket.

"Don't answer the door when I'm not here," he warned her. "I've heard there some strangers targeting houses around here, looking to steal things."

"Alright, son," Lydia said.

Carl went into the garden shed while his mother went into the lounge, and put the bracelet in the black bag.

He returned to the house. His mother had turned the television on to watch *This Morning*, hoping Philip and Holly had returned from their summer break.

He called goodbye, made sure she had a drink by her chair, said he would see her later and set off in his car.

He finished his coffee and wandered around to kill a bit of time before going home. He needed time alone to think. He would tell his mother he had left the bracelet with a jeweller who would send it away for a valuation.

He needed to get back to work so he could earn money. He had been told by Matron that she would be in touch with him. He was dreading her phone call.

He drove home and told his mother the bracelet was with a jeweller. She accepted this, rubbing her hands together saying she hoped it would turn out to be valuable.

She hadn't noticed that the bird clock or magnifying glass had gone. She noticed the blanket and cushions were missing and he told her he had taken them to a drycleaner's. "How thoughtful," she said. She picked up the *Hello* magazine and commented that the next issue should soon be out and could he pick her one up?

"Course I will," said Carl.

Fiona was at work discussing the weekend events with Lynne. She was most interested to hear about Matt and Nancy's visit to Carl's house.

"Lydia was lovely. It will be awful if she finds out that Carl has given her things stolen from the residents," she said.

"I know," replied Fiona.

Lynne told her that she had had a good weekend with Kevin. They had been out for a meal on Saturday evening. "I wonder if he has spoken to the Matron yet. He doesn't discuss his work much and I don't like to ask him."

"I hope he has spoken with her and convinced her to take it seriously," said Fiona.

Dr Johnson had actually spoken to Matron on Saturday morning. He said he had called in the home the previous evening and Sally had told him about the residents' missing items. He asked Matron if she any idea who was responsible. She became flustered and said she was looking into it. "Let me know what you find out," he asked her.

Matron had not yet informed him of Saturday afternoon's events but she was sure he would soon find out. She had rung Carl and suspended him or Sally, Matt or Moira would ask her why she hadn't. She needed to speak with him urgently. She rang him up on Monday morning and arranged a meeting with him. She asked him to come to the home on Tuesday morning at eleven o'clock. She said his shifts would be covered by another carer until this was sorted out.

Carl put the phone down. He needed to think about what he was going to say. His mother noticed he was distracted and asked him what the matter was. "Nothing," he said.

He arrived at the home and let himself in. Matron came out of her office and asked him to come in and shut the door. She sat down behind her desk and pointed to one of the two chairs in front of it. Carl sat down.

"Have you been stealing residents' items?" she asked him outright.

"I borrowed them," he admitted.

"Borrowed them?" she retorted. "How could you just borrow them?"

"My mother is an invalid. She likes nice things. I care very much for her. I thought if I could give her some nice things for a while, it would make her happy. I always intended to bring them back."

"And what would your mother say when they left your house to be returned?" she asked.

"She would accept my explanation saying I needed to sell them to make some money."

Matron looked at him in astonishment. "But they were residents' items. They were very upset when they went missing."

"I know, and I'm very sorry. I will return them all."

"How can I trust you not to take other things?"

"You have my word. I really need this job. I am sole carer for my mother and without my money, we would really suffer financially."

"Some of the staff have been suspicious of you. How would I explain this to them if I let you return to work?"

"Let me apologise to them and show them that I can be trusted."

"I'm not sure they would just accept your apology. You have stolen from residents. It should be a police matter."

Carl was shaking and very pale and on the verge of tears.

"Please don't involve the police. My mother would be devastated."

"Wait here. I am going to call Sally in. She is one of the staff who has made me aware of this and should listen to what you say."

Matron got up and went out of the office.

She returned with Sally who sat down in the other chair in front of the desk.

Matron asked Carl to repeat what he had told her. He did so in a faltering voice.

Sally looked amazed and said, "How could you borrow residents' things and then say you were going to return them? They have been upset at their belongings going missing."

"I know and I'm very sorry and ashamed of what I have done," said Carl.

"So you should be. I can't believe it. I feel sorry for your mother thinking you bought these things for her."

Sally turned to Matron and asked what she was thinking.

"Perhaps we should give Carl another chance. If he returns all the items to the residents and they are told they have been found in the home then they would be none the wiser," replied Matron.

"But how could we trust him not to take any more things?" said Sally.

"I promise I won't," cried Carl. "Please give me another chance. I really need this job."

Sally looked at Matron.

"If he comes back then he must be on trial and if anything else goes missing, I will report it to the police myself. I also want this meeting to be documented as evidence."

Matron listened and then looked at Carl.

"We will give you one chance to redeem yourself. This meeting will be documented and placed in your personnel file. If one more thing goes missing from this home, you will be dismissed immediately and the police will be informed."

"Where did you hide the things?" asked Sally.

"In the shed in the garden. I took them, used a torch. There was a broken slat near the window that opened so I hid them there overnight on a shelf and then put them in my car in the morning when it was light."

"That explains the lights that were seen in the shed. I expect you were avoiding the carpark sensor light that comes on at night? At least that's one mystery solved," said Sally. "I can't believe you are being given a second chance. In my opinion, you should really be dismissed immediately."

"I am in charge here and it's my decision he be given one more chance," said Matron. She stood up and told Carl to report back on duty tomorrow evening. "You can leave now and I will write up this meeting. You will bring all the items back in the morning and sign my documentation as a true record of this meeting."

Carl went out of the office, looking very relieved. Sally shook her head at Matron saying she hoped she could live with her decision. Matron glared at her but said nothing. Sally left the office and went back on shift. She needed to tell Moira and Matt about this and she wasn't sure how they would react to Matron's decision.

She was pleased that at least it cleared up the mystery of the lights at the end of the garden. The next investigation must be about the sudden deaths in the home over the last few months.

Carl got in his car and drove to a nearby layby. His heart was pounding and his hands were damp. He was shaking and realised how extraordinarily lucky he was that Matron or Sally hadn't called the police.

Carl took a few minutes to compose himself. He now needed to go home and retrieve all the items he had taken from the home as he had to return them in the morning to Matron. He hoped his mother would not notice.

He arrived home and let himself in the house. His mother was in the lounge reading a magazine. "Have you seen my magnifying glass?" she asked him. "I thought it was in my bag here but I can't find it. Perhaps I put it down somewhere else but I can't remember where."

"I will have a look around for it," he promised her.

He went into the garden and entered the shed. He retrieved the black bag he had hidden yesterday.

He went back to the house and took it up to his room. He went into his mother's bedroom and opened her wardrobe. He took out the blue lambswool cardigan, a pair of trousers, a blouse and a skirt. He placed them in the black bag. He went into the bathroom and found the makeup bag containing cosmetics. He took the small alarm clock from his mother's bedside table.

In his room, he found John's wallet but it was now empty. The money had been spent as had the loose change he had taken. He hid the black bag in his wardrobe; his mother didn't normally come into his room but he couldn't take any chances. He would need to take the bag out to his car later in the evening when his mother was in bed.

He went downstairs and started to prepare their lunch. He could hear his mother in the lounge grumbling about not being able to see the small print in her magazine without the magnifying glass.

He called her into the kitchen to come and eat the cheese and tomato on toast, which was ready. He poured her a cup of tea.

"I am at work tomorrow night," he informed her.

"I hope you have enjoyed your few nights off," she said as she tucked into her lunch.

"Yes, I have," he replied. He cringed as he said this.

After lunch, Carl went to Tesco's to do a food shop. Money was in short supply so he looked for reduced items or products that were two for one. He found a cheap magnifying glass for his mother that looked very similar to the one he had taken from Gwen.

He went through the checkout and loaded the shopping into the car. He was just returning the trolley to the trolley park when he saw Moira. She was just getting out after parking her car. He recognised her as one of the nurses from the home.

"Hello," she greeted him. He said hello but said he was in a hurry to return home as his mother was waiting for him. She gave him an odd look. He wondered whether she was one of the staff that Matron had mentioned as suspecting him of stealing. He quickly got in his car and reversed out of his parking space.

He arrived home and put the shopping away. He handed his mother the magnifying glass. She assumed it was the one that she had mislaid. "Where did you find it?" she asked.

"It was on the kitchen worktop near the kettle," he told her.

"I'm losing my memory. I must be coming down with dementia! I can't remember taking it in there," she chuckled.

Carl reassured her that a lot of people mislay things but it doesn't mean they are getting dementia.

She said, "You are such a comfort to me, son, I don't know what I would do without you."

Carl hoped she would never find out. He wanted to look after her as long as he could.

Moira was on the afternoon shift. After handover, Sally spoke to both Matt and Moira. They met up in the dining room. All were amazed at Matron giving Carl a second chance as long as he returned the items.

"Surely he can't be trusted?" said Matt.

"I agree," said Moira.

Sally said that they now needed to investigate the sudden deaths in the home now that the mystery of the shed light had been discovered.

"How are we going to do that?" asked Matt.

"Well, we have a list of who were on shift the night before or the day of the deaths," replied Sally. "We need to speak to some of them to find out if they had any doubts about what happened."

"I already spoke to Nick," said Moira. "He was very abrupt with me when I mentioned the deaths."

"We need to speak to the others then," said Matt. "Remind me who was on at all the relevant times."

"Brenda and Annie were the housekeepers, the day carers were Rosalyn, Josh, Jackie and Ken. Nick was the day nurse. The night carers were Alice and Carl. Graham was the nurse on shift on one of the nights and Nina was on three nights," said Moira. "All the deaths occurred in the mornings, some early and some a bit later."

"So there were two different night nurses but all the others were there for all the shifts."

"Don't let's forget as well that two residents, Arthur and Ness, said they were given a tablet by someone, but can't remember who, but fortunately, they didn't die. It made them feel poorly and tired. Was it to keep them quiet?"

Matt scratched his head. "Where on earth do we start?"

"Have there been any drugs missing from the trolley or controlled drugs cabinet?" Moira asked Sally.

"No," she replied. "There have been no missing drugs at all."

"If the deaths were due to a drug being administered then it had to come from an outside source," said Sally.

"But Freda's death was reported to the coroner," said Matt. "Surely it would be discovered if there were drugs in her system?"

"There was no post mortem though. The coroner said her death was due to old age, diabetes and congestive cardiac failure and there was no need for further investigations so the body was released. The three other deaths did not go to the coroner. The death certificates were signed by Dr Johnson," said Sally.

"Did the four residents have anything in common?" asked Matt.

"Oh my goodness, of course!" said Sally suddenly. "Yes, I've just remembered, they all had diabetes."

"What?" said Moira.

"How could I have missed this connection?" said Sally.

"But even if they all had diabetes, how come they died suddenly?" said Matt.

"Overdose of insulin?" whispered Moira.

They all looked stunned. Was this the cause of death?

"How?" asked Matt.

"They were all insulin dependent. They had their individual regimes set out. Their blood sugar level would be checked and the amount of insulin prescribed would be injected via a pen."

"Pen?" asked Matt. "What sort of pen?"

"It's an insulin-filled cartridge in a holder that looks like a pen," explained Moira. "There's a dial on the pen that you turn to the prescribed dose and it injects the correct amount of insulin into the person."

"But surely after death, the cartridges would be kept for seven days in case of investigation. It's a legal requirement that all prescribed drugs are kept for seven days after any death," said Sally.

"Yes, but if it wasn't a suspicious death and the drugs weren't called in for investigation, then the cartridges would be destroyed after seven days and no one would know if too much had been used," said Moira.

"Where is the insulin kept?" asked Matt.

"In the drug trolley at room temperature if the cartridge is in use. Unopened cartridges are kept in the drugs fridge."

"Is there anywhere where the disposed cartridges would be documented?" asked Matt.

"Yes, there's a drug book that itemises all disposed drugs and the quantities," said Sally. "We need to check it out."

Moira went to the drugs trolley and retrieved the drug disposal book from the bottom shelf.

She turned the pages back to the date of the first death, Robert. "He died on May 2nd so the entry here will be on the 9th; that is, seven days after his death. Here it is, a list of his tablets and it says one opened cartridge and three unopened packets that contain five vials, all destroyed."

She turned to August 8th, which was seven days after Mary's death. "A list of her tablets and one opened cartridge and one unopened packet of five, destroyed," she read.

August 18th, seven days after Wilfred's death, recorded one opened cartridge and one unopened packet had been destroyed. August 28th showed Freda's disposed medication as one opened cartridge and two unopened packets of vials had been destroyed.

"It doesn't mean that any was used to kill them though," said Matt. "We don't know if the quantity destroyed was any less than it should have been."

"No, I agree, I think it's impossible to tell," admitted Sally.

"But all this doesn't explain why the four residents died," pointed out Matt. "There has to be more in common with them besides being diabetics on insulin."

"They were all residents that could speak up for themselves from what I hear. If something needed saying then they certainly said it," said Moira.

"Perhaps they saw or heard something that they shouldn't and had to be silenced," said Matt.

"This isn't television or a film!" said Moira with a grin.

"He could be right though," said Sally. "It might explain why they died suddenly if someone was afraid, they would speak up."

"So an unknown person, armed with an insulin pen, injected them without them knowing and they subsequently died," said Matt. "They all died in the morning so could have been injected in the night when they were asleep."

"We need to be very careful," said Moira. The others agreed.

Matron suddenly appeared in the doorway. "I thought I heard voices. What are you all doing in here?" she snapped. "You," pointing to Matt, "get back to work at once. Sally, you should have left by now and Moira, you need to look after the residents for which you are paid for, not to sit around gossiping."

She turned and left the room.

The three of them got up and quickly agreed to all think about what to do next.

Matron left work just after five o'clock. She had arranged to meet her nephew Stephen in their usual place in the park. He was the only son of her sister Barbara. Barbara was ten years younger than her and lived in a council house in Morton with her husband Bill and son.

Barbara was not in the best of health and her husband hadn't worked for years as he had a bad back. They lived off his disability allowance and a small pension that Barbara received from her last job in the Post Office. Matron often gave Stephen some money to help with their finances as she knew they struggled to make ends meet. They were proud people so she asked Stephen not to tell them that she gave him money on a regular basis to help the family out.

Stephen told his mother it was a bonus he received every so often from his boss at the garage down the road across from the park where he worked as a mechanic. Matron knew she was hard on the staff at work and she wasn't particularly liked. It was a lonely position being in charge. The staff would no doubt be astonished to hear she helped her family out.

She met Stephen on the bench in the wooded area of the park. He had come straight from work as well. He was in his overalls and had his usual cap on. She handed him an envelope containing two hundred pounds. He took it from her and said how grateful he was. "The electricity bill is due next week and Mum is worrying how to pay it."

"Remember, your mum and dad mustn't know about this," she said.

"Thanks very much, Aunt Bridget," he said as he put the money away in his rucksack. "You're the best!"

They walked together out of the park, said goodbye and each returned to their own homes.

Matron lived alone in a semi-detached house on the outskirts of Morton. She had lived here for twenty years and had a tabby cat called Minky for company. He was fifteen now and gradually slowing down. Birds and mice could now get away from him very easily. She couldn't bear the thought of him not being around. He greeted her at the door when she entered. He brushed against her legs as she petted him.

"Hello old boy, have you had a good day?" She closed the door and went into the kitchen where she prepared his meal. He used a cat flap in the kitchen door to go outside when she was at work. She put his food bowl down and he slowly ate his fish supper. She replenished his water bowl and gave him a dish of milk.

She went upstairs and took her uniform off. She had a shower and dressed in casual clothes. She looked at her reflection in the mirror and saw the signs of ageing. She didn't know how much longer she wanted to work in the care home. She ought to look around for her replacement. She would like to have time to herself and get on with the rest of her life. She had several interests that she would like to pursue. She enjoyed walking. Perhaps with more time, she could explore the surrounding countryside and go on some coach day trips that appealed. She couldn't leave Minky overnight though.

She liked reading and had recently toyed with the idea of volunteering in the local library. She had only a few friends but could meet different people and form new friendships if she had more time. She would also like more visits with Barbara and Bill.

She would also like to be known as Bridget instead of Matron. *Yes*, she decided, *I will plan my retirement.*

She went downstairs and had a cold supper of ham salad. She sat at the kitchen table with the radio on for company. She washed up, went into the lounge and turned the television on. She sat down and Minky jumped up on the settee and settled on her lap. Matron spent a pleasant evening watching a documentary on the trials and tribulations of past royal families, although the cat slept most of the evening, obviously not very interested in kings and queens.

That evening over supper, Sally told Jack about the suspicions that she, Moira and Matt had about the sudden deaths. He advised her to be very careful who she spoke to. She assured him that she would. She needed to think about what to do next.

She needed to speak with them again in a couple of days when each had had time to think. She knew she should discreetly ask the carers who had been on night shift when the deaths occurred in the morning.

She didn't need to speak with the housekeepers who started work at nine o'clock. The deed had been done by then. But who could it be? Surely it had to be someone who knew what an overdose of insulin would do? Where would they get it from, if not from the home?

She worried about it all evening. Jack could see how distracted she was and tried to cheer her up. They watched an old episode of *Only Fools and Horses*, which normally made her laugh but it didn't amuse her tonight.

She couldn't relax properly so went to bed earlier than usual. She was on the early shift again in the morning.

She arrived at work and took the handover from Nina. Nina had been on three of the night shifts prior to the morning deaths. She had been asked about the missing items but hadn't been asked about the morning deaths. Sally wasn't sure how to approach her. She had reacted defensively being asked about the missing magazine so Sally wasn't at all sure how she would react being asked about something more serious like sudden deaths that had occurred after her shifts. She decided not to mention it until she spoke to Matt and Moira.

Matron appeared at work around nine o'clock. She appeared distracted and replied absently when Sally wished her good morning. She asked Matron if she was alright. Matron asked her to come into the office. Sally followed her in, her heart beating rapidly wondering what she was being called in for. Had she done something wrong?

Matron asked her to sit down.

"I'm considering retiring," Matron said. Sally was stunned as this was the last thing she was expecting to hear.

"When?" she asked.

"As soon as a replacement can be found," replied Matron. "Is a management position something you would be interested in?"

"Not really. Jack and I are planning to travel, probably sometime next year, so I wouldn't be interested in taking on the role."

"If you know of anyone who may be interested, please let me know. I will tell Mr Smith, the owner of the home, my plans and he can put feelers out as well. I know you think I'm hard on all of you but I'm tired and get short-tempered."

Sally actually felt quite sorry for her, an emotion she never thought she would feel where Matron was concerned.

She got up and left the office. What a surprise!

She finished her shift without any problems and handed over to Moira and the afternoon staff. When the carers left the room, she told her what Matron had said about retiring as soon as a replacement could be found.

"Crikey!" said Moira. "I wonder when this will happen and I wonder who the new Matron will be?"

"Would you be interested in the job?" asked Sally.

"I've only been here five minutes!"

"You would be perfect for the role. You are an experienced nurse, the staff like you and your recordkeeping is spot on. I realise there's a lot involved in running a care home but I know you could do it."

"Let me speak with Hugh and see what he thinks," said Moira. "It's a huge responsibility."

Sally left with Moira thinking about it. She got up to see the residents, looking around the home with management eyes. She could do this, she thought, *but do I want to?* I will discuss it with Hugh.

Fiona and Ted visited Aunt Ness on Wednesday evening. They arrived at six-thirty. Rosalyn let them in and watched over them as they signed the visitor's book. Fiona asked where Aunt Ness was and was told she had just gone up to her room. Fiona knocked on the door and heard her aunt reply, "Come in."

They entered the room and the first thing Fiona noticed was that the missing red cushion was back on the chair. She looked up and saw the scenic picture back in place on the wall.

"How did they reappear?" she asked Aunt Ness after kissing her hello. Ted looked amazed as well.

"They were here when I came up after tea," replied her aunt. "It's good, isn't it? I've even found my green purse and my moisturiser is back in the bathroom."

"It's very good to have them all back. Let me check your wardrobe." She opened the door. "All the missing clothes are now back hanging up."

"How very odd," said Ted. "How can they all return as suddenly as they went?"

"The person who took them must have returned them, they must have been found out and told to return them," replied Fiona. "I wonder if the other residents have had their things returned as well?"

They stayed for an hour chatting with Aunt Ness.

"Have you seen any more lights at night?" asked Ted.

"No. It's just dark now, no lights at all in the garden."

"Good."

Fiona went downstairs, leaving Ted with her aunt, to look for the nurse in charge and was pleased to see it was Moira. Moira said she had an update on the missing items and garden lights. Fiona told her that Aunt Ness's things had been returned.

"Yes, all the residents' items have been returned. It was a member of the night staff who 'borrowed' them."

"I hope the person was sacked. It caused a lot of distress," remarked Fiona.

"Matron gave him another chance if he brought everything back. He is being watched very carefully and if anything else goes missing, he will be dismissed immediately and the police informed."

"He should think himself very lucky," said Fiona. "I'm just surprised he is still working here."

"Me too," Moira replied. They arranged for the four of them to meet up at seven o'clock on Saturday night in the Roosters Arms for a drink and a meal.

"It's my weekend off and Hugh is golfing in the afternoon so we shall look forward to it," said Moira.

Fiona went back upstairs and told Ted about meeting up with Moira and Hugh on Saturday night.

"Great," he said.

Fiona said she had something to tell him but it would wait until they were on their own.

They said goodbye to Aunt Ness, leaving her looking at a cookery programme while waiting to watch a repeat of *Doc Martin* starting at nine o'clock. Fiona thought with some relief that her aunt appeared more settled than when she had previously visited.

On the drive home, she told Ted what Moira had said about it being a member of the night staff pinching the residents' things, hiding them in the shed at night which accounted for the lights seen by Aunt Ness, but had now returned them

"And he's also keeping his job apparently. Matron has given him a second chance!"

"I wouldn't have him working there, she must be going soft," he replied. "Let's hope he keeps his sticky fingers to himself in future but at least the shed light mystery is solved."

"I wonder if the thief is the person, we saw her with in the park. She was handing him something, wasn't she, do you think she may be involved in the thefts?" said Fiona.

"Don't know. Perhaps Moira will tell us more about it on Saturday evening," Ted replied.

They stopped at the takeaway and picked up fish and chips to save cooking. They ate them on trays in front of *Doc Martin*.

Next day in the office, Fiona told Lynne about the return of the residents' things after Carl had admitted taking them.

"That's good news but it does seem strange that Matron didn't sack him. I do feel sorry for his mum if she finds out, she was really nice and obviously adores him."

"Yes, it is a good thing that she isn't aware of what he's been doing, it would only upset her. How's Kevin?"

"He's good. I feel a bit bad that I didn't tell him about me going to Carl's house and playing my part in all this."

"There may be a point when you can tell him, but perhaps not yet," said Fiona. "I may know more after Saturday evening as we are meeting up with Moira and Hugh."

"Okay, but let me know if there are any more details!"

They had a difficult day in the office. There was an internal audit in progress at the council and two auditors arrived at Lynne and Fiona's office at eleven and didn't leave until five. The auditors were a lady in her forties, obviously the senior one, and a young lad who couldn't be more than twenty. They didn't say much but just kept asking Lynne and Fiona questions, looking and checking at requested paperwork and typing away on their laptops; the atmosphere was a bit strained.

Both Fiona and Lynne were relieved when five o'clock arrived and they could go home.

Fiona complained to Ted about the auditors being in the office. "It was a bit of a silent day. Lynne and I couldn't talk as we usually do."

"Gossip, you mean," he replied with a grin.

"No, we just talk about what's going on in our lives!"

"As I said—gossip!"

Fiona punched his arm with a smile. "Bet you and Geoff talk a lot too."

"Yes, but it's mainly about sport."

"I'm looking forward to seeing Moira and Hugh on Saturday night," she said. "I want to hear more about Carl."

"I am intrigued as well. Wonder why he's still got his job," said Ted.

They put the television on and watched a repeat of *Doc Martin*.

Friday was forecast to be a showery day. Low grey clouds drifted slowly across the sky. Matt arrived at work and the rain started just as he was getting out of his car. He ran across the carpark and let himself into the home, shaking his head of raindrops. Josh was in the hallway and laughed when he saw him. Matt went to the staffroom to dry off a bit and put his lunch bag away. He went into the lounge to call out a general hello to the residents.

He saw Tom and Arthur sitting with the folded paper between them to start the crossword. Gwen was in her usual chair with a magnifying glass in each hand looking at a magazine. She saw Matt and held her hands up to show him. "I've found my missing magnifying glass, it was in my room all the time so I've now got two," she beamed. The television was not on for a change and the atmosphere was nice and peaceful. John was there looking at his wallet that had suddenly reappeared in his room.

Matt went out and looked in his maintenance diary to see what jobs were in for him to fix. He really enjoyed his role in the home. He liked chatting to the residents and most of the staff were nice and friendly.

It was horrible to believe that someone on the staff could be responsible for the recent sudden deaths. He understood that deaths were inevitably going to occur at the home, it was the nature of the business, natural expected deaths were fine but unexpected deaths shook him up as it did with most of the staff.

He wondered when he would meet up with Sally and Moira to discuss what they were going to do next in their investigations.

Jane was the nurse on shift this morning. She nodded hello but did not speak with him. He went to fix a bedside lamp that didn't work in Room 5. It was the fuse so he exchanged it and the lamp now worked. He then collected undercoat, gloss paint and brushes as he needed to repaint a skirting board in the same room, which was very scuffed. He lay out floor cloths under the skirting board and started to prepare the wood for painting. He liked painting. He found it soothing.

The door opened and Annie entered with her housekeeping trolley. "What are you doing in here?" she asked him brusquely.

Bit obvious, thought Matt but didn't say it. "I'm painting," he replied.

She didn't say anymore but went into the bathroom to start cleaning. Her trolley was left in the room after she removed her cleaning products to use. He saw a magazine tucked in the side of the trolley. *Bet she wanted to come in and read it*, he thought. He hoped she hadn't taken one of the residents' magazines.

She didn't stay long in the bathroom. She went to the trolley and got out a duster and polish and very half-heartedly dusted around things on the dressing table and bedside cabinet. She didn't move anything, which he thought she should be doing. She flicked the duster at a picture on the wall and again at a couple of photographs on the windowsill. She then put the polish and duster back in the trolley and silently left the room. *Ten minutes max*, thought Matt, shaking his head. It should take a lot longer than that to properly clean a room. He applied undercoat to the skirting board and then left it to dry. He would return later to gloss.

He saw Jane coming out of Room 6, which was Frances's room. "Can you fix her curtain as it's coming down on one side?" she asked him.

No please or thank you. It was just his bad luck that the two staff he was not keen on were both on shift. "Certainly, no problem," he replied cheerfully with a wide smile. She looked a bit put out as if he was taking the mickey.

He knocked on the door of Room 6 and waited for the command to enter and went in. Frances was sitting watching *Bargain Hunt*. She looked at him and then pointed at the drooping curtain. Some curtain hooks were on the windowsill where they had dropped off the rail. "I shall have to move the television a bit to the side so I can reach the curtain," he informed her.

"Well, be quick about it. I don't want to miss the programme," she retorted.

He didn't need to turn it off but gently moved the television a bit. She could still watch it while he repaired the curtain.

"I need to go and get some more curtain hooks," he told her. "Some have broken and that's why the curtain is coming off the rail."

He went out and got some from his closet. He then went back to her room and started putting the new hooks on the curtain. He adjusted the curtain and all was fine.

Frances begrudgingly said thank you. He asked her how she was, he didn't know her very well as she never came out of her room.

She sighed and said she was alright, which was more than could be said for some of the staff who worked there.

"Who in particular?" Matt asked.

"Night staff mainly. They rush around and don't give us any time. They just want to get their jobs done and go and sit down."

"Really?" replied Matt. "Anyone in particular?"

"The nurses are the worst. In with the pills, allow us a quick gulp of water to take them and they're out the door in a flash," said Frances.

"That's not very nice."

"No, we pay a lot to be here and should have proper service."

Matt said perhaps she ought to say something to Matron.

"I hardly ever see her, too up herself to visit us in our rooms."

Matt said she really ought to say something next time Frances saw her. He moved the television back into position and left the room.

He went for his lunch break in the staffroom. He switched the kettle on and opened his lunch bag. A cheese and pickle sandwich, salt and vinegar crisps and a nice piece of cherry cake. Nancy did look after him well. The kettle boiled and he made himself a cup of tea.

Josh came in the staffroom and retrieved a bag from his locker. He sat down at the table with Matt and started eating his sandwich.

"Do you ever work the night shift?" Matt asked him.

"I have worked some nights but not very often. If someone's on holiday or sick and cover can't be found, I've been called in to do a shift."

"Do you like doing nights?"

"I don't mind the night shift but the staff are not like the day ones."

"In what way?"

"Not so keen on the nurses, they tend to leave the work to the carers," replied Josh.

"All the nurses?"

"Well, Nina is not particularly hardworking, she just wants to rest and go to sleep. She's got young children that need her in the day."

"That's not good," said Matt.

"No, I agree, the nurse is in charge and should direct the carers, not just go to sleep and let them get on with it."

212

Josh continued eating his sandwich as did Matt. They had a chat about the upcoming football season. Brenda came into the staffroom to eat her lunch, made a cup of coffee and sat down at the table and regaled them with the current happenings in *Eastenders*. Neither Matt nor Josh watched it so didn't know who she was talking about. She was a bubbly character and well-liked by the staff. She was slowing down in her work and looking to retire in the next year, but she would be missed.

Josh mentioned that some of the missing residents' item had suddenly reappeared and had Brenda or Matt known where they had been?

"Not a clue," replied Brenda.

"Do you know, Matt?" asked Josh.

"I don't know either," said Matt. He didn't want to admit to them that he knew about Carl being the thief.

"I think there's something odd going on in the home," said Josh. "Matron needs to be more on the ball and find out what's going on." No one said anything more about it.

They all finished their lunch, left the staffroom and returned to work.

Sally arrived for the afternoon shift. She took the handover from Jane. She wanted to see Matt and discuss recent events. She found him in Room 5 glossing the skirting board. She told him about Matron's decision to retire as soon as a replacement could be found.

Matt whistled in surprise. "Crikey, I didn't expect that. I thought she would be here forever!"

"It was a surprise to me too."

"Any more thoughts on how we progress with our investigating the deaths?" asked Matt.

"Not really. I didn't have the courage to ask Nina the other morning," replied Sally. "Let's see if Moira has any ideas."

Matt repeated what Josh had said about Nina not pulling her weight on the night shifts. "She leaves them to get on with the work while she rests."

"That's not good," Sally agreed.

She left Matt to his painting. Sally went into the lounge. She heard Tom and Arthur talking. She heard them mention Carl's name. "Any problems?" she asked.

"He's a bit odd, we think," said Tom. He looked around the lounge to make sure no one was listening. "He asked if he could buy my bottle of whisky a couple of weeks ago. I told him I'd drunk half so it wasn't a full bottle. He said he would buy it at a reduced price in two instalments. I asked him why he couldn't buy one from the shops but he said he was short of cash. Very odd. I said no, of course. I like my tot of whisky each evening."

Arthur agreed with him. "Do you think he wanted a drink while he was working?"

"I asked him that. I was a bit worried about us being looked after by someone who'd had a drink on shift. That's the other odd thing. He said he didn't drink alcohol and it was a present for someone. Who gives someone a present of a bottle of whisky that's half empty?"

Sally agreed it was very strange. Privately, she wondered whether it would have been for his mother. She asked them to let her know if anything else happened that they considered odd.

"We generally keep our ears and eyes open," Tom assured her. "We've got our eye on a couple of dodgy staff already. Now we have added him to the list."

"Who else?" asked Sally.

"Now that would be telling," grinned Arthur. Sally advised them to be careful and to let her know if there was anything she ought to know about any of the staff.

She went around the room saying hello to the residents. She was concerned about what Tom and Arthur had said about 'dodgy staff'.

She went back up to Room 5 where Matt was finishing his painting. She repeated what Tom and Arthur had told her.

"I wish they had told you who the dodgy staff are. It could be a clue in our investigation."

"I have advised them to be careful and let me know if there's any other odd staff behaviour," Sally said.

Matt collected up his paints, brushes and cloths and followed Sally downstairs. Matron was just coming out of her office. She closed the door and told them she was leaving for the day. She went out of the front door.

"Is the office unlocked?" asked Matt. "Perhaps we ought to have a look at some of the staff records while the coast is clear."

Sally asked what they would be looking for. She tried the door and it was unlocked.

"Not really sure but something might jump out at us," said Matt.

They decided to leave it for fifteen minutes just in case Matron returned unexpectedly. He put his paints and cloths away and Sally went into the lounge. A couple of carers, Sue and Caroline, were in there talking to residents. Sally went to the window where Ness was sitting reading a magazine.

She could see Kirsty in the garden kneeling down, weeding a flowerbed. She hadn't had a lot to do with Kirsty as she didn't often come into the home. She had heard she lived alone and had changed careers to do what she enjoyed doing best, which was gardening.

Sally asked Ness how she was and was pleased to hear her say how she was settling in better now she had been here a while. She said she liked to look out onto the garden.

Sally went out of the lounge, meeting Matt in the hallway.

They went into the office, shutting the door behind them. The staff files were kept in a large cabinet at the end of the office. It was unlocked, which Sally thought was not right. Surely, they should be locked up? These were confidential files and she felt uncomfortable at what they were about to do.

Matt pulled out Nina's file and handed it to Sally.

"I don't think it's right that I look at them but as a trained nurse, you have more clout," he said.

Sally opened Nina's file. It had a CV in the front. She was married with three children under school age. One child had health issues apparently and needed careful watching due to diabetes and asthma, which was why she preferred to work nights as her husband was home in the evening and Nina there in the day. She had trained locally and had worked in two other nursing homes before gaining employment at Goodrest for the past two years.

There was the usual compilation of necessary documents within the file.

Matt pulled out Annie's file and handed it to Sally. Her CV showed her to live with her mother. Unmarried and had worked as a cleaner for most of her working life. No health problems other than a cholecystectomy twenty years ago.

Sally was then handed Nick's file. He was fifty-three and married with two grown-up children. He had worked in hospitals mostly during his nursing career and had been at Goodrest for two years. There was nothing in his file that concerned Sally. Like the others, he had been police-checked prior to working in the home.

Matt and Sally kept a careful watch on the office door. They didn't want to be discovered looking at the files. It would surely be a disciplinary issue if caught.

Matt handed her Alice's file. Her CV showed her to be thirty and single. She had worked as a carer since leaving school. Her ambition had been to train as a nurse but she hadn't achieved the qualifications needed.

She had worked at Goodrest for two years. Prior to that, she had worked at another home near Morton.

Matt handed Sally Nick's file again as he thought he saw something she'd missed. They saw his CV showed he had worked previously in several different care homes. He left the last one for personal reasons. The last one before working at Goodrest had been the same one that Alice had worked at.

"Alice and Nick both worked at the same home near Morton before coming here!" she exclaimed. "I missed that. I wonder why they both left there."

"Is there a reason on the application form to say why she left there?" asked Matt. Sally returned to Alice's file.

"It says for personal reasons," she read. "Nick's reason on his application form says the same. It's a bit of a coincidence."

Matt handed Carl's file to Sally. She knew his home situation so skipped that bit. His CV stated he had also worked at the same care home that Alice and Nick had worked at. He had worked at Goodrest for six months. His police check was clear. "It's a big coincidence that all three worked at the same home and then came here," said Matt. "Why did Carl leave, does it say on his application form?"

"Personal reasons too!" read Sally.

"What's the name of the home?" asked Matt.

"Meadowview Care Home."

"I think we need to go and see this home and see what we can discover about why all three of them left. We know Alice and Nick left two years ago and Carl six months ago."

"I do too. We can pretend we are looking for somewhere to place a relative," said Sally. All the files were put back in the cabinet as time was getting on.

They left the office. It was time for Matt to leave work and for Sally to start the teatime medication round.

"See you soon," said Sally. "We'll have a word with Moira about the next step."

Sally rang Moira that evening during her shift. She told her what she and Matt had found out. It was agreed that Matt and Sally would visit Meadowview Care Home on Sunday afternoon on the pretence that they had an uncle needing care. Sally rang Matt who agreed to meet her there at three o'clock.

Three o'clock on Sunday, Matt and Sally rang the bell at Meadowview Care Home. The home was on the outskirts of Morton. It was a large Victorian house just off the main road. It was answered by a male nurse. "We would like to look around, if it's convenient," said Matt. "We have an uncle who needs twenty-four-hour care as he has dementia and cannot live alone any longer."

"Please come in," said the nurse. "I can show you around."

They followed him inside. He showed them the communal lounge. In the lounge were several residents reading or watching television. There was a male and female carer in there attending to some of the more dependent residents. One was crying out 'help'. He was repeating this over and over and some of the residents were telling him to shut up.

The nurse said there were two empty rooms at the moment. He took them to the first one, which looked over the back of the house onto a garden. Matt and Sally looked out of the window onto the garden. It was quite overgrown and not like Goodrest's nicely maintained lawns and garden.

"What's your turnover of staff like?" asked Sally. "My uncle needs people around him that he knows or he becomes agitated."

"That's like a lot of our residents. We try not to use any agency staff as it can upset residents seeing new faces."

"Are there nurses on duty?" asked Sally.

"Yes, all the time."

"I believe a nurse who once worked here was Nick Wilson," said Matt.

"Yes, I knew Nick," said the nurse. "He was here a short while before he moved on."

"I also know a carer called Carl worked here," said Matt.

"Yes, he left quite suddenly. I was told he found somewhere to work that was a bit closer to his home."

Sally knew that wasn't true as Meadowview was closer and Goodrest further away from where Carl lived.

"How do you know them?" asked the nurse. "If you have visited another home and they are working there then best be careful. They both left here very suddenly. A carer called Alice also left suddenly. Are you really wanting a place for your uncle or is it to find out why these people left here?"

"I think you've sussed us," grinned Matt. "We'll be honest with you. Those three people all work at the home where we work and there are some concerns."

"They all left suddenly but nothing could be proved," said the nurse.

"Proved?" said Sally.

"We had a couple of sudden deaths a couple of years ago that were put down to natural causes but management were not convinced, but not certain enough to involve the police. Nick and Alice left soon after. We also had some thefts but the stolen items were mysteriously returned. I'm not really sure who the thief was, I was never told. It may have been Carl as the times were about right."

Matt said, "We have found out who was behind the thefts at our care home but over the past few months, there have been four sudden deaths, all put down as natural causes but it's aroused our suspicions about some of the staff."

"If any of those three are working at your care home, then keep a careful watch on them."

"We will. The sudden deaths, did they have anything in common?" asked Sally.

"They were both men, diabetics and not in the best of health."

"The deaths at our care home were all diabetics too. It's far too much of a coincidence for them not to be connected," said Matt.

They thanked the nurse for talking with them and apologised for pretending to be looking for a placement for a fictitious uncle. He showed them out and wished them luck in their investigation.

"We need to have a meeting with Moira," said Matt. He rang her and arranged for them to go to her house. They got in their cars, drove off and three miles later, pulled up outside her house. Her husband was weeding a flowerbed in the small front garden. He got to his feet, saying Moira was inside the house and to come in.

He opened the front door, calling for Moira. She came to greet them. Hugh went back to his gardening.

Matt and Sally followed her into the lounge.

It was a large room decorated in eggshell blue. The settee and two armchairs were in a darker blue with cream flowers and navy cushions. There was a large television on the wall above a fire place. A large sideboard was alongside one wall.

218

Moira said she would make a cup of tea and went out into the kitchen. Matt and Sally sat down in the armchairs.

Moira returned with a tray on which there were three mugs of tea. She handed them out and sat down on the settee.

"We have just been to Meadowview Care Home and spoken to a male nurse who told us some very interesting things," said Sally. She told Moira everything that he had said.

"It's far too much a coincidence that there were thefts and sudden deaths there just like at Goodrest and our three worked there. Also the fact that the residents who died all had diabetes in common," said Matt.

"So where do we go from here?" asked Moira.

They were all silent, thinking.

"Right," said Matt, "this is what we know. Carl was the thief so he must have been thieving from Meadowview as well and been discovered so that's why he left suddenly. Probably was told if he went, the police would not be called in and like at Goodrest, the missing things were returned. He is very lucky not to be in jail."

"All three were on shift the night of the deaths at Goodrest so there is that connection as well. All the residents who died in both homes were diabetics so there's the connection too. Nick and Alice left at the same time two years ago."

"We need to find out more about Nick and Alice. We already know quite a bit about Carl," said Moira.

"How about I offer to work a night shift when Alice is on? It's much quieter at night with more chance of talking," said Sally.

"Good idea," replied Matt.

It was agreed that Sally would look at the rota on Monday and see what she could arrange.

Matt and Sally left saying goodbye to Hugh who was now mowing the small front lawn.

Monday morning, Sally took the night handover from Graham. There were a couple of poorly residents who had coughs and colds. They would be staying in their rooms so as not to spread their germs to the other residents.

The night staff left and Moira started her day. She dispensed the medications and checked on the two residents with the colds. They were not too bad, just feeling a bit sorry for themselves.

Once the medication round was over, Sally looked at the staff rota. She saw that Nina was taking an annual leave on Thursday night and the shift hadn't yet been covered. Alice was working on Thursday night. Sally was due to work on Friday morning but she would ask Moira to cover for her. Wednesday and Thursday were Sally's days off. She went to find Matron who was in her office. She told her she could cover Thursday night as Nina was off.

"That's good," Matron replied. "It saves me phoning around. I have enough to do."

"No, thank you for covering it." Noticed Sally as she left the office.

She found Matt later and told him she was working Thursday night and Alice was on shift as well. She would see Moira at two as she was on the afternoon shift.

After handover and the afternoon carers had left the room, Sally told her about working on Thursday night. Moira agreed to cover Friday morning even though it was her day off.

Sally left and Moira was just checking the residents in the lounge when Matron appeared with Dr Johnson.

He nodded at Moira, asking how she was. Matron looked annoyed and steered him away.

"Dr Johnson is going to check on the two residents with colds. I will take him up, you can get on with your work," she told Moira. They went out and went upstairs.

They came down after a while with Dr Johnson telling Moira to give regular paracetamol while they were displaying symptoms. He went into the lounge saying a general hello to everyone. *He's nice*, thought Moira. *He really cares how they all are*. Matron was trying to get him to return to the office but he was ignoring her and taking his time chatting to the residents.

He eventually left, telling Matron he didn't have time for a cup of tea as he was needed elsewhere.

Moira hid a grin when Matron told her that he was such a busy doctor and normally liked to spend time with her after seeing the residents.

Moira handed over to Nina at nine o'clock and told her Sally was covering Thursday night. "She will see how busy we are at night. Day staff believe we sit down all night but that's not the case at all," Nina said.

Moira collected her bag and left to go home.

Thursday night saw Sally taking handover from Nick. He was curt and gave only minimal information about the residents. Sally was relieved to hear the two residents were recovering from their colds and had been downstairs in the lounge for the day.

Sally's night carers were Alice, Ken, Amy and Nadia. They went off to check on the residents while Sally dispensed the night medications. She was pleased to find that very few residents were prescribed night sedation. There was always a higher risk of falls if people were sedated. She went to see all the residents. She found the carers settling them down for the night. A few were in the lounge and were helped to their rooms when they said they were ready for bed. She found Tom having his nightly glass of whisky in his room. "Bottoms up," he teased. She grinned and said what a good job he hadn't sold it to Carl. "No way is he getting his hands on my whisky, what a cheek."

Sally wished him a good night. At midnight, all residents were settled in their beds and most were fast asleep. The carers had some cleaning to do. They mopped some non-carpeted downstairs floors, set up the dining room tables for breakfast and tidied the lounge. Sally helped them with some of the jobs.

At one o'clock, Sally went into the lounge. Alice was sitting watching television. "It makes a nice change having a bit of help from the nurse," she said. Sally said she was happy to help out where needed.

"How long have you been caring?" she asked Alice as she sat down with her.

"Since leaving school at sixteen, and I'm thirty now. I really wanted to be a nurse like you but I didn't get the exams needed for the training. It's not fair. I would have made a good nurse. Dishing out pills and giving injections would have been good. It's easy really."

"Well, there's a bit more to nursing than giving out medication," said Sally.

"It's good giving injections though, isn't it? Especially when they are not expecting it."

"Well, it's not so good for the patient though. A lot of them would prefer not to have them. If an injection is to be given, we always tell the patient when we are about to do it and what it's for."

Alice sighed and said she still would have made a good nurse. "You are respected more if you are a nurse rather than a carer."

"We need people to be carers, you all do a really hard job that a lot of people wouldn't want to do. Giving personal care is not a job for everyone. Which other homes have you worked in before coming here?"

"I've worked in a few others. Some I didn't like at all, bad conditions and not appreciated."

"Why do you work nights?" asked Sally.

"I don't sleep very well and find I have more time doing things I want to do in the day."

"What sort of things do you like to do?"

"That's for me to know and you to find out," grinned Alice, touching the side of her nose.

"I nearly took a post at Meadowview Care Home before coming here," lied Sally. "Do you know it?"

"Yes. I worked there for a bit. It was alright but they didn't appreciate me."

"In what way?"

"I tried to help one of the nurses out and got found out."

"What did you do?" said Sally.

"You ask a lot of questions, don't you?" said Alice. She got up and left the room. The three other carers wandered into the lounge.

"What have you said to Alice?" asked Nadia as she sat down. "She had a face like thunder!"

"I was only making conversation," said Sally.

"Well, watch out, she's a strange one. She's a good carer but thinks she's a nurse at times," said Ken.

"What do you mean?"

"She's always asking Nina if she can give out the medications. Says she looks tired and should rest and leave it to her," said Amy.

"I hope Nina says no."

"Mostly, but not always. Nina has been seen handing over pills for Alice to give to a resident."

"What about when Graham is on?"

"She wouldn't ask him, she knows he wouldn't let her," Ken said.

"Good," replied Sally. She was concerned about Nina giving Alice tablets to give to the residents.

A call bell sounded and Ken got up to answer it. Nadia and Amy went out to make a hot drink, asking Sally if she wanted one. "A cup of tea, milk, no sugar, thanks," she replied.

Alice came back into the lounge a bit later. She glared at Sally but didn't say anything. She sat down by the window and picked up a magazine and started reading it. Sally and the other carers chatted amongst themselves, but didn't converse much with Alice as she appeared to be ignoring them.

The rest of the night passed quickly. A few bells needed to be answered but most of the residents slept well.

Sally handed over to Moira in the morning. She gave the day staff a good report of the night shift. When the carers left the room, she arranged to ring her in the afternoon after she had had a sleep and Moira finished her shift.

Sally collected her bag and with a big yawn drove home. It had been some time since she had worked a night shift and had forgotten about the morning tiredness. She saw Jack briefly for a hug and kiss as he was just going off to work. "I missed you," he said. "The bed was too big for one!"

She grinned and said she would be back in there tonight. "Good," he replied with a leer.

"Go to work!" she said with a light punch on his arm.

She slept until one o'clock and then got up for a shower. She had a lunch of a tuna sandwich and cup of coffee. It was a nice day so she took it out into the garden and sat on the bench.

At half past three, she rang Moira.

She told her about her conversation with Alice.

"Do you believe she may have injected the residents causing their deaths?" asked Moira.

"Well, I wouldn't put it past her after telling me how she wants to be a nurse and dish out pills and give injections. If she did though, where would she have gotten hold of the insulin?"

"The previous care home perhaps?" replied Sally.

"Don't forget we couldn't establish how much insulin was left in the disposed cartridges at Goodrest."

"True," said Sally.

"I still think we are missing something. I have a feeling there is more to find out," said Moira. "Remember as well that Arthur and Ness said they were given tablets at night that made them unwell and Alice was on those nights. Nina was on shift so she may have asked Alice to give out their proper medication and Alice could have slipped them something else."

"What for?" said Sally.

"To see what happened after she gave them? She would then have to nurse them and look after them as a nurse might," said Moira.

Sally said she had heard that both Arthur and Ness had said they were well looked after during the night they were given the tablets.

"Have you given any more thought about taking over the Matron post?" asked Sally.

"I have actually. I have discussed it with Hugh and I think I may go for it," replied Moira.

"Brilliant!" said Sally. "You would make a great Matron!"

"I will speak with Matron tomorrow and see what I would have to do to take on the role," said Moira.

They chatted a bit longer and then rang off.

Next day, Moira approached Matron about taking over her role. It was Saturday and normally a day that Matron didn't work but she had come in to collect something. Matron was pleased to hear this and said she would speak with Mr Smith and arrange for them to meet to discuss the next step. "I am ready to retire so this would be a very good outcome," said Matron. "I will let you know when he can come and see you."

Moira returned to her duties. Josh was on shift and said he wanted a quiet word with her. They went into the dining room where they could speak without being overheard.

"I found Annie in Ness's room fiddling with her radio. She was re-tuning it to another station. I didn't know she was in there when I went to fetch a magazine for Ness this morning. I asked her what she was doing and she was surprised to see me. She admitted she altered some of the residents' radios just for fun. I said it was not acceptable to do this but she just laughed at me. I said I was going to report her. She told me to go ahead. She said it was not serious and I would just be seen to be causing trouble and would probably be disciplined."

Moira said he had done the right thing in telling her and she would speak to Matron.

Matron was still in the home and listened to Moira and said she would speak with Annie. She sighed and said, "This is why I want to go; I have had enough of sorting out trivial problems."

Moira offered to speak with Annie but Matron said she would deal with it.

Moira left the office and returned to her duties. A bit later, she saw Annie being called into the office.

Moira kept an eye out and ten minutes later saw Annie come out of the office and head towards the staffroom. Matron beckoned Moira to come into the office and said Annie would be leaving without working her notice. "I have had several reports of her not doing her job properly and she had been seen looking in residents' drawers and cabinets. When I questioned her, she just shrugged and said she wanted to leave anyway. She admitted changing residents' radio stations for a laugh to wind the residents up. She also moved their photos and ornaments around. I told her that was malicious and not acceptable."

Five minutes later, Moira saw Annie with her jacket and large bag leaving the home, slamming the front door behind her. Matron left a bit later.

The news soon got around. Thelma said she never had gotten on with Annie and was pleased she wouldn't be working with her anymore. "I never did like or trust her. I have a cousin Maureen who would like a housekeeping job here so I will ask Matron for an application form," she told Moira.

Moira handed over to Nick at two o'clock. She didn't mention Annie leaving but overheard one of the carers telling another what she had heard from a morning carer. *News soon gets around*, she thought.

She left the home and drove to Tesco's to do a food shop.

She and Hugh were meeting Fiona and Ted for a meal and a drink that evening. She was looking forward to it. She was off work the next day so didn't have to worry about being a bit later going to bed and setting the alarm. She put the shopping away and then sat in the garden for a couple of hours. It was a warm day. Autumn would soon be here though. The flowers were still colourful but leaves were starting to fall now.

Ted was playing a round of golf with Hugh. He arrived home at five, told her about how he had played and then showered. They then had a cup of tea together. Fiona showered and got ready for the evening out. She dressed in a floral dress and pink cardigan. Ted looked smart in his chinos and green polo shirt. He kept chatting about how his golf swing and how it was improving with practice. Fiona listened and was pleased he had enjoyed it.

They met Moira and Hugh at seven. They were trying out a new pub called The Royal Oak just outside Morton. It had recently been taken over by new management and reports were good.

They found a table away from the bar where it was a bit quieter. Ted got the first round of drinks in.

The door opened and to Fiona's surprise, Lynne and Dr Johnson walked in. Lynne spotted Fiona and waved. They went to the bar, bought their drinks and wandered over to Fiona's table. Introductions were made and Ted suggested they join them unless they preferred to be on their own. Lynne looked at the doctor who told them to call him Kevin and certainly they would like to join them all.

He immediately pulled up two chairs to the table and they sat down. *Lynne looked really happy*, thought Fiona. She deserved it, she was a lovely person and Fiona was glad to call her a friend as well as a work colleague.

They all chatted and then ordered their meals with Hugh choosing medium rare steak with all the trimmings after much deliberation. Fiona and Moira laughed and Ted said he wondered why he even looked at the menu when everyone knew what he was going to order anyway!

"I may surprise you one day and order something else. I like to weigh up my options!" Hugh grinned.

The meals arrived and Kevin bought a round of drinks for everyone. He was good company, appearing more relaxed than when he visited the care home.

Hugh mentioned that Moira was interested in taking over the post of Matron at Goodrest when the current one retired.

"That's excellent news. I can see us working well together," said Kevin to Moira. "I think Matron is ready to retire as soon as possible." Fiona was very pleased to hear the news too.

"Did you hear that the residents' missing items were returned by the person who took them?" asked Moira.

"Yes, Matron told me all about it. I was surprised she gave him a second chance."

Moira wondered whether to mention about her, Sally and Matt looking into the sudden deaths but thought it was not the most appropriate time. She didn't want to put a damper on the evening.

They all enjoyed their meals and rounded off the evening with coffee. They left the pub at eleven o'clock and drove home their separate ways.

"What a nice evening," said Fiona. "I'm so pleased for Lynne. Kevin is really nice."

Ted agreed. "I wonder if he plays golf. I should have asked him."

They went straight to bed once they reached home.

Carl was not on shift on Sunday night. He spent the morning in bed after his Saturday night shift, getting up at one o'clock and then mowed the lawn. He told his mother he was going for an afternoon walk. Lydia was happy watching a film on the television. He made her a cup of tea saying he would get their meal when he returned. He patted his jacket pocket as he left.

He got in his car and drove a couple of miles before parking up in a secluded layby where a meeting had been arranged.

A car pulled up five minutes later behind his car. Carl got out and went to the car window that was being wound down.

"Glad to see you, Carl."

"I said I would be here," replied Carl.

"Have you got my money?"

"It's all here," said Carl as he handed an envelope through the window. "You don't need to check it."

"Can't be too careful. You are lucky to still have your job from what I hear."

"Yes, I know," said Carl.

"I hope your poor old mum never finds out about it."

"Please don't tell her. Our arrangement doesn't have anything to do with her."

"As long as I get my money on time, she won't find out from me."

The window was wound up and Carl stepped back as the car drove off. He got back into his own car and sat for a while without starting the engine. If it wasn't for his mother, he would move away and start afresh where no one knew him but he knew that wasn't an option while his mother was dependent on him. He wished he had someone to talk to. He did wonder about talking to Moira. It was a false hope though as he knew he wouldn't want anyone knowing what else was going on besides taking residents' items.

He knew that the taking of residents' items had been wrong but he had only wanted to please his mother by giving her presents. He couldn't afford to buy her nice things. He knew he was exceedingly lucky to still have his job. He needed to work to pay these instalments. He hadn't been told how long he would be expected to keep handing over money.

He sighed and started the engine and drove to a park where he took a short walk. His mother would ask him where he had been and he didn't want to lie anymore to her. He took note of people and surroundings so he could give an honest account of what he had seen on his walk.

He arrived home at four and as he expected, his mother asked who he had seen and where had he been for his walk. He gave a good account that satisfied her. He prepared their evening meal of pork steaks and vegetables.

They ate at six and spent the evening watching television.

Moira, Matt and Sally met up on Monday evening at Sally's house. Sally made a cup of coffee and they sat at the kitchen table. Jack was still at work.

Moira said she thought she should tell Dr Johnson about their suspicions about the sudden deaths. "We need to have help with this and he is the obvious person." She told them that she had met with him socially on Saturday evening and she thought he may help them either find out what really happened to the residents or to allay their suspicions.

Matt agreed and asked what Sally thought.

"I suppose so. We don't seem to be getting anywhere on our own," she said.

Moira said she would find a good time to speak with the doctor when he came into the home.

Matt left first, leaving Moira and Sally talking. Moira told Sally she was hoping to meet with Mr Smith sometime this coming week to discuss the Matron's post. "I really hope you get it," said Sally.

Jack arrived home from work. He had on dirty oily overalls that gave off a strong smell of engine oil. Sally said to go in the shower and freshen up as she didn't want to smell oil all evening! He grinned and kissed her, enjoying her reaction of batting him away from her. "Put them straight in the washing machine!" she ordered.

He stripped them off, leaving him dressed in a T-shirt and boxers. "I didn't mean right now in here! Go now, Moira doesn't want to see you like that!"

"I am a nurse, I've seen it all before," said Moira, laughing. "At least Hugh has an office job so doesn't come home smelling like that. The only smells I get are after his runs or sports and that's a healthy sweaty smell!"

Jack shoved the overalls in the washing machine, putting soap powder in the dispenser and switched it on and then ran laughing upstairs.

Moira was still smiling as she left to drive home.

Hugh was at home and had started getting their supper. She was laughing as she told Hugh about Jack and his overalls. She poured a glass of wine for each of them. She loved Hugh and had ever since their first date and couldn't imagine life without him. She put her arms around him and kissed him. "I love you," she said. Hugh told her how much he loved her too.

They ate a very companionable meal, watched some television and had an early night.

Moira was on the early shift on Tuesday. She had the handover from Nina. All was well with not much to report. Matron arrived at nine and told Moira that

Mr Smith was visiting the home on Thursday morning and would see Moira to discuss the Matron's post. Matron appeared to be in a good mood. "Dr Johnson is coming in later to see the residents," she told her.

That's why she's in a good mood, thought Moira.

At eleven, Moira was enjoying a coffee break in the dining room when Dr Johnson arrived at the home. "I will accompany him seeing the residents," Moira had been told earlier by Matron.

An hour later, he had finished seeing all the residents. There was no one unwell at present, which was good.

He saw Moira in the lounge. "All's well," he said.

"Can I have a private word with you?" she asked him. Matron looked at her and asked what she wanted with him. "I'd prefer to discuss it alone with the doctor. It's a personal matter," replied Moira.

"Can we use your office?" he asked Matron. She huffed a bit but said yes, she supposed so.

Moira and Dr Johnson went into the office and he closed the door behind him. They both sat down and he asked what the matter was.

"I'm not really sure where to start," she said.

"At the beginning," he smiled.

"I am concerned about four residents who have died at Goodrest in the past few months. They apparently were reasonably well but died very suddenly. They all had type 1 diabetes in common and I have a gut instinct that all were given a high dose of insulin that killed them."

"Good lord!" he said. "Which residents are we talking about?"

"Robert was the first, then Mary, Wilfred and Freda."

"Yes, I remember all of them. They all had underlying health conditions as well as diabetes, all of which were documented by me on their death certificates, if I remember rightly," he replied.

"But they were well the day before their deaths and the next day were gone. Sally and I have identified the staff on shift at the relevant times and the same staff were on duty at the time of each death. I am frightened that one person injected them with insulin outside of their normal dose," explained Moira.

"An insulin overdose would be hard to identify without a post mortem and none of them had one. They were all cremated as well so there is no body to examine. I didn't have any suspicions about their deaths or I wouldn't have signed their death certificates. A lot of elderly people can suddenly die but it's not generally suspicious. Most have conditions that can exacerbate suddenly. What are you asking me to do?"

"I think we should speak with the staff and see if there are any clues. Were they ill in the night but it was not reported to the nurse? You are probably right but for my own satisfaction, I think we should make enquiries."

"I agree with you. Can you give me the names of the staff and together we will speak with them."

"I can give you the list, Dr Johnson. Matron doesn't know I have any concerns. I haven't spoken to her about finding out who was on shift the night prior to the deaths."

"We will keep this between ourselves for the moment," said Dr Johnson. "And just for the record, please call me Kevin when we are not in front of the residents. I did enjoy our time at the pub on Saturday night."

"Yes, it was a good evening. We all enjoyed it."

Dr Johnson stood up and said, "Arrange for the relevant staff to be called in, one at a time, so we can see them. I will make myself available whenever you arrange it. Here is my mobile number so you can contact me."

He wrote the number down on a piece of paper and handed it to Moira.

"Thank you," said Moira. "I will be in touch soon." He left the office and went out of the front door. Matron was hovering in the hallway and immediately rushed to ask Moira what they had been discussing. "I can't tell you, it's personal," replied Moira and went along to the lounge. Matron looked very displeased.

Moira handed over to Sally and her afternoon team at two o'clock. After the carers had left the room, she told Sally about speaking with Dr Johnson.

"Well done, we might get some answers soon."

Moira said she would contact the relevant staff asking them to come in for a meeting.

She rang Alice and asked her to come into the home on Thursday at two-thirty for a meeting. Moira was on early shift and hopefully would be meeting Mr Smith in the morning so would be free to stop on after her morning shift. Alice asked what it was about but Moira said it would be explained to her when she arrived on Thursday.

She rang Carl and asked him to come in at three-thirty on Thursday. Carl sounded worried about the meeting but she said it was not about the recent missing items but another matter.

Moira also rang Nina to come in but she said she could not come in for a meeting in the day on Thursday due to child care but was in on Wednesday night shift. Moira said she would see her at handover as she was working an afternoon shift. She didn't say Dr Johnson would also be there.

Moira found Matt and told him about the proposed meetings. She then rang Sally at home and told her. "Do you want me there as well?" she asked.

"Probably best not. It could intimidate them having three people against one," said Moira. "I will let you know after the meetings how they went."

Moira rang Dr Johnson and told him the times of the three arranged meetings. He said he would be there for all of them.

Wednesday afternoon, Moira worked her shift. She was a bit nervous wondering how the interview with Nina would go. Dr Johnson had rung Moira to say he would arrive at eight forty-five, ready to see Nina at just gone nine o'clock after handover.

Nina and her night staff arrived. Dr Johnson was in Matron's office after arriving at eight forty-five as arranged. Carl and Alice were on nights off. This was a good thing so Nina wouldn't be able to discuss the meeting with them. She could ring them but Moira thought she probably wouldn't as it would be late in the evening.

After handover, Moira asked Nina to go into Matron's office. Nina asked what it was about and what right had Moira to ask her into the office?

"Dr Johnson is in there. We would just like to ask you a couple of questions."

The office door was closed after Moira followed Nina in. Dr Johnson was sitting at the desk and asked Moira and Nina to sit down.

"We should like to ask you about four nights over the past few months when we had four deaths in the morning after the night shift," said Dr Johnson.

"What are you accusing me of?" asked Nina, springing up from her chair. "How dare you insinuate I have murdered these residents? I am a good nurse."

"No one is accusing you of anything. Please sit down. We are hoping you may have some information that wasn't reported or appeared relevant at the time."

Moira said the first death was Robert on 2nd May. "Carl and Alice were on shift with you. Did they report anything to you? Perhaps that he was feeling ill?"

"No one reported anything to me."

The other sudden deaths were Mary, Wilfred and Freda. Graham was the night nurse on shift when Mary died so we know you were not there. Carl and

Alice were on shift on the nights prior to all the deaths. We need to ask if you have any suspicions about either of them.

"Well, Alice has aspirations to be a nurse. She's always asking if she can do the medication round. Carl is a bit quiet. I don't know too much about him. He works well, but often disappeared and it was difficult to find where he was. Lately though, he's been around a lot more."

Moira wasn't going to tell her the reason why.

"Did Alice ever give out medications? If you were feeling tired or were busy?" asked Moira.

"Well, a couple of times I said she could give some tablets out. I get tired because I have young children that I need to stay awake for in the day because they need me."

"That was the wrong thing to do. You must never do it again. Did she ever mention giving injections?"

"She said it was a shame there were no injections to give on the night medication round. She said she would be good at giving them. She said it's easy to do."

"It sounds like she has actually given injections if she says it's easy to do," said Dr Johnson.

Moira asked Nina if she could recall anything else that Alice had said or done.

"No, can I go now? The night medications won't give themselves and I'm going to be late with the round now."

She stood up and left the office. Dr Johnson and Moira looked at each other.

"It will be very interesting to speak to Alice tomorrow afternoon," he said.

They both left the home, agreeing to meet at two-thirty the next day. Moira went home and gave Sally and Matt a quick call to tell them how the meeting with Nina went.

Matt was off the next day as he was going with Nancy to an eye appointment. "Keep me informed," he asked.

Next day, Moira was on the morning shift. She wondered where the meeting with Alice should take place because Matron was in the home and would be using her office. Perhaps the staffroom would be free. Dr Johnson arrived at two o'clock, which surprised Matron as he normally would tell her when he was visiting.

They had a cup of tea together before he went off to find Moira. Matron got up to go with him but he said he needed to speak with Moira alone. She did not look too happy with this but sat down again at her desk.

Moira handed the shift over to Nick and the afternoon carers.

Alice arrived at two-thirty. Matron saw her come in through the door and asked what she was doing there. Alice replied, "She had been called in for a meeting with Moira."

"Whatever about? I have not been told about any such meeting," asked Matron.

"Not sure," shrugged Alice. "It better not be long because I have things to do later."

Moira and Dr Johnson saw Alice, thanked her for coming in and after a look in the staffroom, which was free, decided to hold the meeting there. Moira asked Alice to sit down. She explained that they were looking into four deaths that appeared to have happened suddenly. She told Alice the names of the four residents.

"I remember all of them," said Alice with a shrug. "They were all old, hadn't got much to live for."

"They may have been elderly but they had a reasonable quality of life even with their health conditions."

"They were diabetics and some had dementia," said Alice. "That's not good, what quality of life did they really have?"

"That's not for you to say. You are a carer supposedly looking after them, regardless of their health conditions," said Dr Johnson.

"We have heard you wanted to be a nurse but didn't have the qualifications for the training," said Moira.

"I would make a good nurse. It's wrong that I couldn't train just because I didn't have the exams needed. It's not fair," said Alice.

"We have also heard that you offer to give out the night medications but are disappointed there are no injections to give. You have also been heard to say giving injections are easy. Can you tell us if you have ever given anyone an injection?"

"I might have," replied Alice, running a hand through her fair hair. She was looking a bit flushed.

"When?" asked Dr Johnson.

"Can't remember."

"Did you give any of the four residents, Robert, Mary, Wilfred and Freda an injection?"

"What if I did?"

Dr Johnson and Moira were stunned.

"What did you give them?" Moira asked.

"They were not feeling too well when I checked on them so I thought I would top their insulin dose up. I recognised the symptoms of hypoglycaemia. See, I even know the medical term for low blood sugar. I'm not stupid. I know the spare cartridges are kept in the fridge. There are spare pens in the medicine cupboard so I know how to attach the cartridges and turn the dial for the dose. I wasn't sure what dose they usually had so I had to guess. If I had trained as a nurse, I would have known. I told you it's not fair. They would have been alright if I'd known the right dose to give them."

Moira asked if she had given Arthur and Ness an extra tablet one night. They had been poorly for a couple of days afterwards.

"Yes."

"What was it?"

"Diazepam. I didn't take them from the home. I was prescribed them some time ago but didn't take them after the first one as they made me very tired. Arthur and Ness had both annoyed me on my previous shift. I told them the tablet was to prevent a heart attack. They soon gobbled it down! I said Matron had ordered it for them. They didn't argue, just took it!

"Quite funny really, they were very grateful they said, as neither wanted a heart attack. It was interesting to see how long it took for them to get over having the tablet. I thought Arthur was going to tell someone that I gave it so I told him I would give him another one that would really make him ill when he wasn't aware, unless he said he was mistaken about having the first one. I also told Ness to keep quiet." Alice then started laughing.

She's quite mad, thought Moira. She looked at Dr Johnson who nodded at her. He got up and asked to be excused. He went into Matron's office and dialled 999 and asked for the police. Moira stayed with Alice who was still laughing hysterically.

Matron spluttered, "What is happening?"

Dr Johnson didn't reply but spoke to the operator on the end of the line. He requested that the police come as soon as they could as they had just been made aware that four murders had been committed in the care home.

"What?" said a shocked Matron.

"I will explain soon but I need to go back to Moira," he replied. He went back to the staffroom. Some of the carers had tried to enter to have their break but Moira asked them to use the main kitchen and dining room instead.

Alice had calmed down and tried to exit the staffroom. Moira and Dr Johnson held her back and told her to sit down.

"The police are on their way," he told her.

"No, no!" cried Alice. "You can't do this to me. I need to go now. I have things to do."

Moira looked at her, shocked and bewildered.

"Why did you do it?" she asked.

"I should be a nurse. I'm just as good as you are! Why should you be paid more just because you did some training?"

Sirens were heard in the background, getting closer to the home. Dr Johnson asked Moira to let them in while he stayed with Alice.

Moira got up and let the four policemen in the front door. She asked them to follow her. Matron and staff were standing around open-mouthed, wondering what was going on. Arthur and Tom had come out of the lounge asking the same thing.

"It's a raid!" said Tom excitedly to Arthur. "It must be drugs. It's like being on the telly!"

Moira took the police to the staffroom where Alice was being restrained by Dr Johnson. They were both standing up with Alice trying to get free from him.

The police took over and sat Alice firmly down in a chair.

Moira quickly explained the situation.

"Police station for you, Miss," said one officer to Alice. He read her rights that Alice said she understood even though she was innocent and didn't know what was going on. She was shouting it was all a mistake and lots of lies. The policeman asked Dr Johnson and Moira to make their own way to the station to make their statements.

The policeman put handcuffs on Alice and led her out of the staffroom. Matron, Nick, care staff and some residents followed the proceedings with their eyes, not saying anything, hardly believing what they were witnessing.

"Always thought she was a rum one," said Tom after the front door closed. Sirens were heard with them getting fainter and fainter as the police cars drove away.

"She always was on our watch list. She was one of the dodgy ones," agreed Arthur.

Matron shooed them back into the lounge and told the staff to carry on with their work and calm the residents down.

Dr Johnson and Moira went into Matron's office to tell her what had happened. She had to sit down quickly as she felt quite faint when she heard.

The front door opened and Carl appeared for his three-thirty meeting. Moira said the meeting would need to be postponed and she would be in touch with a new day and time. "What's happening?" he asked, his heart beating fast. "I've just seen police cars leaving here with Alice."

"All will be explained but for now, can you leave as there is no meeting," said Moira.

Carl left as requested. He had nearly had a heart attack when he had seen the police cars with Alice in the back of one of them. He needed to know whether his name had been mentioned in connection with the thefts but surely if it had then he would be travelling in a police car with Alice or even worse, a police car going to his house.

Dr Johnson and Moira got in their cars and drove to the police station in Morton. They were met by an officer who told them his name and rank and then showed them into a side room. It had four chairs around a table. Another officer entered the room, identified himself and sat down, indicating Dr Johnson and Moira to do the same. They were asked if this meeting could be recorded. Moira and Dr Johnson agreed that it could.

"She's protesting very loudly that it's all lies and a setup. It gave the officers who were in the car a right headache. She wouldn't keep quiet all the way to the station," said the first officer.

Dr Johnson reached into his jacket pocket and withdrew his mobile. "I have it all recorded on here," he told them.

Moira could have kicked herself. She should have thought of recording the meeting herself but thank goodness, the doctor had done it!

Dr Johnson pressed Play on his mobile. The whole recorded meeting with Alice was heard in silence by the four of them.

"No doubt about it," said the second officer. "It's all down there; well done. What made you suspect her causing the residents' deaths?"

"I, along with two other staff, have been concerned for a while but without evidence couldn't prove anything. I alerted Dr Johnson who agreed to have a meeting with me and Alice. You also need to go to Meadowview Care Home where she previously worked. Apparently, there were two sudden deaths there. Both residents were diabetics just like the residents at Goodrest," replied Moira.

"We certainly will pay Meadowview a visit. Thank you for telling us."

She and Dr Johnson made signed statements that were read by the officers. They took a recording of the meeting with Alice off Dr Johnson's mobile.

"Thank you. We will keep you informed as to what happens next. You are both free to go now."

All stood up and went out of the room. Outside the police station, Moira turned to Dr Johnson. "I hope my heart slows down soon. I've never been in a police station before. I need to go home and wind down. I can't believe this is happening. Those poor residents who died at her hand. It's awful."

"She is in custody now so won't be free to do more damage to anyone," he replied. "Well done to you for finding it out."

They said goodbye and each drove home.

Moira rang Sally and told her everything that had gone on. "Wow," said Sally. "We were right after all! How awful. Just because she wanted to be a nurse. It's unbelievable."

Moira rang Matt and told him too. "I wish I'd been there to see her carted off in handcuffs!" he said. "I wonder what happens next?"

"I'm not sure, but the police said they would let us know. I hope they don't release her on bail."

"Surely not," he replied. "They've got her on record admitting it."

Moira told Hugh all about it when he got home.

"They have the doctor's recording so it can't be dismissed," he said. "I've seen things like this on the television. They will hold her in custody and she will be up before a judge in the next day or so."

He saw Moira was upset and distracted so he prepared their supper and pampered her with running a hot soapy bath where she could relax. It did help but Moira still went to bed earlier than normal.

Sally was on the morning shift the next day. As soon as she arrived in the home, the carers told her what had happened with Alice the previous day. They did not know exactly why she had been arrested but all sorts of ideas were being bandied around. Sally listened but did not comment other than saying, "I'm sure we will know about it in good time."

Matron came in at nine and immediately found Sally to ask what she knew about yesterday.

"As much as you," she replied. Sally knew Moira and Dr Johnson had told Matron why Alice had been arrested. "Alice has admitted giving four residents an overdose of insulin that caused their deaths."

"I can't get my head around this," said Matron. "How could I not know? am now even more than ready for retirement. Don't forget Mr Smith is coming to see you tomorrow."

She looked very sad and went into her office, closing the door behind her Moira felt quite sorry for her.

Arthur and Tom were full of it. They were telling anyone that listened all about the events of yesterday but embellishing it as they told their story. "We knew there was a murderer on the loose here. We slept with our eyes open."

"Let's all settle down now," said Moira.

She saw Matt a bit later when he arrived at work. They had a chat, making sure no one could overhear them.

"Thank goodness it's all over now," he said. "She should be put away for life."

Moira agreed with him. "I can't help thinking about those poor residents being injected probably as they slept. It must have been a massive dose of insulin for them to die. There will now be an inquest into each death."

She finished her shift, handing over to Nick. *He was a strange one*, Moira thought. He didn't even mention Alice even though she had heard Josh telling him about it all.

Moira went home and spent a couple of hours trying to relax in the garden It was warm but with a slight breeze. She felt cold thinking about recent events She also rehearsed what she would say to Mr Smith tomorrow. She really wanted the Matron's post as she knew she could do it well and look after the residents as they deserved to be.

Carl was worried. He had been, ever since seeing Alice being carted off in the police car. It could be him next time. He had no idea what was going on. He hadn't received any phone calls that he was surprised about. Surely, they would have heard about Alice being taken off in a police car and would want to discuss it with him probably frightening him in the process.

He was working the night shift so should find out from the other staff what had happened. He didn't know why he had been called in by Moira yesterday either. He didn't mix with the other carers outside of work so couldn't ring anyone to find out. His mother noticed he was distracted and asked if he felt alright and she hoped he wasn't coming down with anything. "No, I'm fine," he reassured her. He acted as normal, making their tea and watching television before he got ready for work. He was in his bedroom, putting on his uniform when his mobile phone rang.

"Have you heard what's happened?" he was asked when he answered it.

"About Alice being arrested?" he replied.

"It could have been you sitting in the back of that police car if they knew what I know."

"I know it could, but you are being paid good money to keep quiet. Please tell me how long you are going to be fleecing me. I can't keep making these payments. You are breaking me. Surely I have paid enough to you now."

"Our arrangement still stands as long as I want it to." The phone was put down.

Carl sat down on his bed with his head in his hands. How much longer was he expected to pay? He was only just surviving to pay the bills and pay for their food shopping. His mum deserved better than this.

He finished getting ready, said goodbye to his mother, making sure she had her evening cup of tea, and drove to work.

He arrived at work and was immediately told what had been going on in the home. He listened to Nadia who was full of it. He didn't tell her that he had seen Alice yesterday in the back of a police car.

"I can't believe I worked with her and didn't suspect anything. Did you think anything was going on?" she asked.

"No," he replied. "I didn't suspect anything at all."

Nina was the night nurse who Nick handed over to. Nina tried to pump him for information but got nowhere. Carl looked at Nick and thought what a cold fish he was. No emotion, deadpan face and probably not someone you would want to cross. He had a temper that many carers had experienced if he thought they were slacking. He was actually a good nurse but personality was missing.

Carl didn't think anyone would want to confide in him. He knew Nick had been asked to leave Meadowview care home because of his surly attitude. Some staff had refused to work the same shifts with him so he had been asked to leave as it was creating shift problems. He had improved slightly since being at Goodrest, probably because he didn't want to lose his job again. Nina was nice even if she was a bit lazy. He felt sorry for her knowing she couldn't sleep after a night shift as she had young children to look after.

Nadia, Ken and Amy were on with him tonight. They were all good carers and helped each other out.

He liked the job at Goodrest and didn't want to leave. He was shocked about what Alice had done. The residents did not deserve it. He supposed there would be a full investigation and possibly he may be interviewed as he had worked with Alice on many night shifts. How deeply they would investigate the staff was very worrying. He just hoped the residents' missing items did not crop up in the investigations.

After handover, he and the other carers left the dining room to attend to the residents. He was truly sorry about taking things from them and swore to himself he would never do it again. *A clean sheet from now on*, he promised himself. If only he could draw to a close his other problem. He was going to have to work on it.

The night passed smoothly. The residents who were aware of what had gone on recently were a bit nervous that it could happen again with another member of staff. Lots of reassurance was needed that he hoped he and the other carers could give them.

Morning arrived and Moira was the nurse having handover from Nina. Nothing much to report, she said. She wanted to talk about Alice but Moira didn't supply any information.

Moira dispensed the morning medications and Matron arrived at the home telling her Mr Smith was due at eleven to speak with her about the Matron's job.

At eleven, Matron found Moira to tell her Mr Smith had arrived. She was invited into the office. Matron sat at her desk and Mr Smith stood and shook hands with Moira.

They sat down. Mr Smith said he understood that Moira was interested in taking over from Matron when she retired. They had a good chat. Mr Smith asked her many questions about her circumstances and how she intended to run the home if she was given the post.

Moira was confident in her replies and felt that the interview had gone well.

He stood up and said he would be in touch. He needed to speak with the care home regulators who would also want to conduct an interview with her. Matron hadn't said much during the interview but gave her approval and said she would be happy to hand over to Moira over a period of two months, after which she would leave.

Mr Smith then thanked Moira for investigating the recent events saying he was devastated to hear of the deaths at the hand of one of the carers.

Moira left the office, feeling that all had gone well.

She handed the shift over to Sally and told her about the meeting with Mr Smith. Sally was thrilled for her and told her so. Moira left and drove home.

She rang Fiona later and told her about the interview and how she hoped she would be successful in becoming the new Matron.

"It will be a relief to me and probably the staff and residents when the current Matron has gone. She doesn't have much compassion at all from what I have seen," said Fiona.

"I think she's just had enough. She may have other things she wants to do with the rest of her life," said Moira.

She also told Fiona about how the investigation into the sudden deaths at the home had reached its conclusion with a member of staff being arrested. She needed to tell her because it would surely be in the newspapers at some point. Fiona was horrified to think how someone could do such a thing.

"It's shocked us all," replied Moira.

Carl got up at one o'clock after a morning's sleep. He had come to a decision that he was not going to pay any more money over. It had been going on for six months now and enough was enough. Blackmail was a very nasty business and surely an offence. Yes, he had done something wrong but it worked two ways. He would not turn up for the next meeting when he received the phone call saying when and where it would be.

He made his mother a sandwich for lunch. He wasn't hungry as all he could think about was his decision in not paying up anymore. He sat with her and watched the lunchtime news. The newsreader was talking about a female carer being held on suspicion of murdering four residents in one care home and two in another. No names were mentioned. "How dreadful," said his mother. "I hope things like that don't go on at Goodrest."

Carl didn't answer as he didn't know what to say.

His mobile rang. He took it out of his pocket and looked at the number displayed. He got up to go out of the room to answer it. "Who is it?" asked his mother.

"Just work," he replied.

"Saturday, same place, same time," he was informed and then rang off.

Carl went hot and cold thinking about what would happen when he didn't turn up for the meeting. He was determined not to go.

He worked the next couple of night shifts. He had the weekend off. The staff were still talking about Alice and what she had done. Nina said she always thought something was not quite right about her. She resolved to be more attentive to the staff and residents in future. She would cut out one of her nights so she would be less tired. She had told Matron who said Graham was looking for extra shifts so he could take over one of her nights.

Matron had also informed the staff that she would soon be retiring and hopefully Moira would take on the role. This pleased the staff who all liked Moira. It would be a new beginning for Goodrest.

Carl got up at lunchtime on Saturday after his night shift. He had not slept well thinking about not turning up to the meeting place to hand over any money.

He told his mother he was going out to do some shopping. He needed to be doing something rather than sitting at home. She asked him to pick up a *Hello* magazine and a packet of jelly babies.

He got in his car and drove into Morton. He kept looking at his watch. The time reached when he should be in the layby for the meeting. He parked up and purchased the magazine and sweets from a newsagent shop and then drove to the park and went for a walk. It was a warm day and there were lots of people in the park. He saw happy families enjoying themselves and looking as if they had no worries at all. Children raced around and he saw some playing on the swings and slides with parents watching them carefully. It was a perfectly normal Saturday afternoon for most people, except for him.

His mobile rang at three o'clock. He looked at the number but didn't answer it. He then heard a message alert. He read the message that came through.

"I am waiting, where are you?"

He turned the phone off. He carried on with his walk. He wondered what would happen next.

He returned home at five. He handed his mother her magazine and jelly babies. "What else did you buy?" she asked.

"Nothing, I went for a walk instead, it was too nice a day to spend shopping," he replied.

He switched his phone back on. There were seven messages, all becoming more threatening with each one he read.

242

He made their tea of fish fingers and chips and sat with his mother eating on trays and watching *Catchphrase*. His mother was good at answering the phrases and chuckled away when the contestants were stumped and she had gotten them right. "I should go on this programme," she laughed.

"Yes, you should," Carl said. He enjoyed seeing his mother happy. He would do anything for her. He was so grateful for all she had sacrificed in bringing him up on her own since his father died. He had proved this over the last few months.

His phone remained silent for the rest of the evening. He knew he would be contacted again before too long.

The next text message came through at ten the next morning.

"Meet me at eleven-thirty this morning at the usual place or else all will be revealed and you know what that means."

Carl was undecided as to his next move. He had no money to hand over. He thought about what to do and then decided to go to put an end to this whole sorry business. He couldn't take any more. He told his mother he was going out to meet a friend and wouldn't be too long.

He drove to the layby and waited.

A car pulled up behind him. He watched through his rear-view mirror as the door opened and the driver got out coming over to his car.

Carl wound his window down.

"Where's my money?" he was asked.

"I am not paying any more," said Carl.

"You know what will happen if I don't get it."

"I don't care anymore. I've had enough of being blackmailed," Carl answered.

"So you want your mum to go to prison?"

"I will explain everything to the police. I'm sure they will be lenient with her. She an old lady."

"It's your call. I will now go to the police and tell them everything."

"Do what you want. I can't take anymore," replied Carl. He wound the window up, started the car and drove off. His heart was thudding in his chest. He felt quite faint so drove home very carefully. It wouldn't do to have a crash. He knew all too well how that could end up.

He reached home and his mother asked him if he'd had a nice time with his friend.

"Very nice, thanks," replied Carl.

The rest of the day passed without any more messages or phone calls.

The next morning, there was a knock on the front door. Two police officers, one male and one female, stood there. They identified themselves.

"We have had some information relating to a car incident six months ago. May we come in please?" said the male officer.

Carl opened the door so they could enter. "Is your mother in?"

"Yes, she's in the lounge," said Carl. He closed the door after them, took a deep breath and led them into the lounge where his mother was reading her *Hello* magazine.

"Mrs Lydia Small?" asked one of the officers.

"Yes, that's me," she replied as she put the magazine down. "Please sit down. How can we help?"

"We have received some information about an incident in your car that you may have been involved in six months ago. We have been told you were driving at the time and that two cars crashed. The other driver took himself to hospital and he died three weeks later. Can you tell us if you were the driver at the time?" the female officer asked.

"Yes, I was involved in a car accident. I should have reported it but I drove off after speaking to the other driver. He seemed fine. I was scared, I didn't want to lose my licence," Lydia said. She went very pale and looked at Carl.

"Were you aware of this incident?" asked the male officer looking at Carl.

"Yes, but not that she had spoken to the driver. I really believed she hadn't stopped. I thought the crash was her fault," admitted Carl.

"So you believed that, but still didn't come forward?"

"I know I should have. My mother has been mostly housebound ever since. She's nervous in a car now even when being driven. She told me about the incident. I really thought it was hit and run so I kept quiet. She hasn't driven since. Someone said they witnessed it as a hit and run and started blackmailing me. I was told if I didn't pay, Mum would be going to prison."

The male officer said, "The man who died didn't actually die of any injuries from the crash. He had a small cut to his forehead apparently, nothing life-threatening, but actually died later of an existing heart condition. He had a very limited time left because of his heart condition. He should have not been driving. His licence had been revoked due to his illness. The actual accident did not cause his death. It was not hit and run."

Carl looked stunned. "So Mum didn't cause his death?"

"No, but the incident should have been reported to us and the insurers."

"I am very sorry I didn't report it," said Lydia. "His car crashed into mine but he got out and came to speak to me, saying it was his fault as he had pulled out of the road and hadn't seen me. There wasn't much damage to his car that I could see. Carl arranged for my car to be repaired as the passenger side was buckled and we paid for it privately so the insurers wouldn't find out as my insurance premium would go up. I thought at the time I would continue driving but didn't realise how much it had shaken my confidence."

"This witness who has reported it to you, what are they saying?" asked Carl.

"The person told us they thought we ought to know what had occurred. They did admit to seeing the man getting out of his car and talking to your mother. It was assumed by them that the crash resulted in the man's death three weeks later."

"So I have been blackmailed for months without any reason. I was told Mum hit the car and drove off without stopping," said Carl.

"Blackmail is a very nasty business so we shall look into this but your mother is in the clear. I'm glad you're not driving anymore, Mrs Small. It must have shaken you up."

"It did make me decide not to drive anymore. We sold my car after it was repaired. Carl is the only driver in this family now."

"Good," said the female officer.

"We will leave you now and investigate the blackmailing. We will be speaking to this person and then will need to interview you, Mr Small, but in future you must report any car accidents," the male officer said.

Carl showed them out. He could hardly believe all this. All the money he had paid over the last few months!

He went back into the lounge. He then told his mother about being blackmailed because he was told that his mother was responsible for the other driver's death and he didn't want her to go to prison.

"Silly boy," she said. "I could have told you the other driver was alright after our car crash if you had asked me at the time but I was shaken up, as you know. Who was blackmailing you?"

"I will let you know after it's been sorted," he promised her.

He sent a text. "You are the one in trouble now. Police have been here and Mum was not to blame for the man's death."

He did not receive a reply.

Tuesday morning, he was asked to go to the police station at eleven to make a statement about the blackmailing and could he total up how much money he had paid over.

He arrived at the station at eleven. He was shown into a small room that held a table and two chairs. A police officer sat with him, recording the interview while Carl made a statement and told him that he had handed over four thousand pounds in all.

"What happens now?" Carl asked.

"We will compare statements from both of you and be in touch. It's a very serious offence to blackmail someone and could end up with a prison sentence for the blackmailer if it's proved," he was told.

"I do have my bank statements to show the withdrawals. It's for the same amount on a regular basis," Carl said.

"Please bring a copy in for our records," he was asked.

Carl left the police station. He felt such relief telling someone about it after all the months of worry. He wondered when and if he would be contacted by the blackmailer.

He drove home and told his mother about the interview. She admonished him for not telling her about being blackmailed but said she understood. "No more secrets," she said.

"Promise," replied Carl. He would never tell her about thieving items from the care home but from now on would not keep anything more from her. He was so relieved that she wouldn't be prosecuted, relieved but angry at having allowed himself to be blackmailed over the last few months. *A new start from now on,* he promised himself.

Moira had a phone call from Mr Smith on Monday morning whilst she was at work. He said he was delighted to offer her the post of Matron. He would put it in writing with the terms and conditions attached to the role. He had arranged for the care home regulator who inspected Goodrest to come on Wednesday morning to interview her. He said she would need to complete a management course but he had every confidence in her achieving the qualification.

Moira was very happy to hear from him and accepted the position. She went to see Matron in the office, who also expressed her delight.

"I will speak with you after your Wednesday interview and if all goes well I will start the handover immediately. We will need to employ another nurse to take over your role. I will put out an advert as soon as I can," she was told. "I will take about two months to hand over and then I shall retire, leaving you to it."

The staff at the home were pleased to hear about Moira's new role. They assured her that they would work well for her and give her their full support.

The interview on Wednesday went well and the Matron's position was secured for Moira. It would be a new start for Goodrest and all the horrors of the last few months would be in the past. There was to be an investigation into the deaths but because Alice had admitted to being responsible, it would not infringe on the current day-to-day running of the home. Residents would be safe. Now the mystery of the residents' missing items had been cleared up too. Moira was convinced Carl had learned his lesson and would be a model employee from now on.

Sally was very pleased to hear Moira's news and suggested they meet up with their other halves on Saturday night to celebrate. "Let's invite Matt and Nancy as well."

Moira also wanted Fiona and Ted, Dr Johnson and his lady friend Lynne to be included in the celebration. After speaking with the others, it was arranged they all meet up in the Roosters Arms for a meal and drink on Saturday evening at seven.

Carl had not had any phone calls or messages. He needed to arrange a meeting so that he could bring closure to the whole affair. He wondered how the police interview had gone. He texted a meeting place with a time for Saturday afternoon. He knew their working hours and that weekends were free for meeting up as it was always a Saturday or Sunday when he had handed the money over. He received a reply confirming the meeting place and time.

The police had been in touch with him and said the investigation into the blackmailing allegation had been closed. He was not at all happy with this conclusion and wondered why it was not being investigated further, but he would have to live with it. It was good it was at an end even though he was four thousand pounds out of pocket. At least he could breathe easier now and not wait for the dreaded texts and phone calls. He blocked the number so he wouldn't ever have to see it again.

He was at work Thursday and Friday night. The residents were all in reasonable health. From this week, Graham had taken over one of Nina's night shifts so both were happy with this. The atmosphere was a lot better in the home now. Staff still talked about what Alice had done and he knew it would be talked about for a long time to come. To actually have worked alongside a murderer was gossip fodder and he was sure it was being talked about outside their working hours. *Their claim to fame*, Carl thought with a shudder.

Saturday afternoon at two, Carl waited in the layby as arranged. He watched the car pull up behind him through his rear-view mirror. Carl got out and walked to the car. The window was wound down.

He put his head near the open window and said, "Hello Kirsty. Nice of you to come."

Kirsty looked at him and said she never wanted to see him again after today. She had been questioned at length by the police. There was not going to be any further action as there was no real evidence; she had told the police that Carl had been lending her money as she was in debt and he was a friend helping her out.

"What rubbish to say we are friends and making the police believe it," he replied. "I hate you for what you have put me through but at least it's all over now. You are a liar and I hope you can live with yourself with what you have done and I never want to see you again either." He walked off quickly, got back in his car and drove off without looking back.

Kirsty looked at the disappearing car. She wondered whether Carl would tell anyone about what she had done. Now it was over, she couldn't take the risk of him telling anyone and have fingers pointed at her, she couldn't stand the humiliation, so she would move away and she and Joey would make a new life somewhere else. She wasn't sorry she had blackmailed him.

It had been an easy way to make a bit of cash. It served him right for being so gullible. She had seen his mother at a coffee morning in the local community hall where the elderly met weekly for coffee, cake and chat. Her own mother had attended weekly as well before she became ill and died last year. Her mother and Carl's had become quite friendly and Lydia spoke often about her son Carl who worked nights at Goodrest care home.

Witnessing the crash whilst out shopping and recognising Carl's mother had been too good an opportunity to miss after hearing that the other driver had died later. She had also seen Carl and his mother shopping in Tesco's on quite few occasions. She had heard at Goodrest how devoted Carl was to his mother and it had been all too easy to convince him that it was a hit and run.

Good gardeners were hard to find so she was sure she could find another post quite easily. She would phone Matron on Monday and tell her that she was needed immediately to go and look after an ill relative and couldn't work any notice and start looking for employment miles away from here. She still had the four thousand pounds that she had extracted from Carl so she would be alright for money for a while. She would miss looking after the gardens at Goodrest and hoped the next gardener would look after them as well as she had.

She started the car to drive home to Joey and start packing.

Saturday evening saw the party of eight gathered at the Roosters Arms. They had found a large table to accommodate them all. A toast was made to Moira and she was wished the very best in her new post as Matron of Goodrest Care Home. "We shall work well together," said Dr Johnson. He turned and smiled at Lynne.

Their relationship was going really well, thought Fiona, seeing the smile they shared and hoped it would lead to a permanent partnership. She hid a smile. She had found out some good news herself before leaving for the evening out. She would have her own announcement to make soon but needed to tell Ted first, which she would do later when they were alone. She knew he would be as delighted as she was.

Sally and Jack were telling them that they were going to go travelling in six months' time and when they returned would be getting married, to which they were all invited. "Another toast!" said Ted, raising his beer glass.

Matt and Nancy were also celebrating as their son and family were moving to live nearer to them. George had been given a promotion and was able to locate to an office with the same firm in Morton. They would see much more of their granddaughters in person rather than on video. "Another toast!" cried Sally as they laughed and raised their glasses.

"Now let's look at the menu," said Moira. "All this toasting is making me hungry!"

They read the menu options and seven chose what they wanted, except for Hugh who was still studying the menu and as usual was the last to say what he was going to order.

"I think I might go for the—"

"Medium rare steak and all the trimmings!" Moira, Ted and Fiona interrupted with laughter. "Let's give Hugh a toast for never letting us down!"

Eight glasses were raised.